P R A I

# *Unsettled*

"One chapter to the next feels like walking, step by step, into a haunted house. A great read: Once you start, it's hard to stop. Even when you meet a ghost."

—Michael Lesy, author of *Wisconsin Death Trip*

. . . . .

"*Unsettled* is an old-fashioned novel, filled with characters as familiar as family pictures, as touching and as terrifying. Reis writes with assurance about the kinds of secrets that destroyed families generations ago — and maybe still do."

—Jacquelyn Mitchard, author of *Deep End of the Ocean*

. . . . .

# Unsettled

*A Novel*

## PATRICIA REIS

Sibylline
PRESS

AN IMPRINT OF ALL THINGS BOOK

Sibylline Press
Copyright @ 2023 by Patricia Reis
All Rights Reserved.

Published in the United States by Sibylline Press,
an imprint of All Things Book LLC, California.
Sibylline Press is dedicated to publishing the brilliant work of
women authors ages 50 and older.
www.sibyllinepress.com

Distributed to the trade by Publishers Group West.
Paperback ISBN: 978-1-7367954-8-4
eBook ISBN: 978-1-960573-05-6
Library of Congress Control Number: 2023935646

Book and Cover Design: Alicia Feltman
Cover Art Courtesy of The Cleveland Museum of Art:
*Gray and Gold,* 1942. John Rogers Cox (American, 1915–1990).
OIL ON CANVAS; FRAMED: 116 X 152 X 12.5 CM (45 11/16 X 59 13/16 X 4 15/16
IN.); UNFRAMED: 91.5 X 151.8 CM (36 X 59 3/4 IN.). THE CLEVELAND MUSEUM OF
ART, MR. AND MRS. WILLIAM H. MARLATT FUND 1943.60

*Unsettled* is a work fiction; some place names may not match
exact geographical areas.

# Unsettled

*A Novel*

## PATRICIA REIS

"All the departed may return, but some are destined to haunt."

—Nicolas Abrams, *The Shell and the Kernel*

*For John*

# PART ONE

# The Family Portrait

# MADISON, WISCONSIN

THE REAL ESTATE AGENT'S MESSAGE WAS CURT.

"We have a showing at one this afternoon. The house needs to be completely cleared out by then."

Van Reinhardt stuffed her briefcase with final exams, left a note on her office door saying she would be back after one, and hurried to the staff parking garage. She tossed her briefcase into the passenger side of the Honda and wheeled out in the direction of her father's house. The high pulse of urgency made her buzz like too much caffeine. She headed toward the west side suburb of Oak Crest where she had spent her childhood, a tree-lined neighborhood on the outskirts of Madison. The house had been built in the post-World War II boom—a three-bedroom ranch, solid, respectable, unremarkable. The neighborhood had once abutted farmland, but now was surrounded by designer communities boasting large lots, two and three-story houses, curving driveways and names like Meadow Lark Estates. Her father had refused to move.

Martin Reinhardt had died a classic old man's death, the kind people warn you against. A freak April snowstorm sent him outside armed with a shovel. The heavy wet spring snow made shoveling difficult. A heart attack took him—quick, clean, and fatal. He had been 88. A month later, Van's internal seismograph still registered aftershocks. Her father's presence had dominated her life; his absence rearranged everything.

A house changes after someone dies. The ranch house had always felt claustrophobic, deprived of air; windows unopened even in the summer, curtains perpetually drawn. The first thing Van did upon unlocking the front door was to throw open the windows. After her mother died, her father had sealed off rooms, claiming it saved on winter heating bills, but Van thought he meant to extinguish the memory of those who once had lived with him. The shades in her mother's bedroom were pulled, as they had been when she was alive. The light had bothered her, Mother had always complained, aggravated her condition. Immediately after her death, the army of orange bottles that had crowded her night table like pieces on a chessboard—medications meant to ameliorate or ward off symptoms of some undisclosed disorder—disappeared, leaving no sign of their former occupancy. Across the hall, the only vestige left in Van's bedroom was the skeletal frame of her childhood bed

Her father had contracted his living space into three rooms—his study, the kitchen and the spare bedroom. For the past month, she had spent weekends in these spouseless quarters, gathering up old-fashioned tweed jackets, buttoned wool vests and trousers, skinny ties and leather oxfords to take to Goodwill. She boxed up his books and papers and took them to the geology department to be archived. His old Selectric II typewriter and a box of ribbons she donated to the battered women's shelter. He had scorned computers and never owned one. Van was all business, made to-do lists, and willed herself not to get emotional.

Parents die, she told herself. It happens.

The three of them had moved into the newly constructed house in 1950, the year Van was born. The place had never been remodeled, nor had her parents purchased any new furniture. Her father never cared about such things. Her mother only cared about where to get her next prescription filled. The house was a 1950s museum—pink and gray bathroom tile, red kitchen linoleum. Goodwill had taken the brown fabric couch and the cracked leather chair that bore the imprint of her father's body. The rarely used maple dining room set and the faded flower rugs went to a consignment store.

From more than a thousand books, she kept one, an 1871 volume of Longfellow's poems covered in forest green cloth with a worn gilt design on the spine. The elegant signature of Elizabeth Konrad, her father's mother, her grandmother, graced the title page. Van had never met her. What could she tell from one book? That she was literate, that she appreciated poetry? She supposed her grandmother's hands had once held this relic, the only piece of literature in her father's over-stuffed bookshelves. It contained Longfellow's first epic poem, *Evangeline*. She must have read the poem to her father. Why else would he have given her that name?

You discover things when you clean out a house after a person dies unexpectedly. For instance, there was no sign of alcohol, not even a lone bottle of port or sherry, the preferred beverage of her father's aging colleagues. Martin had never mentioned anything to her about his abstinence but it made sense. Van attributed his lack of criticism over the last few years to the mellowing, the wearing down of old grudges that was supposed to accompany old age and was grateful that they had established a kind of demilitarized zone in their phone calls. Even her position in women's studies no longer piqued him, nor did he rebuke her about his lack of grandchildren. She wasn't sure when her father had stopped drinking, but she knew when he had started—thirty years ago, the night of her mother's funeral, the last night she had slept in her childhood bed.

After the funeral, Van had stayed in the house with her father. She woke in the dark with the familiar sense of someone calling her. They had called it sleepwalking when she was a child, but she always knew she was not sleeping. Her forays were just long enough to take in the night air, look at the winking stars and the great white swath of Milky Way. Sometimes the moon was visible, but the best was when it wasn't, for then the stars became more numerous, sharp and glittering in the night sky. After a while she would go back to her bedroom satisfied that she had made her appearance to whatever had summoned her. She distinctly recalled the feeling of cool dampness on the soles of her feet as she slid under the covers and reentered sleep.

The night of her mother's funeral, this childhood habit got her out of bed, and she padded barefoot through the darkened house heading for the back door. She was stopped in her tracks by the shadow of a hunched figure sitting at the kitchen table. She could smell the whiskey before she made out the shape of the bottle planted firmly in front of him, his hand holding a water glass.

"Dad? What are you doing up?"

"Go back to bed, Vangie," he said in a thick voice. "Leave your old man to grieve in his own way."

She had obeyed his command for the next thirty years.

They were not so much estranged as they were restrained around each other, held back, as if approaching the molten core of loss and love would set off a mutual conflagration, that sudden eruption of scorching anger and searing disappointment. The last time it happened was after she won a prestigious scholarship for graduate school at the University of Chicago. She called her father to tell him about it, but also to say she had fallen in love and was going to take the summer off to canoe in the Boundary Waters. Then her mother was suddenly and inexplicably dead.

Later, when she told her father she was deferring her scholarship for a semester, letting him believe it was due to her grief, he wrote her a scathing letter enumerating his failures as a husband and a father. He had computed his only daughter into the sum of his losses—one too many, by his accounting. Martin retreated into himself and grew into a sorry, solitary, wounded old man. There were no other women in his life as far as Van knew—a few longtime, long-suffering colleagues from the university invited him for the occasional dinner, there were lengthy correspondences with some of his past students, but nobody grew close enough to heal the invisible wounds. They had scarred over, and Van knew not to touch them.

She pulled her Honda into the driveway where the Dumpster loomed. The big oak in front of the house was leafed in mid-June green. Next to it a *FOR SALE* sign was staked in the ground. The two words felt bruising, as if she had been punched. She wondered if the house retained memories of the lives once lived inside its walls. Or, like a body emptied of breath, did it, too, suffer a death?

She checked the time. She had less than an hour. The house was stripped bare, right down to the hardwood floors and painted walls. Only two items remained in the study, the place where her father had spent uncountable hours. She took one last look at the oversized oak rolltop desk, and decided it had no future with her—she had no room for it, not in her studio apartment, nor in her heart. His four-drawer file cabinet was the last thing to be sorted. The top drawers yielded yellowed manila file folders with syllabi dating from 1950, old conference announcements, lecture notes, the debris of Professor Martin Reinhardt's long academic career—nothing worth saving. This lot she consigned to the waiting trash bag.

The bottom drawer stuck. Van knelt and pulled, nearly tipping the metal cabinet onto herself. It was locked. What the hell? She rummaged through the desk for the missing file keys. Nothing. She hurried to the car, opened her toolbox, grabbed the hammer, and went back into the study. With a couple of sharp hits, the mechanism gave. The drawer gaped open. She jumped back as if something alive lurked in the drawer, some creature with teeth. On top of several fresh manila files was a yellow sticky note: "Talk to Vangie." The little hairs on her arm rose.

A hot fury made her heart pound. "Talk to Vangie," she said aloud. "How dare you snag me now with a promise of an explanation? You're dead and properly buried next to Mother. Whatever talk you wanted is *never going to happen*." She glanced at the files neatly labeled in her father's precise handwriting—Family Portrait, Road Map of Iowa, Important Addresses in Maple Grove. Her watch said five minutes to one. Van shoved the map and folders into a large brown grocery bag. She left the house keys on the kitchen counter with a note for the agent, saying she would call the appraisers to come for the desk and file cabinet.

Van had no regrets pulling the door shut. She was officially an orphan. *Fine.* She had felt like one for most of her life. Besides, didn't being an orphan have its benefits—no parental deities hovering? She eyed the Dumpster and dropped the trash bag and the grocery bag with the map and files into it and got into her car. *Done! Finito! Freedom!*

She backed the Honda out of the driveway. She had finished all the remaining tasks; the house was on the market, she had purposely made no plans for the summer, she needed open space for once, no extra summer teaching, no conferences, only one overdue paper to submit, then a much-needed sabbatical. But self-reproach and a primal grip of filial obligation slowed her down. She put her foot on the brake. Was it wrong to dispose of the files without at least looking over what he had assembled? After all, those were his last words addressed to her. She jammed the car into park.

The rented Dumpster was large and grotty from years of use. Van hoisted herself over the edge of it, reached down for the grocery bag and lost her balance, landing in a pile of rubbish—the rusted-out toaster oven, a 1950s aluminum coffee percolator, chipped plates and stained coffee cups, grey mop heads, dishrags, the kitchen sink drainer, wire coat hangers, worn towels, bathmats, moldy pillows and comforters that had lost their puff. Her knee scraped the Dumpster's edge and left her with a burn. She sat in the bottom of the filthy Dumpster catching her breath and cried like a girl who had fallen off her bike, sad, whimpering cries. At last, embarrassed and furious, she grabbed the grocery bag, did a pushup against the edge, threw a leg over and leveraged herself out of the Dumpster, hoping to God no one saw her. She tossed the paper bag into the passenger seat on top of her briefcase, and drove a half hour to Picnic Point, the finger of land that jutted into Lake Mendota. Underneath her jeans, the scraped knee stung.

In the empty parking lot facing the lake, she glared at the bag of files. They felt radioactive. "Talk to Vangie." Anger and tears were a terrible combination. Nobody ever tells you rage can be a part of grief. Anyway, now it was too goddamned late to talk. Gripping the steering wheel, Van stared at the open water. The lake seduced her like a bad relationship with its changeable moods, its wild unpredictability—smooth and sparkling with sunlight one minute, dark and choppy the next. Today the water showed its beneficent face, sunlit, lapping the shore like a kitten. She wished for a violent storm to match her mood.

Van reached into the bag and opened the top folder, revealing a large sepia portrait of the Reinhardt family. On the back her father had penciled in the date, 1900, and the names of his grandparents, Adam, Elizabeth (Letty), and the names of their eight children. Out of the whole assembly, she identified Jacob, the handsome young man who anchored the far right of the group. Martin had once pointed him out as his father, her own grandfather, whom she never met and knew nothing about. Jacob was obviously the oldest of the children and looked slightly out of place.

Although carefully labeled, the other file folders were empty, except for a typed sheet with addresses for the Maple Grove, Iowa, town office, the Ida Grove courthouse, and the location of the cemetery. A Post-It note was stuck onto a folded map of Iowa: "Ask Vangie to do some research." Her father knew her reputation for being inquisitive—nosy and meddlesome, he had called her—which made her a troublesome daughter but a good researcher. Now he was taking advantage of her from beyond the grave.

Van opened the map where yellow highlighter marked a route from Madison to Maple Grove in western Iowa. Had he been planning a trip? He had never mentioned it. As far as she knew, once he left Iowa for the University of Wisconsin, he never returned. He was the youngest of a large family. He had never said much about the people in the portrait; a few scraps of words recalled here and there—German, immigrants, pioneer farmers—hardly enough to make a whole sentence.

She got out of the car and sat on a bench by the lakeshore and looked over to the forefinger of land. Picnic Point. She always figured she had been conceived there, months before her parents' marriage took place. The sparse family album held a black and white photo of her father and mother in a canoe on Picnic Point, the two of them shining and beautiful, her father with his dark almond eyes and suntanned skin that had earned him the football team's nickname of "Indian." It was her father who had paddled the canoe. As a child, she thought the picture showed her parents in love. As an adult, she thought they were probably in post-coital bliss. Outside that one photograph, she never recalled that expression on either of them during her lifetime. Scowls and grimaces, theirs and hers, predominated. As far as she could remember, her parents always had separate bedrooms. To her knowledge, they had never owned a canoe.

The lapping water was like a heartbeat and the pungent tannin of late spring lake water was deeply familiar. Van let the lake pull her down and back. Since childhood she had loved to time-travel. Whenever her father had suspected her of daydreaming, he chastised her, as if it were some reprehensible defect in her character. She learned to hide her penchant, but never completely lost the habit. Living alone, Van talked out loud to her cat and often to herself, long disquisitions on life's few pleasures and innumerable vicissitudes.

At the edge of the lake, she imagined the Hočąk, the Winnebagos, who had pitched their birch huts and tipis and made their living along the very shore where she was sitting. She knew well their sad history and how they were pushed north and then west, away from their traditional homeland. How they must have longed for the waters of the four lakes of their birthplace in the dry, lakeless regions of their reservations. If she walked the path to the end of Picnic Point, she could find evidence of the earlier and more enigmatic effigy mound-builders that had claimed the ridge tops facing the lake as their sacred burial places. There were other large earth monuments that astonished her when she came upon them unexpectedly amidst the modern campus buildings—these protected mounds rose up in archaic shapes, mute testimony to a mysterious past. The lake itself was the signature of that even more distant master sculptor who worked in ice and had cast a caul of frozen water many hundreds of feet thick across this part of the earth.

Ice. That was her father's domain, both intellectually and emotionally. Geology had drawn him to this campus where he had built his career. Primordial glaciers were his specialty. The subject suited him. Remote and cold. Van rubbed her upper arms, shook her head to clear it, and checked her watch. Now she was too late for her office hours. Her briefcase bulged with final exams.

Back in the parking garage, she picked the Iowa map from the paper bag and shoved the rest in the trunk as if she were hiding a criminal act. She walked down the hill from Bascom Hall to the student union. The long trudge up the hill in winter boots, heavy coat, scarf and mittens, punctuated by white puffs of frozen air, was easy to forget in the lush blossoming of early June. She ordered a large draft beer at the student union and walked onto the terrace where a skirt of paving stones and grass fronted Lake Mendota. These were the reasons she loved this campus: the bright orange, yellow, and green metal tables and chairs spread across the terrace like a flower garden—and you could buy beer in the union, even though it was only 3.2 beer and tasted thin and pissy.

She found an empty table and took a long swallow of cold beer. "Talk to Vangie." The note bugged her. That sure as hell would have been some conversation. She opened the highlighted map. "Were you actually expecting me to take a trip to Iowa with you?" she muttered. The thought of the two of them held captive for hours on a car trip was unthinkable. Yet there it was: "Ask Vangie to do some research," his last wish, written in his hand. Would it plague her for the rest of her life if she refused to honor it?

Her teaching career was her whole life. Although Van had cracked open a few doors in women's studies, she kept bumping into the walls of academe. She had hopes that a sabbatical would give her room to consider her next possibilities. Iowa had not been in her plan. Despite feeling like an orphan, her father's death left her oddly untethered—no parents, no siblings, no partner, no children, no existing family ties. Mother had been an only child and Van never knew any of her grandparents. She had learned to never ask for what she couldn't have and later learned to shut off wanting altogether.

The people in the Reinhardt family portrait stirred an old longing. Maybe some of their descendants were still living in Iowa, some folks who would be happy to claim her as their own long-lost relative. Van pictured family reunions, picnic suppers, stories, cousins, and people who looked like her. Maybe there was still a chance for kinship. Outside of his cryptic notes, she wasn't sure what her father expected, but maybe there was something in it for her. She looked at the map. "Okay, okay, I'll go, dammit." The couple at the next table glanced her way. She was talking out loud to an empty chair.

Back in her apartment, Van inspected her knee and iced it. Nothing too serious, just a raw patch. She washed yesterday's dishes, fed Mister, and called Emma at her office.

"Dr. Cooper here."

"I know this is short notice, Em, but can you cat sit Mister for a few days?"

"Sure, Van. What's up?"

"It's a long story. I'll fill you in later. I'm going out to Iowa to settle a few things for my dad."

"No problem. Where's the key?"

"I'll put it back where we used to keep it, under the big rock near the front door."

"Okay. It'll be great to see Mister again."

There was a brief silence. Van could hear Emma breathing. She pictured Em in her cords and cardigan, sitting at her desk in the humanities department surrounded by stacks of papers, a brown sparrow in her nest.

"Thanks. I'll be leaving first thing in the morning. Cat food is in the usual spot in the cupboard. I'll give you a call once I am out there. I should be back in a few days."

Van hung up and looked at Mister. "Em's coming over while I'm gone." The tabby circled her legs and purred. Even though they had broken up, Van could still count on Emma.

The next morning Van put her thick hair into a braid that hung halfway down her back and pulled on a pair of worn jeans and sneakers. She loaded the Honda with her tent and sleeping bag retrieved from the back of her closet where she had shoved them years ago after her last camping trip. A small backpack held toiletries and a change of clothes—just enough get-away gear for a few days. A cooler filled with bottles of spring water and lemons and a bag of trail mix went into the trunk. She moved the paper bag with the map and file folders to the car's passenger side and started up the car, then put it in park and went back into the apartment.

"Sorry, Mister, I'm just back for a second. Em will be coming later." She pulled a blank journal from the assortment she kept on the bottom shelf of her bookcase. As a historian, she coveted every woman's diary she could lay her hands on. Women's experience was seldom recorded, their words seldom heard, the intimate details of their lives left blank. Even when buried in stiff, stoic religious language, she searched for clues to their hidden stories, she probed the edges of their silences. In bookstores, she bought herself beautiful journals with bright blank pages but never found time to write in them, simply added them to her growing collection.

These days Van figured the details of her life were just too boring, and recording her inner thoughts felt creepy. Someone might find it, or more truthfully, she wouldn't be an honest reporter, and then what was the point? On the other hand, maybe keeping a diary of this trip would give her a chance to begin. She could use the journal to record her findings, fill in the gaping holes in her father's history. Wasn't that what he wanted? She picked out an unlined journal with a faux brown leather cover and stuffed it into the paper bag. "Okay, Dad, you want research, you want to talk? Great. Looks like it's going to be a one-way conversation."

The car had a full tank. She checked the map. The highlighted route was a straight shot from Madison to Dubuque on Highway 18. How typical. *Sorry, Dad, I'm the one driving, so we're going to take the scenic route.* The radio was tuned to WIBA. Bon Jovi came on with, "It's My Life." She turned the volume up and sang along in a rush of energy. "It's my life. It's now or never. I ain't gonna live forever. ... My heart is like an open highway."

Van drove west on Highway 14 to Mazomanie and then headed for Spring Green and the Wisconsin River. She was always drawn toward water—lakes, ponds, river water—only fresh water, never salt. The Wisconsin River had once been used as a highway for the French trappers who paddled down the waterway from the Great Lakes centuries before. Her research had uncovered old illustrations of their big freighter canoes piled high with shiny fur skins, the Native people in canoes with blanket sails, the French-speaking *voyageurs* with their red-tasseled toques bringing in the season's load of skins. The Wisconsin River was a throbbing artery, a yearning, shifting flowage with sandbar islands and channels that carved a landscape of hills, bluffs, and valleys, until it joined the Mississippi. If lakes were moody and tempestuous, rivers were ardent, inventive, and full of longing.

A flash of brown shot out from a field of high grass on her right. She slammed on the brakes and swerved toward the ditch as the deer made high arcing leaps across the road and disappeared into a group of oak trees. She gripped the steering wheel, her heart banging high in her throat. Why do deer choose that exact moment when they are most likely to get killed? Luckily, she had not collided with the animal or crashed into the ditch. She pulled onto the side of the road and put the flashers on. Her jaw was clenched and her breath took time to reclaim its normal rhythm. She felt scared. What had she been thinking?

Van purposely hadn't been back in the area for more than thirty years. Now she remembered why. The pastoral beauty of the Wyoming Valley was haunted on too many levels. Down the road was Frank Lloyd Wright's restored home and architectural studio. Taliesin never ceased to draw visitors who were captivated by its artistic splendor and horrific history. In 1914, the original living quarters had been set on fire by a deranged servant, but not before he axe-murdered Wright's mistress, her children, and a number of other workers. Wright rebuilt only to have the next building burn due to bad wiring. Again, Wright stubbornly built against fate, and now Taliesin stood as a monument to his willful genius, a survivor of its traumatic past. Wisconsin Gothic.

Was it admirable or arrogant for Wright to persevere in the face of such bloody madness? Wasn't he haunted by guilt? Maybe the ghosts of the murdered still roamed Taliesin. There was something sinister in Wright's ability to keep on building. The pain from the past does not so easily disappear. Some people cannot stay buried. They leave traces. Wasn't her father like Wright? Wasn't it perverse of him to ignore the danger signs and then erase all memory of her mother after she died? Hadn't Van done the same with parts of her own life?

The deer was young, a yearling. It was a bad omen. The close call loosened some internal safety mechanism. She started the car and headed toward Spring Green while the wires of her nervous system sizzled like a lightning-struck transformer. She already regretted her choice of routes.

Down the road from Taliesin was The House on the Rock, Alex Jordan's fever dream, a complex stone and beam shelter built atop a monolithic rock. In Van's student days, before it was turned into a tourist attraction, it had been a place to party. An electronic stairway dropped down to bring invited people up and then retracted so there you were, atop an aerie sixty feet off the ground. The parties often lasted for days. They drank and smoked weed, took LSD, and retreated into nooks and crannies for sex. It was amazing that no one ever fell to the ground. In those days Van passed up the more serious drugs, rather, she had been the queen of one-night stands—until she met Len.

Instead of climbing the staircase to get high, Len took her down to a secluded place on the Wisconsin River where the water was shallow, and they could avoid its strong and dangerous currents. They waded out to the sand bar islands for the afternoon, escaped the mosquitoes, and made love on warm sand surrounded by water.

Van put on the brakes and pulled over to the shoulder. She felt ambushed. Hadn't she been just like the deer in those days? Risking her young life, for what? She closed her eyes. The flashbacks were fragmentary, heavily redacted, but the old anguish cut deep as a newly sharpened knife. She knew there was more. She could not go any further with these memories, especially with her father sitting in the passenger seat. Or what was left of him. She had never told him anything about those days. And anyway, wasn't she on a quest to uncover his past? She was not about to be bushwhacked by her own.

What was it that Faulkner had said? The past is not dead; it's not even past. As a trained historian, Van well knew the truth of that. Under the gauze bandage, her knee stung, and despite her fried nervous system, she wanted a cup of coffee. She stepped on the gas and drove away from Spring Green, south on Highway 61.

Prairie du Chien was a prettified tourist destination located on the confluence of the Wisconsin and Mississippi rivers. At a conference last fall, Van gave a paper on the little-known history of the place. Once a rendezvous point for Native peoples and French fur traders, it had been home to a diverse community of people of mixed ancestry—French fur trappers, Scots-Irish traders, free Blacks, Native women of different tribes—people who intermarried and lived peaceably together on the fertile land that abutted the river. That was Van's angle, how a diverse community could harmoniously live together. The peaceable kingdom didn't last long; its story was eclipsed by those who wrote about Prairie du Chien when it became famous as the site of collisions between government officials, demoralized and desperate Natives, greedy fur traders, land-hungry new Americans, and bitterly contested Indian treaties. Surely the old stories slept a restless sleep under cover of revisionist history. The paper she had given at the conference needed to be submitted to the journal proceedings for publications and was long overdue. The editors were impatient. She would get to it this summer, she promised. But since her father's death, Van had lost traction, or was it her appetite for academic proceedings?

At the coffee shop she checked the map. She could go south on Highway 52 and cross the Mississippi into Dubuque, Iowa. From there it was a straight shot to Maple Grove on Route 20. She checked her watch. She had a cup of coffee and now she needed to burn off her nervous energy. Back in the car, the radio station played country and western songs of unrequited love. She turned the radio off and announced to the passenger seat, "Okay, we can get there in four hours."

* * *

Maple Grove was a relic, not a town where young people with ambition remained. Along with shuttered storefronts and dusty *For Rent* signs, Main Street featured the basics: a working laundromat, a bank, a library, a church, a tavern, a beauty parlor, and Dee Dee's Diner. Van went into the diner and took a seat on a worn red leather swivel stool at the counter. It was mid-afternoon. A sturdy middle-aged woman with a beehive hairdo and apron assumed to be Dee Dee was still serving farm breakfasts, complete with eggs, ham and biscuits. Her elderly clientele—men in jeans, plaid shirts and suspenders, and women in dresses, their white hair tinted the same shade of blue—probably folks retired off their farms with time to meet for a late breakfast, small town people with manners.

"What do you want, hon?" Dee Dee's question left Van speechless. She drew a blank. Had anyone ever asked her that before?

"Still got the full breakfast going on the griddle, or I could make you an egg salad sandwich."

"I'll take the sandwich, thanks. On whole wheat bread if you have it. And coffee—black—to go, please."

"Where you headed? We're a little off the beaten path, so to speak. Did you lose your way?"

"I'm going to Storm Lake but thought I would visit Maple Grove—to pay respects to my relatives."

Dee Dee scooped egg salad onto bread and cut the sandwich in a diagonal, wrapped it in wax paper and placed a large dill pickle on top. "What's the family name?"

"Reinhardt. They pioneered a farm near here, sometime after the Civil War."

"Name doesn't ring a bell. I reckon none of them live here now. I would've heard of them."

Disappointment tightened her throat. So much for family reunions and the return of the prodigal. Van should have known better than to let her fantasy of kin take hold. If there was nothing to find, she could turn around and go home—to what? Dee Dee's question rang in her head. *What do I want?* There was always pain in wanting. All of a sudden, the unplanned summer loomed empty.

Dee Dee filled a to-go coffee cup and called out to the table of folks lingering over their meals. "Helen, you ever heard of any Reinhardts living in Maple Grove?"

The elders conferred, frowned and shook their heads. "No," one of the blue-haired ladies replied. "Can't recollect them. Lots of those early folks left off farming, their kids moved away. Cemetery's probably your best bet."

Another woman piped up. "We were lucky our boys stayed on the farm. Farming's not for everyone these days. It's all big business; most youngsters don't like to work that hard, right, Fred?" She elbowed the man in the John Deere cap.

"Guess, you're right about that, Marge."

Van felt drained and deflated, not up for an afternoon chat, something she was never good at. A hot dry wind was blowing from the west, good weather for growing corn but hard on a woman longing for water. She needed to get to Storm Lake, but first the cemetery.

Dee Dee handed her a paper napkin penciled with directions to the cemetery, along with the lidded cup of coffee and the bag with the sandwich. "Good luck on your search, hon."

Off a paved road, on a small rise outside of Maple Grove, the cemetery replicated the chauvinisms of the old country: Swedes and Norwegians in one section, a small grouping of Irish in another, and a great congregation of German Catholic dead settled into the largest portion. The tombstones assembled according to family names, the generations keeping each other company. The various fashions in markers distinguished the most recently dead from the more antiquated. She found the Reinhardts in the oldest section, a small contingent of granite ghosts.

Dates were a place to start. Born and died. Incontrovertible facts. She noted them in her journal and made a rough sketch of the gravestones' shapes and placement. As befits a patriarch, Adam Reinhardt's stone was the tallest: a grey monolith decorated with a peaked roof, and an engraved trefoil oak leaf topped by a cross, bearing his name and dates, 1842-1901. A smaller gravestone similar to Adam's bore his wife's name and dates: *Elizabeth Bauer Reinhardt, 1856-1909*. She must be Letty in the family portrait, which was probably how her family knew her. Between them was a flat stone with a barely legible inscription: *Johnnie, 4 Jahre, 22 Marz. 1887.* Her heart involuntarily sank. Johnnie, not John or Johannes. He must have been a beloved son, dead so young, certainly not an uncommon event in those days, but the blunt fact of it still hurt. Her grandfather Jacob Reinhardt's stone featured a draped granite cloth drawn back to reveal an open book with dates, 1869 -1947. He had died three years before she was born. An open book. *How symbolic.* Undoubtedly a 1940s tombstone model, but Van hoped it meant what it promised. A cemetery is a mute crop, headstones frozen in time, revealing little beyond the fashion in monuments and dates. What happened in the hyphen between birth and death was what she was after—the stories, the lives lived.

Back in the car Van pulled out the family portrait and compared the people with the dates on the tombstones. Oddly, Adam was either fifty-nine or sixty when he died, only a year after the photograph was taken, when he looked quite robust. Of course, there were myriad ways a farmer could perish. He was fourteen years older than his wife. Was Letty a second marriage for him? She made a note in her journal.

Letty was forty-four when the portrait was made. Van turned over the portrait to where her father had identified the eight children: five girls and three boys. They fell into two groups, four older and four younger. Probably the time of grief for little Johnnie accounted for the gap of years between the two sets. The oldest by far was her grandfather Jacob, followed by sisters Kate and Mary, brother Otto. The youngest were close in age: Lizzie, George, Margaret and Lena. These children would have been her father's aunts and uncles. People he never spoke about. Outside of Jacob, did he even know them?

Using the available dates, Van calculated that after Adam's death Letty lived for seven years as a widow with the younger children. Again, not that unusual. Letty was fifty-two or three when she died. Of natural causes from a hard life on the prairie? After her death, the four younger children were orphaned; maybe the two older sisters folded them into their families. Another widespread practice. The one thing that didn't add up was Jacob, the only of their children besides Johnnie to be buried in the cemetery. From what Jacob's birth date indicated, Letty would have been thirteen when he was born. Not impossible, but unlikely. Perhaps he was Adam's son? An earlier marriage? An adopted child? Beyond guesswork, there was nothing more to gain from the cemetery.

Van automatically pieced together these meager bits. Even scanty evidence was enough to generate a narrative. It was common knowledge that hardship and heartache were a given for pioneer farmers, but without the specifics of their daily lives, it remained generalized conjecture. Her chin jutted out in a familiar gesture of determination, Van propped the family portrait up in the passenger seat and drove north, eating her sandwich along the way. "Somehow I'm going to fill in those spaces between the hyphens," she announced to the somber-eyed people next to her.

At Storm Lake, she checked into a Super 8 motel. She couldn't get the door to open. "Damn!" She turned the key around until it finally gave, and she entered the room. She could have been anywhere—polyester spreads in a drab, unidentifiable color on the two double beds, the floor's dark gray indoor/outdoor carpeting, a generic framed landscape print on the wall revealing no particular location, the air conditioner set in a window that didn't open. Van preferred these kinds of rooms for their complete predictability, their absolute anonymity. No surprises, nothing to disturb your mind or make you wonder who last inhabited the space. A clean bathroom, hot water and a few fresh towels were things she did not mind paying for.

She pulled the blank journal out of her pack.

*Storm Lake, Iowa*
*Monday, June 12, 2000*
*Day One*

*Not much news from here. Pretty quiet. Seems strange that Maple Grove locals don't seem to remember the Reinhardts. I guess I will have to find them in the places you suggested. Feel disappointed—am actually a bit shaky since the close call with the deer—*

She crossed the last words out and looked around. *What the hell am I doing here in a third-rate motel in the middle of Iowa in the oppressive heat of summer, writing in a journal addressed to a dead man, talking out loud to an old family portrait, searching for people I've never met?* And, it looks like the only Reinhardts in the area are in the cemetery. *What a pipe dream to think I could find long-lost relatives who were still alive.* Dee Dee's patrons had quashed that fantasy.

"Dammit, Dad," she said aloud. "You knew that the research part of your note would get my attention." The accusation betrayed the fact that she was a beagle hound, a single-minded tracker, helpless against the call of a hunt. She hankered after the long chase. But this time there was a limit to what she was willing to do. In any case, there was no one to bring the prize back to, so no use running herself ragged across the cornfields looking for something or someone that might not even exist.

"I'm giving you one week for this research. After that, I am signing off. "It's my life. It's now or never, I ain't gonna live forever—"

She propped the Reinhardt portrait on the wooden dresser. Taken one hundred years ago at the turn of the 20th century, the framed photograph had hung in the shadows of her father's study for years. Along with Longfellow's book of poetry, it was the only ancestral artifact. No stories were attached to the people. Formal photographs never registered loss or absence, no empty spaces were made for the missing, like little Johnnie, and one could never ascertain the true nature of a person from a fixed middle-distance gaze or the calm placement of hands.

"I bet it took a lot of money and planning for all you folks to come together for a formal photo shoot. Dressed in your finest, you don't look at all shabby." Did she imagine it, or did Letty's eyes just slide her way?

# SIOUX CREEK FARM, IOWA

## DECEMBER 31, 1899

CAREFUL NOT TO DISTURB HER SLEEPING HUSBAND, Letty inched noiselessly out of bed, wrapped her shawl around her nightgown, and tiptoed barefoot down the stairs. Her nerves were too jumpy for sleep. In the kitchen, she adjusted the wick in the kerosene lamp to give just enough light for her task. The cook stove still held embers and she tossed in a few dried corncobs for extra warmth. The clock hands were nearing midnight. She was born at this hour—a strange and uncanny moment to enter the world, her mother always said. In the blink of an eye, she would turn forty-four years old, and the world would enter the twentieth century.

On the high cupboard shelf, away from any greedy little fingers, she stored the glass canning jar that contained all her extra egg and creamery butter money. Filled to the top with pennies, nickels, and dimes, she emptied it onto the kitchen table and sorted and stacked the coins. For the umpteenth time, she counted it out—three dollars, a veritable housewife's fortune. Satisfied that her addition was correct, she scooped the coins into a blue velvet coin purse, ready for tomorrow.

Months ago, rumor had reached her that Heinrich von Schimmer, the famous portrait photographer from Des Moines, was going to set up a studio in one of the storefronts in Maple Grove. Town folks and farm wives for miles around were clamoring to get a family portrait made as a souvenir to mark the end of the old century and the beginning of the new. Except for the commonplace one taken of her marriage, her family had no reason or money for photographs charting their past twenty-three years of building up their farm, so she was dead set on making a record of their accomplishment. Letty had given advance notice of the exact time they were to meet at the studio. Sister Kate and Mary lived in Maple Grove. Her oldest girls were reliable women now; their timely presence was guaranteed. Jacob and his family also lived in town, and he had been informed that his presence was expected. Otto had an establishment some miles north in the town of Early, but he had promised he would be there on time. She would have to trust him. The four younger children sleeping upstairs had their finery all set out.

With the coins safely secured, Letty sat at the kitchen table, threaded the needle and put the finishing touches on Adam's new wool vest, lining it with a chestnut-colored silk, the very color of his eyes. Over the years he had let his beard grow long. He was still dark-haired, even though he was fifty-eight years old. Farming had kept him strong, although lately he complained of stiffness in his joints upon arising and her concern for him nagged, along with aching remorse that she had not given him more sons. The silk lining was a great extravagance if not a reward, as was the family portrait that would serve as solid proof that their family had stayed the course and prospered despite the lack of sons.

Beyond that, in the darkened chambers of her private mind where she worked her thoughts, there dwelled other reasons for making the photograph. She cut the thread with her teeth and hung the vest on Adam's chair where he would find it in the morning. She checked the cobs in the cookstove, making sure there were enough embers for Tante Kate to get the fire going again in a few hours. Still half asleep, she snuffed the lantern wick with the tips of her fingers. *Ouch!* She was so careless, always burning something.

From out the kitchen window a shroud of whiteness covered the corn-stubbled fields and veiled the trees. Adam would have to hitch up Pet and Bucky to the sleigh for their ride into town. The snow glowed as if lit from within. The cold windowpane soothed her burnt fingers. Her eyes caught a darting shadow move in the woods. It was not an animal, but someone on foot. A chill passed through her. She clutched her shawl closer. A creak in the floorboards caused her whole body to jump. Tante Kate stood in the kitchen doorway holding a lit candle. She looked like an ancient wraith with her loose braid and long nightgown.

"Goodness. You gave me a fright. I didn't hear you come down."

"What are you doing in the dark at this hour? And in your bare feet, too," Tante Kate chastised, as if Letty were a child caught in some misbehavior. "It is no good staying up all night. Tomorrow is almost here. There is nothing more for you to do except go back to bed and get some sleep."

Letty's shoulders hunched in deference. "I'm sorry. I couldn't sleep, there's so much to get ready for tomorrow. Now I've ruined your sleep, too." Following Tante Kate upstairs, she reiterated her apologies. "I am very sorry you aren't going with us—to be in the picture. I told you the photographer said it was outside convention to include anyone else—just the husband, wife, and children—"

"*Das ist doch egal.* It does not matter to me," Tante Kate snorted. "I have almost seventy years of age. Do not even think of it. Certainly, I do not want to spoil your picture, or break the camera, or scare the photographer out of his wits with my homely old visage. I have two pictures. I don't need any more to know that I exist."

After all these years Tante Kate still scolded in German. Nothing worked faster to stopper Letty's mouth.

"Come, let's get you back to bed, before you catch your death." Tante Kate led the way up the stairs, holding her candle aloft. Letty shivered, pulled her shawl closer and padded behind her. At the top of the stairs, Tante Kate turned and pressed her forefinger to her lips. "Shush, don't wake Adam."

Even under the covers, Letty's feet were freezing. What a ninny she was. Why hadn't she pulled on her thick woolen socks? She moved her cold feet closer to Adam's warmth without disturbing his rhythmic breathing. Even as she closed her eyes in hopes of sleep, her mind raced backward.

Shortly before they had married, Adam informed her that his sister Katharina would be making a permanent home with them. He had shown her the two studio photographs, the same as Tante Kate had just mentioned. They were unforgettable. One showed Kate as a young woman in Germany. She stood next to a table, her hand resting on a book. The powerful frame of her body was tightly cinched at the waist, while a muscular force pushed against the constraining sheath of tucked and darted cloth. Her formidable will was undeniable in the forward set of her chin and jaw, her frontal gaze threatening an assault on the camera. The other portrait included Adam as a young man and was taken some time after their arrival in America, before they had turned up at Letty's family farm in Illinois. In this photograph, Adam was in his early twenties, full of youthful vigor and promise, while Kate, fifteen years older, sat next to him, doleful as a funeral goer. Adam never said, and she had never asked, what had transpired for Tante Kate in the years between the two portraits, but it looked like it had been something dreadful. Letty never saw the pictures again.

* * *

Why did Letty have to apologize again about the portrait? Celebrations of accomplishment put a chill in my blood. I do not think it wise to stick one's head up too high. I question the importance people place on looking at themselves. Of what significance is capturing a few seconds of existence on a glass plate when my memory can fashion endless pictures? In sum, I figure the family portrait to be an expensive and deceptive fancy. I have two pictures already and they are enough to last my lifetime. Anyway, most of what people call *real life* passes by unrecorded.

I keep the lit candle on the night table and quietly slip into the narrow bed that barely fits my wretched body and adjust the quilt over my feet, careful not to wake the three younger girls. Margaret and Lena sleep clasped in each other's arms, while Lizzy sleeps alone on her cot, flat as a board, her blanket up to her chin—such biddable girls, so unlike their mother who requires constant vigilance. What had Letty been doing up at this hour, barefoot, bug-eyed, roaming the house like a ghost? She'd burnt her fingers again. She bears constant watching.

No one can reproach me. Hasn't my whole life been devoted to others? Except for once, more than thirty years ago, when I tried to steer it otherwise. And who is to say if I was right or wrong? I suppose the Great Almighty, if there happens to be one, will be the judge when my time comes.

My mind drifts. Years ago, I determined to keep my own counsel about the time I went away, never revealing my actions or whereabouts, not even to Adam. He had no other choice but to accept me and the baby I brought back with me. What else could he do? Adam was my brother, and I was his only living kin in America, and what had happened to me was beyond explaining.

"*Der Junge ist ein Waisenkind.* The child is an orphan. His name is Jacob. He was put into my care. It is a common occurrence. Surely, I cannot abandon him!"

It was not an outright lie, more a convenient untruth. He was my child. How he came to be mine was my secret. I did not bear the look of a married woman, and Adam surely knew I did not marry because he knew my feelings on the subject clear enough.

Before getting to sleep, I reach for where I store my best memories. As a girl, I had kept a small diary of my secret heart. Poor little book. I burned its pages in our family's cookstove before Adam and I set sail for America. At Bremen port, I bought a Staedtler pen and a *Reisealbum,* a travel memory book, thinking I would make an account of our ship journey. My one photograph was tucked into the pocket of the album for safekeeping. Even now I groan to recall that frightful two-month sea journey, how poor and insufficient the food was—seven pounds for each person of mostly bread, biscuits and potatoes. Adam and I suffered only mental and moral disgust at the quality of the provisions and the unclean water that smelled of turpentine and vinegar. Our strong constitutions barely kept us from the scourge of dysentery that swept through the cramped quarters in steerage. I had no inclination to make dainty notes in a travel book that was just as likely to go with me to the bottom of the sea.

After I came back to Iowa with the baby Jacob, I wanted to write down how it transpired. I found the empty album where I had left it, at the bottom of the steamer trunk. Over time, the ink had dried so I swiped a pencil from our landlady's desk. Pinching private moments before bed, I licked the lead of the pencil and hastily recaptured the past before it became forgotten in the rush of days. I wrote in French, the language of my mother, the language of heart and love. I finished recording my journey by the time Adam and I arrived at Bauer's farmstead in Illinois. I hid the book from sight, but always close to hand.

Over the passing years, there was seldom a second to spare for rereading what I had written. But with Letty's recent campaign for capturing the family in a portrait, an urge arose to remember my secret self. In the flickering candlelight, I pulled the book from its hiding place underneath the cotton-stuffed mattress. The second photograph fell out. Adam had insisted on a memento before I left for my journey to the North Country. How dour I looked. Ever afterwards, I refused to be placed in front of a camera. My words sufficed as a true portrait.

It took some minutes to decipher what I had written more than thirty years ago. French was a faraway music, a melody never heard in our farmstead.

*No one knows I have a secret story. If I don't write it down, my life will be nothing but an empty space between the two dates on my gravestone. Dear book, you will be my witness as I have no other.*

*Adam and I had been in Illinois for the winter months. In the spring, he hired out to labor on a farm in another county and we determined it best if I could reach some distant relatives who had settled farther north. Being so alone in the new country of America unmoored me. I was like a kite cut loose from its tethering string. When the early spring days turned fair, I went to town for the purpose of finding a suitable family to travel with.*

*The town was hardly deserving of a name. Stern-faced men and tightlipped women with their broods headed west for an unknown destiny with terror and determination at equal parts. I stepped aside for an old trader whose Indian wife and their assorted children filed past with their bundles of supplies. A sorry collection of half-starved Indians huddled in their blankets up against the trading post. Indian agents and deputies with guns on their laps sat in rickety chairs outside the Mercantile along with several soldiers dressed in ragged uniforms from the country's recent war.*

*"The Iowa prairie is just waiting to be settled," a man proclaimed to a group who had gathered to hear him. He handed out a broadsheet extolling the Garden of Eden awaiting them in the west. "The land is cheap and fertile and truly meant for the white man's way of farming."*

*Someone called out, "What about the red Indians?"*

*Another voice answered, "Indians can't be taught to farm. They only know the warpath."*

*"There are no Indians left in Iowa," the promoter assured.*

*The merchants and traders had set up stores that supplied all and sundry with necessities for those migrating west toward the open prairie land. They always knew who was headed where, and I hoped they could locate someone fitting to take me north.*

*I heard him before I saw him, talking a kind of country French inside the Mercantile. Maybe it was the sweet sound of my* maman's *tongue that pulled me towards him as he was striking a bargain at the counter. Before I knew it, I found myself conversing with a stranger in the language of* maman, *caring nothing for the merchant's frown and the disapproving glances given me by those bonneted women with their pursed lips.*

*"I want to go up North. Will you take me with you?"*

*He took my measure, seemingly weighing the strange proposition in his mind. I did not want him to think about it for too long so I held my purse in front of his face. It was plump with a roll of cash that Adam had left me. "I have some good money to pay you for your efforts."*

I pushed the notebook back under the mattress and blew out the candle. How strange to have this language and these times come so alive now; they warmed the cold chambers of my heart. With a smile on my lips, I fell into a dreamless sleep.

* * *

Agitated from Tante Kate's scolding and still fearful about that shadow in the woods, Letty was unable to sleep. She burrowed deeper under her mother's worn coverlet, hoping to hide from the dreads. In their place came unhappy thoughts of her mother who occupied her mind more often these days, as she had just turned the exact same age as her own mother when she had died.

Letty was twelve years old when her mother stopped eating. As much as Letty pleaded, "One more spoon of broth, please," she could not make her mother open her mouth once she had clapped it tighter than a bolted barn door. The end was terribly slow in coming. Poor Mother, in her nightclothes all day in a darkened room, her mind gone permanently underground with the little coffins of her babes. The doctor brought brown glass bottles of medicine that were supposed to help. The closed air in her sickroom was soaked with the dark smell of that rank potion. Not that the medicine ever really helped. Probably it made her worse. Maybe it made it so she couldn't scream and cry and vent the fury that was surely in her, and maybe such a stifling is what killed her in the end. At least that is what Letty believed.

The doctor had recommended some kind of hospital, but her father said, *Nein,* and her mother became fierce in her silence while her pale flesh melted away. When a last fugitive breath slipped through the bars of her clenched teeth, her lips remained clamped, as if her spirit had glued them together. Unlike in most dead people, those muscles never did slacken.

Her two brothers lowered her coffin into the dug earth in the small Catholic cemetery on the hill. The priest claimed her mother was finally at rest. How did he know? In Letty's private mind, she doubted her mother was resting, with the little ones next to her, lost babes with their little flat stones marking their dates, hardly a few seasons having passed between them, mother and two infants.

And didn't her mother's unspent fury hollow their family to the core? Still a girl in braids and apron, Letty reluctantly hoisted the household burdens of a farmer's wife onto her shoulders. Each night through fall and winter, her father and brothers sat at the table and ate her chicken and potato suppers in silence. Mother's death had turned her father into a cold and merciless stone.

Letty's brothers were happy in the fields working the forty acres of corn, wheat and potatoes. Even under their father's harsh directives, which often included sessions with the leather strap, at least they had each other. She was alone, the only one in charge of chickens, cow's milk, sweet butter, and all the endless womanly chores, mostly unnoticed by her father and the boys unless they grudged about some chore that went undone. And then in the spring they came, these Reinhardts who changed her life forever.

One morning in early April her father asked her to handprint a sign in English and in German asking for an extra farm hand to help with spring planting. He took it to the Mercantile and two days later an ancient black buggy drew up in a splatter of mud from the rain-puddled road. Letty peeked through the upstairs window curtain and watched a tall young man swing off the wagon. Two others stayed in the carriage—a small boy and a woman who sat straight as a post with only her profile showing, her nose a hook, her chin jutting like a spade.

Huddled on the top stair with knees to her chin, Letty could hear the man and her father as they spoke in the parlor. The man was soft-spoken but insistent. He would only hire on if he could bring the woman and the boy. She pictured her father eyeing the young man like a horse, calculating the use he could get out of him while estimating how much it would take to feed the woman and boy. "*Nein.*" He wanted the man, not the woman and child. Letty understood too well that he was tired to death of women and the sad trouble they bring, and she was afraid he would not want the little boy, who would be a constant reminder of the sweet-smelling little babes he had lost.

The young man pressed his case. "Despite her age, my sister's labor is equal to half a man. She can more than make up for feeding the boy. You will see for yourself. I am strong and willing to work. You will not be disappointed in us."

Letty crossed her arms against her chest and prayed father would agree. Wasn't there always a need for more hands on a farm, men's hands, women's hands, even little boys' hands fit for holding one egg at a time? Surely, he must know she needed help with the chores and was desperately lonely for company?

She closed her eyes in relief when her father said, "*Ja,* I will take you on for a season, and the woman can help the girl with household chores." They were given sleeping quarters on straw mattresses in the out-building where the Bauers stored tools and housed extra hires during harvest.

When Letty dared to ask about them, her father said, "They sailed from Germany, some three or four years past. In the Old Country, a son in a family too large to sustain itself on a small patch of leased farmland has no choice but to leave." An uncurious man, he had not inquired further; Letty was not privy to what happened to the rest of the Reinhardt family, what remnants of parents, sisters, brothers, aunts, and uncles remained in the Old Country. She figured they had swarmed like bees when the hive got too crowded, taking the queen and lighting out for new territory. And the woman, Kate: She was the queen bee, all right.

Nothing happened in the house until Kate said, nothing moved until she did, nor stopped until she said stop; her black billowing taffeta skirts in full sail or at rest were signals to the actions of all others. Even then she was a big woman, and her bigness filled any room she was in. It was still so. Of course, at the time, Letty had no idea the young man, Adam, would someday be her husband, and the boy Jacob would be her first child, and Kate would become Tante Kate and still be ordering their lives all these years later.

Letty reached over to touch Adam's shoulder. She didn't want to arouse him, just needed his reassuring warmth. All the children granted her were already born, little Lena being the last. After her birth, Letty informed Adam there were to be no more. They had all heard of women who kept bearing until they were fifty, but she had no aspirations to be one of them. That she had not made enough boys was her shame.

"Be grateful that all but one of your children survived, as have you," Tante Kate reproached. It was true. As her own mother and the local cemeteries attested, many children didn't last their first years and many women didn't live through their childbearing years. Not counting an unformed bloody clot, she had lost only the one babe, little Johnnie.

Thoughts of Johnnie gave Letty vertigo. With her face turned to the wall, a whirlpool of sadness pulled her under. Their family picture would be missing little Johnnie. He should be standing next to his brother. Ott was two years younger, but sturdier and more robust. Of course, only the living can be portrayed in a family portrait, while the dead go unrepresented. The unknown future sits in the dark behind the eyes of those who look out at the camera.

"Unwholesome thoughts," Tante Kate would have scolded and shaken her forefinger.

Letty chided herself to stop maundering. "I am a forty-four-year-old woman with a husband and eight living children. Married for twenty-five years." She could hardly believe it herself.

The windowpanes showed gray light. The snow had stopped. As much as she had anticipated this day, her body was weighted by heavy memories. She pulled the often-patched quilt up to her neck and sucked on her burnt fingers. She had discovered that pain brought a strange pleasure. Sometimes she purposely bit her knuckles until the skin broke or picked at scabs until they bled. Tonight, she had burned her fingertips and let her feet get too cold. But if the hurt was strong enough, the taunting voices that swarmed in her head receded to their lair, satisfied.

Like some great rustling bird settling her feathers, the sound of Tante Kate descending the stairs told Letty that it was time to rise. The iron lid of the cookstove came down with a clang while Tante Kate fed it cobs. The rooster crowed and the back door opened and slammed shut. Tante Kate would feed the chickens and go to the cow barn to milk. Letty examined the red tips of her fingers and put her hands over her face. The photographic studio had been very strict about having only the immediate family represented in the family portrait. Even so, excluding Tante Kate felt deeply wrong, as if the picture would be telling a bald-faced lie, denying the very solid central beam that had held their family steady and upright for the past twenty-five years, but in her innermost mind where she kept her unspoken thoughts, Letty was glad that, for once, she would be placed in the center of her family.

# MAPLE GROVE, IOWA

## Tuesday, June 13, 2000

"Ask Vangie, to do some research," the note on the map said.

"Vangie." Van made a face. Even her father couldn't come to terms with the extravagant name he had given her, taken from Longfellow's long rhyming tale of *Evangeline*. The poem was redolent with nineteenth-century romantic sentiment—the French Acadian deportation, the star-crossed lovers unknowingly passing each other in the night, who, when finally reunited, die in each other's arms. When she was old enough to read it, she had no immunity against this bittersweet strain of nostalgic romance. One drop was potent enough to infuse her earliest love fantasies with dark endings and unfulfilled longing. She had attuned herself to the slightest hint of warmth lurking under her father's coldness. If his mother had read him poetry, and he kept her book, maybe he would have fallen in love with her mother's poetical nature and had once been sentimental enough to name his only child Evangeline.

Pure conjecture. Neither parent ever used her full name, and Van was stuck with a moniker that took up too much space.

When she was a graduate student, her professors insisted

on her full name. The elaborate French Evangeline clinging to the solid German Reinhardt was both embarrassing and cumbersome. She asked colleagues to try variations—Eve, Ev, Vange, and Evan—and finally saved up enough money to legally change her name to Van. In the beginning of her career *Professor Van Reinhardt* provided camouflage, made it easier to get published, to pass through the screen of gender discrimination that was still operative in her field. The three strong syllables had a pleasing consonance and gave her a sturdy, more forthright platform on which to stand. Later, when she became known for her feminist analyses of early American history, it distanced her from the 19th century romantic associations of *Evangeline*. Lately, she liked the name Van for its borderline quality, suggestive of something in between, which felt satisfying and truer to her nature. She never told her father of the name change. He had never called her Evangeline. He only ever called her Vangie.

Despite the one instance of Longfellow *Weltschmerz*, Martin was hardly a romantic. In fact, he loathed anything that smacked of fantasy and was not hard, provable science. Even as a high school student Van had had to read her English literature assignments in the library to avoid his scorn. He had left Iowa after high school and carried nothing of his childhood with him except the Longfellow book and the family portrait. He must have needed to reinvent himself.

She looked at the files. "Why at your age did you need to look into the past? Had you left something behind or had something finally caught up with you? But what?" Perhaps this is what happens to old people when they near the end of their lives, the urge to harken back. *But why recruit me into your nostalgic project?*

Her watch said midnight. Van was over-tired, but her body still buzzed with too much caffeine. Tomorrow she would go to the Maple Grove town office and see if she could locate the plat map of the original Reinhardt farm and the early census records. Then she would stop at the library. Archives were her resource and refuge. Without any living Reinhardts in the vicinity, maybe she could wind this trip up soon and head back to Madison, although what she would do when she got there drew a blank. "What do you want?" Dee Dee had asked. The question nagged at her. Maybe Em would be up for an adventure. They could find some interesting place for a summer getaway. They could still do that, couldn't they? They didn't have to sleep together.

Van woke with a chill, got up and turned off the air conditioner. She rummaged in her backpack for the worn, over-sized sweatshirt with the Bucky Badger logo and got back into bed. Ordinarily she relished the leisure and comfort of the morning where she could drift between waking and dreaming. Often this was the time when her ideas formed themselves. But something lingered from sleep that was disturbing. She couldn't quite put her finger on it. She felt edgy. Then she remembered her dream.

Near the river, a feeling of imminent danger, a threat. A frantic search for a telephone, trying to dial 911 on a strange phone pad with symbols instead of numbers. A phone ringing. A man's voice answering. She could see him, a dark man with black hair tied back into a ponytail. "I need your help," she said.

Now she was sweating. Had she been calling Len? What a bizarre thought. They hadn't seen each other or spoken to each other in years. Seeing the Wisconsin River must have triggered the dream. She checked her watch. She pushed the dream from her mind and went into the bathroom, where she took a long, purposeful look at herself in the mirror. "What are you after, my girl?" she inquired of the face looking back at her. "What *do* you want?"

Van was what people called a handsome woman. Even in the early summer her skin turned a reddish brown, the color set off by her thick graying hair. Her eyes were her best feature, she was told: a startling and intense blue, clearly a gift from her mother. Her high cheekbones and beaked nose were from her father's side. The impression of her face, however, was marked by a slight underbite, a feature of unknown origin that set her chin in such a way that if she weren't smiling, people usually read her as a stubborn woman. "An underbite is unattractive on a woman," her dentist once told her, and offered to fix it for a small fortune.

She had pushed her chin out further and replied, "No, thank you. I'll learn to live with it." This morning she noticed the tiny lines around her mouth were becoming more pronounced. Her hair had pulled out of its braid and perspiration dampened her forehead and upper lip. "You're a mess!" she told the mirror. "You need a good, long shower."

The warm water washed over her as she lathered her body with the cloying motel soap. She supposed she was in good shape for a fifty-year-old woman, her legs and arms still strong and muscular, and yet she was womanly, too, with full breasts and a soft curve of belly. She was not always comfortable in her skin, but she was healthy and capable, able to rise with the heat of passion under the right circumstances, which hadn't happened lately.

She pulled the gauze bandage off her knee, put on her cut-offs, a clean T-shirt, and sneakers, rebraided her hair and grabbed her backpack along with a sun visor and dark glasses. She took the sepia photograph from the dresser. "Okay, people, you're coming with me. Yield up your stories and your secrets if you have any. Don't waste my time."

Van reserved the room for another night. The bored guy at the front desk took her money without a comment. The humid heat hit her as she walked across the parking lot to her car. She propped the family portrait in the passenger seat. She reminded herself that these were her ancestors, great-grand-parents, great aunts and uncles, her grandfather. She searched for some resemblance in the women's faces—a familiar tilt of a head, the set of a mouth, the placement of hands—but could find nothing.

"How did you women ever manage this weather in heavy stockings, corsets and long dresses?" she asked Letty, daring her to move her eyes again. Turning on the air conditioner, Van drove south toward Maple Grove and the town office. She checked her watch. It was already mid-morning.

A stout, grandmotherly woman in a flowered dress heaved out of her office chair and stood behind the counter where a small oscillating fan moved the warm air and ruffled a stack of papers.

"What can I help you with, dear? You look like you're not from around these parts."

"My name's Van Reinhardt. Drove here from Madison, looking to do a bit of genealogical research of my Reinhardt ancestors."

"Nice to meet you, Ms. Reinhardt. I'm Lillian Grob. Now what is it you're looking for?"

"I was hoping to locate the original plat map of the Adam Reinhardt farm. It was probably purchased in the mid-1870s. And maybe you can tell me where to find census records from around that time."

"That's a pretty tall order, dear. Don't rightly recognize the name. Might take some time. Not sure I can lay my hands on them. Files back there haven't been touched in years. But I'll see what I can find."

Lillian shuffled into a back room and emerged trium-phant fifteen minutes later.

"Here's the plat map. Thought you might want to take a look at the rest of this stuff while you're at it. It's going to take me longer to locate the census records. Got nothing else to do this morning. But I can't promise. Otherwise I'll try to get them faxed from the county. Can you come back in the morning?"

"No problem. Thanks. Would you mind making copies of this material?"

Lillian shook her head at the dollar Van offered for the copies and fax. "On the house, dear."

"By the way, do you know where I can get a topographic map of the area?"

"Maybe the Carnegie Library. It's just down the street. Wait. Come to think of it, one of those developer fellas was in the other day and I think he left one of them maps on the counter. I stuck it in the desk drawer."

Lillian rifled through a drawer and handed Van a folded map. "Is this what you're looking for? You might as well have it. Too bad for the fella. Between you and me, I don't much like those guys. Good luck on your search, dear. I'll get to work on the census records. And if you want some good home-cooked food, go across the street to Dee Dee's."

"Just where I was headed. You've been a great help, Lillian. See you tomorrow."

At Dee Dee's, a few new faces had joined the crowd from yesterday. Blue-haired Helen waved as Van walked in.

"Didn't catch your name yesterday, dear."

"Van. Van Reinhardt."

"Interesting name for a girl."

"It used to be Evangeline," she said, as if that could explain anything.

Dee Dee was all smiles. "Am guessing you might want something more substantial than an egg salad? Got a few pancakes left." She gave Van a sidelong look. "The bacon is local."

"Sounds good. Thanks. And coffee. Black, please."

Dee Dee poured batter onto the grill, and added a couple slices of bacon. "Any luck at the cemetery?"

"I found some grave markers with dates. I guess it's a start. I got a plat map of the original farm at the town office from Lillian Grob. She's looking for a census record. She also gave me a topographic map someone had left on her counter, which was really kind of her."

"That's my Lillian for you. She tends to take her work seriously," Dee Dee said, while she flipped the pancakes and poured the coffee. "You go find a seat at that back table. I'll get this to you in a jiff."

Decades of frying grease permeated the atmosphere. Van welcomed the empty red Formica back table, the only one that seated two. She did not want conversation. She needed to focus on the task at hand. Dee Dee delivered the plate of pancakes and bacon, along with a giant bottle of orange corn syrup and a mug of black coffee.

Van examined the copies Lillian had given her. The photographs were of Maple Grove's prouder days when the Chicago and North Western Railway was the major means of transportation. Remnants of those prosperous years were still in evidence: a Carnegie-endowed library with its original white pillars; a marble-faced bank building; a small public park; Catholic and Lutheran churches, and the towering grain elevators.

The broadside was from an old railroad company promotion.

### "WANTED, THIS SPRING, 10,000 FARMERS!"

"To improve 1,700,000 acres of the very best Farming lands in the World, which can now be had at Present value on long time, with six percent interest on deferred payments. These lands comprise the

Government Railroad grants along the Central and Northwest, Illinois Central and Sioux City and Pacific Railroads, and are mainly located in the middle region of Western Iowa noted for its salubrious climate, fever and ague being unknown—and inexhaustible soil—a finely watered yet perfectly drained district in the best agricultural state of the Union."

This kind of boosterism must have been what drew the Reinhardts, along with thousands of other migrants, to western Iowa.

She pulled her journal from her pack.

*June 13, 2000*
*Day Two*

*I've only been here one day and am being treated like a local. The town itself is in steep decline. Unsurprising. Looks like the old stone Catholic Church has been replaced by one with angular architecture and garish stained glass made popular in the 1950s. The old schoolhouse where I figure you went to school is gone— now it's just a generic two-story brick cube.*

*I got the plat map and am going to see if I can find the old farmstead. I need to put my feet on the land. The weather is hot for humans—good for corn and soybeans, I guess. Everything looks pretty normal.*

Van ate the last syrup-soaked pancake and was about to close her journal. Questions banged in her mind. Although it was her longstanding habit, she figured that talking out loud in Dee Dee's Diner to someone who wasn't visible was not a good idea. Instead, she wrote in a fit of pique:

*Why did you leave Maple Grove and never return? Did you kill someone? Did you get a girl pregnant? What were you running from? And what did you expect me to find? This assignment came with a cryptic note and no other clue as to what you were after. It still makes me angry. All of it!*

Before closing the journal, she drank the last swallow of coffee and wrote:

*Note to self: I think Len is stalking me in my dreams. Why? I don't like it. Anyway, this trip is not about him or me.*

Back in the car, Van regretted the pancakes—a terrible choice for a hot day. She turned on the air conditioner and addressed the family portrait. "'Salubrious climate,' my ass! Sorry folks, but who were those land-boosters trying to kid? I bet you sweated plenty in those long dresses."

As she drove through shimmering acres of cornfields, she realized her father had never owned land beyond his small suburban house lot. Instead, he possessed the earth by grasping and naming its hidden parts, fathoming its secret turbulence, apprehending its ancient convulsions. His lessons in ancient geology were downright violent, elemental, impersonal—primordial seas, howling winds and glacial ice without benefit of human company. They had scared the wits out of her as a young person and still evoked a sharp and terrifying kind of loneliness.

Reciting names in a holy litany—sandstone, limestone, dolomite, shale—he had explained how millions of years ago, a primeval sea had covered the land with shallow waters and, as the sediment settled, it layered itself onto the ancient sea floor. When the glaciers melted and the seas evaporated the pebbly clay, sand, and gravel were blown and abraded by a ferocious wind, forming the abundant silt that made up

Iowa's loamy soil. "Loess." Her father had pronounced the German word *Luss*. "It was loess that made Iowa soil such a goldmine for farmers."

From such unlikely material she had made up her own bedtime stories. An imaginative child without grandparents, she had pictured loess as Lois, a wizened old woman, a fantasy grandmother, with wild grey hair, warm sparkling eyes, and a big apron, who lived near a terminal moraine and had six drumlins to do her bidding. It was Lois, a kindly being with supernatural powers and human needs in mind, who watered, baked, froze and thawed, weathered and matured the earth through thousands of seasons. When she was seven, she wrote and illustrated the story for her class and won a prize. She ran home to show her parents.

Her father was furious. "Sheer fantasy," he scoffed. "Nothing scientific about it. Don't bother your mother with this nonsense. Your teacher shouldn't be rewarding you for such silly ideas."

It took years before Van comprehended: Martin had never related to her as a child, only as a student of Ice-Age geology. She had barely understood the language of his lectures, but she did absorb the chill that emanated from them. She had no name for what his lessons lacked: the warmth of human connection. For all she knew, it was that absence which sent her packing into the warm-blooded study of history. Frequently harsh and unforgiving, history had never left her feeling desolate. Whatever her father's personal demons were, they had been perfectly expressed in the ferocious ways the earth was formed. There was violence in him. She knew this now.

Her father had pressed on her mind like the last great Wisconsin glacier, and, like the retreating ice, his death had released her from the tyranny of his frozen world. But without his influence she felt unsure of her own shape. Weren't most people confused about their parents? Probably. But she didn't think they were afraid of them.

# SIOUX CREEK FARM

## New Year's Day, 1900

THE SUN HAD NOT YET RISEN ON THE MORNING. The family was scheduled to sit for the studio portrait in Maple Grove and I had work to do. The kerosene lantern was filled and lit and a pail of chicken feed and scraps was at hand. I pulled on barn boots, wrapped my head and shoulders in a thick winter shawl and headed to the cow barn, that great *Kuh* cathedral with its familiar smell of warm animals, hay, and manure. The lantern, set on a far bench away from the cow's rear hoof, made a small circle of light. I tied the first cow to her stanchion, positioned the stool and tin pail and began to milk, letting the cow's teats warm my hands. Milking was my job. Not that I ever minded it. The cows know my touch and give freely. Milking is rhythmic and conducive to mind-wandering, and I let my thoughts seek the past. I had milked cows for more than thirty years, since we had arrived at Letty's family farm.

Grief must have crooked its bony finger and beckoned us to that lonesome Illinois farmstead. On our first meeting, I saw that Farmer Bauer's face carried a widower's sorrow, and that bitterness had carved his down-turned mouth. With his wife newly dead there was no woman in the house, only a girl in braids. This would be to our advantage. Every farmhouse needs a grown woman.

It was plain the girl could use a mother, but I had no intention of making a mother-daughter bond with her, although our ages would have permitted. No, I was not about to take another helpless thing under my wing. If I hadn't used up all my caring on *maman* then my year away had surely sucked out whatever warmth remained in my heart. Grief still lived in me as a cold emptiness.

Newly acquainted with bereavement myself, I suspected old man Bauer had spent his limited supply of finer feelings on those who had died. His two sons did not resent their father's bleak demeanor for they had each other, although they were not spared his wrath. As for the girl, the old man acted as if she was the cause of his suffering. Adam told me that her brothers said the girl resembled her dead mother in looks and gesture. This was hardly the girl's fault, but it could be counted as her misfortune.

Beyond this comment, I had wondered if Adam took notice of the girl. Most likely he had not. She was merely a flash of apron pinafore, a switch of braids. Nor did she appear to register his existence. Who was he to this motherless girl? Another farm hand, another plate set at the long wooden table, another mouth to feed, just another man in the house. In the winter, after Bauer extended our employment and gave us a place to live inside the farmhouse, Adam and the old man anchored each end of the family dinner table, both of them silent as dirt. That suited me just fine. I always preferred silence to speech. It was more honest.

I untied the cow and got the next one moved to the stanchion. This one would take some hard pulling to get the milk to flow. My hands were getting arthritic, and I hoped that milking would help to loosen them. There was still a good supply of willow bark from my harvest last summer and I would make some tea for the pain. I had not always needed such remedies. I had not always been this old.

When the big migration to America took place in 1848, I was a young woman of marrying age. I could have gone then, because I had a craving for something larger than all the smallness I saw around me, but I had refused to marry one of those wretched '48ers. They were a desperate lot, driven to the boats by hunger and despair, willing to gamble their pitiful lives on the promise of land, and a hope for a new start. Hadn't I watched girls in our village take on the marriage yoke like dumb oxen, their bodies shaped by the weight and strain of it? The minute I started to bleed, I foresaw my future possibilities, and they were not going to include some clumsy old farmer having proprietary rights over my body. I was not going to be someone's ox or make babies like rabbits one right after the other, sometimes dying from the sheer misery of it all. And for certain, I would never enter the convent like some pale and homely girls I knew. No soft-handed, red-faced priest would ever tell me what to do or how to live and think or pray.

I had managed to stay clear of a husband by being tight-lipped and strong in my will. No man wanted a woman like that, at least no man in our village of Heidesheim where they liked their women meek and obedient as sheep, no matter if that docility froze their hearts and made their mouths empty as a widow's purse. When I agreed to join Adam aboard that stinking, creaking vessel headed for the shores of America, our parents were dead, and I was thirty-five, well past marrying age.

Even later with the boy, Jacob, I did not let my heart soften, not that I didn't care for him in ways that befitted my position. I stifled my womanly nature, never letting my hands reach out in a tender touch, nor did my lips speak any sweet words. If withholding maternal feeling was my failing, it was purposeful.

I poured the pail of cow's milk into the large metal milk can and got the next cow. Holsteins. Adam chose his cows well, good reliable milkers. I had heard of mechanical milking machines but could not imagine a cow putting up with a new-fangled thing like that. I placed my cheek against the cow's flank and spoke softly to her in German while I milked.

We must have been at Bauer's farm for four years when Letty's narrow waist revealed the curve of her hips, and pins and rolls replaced her girlish braids. Ever vigilant, there was not one moment when everything changed, but like the crops at the end of summer, one day the girl appeared ripe and full. I marked how Letty stared at Adam with her hard blue eyes, her look no longer the downturned glance of a shy young girl but the complete, assessing gaze of a woman taking inventory and weighing out her chances in a game she had never played. Her eyes had contained no modesty; it was as if they belonged to some kind of animal, curious and hungry. Adam flushed under her scrutiny and fled the house each morning for the fields, rushing to break up clods behind the team.

One morning when we were alone in the kitchen, I spoke to Adam.

"Adam, Adam, *hör mir zu!* Listen to me! Maybe as her lawful husband you could regain some of your strength and recover your self-respect. Put an end to this feeling that you are her toy at the end of a little stick, bouncing up and down at her whim."

Adam sat in the kitchen chair and put his head in his hands. Why did he look so mortified? Really, I thought, I caught him in a trap of his own devising. Hadn't he encouraged and enjoyed his little cat and mouse games with Letty?

"Adam, you are old enough to be your own man by now. *Bitte, es ist Zeit dass Du heiratest!* Please, it is time for you to take a wife!"

"*Nein, Nein,* Katharina!" he pleaded, his face going scarlet at my proposal, whether from embarrassment or fear or both, I did not know. "Katharina, please, please do not pursue this any further. Anyway, she is too young for me."

"Her age is to your advantage. And furthermore," I countered, "I do not think it natural for a man like you to live out your days without a wife, although we know that many others have done so by choice or by circumstance." I purposely softened my tone. "Look at it this way. We have already formed ourselves into a regular family over the time we have lived here, so her father will have no objection and this blessing from the priest is really not too much to ask." I sweetened the marriage idea by assuring Adam that I would always make my home with him.

This was a long speech and Adam was nailed to the chair by the force of it. I waited for him to see the wisdom in my plan. Well, what could he do about it anyway? My mind was fairly well set upon it. I had been mulling it over for months.

In my estimation it did not sit well for a man to live without a wife. Had I not seen those bachelor farmers sitting outside the Mercantile? There was something not right about them—either they took to drink, or they took up with their animals. And I did not want my younger brother to become one of them. For a man, marriage gave a clear benefit. Of course, it was not the same for a woman like me. Truthfully, I harbored a sheer dread of marriage, worse than my fear of diphtheria or even plague.

Stubbornness was not thought to be a virtue for a woman, but it had proved to be my salvation. I was not opposed to men in a way most would notice— not full of high tempers and dark storms—but deep down in the place where I carried my secrets, I set myself against them and there was no changing that. My brother was the only living man who had ever found a place in my heart.

Well, that was not exactly the truth. There had been one other.

As a matter of fact, Adam and Letty's union proved a practical remedy for my larger concerns. I would always have a place to live with them, and Jacob would be provided with what I could not give him, the shelter of a proper mother and father. Since he first formed words, the boy had taken to calling Adam *Papa*, and the girl *Mama Letty*, so the pairing seemed nature-made. When the census man came round to the Bauer farm, I kept my tongue when Letty lied through her teeth and designated Jacob as her and Adam's son. That is how Letty became Jacob's official mother and I became Tante Kate, maiden aunt, although at that point I was not a maiden and no one's aunt at all.

There were ten cows left to milk. I made note to tell Adam that the young cow was dried out and would need to be bred. The tin pail was hardly full. I pitchforked extra alfalfa into her trough.

As certain as I had been that marriage would serve them, I harbored fears that it might work against Letty, that whatever troubled that young woman's mind would not be settled by becoming a wife. No, I had not considered her when urging Adam to marry. I hoped Adam would find his way with her. But women were never within his ken, especially not a one such as her. A mule or draft horse would have surely bent to him, but Letty did not. I determined it best to let nature take its course. And nature was not always something you could predict, as I soon found out.

We were still at Bauer's farm after the marriage took place. I was putting straw on the kitchen garden beds, preparing them for the winter snows that were already in the air when Adam ran from the barn, tears streaming down his face.

"*Was?* What is it?" I could not imagine what had put him into such a state. I saw no blood or broken bones.

"Bauer." Adam choked the name out.

"*Was?*"

"Hanging from the barn rafters."

In a flash I pictured the scene. "*Wo ist er jetzt?* Where is he now?"

"I cut him down."

"Take me to him. And stop blubbering before anybody sees you."

Bauer's body lay unnaturally twisted on the barn floor. Next to him was the thick rope and the hacksaw Adam had used to cut him down. I had not seen my brother sob like this since he was a small child, not even when our parents had died. He sat next to the body patting the old man, imploring, "Why didn't you come to me? What will I say to Letty?"

"Listen to me, Adam. You are not a boy any longer. We mustn't let anyone know how he died. Otherwise, he will never get a Christian burial. We have to say he had a stroke and fell from the hayloft. Hide the rope and pull his collar up to cover his neck. Tell her brothers first. They will build the coffin, and then we will tell Letty."

Adam followed my lead. I knew best.

Life on a prairie farm was often hard beyond reason and its toll frequently more than the human mind wished to bear—crops failed, farms were lost, men turned bitter, and children died too young and too often, leaving women hollow-eyed and empty hearted. Others had met their end by their own doing. Women, too. There were many ways a person could end their life, and hanging from the barn rafters was surely cleaner than a firearm, carbolic acid, or kerosene. Of course, there was always shame cast upon a death by one's own hand. I presumed religion gave some a stronghold, but you never knew when a person's breaking point would come. Maybe Bauer had some incurable illness and wanted to spare the family the time and energy it would take to care for him. Whatever his reasons, the church declared taking your own life an ungodly sin and refused burial in consecrated ground. I was adamant that no one but Adam and I would ever know the truth of his dying. It remains a secret between us.

When Adam told Letty her father had died from a stroke, her hands flew to her swelling belly as if to protect the child in her womb. I feared Letty might lose the baby with the shock, but she betrayed no other feelings. Her father had long turned away from her, so this fresh sorrow must not have entered her heart as anything new. In truth, I even imagined Letty straightened her spine, as if a cold wind had finally ceased, and her body could resume its natural shape without his baneful influence. I, myself, did not miss the ill-tempered old man, either.

Letty's baby was born soon afterwards and to my surprise, Letty named her Kate. Not the German, Katharina, of course, but the American style, Katherine. In doing so, I believed Letty was making up to me for boldly claiming to the census taker that she was Jacob's mother. At the time I had raised no objections. I just played along. I reckoned it was easier that way for everyone. No judging looks or questioning remarks, nothing for rumors to feed on. Shortly after Bauer's death, Adam informed us of his decision to buy land in Iowa. I was all for leaving that doomed farm in Illinois.

The last cow nudged. Milking always gave me the reveries. Morning light cut through the slats in the barn and the urgency of the day goaded me on. I took the milk pail into the cold room and went into the hen house to gather eggs. My tasks marched in front of me—make the quick bread, fry the bacon and cook the eggs, get young George to slop the pigs, fetch the water, and feed the geese, wake the girls and get them dressed, make sure everyone gets into the sleigh and off in time.

* * *

Letty heard the back door slam. Tante Kate had taken longer than usual milking the cows. Still Letty lingered, grateful for a few extra minutes in bed, for the heat emanating from her husband. Her husband. Even after twenty-seven years it was unbelievable that she had gotten a husband. Of course, she hadn't had much say in the matter.

She had just turned seventeen the afternoon Adam came into the family parlor after Sunday dinner to talk with father. Grabbing a fistful of skirt, she ran upstairs and crouched on the landing so she could overhear them.

"I wish to marry your daughter, Herr Bauer. I hope you will give me your approval. You have known me as your hired hand for the past four years. Now, I wish to be your son-in-law. We will make a good match. Young Jacob and my sister Kate will be part of our family, and yours, too."

"*Ja*, it would be good. Do as you wish."

Letty's whole body was shaking as she ran into her mother's old room. She was barely yet a woman, only three years into her monthlies, and Adam so grown and rough from working the farm. She knelt at the edge of the bed and buried her face in her mother's quilted coverlet. Father had agreed to the marriage—a little too quickly, she thought. But no other plans had been made for her. Even her mother would have told her that marriage was an expected thing for a woman, and hadn't she already lived with Adam in the same house since she was a girl of twelve? At least he was not a complete stranger.

Letty harbored a foreboding of the marriage bed even before she knew all that happened there. Was it not unseemly, this coupling of bodies? Living on a farm she was eyewitness to plenty of it in the barnyard and maybe that was the source of her nerves, or maybe it was the indecorous nature of those acts that offended her so. How her brothers laughed as the bull clumsily mounted the cow, how they cheered him on, and how the cow just stood there blank-eyed and took it. Surely the embrace of a husband and wife would be different.

As to be expected, married life altered her in ways, some visible and some concealed. As the newly married, she and Adam were installed in her parent's bedroom with the big wooden bedstead, the very room she was birthed in and the very bed her mother had died in. In that room, with its four-paned window and white-sash curtains that looked out onto the orchard, was where her struggles commenced. And it was in that bed under her mother's handmade coverlet where the unseen changes took place.

In the first days of marriage her body took to trembling the minute Adam laid his hand on her. He tried to gentle her as if she were an unbroken horse: "Letty, Letty, *meine Braut, komm zu mir.* Letty, my bride, come to me," he would whisper. But his want always pressed on him so hard, and he was not inclined toward delicacy, being a big man with farming hands and an urgency he did not seem to understand himself. Most of the time he did not linger long, and she soon learned it best to let him have what he would and put her thoughts elsewhere—away from his hoarse breathing and the strange and desperate convulsions of his body, and the pitiful bleats coming from her own mouth.

Her womanly resistance was soon worn down by the larger dominion of her husband's flesh. Poor Adam, his need was always so great and her offering so puny and oftentimes withheld. It took a year of those nighttime thrashings before her body accepted the start of a new life. She heard sneering voices that stormed her mind. But she did not possess the power to refuse the task altogether. The force of nature was mightier than any one poor woman's thoughts. The birth had been a ghastly matter. She howled and bit like some rabid dog. Dr. Ziegler held her down and tied her with torn up sheets. When the baby finally came whole into the world, Letty was triumphant and put the horror of her birth behind her, all that blood, her arms and legs bruised blue from being trussed up like a turkey.

Letty was regretful she did not give Adam what it was he truly craved. But beyond sons, she was not sure what that was. It was always a surprise to see him in the early light of morning, his body soft and almost boyish in his sleeping, and so very peaceful in his even breathing.

Back from milking, she heard Tante Kate drop fresh cobs into the cook stove. Sliding from under the quilt without waking her husband, Letty stood barefoot in her winter nightgown, splashed cold water on her face and stared into the silvered mirror. Her face was not fit for the photographer. There were shadows under her eyes. Dark shapes still flickered in the background; unwanted visitors left from last night's vision. She willed herself toward the day. If Tante Kate and poor dead Johnnie were not included in the family portrait at least Jacob would be. He daren't miss it. Surely his wife would see that he arrives on time. Thoughts of Jacob these days put her in a state of nerves. She never knew what effect he would have on her— heart palpitations, shortness of breath, love, fury.

* * *

Jacob could hear his wife downstairs tending to the babies and getting breakfast ready. She had let him linger in bed, knowing he didn't have to be at the photographer's studio until late morning. On the wardrobe closet she had hung his freshly pressed wedding suit. Beyond his wedding day six years ago, he couldn't remember the last time he wore it. He hoped it still fit. He would find out soon enough.

Unused to the luxury of the morning bed, he stretched and scratched his chest under his itchy flannel nightshirt. Without looking, he knew it had snowed in the night. He always knew about the weather. No one had ever instructed him. Maybe it was as Tante Kate once said; he was born knowing it. The weather was harder to read since he moved into town. But as a child on the farm he could guess when storms were coming and from where, even when the skies were still bright blue and clear. The breezes whispered to him about the kind of moisture in the air, and he could feel a winter blizzard long before it blanketed the land, putting everything to bed in silent whiteness. He knew if the coming winter would be long and hard or give them a blessing of light snows and little winds. When the buzzards took to the sky, it was a sure sign that winter had finally come to an end.

Summer dry spells were the easiest to predict as they gave his skin and hair a vexing irritation, like when a thing is rubbed against its grain. He could tell what the big summer storms carried with them, what kind of lightning they were bringing—the kind that splinters the sky like shattered glass or the kind that cracks the heavens in two with one jagged bolt. Sometimes a storm carried balls of fire named after a Christian saint, and they made people and animals on edge as they portended great danger and were awesome to behold. The sweet gentle rains that give early crops exactly the nourishment required were felt as a sheer happiness and made him joyful because he could tell Papa Adam they were coming, and everyone would feel the gladness they brought. And then there was the terrible drought.

More than getting himself into his wedding suit, he dreaded the upcoming ordeal at the photographer's studio, and later, back at the farmstead. Unlike the weather, he never knew what people would do next. But there was no use protesting Mama

Letty's demand for his presence. How very strange she had become over the years. She wasn't always that way, was she?

His earliest memories of Letty he recalled with pleasure. At the old Bauer farm there were only grownups—Papa Adam, Mama Letty, Tante Kate, Grandpapa and the big boys. He was the only child and Mama Letty made up games and that is where he'd learned his first words in English. He smiled to recall how he loved to play with her. They were often left alone as all the others were up and working about in the fields or the barn by early morning. Sometimes she chased him, and he hid, then she would find him and they would laugh and laugh. When Old Tante Kate was in the kitchen, well, then they didn't play so much.

She always felt old to him, that Tante Kate, and he guessed she was, compared to Mama Letty. But old is more than age, and maybe he learned it then. It had something to do with how a face was set and Tante Kate's was fairly shut, and smiles were hard to get from her. But not Mama Letty. Was it he who began to call her that? His little boy's mouth unable to fashion her proper name, Elizabeth? It seemed everyone always called her Letty, but he was the only one who ever called her Mama Letty. Those words were a song to his ears— *MamaLetty, MamaLetty*—like some secret tune they shared. Like all little ones who go toward what feels like warmth and love, so it was that he hung onto Mama Letty's skirts. The smell of her was like the clothes she hung out on the line to dry, fresh and clean, as if the whole sweet fragrance of the prairie was in her. There were later times he wondered: Was she his true mother? A question that hardly mattered. She was the only mother he ever knew.

Their lives on the old Bauer farm were as far back as he could remember. Even as a small boy he had his chores; every hand was needed, they said, and it helped him to feel big. At first it was just the chicken coop. And this was not easy for a little one; there were many things to learn if you were going to come out of that coop with the eggs still warm and whole. You could not just walk right in there bold like or the hens would set up such a racket and fuss and the rooster came at you something terrible. You had to go in like a little fox, singing low, humming sounds to match the brooding hens. The coop was always a warm place of straw smell and feathers with little sunlight except for the beams that slanted through the cracks in the boards giving just enough light to see where the hens were bedded.

Slowly, carefully—no fast movements—you could reach under their soft-feathered breasts and feel the smooth warm shape of an egg in its straw bed. It was work meant for a woman or a child; not a man or even a big boy could do this well, nor did they want to, as it was considered unmanly. And it was truly a tender thing that bore no roughness, or the eggs would be lost, and the hens sent off their laying. How Mama Letty praised him for coming back with no broken eggs. She would hand him something sweet as a prize for his good work, but it was always her smile that was the sweetest to him.

When Grandpapa Bauer fell dead in the cow barn, the grown-ups whispered amongst themselves, and he thought it was something fearful that had happened although he knew that death itself was not; it only left an empty, quiet feeling that made your heart feel lonely, like when his favorite barn cat died. But Bauer was an old man and never had given Jacob much mind. The boy did not see Mama Letty cry after her father's death, and so he did not cry either, and by that time he knew that boys were not supposed to cry about anything.

For months he had watched Mama Letty's stomach grow and Jacob knew she was making a baby for them. She seemed happy then even though Grandpapa had just died, and so he tried to feel happy with her. But soon after baby sister Kate came, Mama Letty turned all broody and dark and Jacob did not know why. Maybe she didn't like the baby that came; maybe it made her work too hard and did not let her sleep at night. Having a new baby in the family meant he was more grown up and Jacob did try his best to help Mama Letty, even though the little one was always taking her away from him.

Jacob had just turned nine when Papa Adam said they were getting their own farm in Iowa and leaving Bauer's for good. Jacob was afraid it might be sad to leave because he had felt such happiness there with Mama Letty and the chicken coop. Maybe his happiness was because he was so young and had no worries, and he had Mama Letty all to himself. Or maybe that was just how childhood felt when the cares and troubles that haunt the world of big people are kept from you.

So many things had come upon them all at once. They were caught up in that eerie time between old Grandpapa dying and the new baby, and that was when the big changes swooped down on them like one of those sudden prairie twisters where everything gets turned upside down. And before he knew it, everyone was planning for a move west.

When the schoolhouse opened that fall in Iowa, he heard Papa Adam tell Mama Letty that Jacob was past the age for book learning. Mama Letty had other ideas. In the evenings, she used her family Bible to teach him the meaning hidden in the black marks inscribed upon those thin pages. Maybe his mind was already filled with the teachings the earth and sky offered each day, for he never could find a way to truly cipher those marks. They left him with a small and cramped feeling, as if they might get caught in his throat like chicken bones.

Mama Letty was not happy. "Jacob," she scolded. "You must learn to read and write. Otherwise, you will end up ignorant!"

He knew this was something shameful, so to please her he let her take his hand with the pen in hers, guiding him to inscribe his name in flowery script. But his hand felt dead with that thin writing pen, not at all like when he had held the living, singing willow stick and found the source of water on their land.

"*Lass ihn in Ruhe!* Leave him in peace!" Tante Kate reproached in a sharp voice. "He is not meant to be a book-learned scholar!"

"Clearly not!" Letty grumbled. "Look at you! Even though I know you can, you refuse to read or speak the English language!"

Those two carried on a terrible disagreement until Mama Letty muttered, "He might just as well be a savage," and Tante Kate left the room in a huff. Shame cast a shadow into him. Maybe Mama Letty was right to try to teach him proper reading and writing and maybe there was something bad in him that would not let her.

"There will be times in your grown life," she warned, "when being able to read those black markings will give things a better outcome."

His mind never did find it favorable to be locked up in those small words on a printed page. To this very day, it made his breath come short.

"Jacob! Jacob!" His wife called from downstairs. "Your breakfast is ready. You need to get up. Don't forget to trim your beard and scrub your nails."

Now his heart does not know which way to go; one way it is filled with his boyhood happiness and joy like a summer day, another way and there are dark rainless clouds, a pain so sharp that it clutches at his heart, and he is like a mouse in the talons of a hungry hawk. But that all came later, much later, and he knew nothing of the sorrows to come when he was a young boy.

His wife Elizabeth called from the kitchen. "Jacob! Please get up and come for breakfast. You don't want to be late to the studio." He pushed the blankets aside and planted his bare feet on the floor. He would be turning thirty-one some-time this month. No one was ever sure of the exact date. He was a grown man with a wife and children, yet he needed fortification for the day ahead. He did not know where to find it except in his wife's kindness.

*     *     *

I hurried from the cow barn feeling peevish about all that had yet to be done so the family could leave on time. For the first time in memory Letty put herself in charge and I had to hand it to her. Her obsession for the turn-of- the-century portrait was unusual, for I did not know Letty to be a craving or covetous woman. Despite her needs, she had so few wants. Except for Jacob. Hadn't she sought him as if he were life's breath itself? As a girl, she had taken possession of him with a tenacity I deemed *ungesund*, an unhealthy hunger for a girl of thirteen. Having released my claim as his mother, I steeled myself against intervening; hoping Adam would eventually make a man of him.

I woke George and went into the kitchen to make the quick bread. My stiff hands complained as I kneaded the dough. How did I get so old? There were so few occasions to calculate the passing of the years. An occasional glance in a mirror from time to time to straighten my hair or smooth my apron had not registered my age. My hair was still dark au-burn, as was Adam's, and my figure thicker set but not overly stout. Despite my knobby fingers, I still had the great good fortune of unflagging health and had never been stricken by any of the epidemics that had raged through their farming community, culling out the weak and the able without discernment. My constitution proved to be one of my finer assets for the family. Hadn't Adam once claimed I could work like a man? And wasn't he right about that?

The table was set with biscuits, butter and jam, eggs and bacon, so the family would be well fortified for the sleigh ride into town. I climbed back upstairs and woke the girls and laid out the two dresses I had made for young Margaret and Lena, secretly admiring my own handiwork, the elaborate smocking I had stitched into the bodices. My crooked fingers had conjured the memory of this dainty craft from someplace in my ancient past, astonishing everyone.

During the first year on our new farm, Adam often called me to work in the fields, but in truth, neither farm fields nor fancy sewing was not what I was meant for. My rightful place was at Letty's side. When she stared into the distance, let a pot burn on the stove, or did not respond to her baby's cry, if she saw things that weren't there or conducted breathless arguments that were not meant for anyone's ears, I touched her arm to bring her back from wherever her mind had taken her and brewed herbal teas.

The necessary routines of daily life were what I held to because it kept the family on an even keel. I made certain Letty and I were together at the kitchen table, the barnyard, the kitchen garden, the water pump and washtubs. All the homely toils of scrubbing, sweeping, laundry, meal preparation we did side by side. Always mindful not to tax Letty beyond her capabilities, we labored in silence in order to conserve our united strength, as the work often surpassed our combined efforts. Chores had to be performed sick or well, and I preferred that we remained well. I tutored myself in Letty's moods and changes, learning to sight them coming from a distance, and worked persistently to head off calamities by foreseeing them and taking action before they befell. Small everyday arrangements kept us from an abyss I could not name but constantly defended against.

I was thankful to whatever god there was that he had not meant me for the constant bearing of children. Once was enough. But I could not escape that part of woman's work altogether, and midwifing Letty became my piece of the business. I had assisted Dr. Ziegler when he delivered Letty's firstborn at the Bauer's farm and was convinced I could do it with more tenderness. Once we were in Iowa, the Maple Grove doctor was miles away from their farmstead, and neighboring farmwomen were not always reachable in bad weather. Letty was fearful of strangers, and I pretended my English was not good, so it was just the two of us who brought the second child, Mary, into the world.

My pharmacopeia of plant tinctures and infusions meant I could lay my hands on remedies as soon as I diagnosed the ailment. I had learned wild-crafting plants and herbs that year away, although I never followed the practices for gathering plants as I was shown. I did consider the various bushes, flowers, and herbs as friends, as surely as if they were flesh and bone beings. Sarsaparilla was thought to be all the fashion for female problems. But I banked on my own concoctions of wild red raspberry leaves for pregnancy and labor, and combinations of yellow dock for rejuvenation of low spirits that were a sure sign of danger. I was convinced my herbal ministrations kept Letty's mind steady and her constitution robust.

George came in from his chores, leaving his manure-crusted barn boots on the stoop and hung his coat neatly on a hook. I took his pail of pumped water and shooed him upstairs to get ready. He returned reluctantly dressed in knee pants and long stockings. Letty had insisted that his outfit needed an extra fillip, so she fashioned a large, checkered bow tie for him to wear. He looked so mournful in this unusual outfit that I could barely quench my desire to cut the elaborate bow off with the kitchen scissors just to give the poor boy some relief.

Margaret and Lena skipped into the kitchen. I always figured these two were Letty's final attempt to make more boys. Just five and four years old, they held hands and curtsied in their new dresses, the ones embellished with my fancy smocking. Lizzie stood to the side watching them show off. Her head tilted into her shoulder. This morning, I felt a momentary pang for this ten-year-old girl who was wearing a worn, grey wool plaid dress passed down from her older sisters. In a last-minute addition, Letty had attached two large mother-of-pearl buttons as a special decoration so Lizzie would not feel left out or uncared for, although she was often both these things.

Lizzie's cheerless appearance caused my mind to cloud over. My doctoring had met its limitations with the boy born before her. Little Johnnie was barely four years old when his body contorted with ceaseless pain. Our cherished, robust baby boy had turned into a red-faced, howling demon. He raved in a hellish pain that could not be relieved, no matter what tonics I desperately administered. I suspected a burst appendicitis.

"Would it not be most merciful to suffocate him with a pillow and put him out of his agony?" Letty had pleaded. I imagined she was capable of such a thing and never let the child out of my sight after that. The child's suffering was severe but brief. When it was over, the whole house fell into a benumbed silence. Adam and I watched Letty close the infant's sunken eyes with shaking fingers and lay him in his little satin-lined wooden coffin with one of her mother's embroidered linen pillowcases pulled up to cover his shrunken body. She arrayed some dried wild roses around his small moon-white face and folded his pale dimpled hands together facing each other. Then she collapsed.

It took all my ministrations to bring her back to her senses.

"Letty, *Du musst dich anstrengen!* You must make an effort! You are still young," I admonished. "You can make many more children. We need you to be well."

After the little one's death, our family lurched forward under the burden of loss like a wagon with a broken wheel.

As I had predicted, Letty was soon carrying her next child, born right on the heels of little Johnnie's untimely departure. One boy gone, and a girl appearing in his place. Poor little Lizzie, Letty's own namesake, came shrieking into the world eyes wide open as if sorrow and loss and death were all that awaited her. That babe was surely suckled on her mother's grief, and it showed.

# MAPLE GROVE, IOWA

## WEDNESDAY, JUNE 14, 2000

LILLIAN GROB WAS WEARING THE SAME FLOWERED DRESS. Van wondered if she slept in the back room of the town office. She did not wear a wedding ring. Probably a single woman. Devoted to her job, Dee Dee had said.

"Glad to see you, dear. I found the Reinhardts in the 1885 State census record. They are often more accurate than the Federal ones. I made a copy for you. Hope it's helpful."

"You've been a great help with everything—especially the diner recommendation."

"You bet. Dee Dee said you've been in. People say you need to have a hearty breakfast and she sure makes a good one. Good coffee, too!"

"That's just where I'm headed. Then I'll drive out to see if I can find the old farmstead."

"I'm warning you; it probably won't look anything like the old days, everything all modernized, just fields of corn and soybeans now."

"I'll let you know how it goes. Are you here every day?"

"No one else but me, dear. Nine to five, Monday through

Friday. I eat an early breakfast at Dee Dee's and bring my lunch."

Lillian flipped the switch on the fan and pointed it toward her desk. "Sure is a scorcher today. Rain predicted for later. You always hope it will cool things down, but it only makes it muggier. By the way, I was just thinking, you might want to stop over at the library and check the past issues of *The Chronicle*. The newspaper shut down a few years back, but it was the best source of local news for over a hundred years. Marion works at the front desk. I'll give her a call and tell her to look out for you."

"Thanks for the tip, Lillian. I'll check in with you tomorrow."

At Dee Dee's, Van took occupancy of the empty back table. Dee Dee delivered her order of scrambled eggs, dry wheat toast and black coffee.

"Lillian's been working overtime for you, hon. Things can get pretty boring over there. Besides the occasional out-of-towner who pesters farmers to sell their land, she doesn't get too many requests."

"She's been really helpful. Located the census for me, along with the old plat map."

Van pictured a women's grapevine that telegraphed the Maple Grove news. Even if there were no living Reinhardts in the area, Van felt welcomed into the town like one of their own. Never having had siblings, or cousins for that matter, it was a new feeling, a nice feeling. Like having a family, she thought, although she had nothing to compare.

There were eight children in the Reinhardt portrait—three boys and five girls. Historically, farm families tended to be large out of necessity, certainly all that labor needed to be shared. She envisioned a lively household of brothers and sisters, a living, interdependent organism where everyone helped out and cared for each other, a dining table that could hold ten for dinner. Maybe it was just her imagination—wish fulfillment, her psychologist colleague Pam would ᴗᴗᴗ Maybe they all secretly hated each other.

"Happy families are all alike, but every unhappy family is unhappy in its own way." Wasn't that Tolstoy? High School English class? From the looks of them, she questioned whether the Reinhardts were happy. For some reason, she doubted it. But what was the particular nature of their unhappiness? Their faces were close-mouthed and felt subtly defiant.

Between bites of breakfast, Van went over the census record. Official documents always grounded her; they were her building materials, her bricks and mortar. Once she assembled her structure she could go after the stories that lived inside the facts and figures. She studied the 1885 census. Adam and Letty had farmed their land for ten years and had five children listed—Jacob, Katherine, Mary, Otto, and Johnnie, who, according to his gravestone date, would be dead in 1887. Letty must have had babies every two years. When the portrait was made in 1900, the family included the four younger children, Lizzie, George, Margaret and Lena. That was a lot of pregnancies one after another.

Jacob was designated as Adam and Letty's son. She did the math again. According to the dates, Letty would have been thirteen, at most, when she gave birth to him. Strange. Was he a foundling they had adopted? A quiver of nervous energy ran down her arms as if her shovel had touched the hard edge of a buried secret. Was it possible that her father's father, her grandfather, wasn't really a Reinhardt? That would send this whole project into the ditch. Something didn't line up. She penciled a question mark next to Jacob's name. She would have to see if *The Chronicle* listed past obituaries.

Van squinted at the sprawling script of the census taker. At the bottom of the list there was one name she had not seen before—not in the cemetery or on the back of the family portrait: *Katharina Reinhardt, maiden lady, born in 1830 in Heidesheim, Germany.* She penciled a question mark next to Katharina's name. Something made her nose wrinkle. She was probably a relative, maybe Adam's older sister, an unmarried aunt living with the family. Van pulled the journal from her pack.

*Wednesday, June 14,*
*Day Three*

*Note to self: Gathering information. Got the census. Am collecting a lot of question marks. I hope I'm not going crazy. I don't know, maybe the heat is getting to me. Things feel unsettled, I feel a bit spooked.*

A cool blast from the air conditioner gave her chills. She felt her father peering over her shoulder. She stopped writing and crossed out the crazy part. She did not want to provoke him or stir up his dread of anything irrational. Nor did she want to gin up the old fear that her mother's strangeness had been passed on to her. She shook her head. He's not here, he's dead. *I am a professional historian.* Just assemble the facts like you've been trained, she counseled herself. They always lead somewhere.

*I located the Reinhardt plat map and today I am driving out to find the old farm. Am assured by the locals it will be nothing like the old days. Dad never lived there. He was a town boy, no farmer in his blood. Maple Grove has a smalltown atmosphere, everybody knows everybody even though nobody can recall any Reinhardts, which is odd. Where did they all go? I will say the folks here have been more than helpful. The topographic map I got from the town office is right up Dad's alley.*

Van stopped. She wanted to write her dead father a post-card from Maple Grove. "What the hell am I looking for, Dad? What were you hoping I'd find?" But she didn't know to what glacial realm the card should be addressed.

Van finished her breakfast, drank a second cup of coffee, and said good-bye to Dee Dee. In her car she automatically turned the air conditioner on and looked at the sepia photograph of the Reinhardts. "Okay, folks, we're going out to see your old farmstead."

Usually, she was excited to be off on the hunt, but today she felt wary. She reminded herself that history was nothing but stories of dead people. Years ago, when they were students at the university, she had told Len about her pioneering ancestors. She knew nothing about them, but since she had no other relatives, she thought it something to be proud of like *The Little House on the Prairie*, the books she read as a child in her school library. She remembered how much pleasure he took in disabusing her of that fantasy.

"Those people were living on stolen land," he said. "That whole prairie is one big boneyard. And most of those bones won't be found in your tidy white man cemeteries. That land is peopled by restless dead. Their unsettled skulls are fierce enough to bite through all those pretty cornfields." It irked her to recall his almighty pontificating. She could never counter his lofty proclamations. She had hardly given him a passing thought in all these years and was irritated to find him occupying her mind. She checked the map and stepped on the gas.

The road was straight as a plumb line, the rolling land divisible into plowable acres and made accessible by surfaced roadways engineered to handle big farm equipment. Small islands of maple, cottonwood, and oak surrounded farmhouses; red barns and silver silos floated in the midst of a blue-green sea of crops. It was mid-June; a month later and the road would be nothing but a tunnel between colossal cornstalks. How serene and pastoral it all appeared, the dutiful earth producing corn and soybeans as if it were the only thing it ever had on its mind, as if it had always done this since time immemorial. She knew better.

Just as Lillian had warned, what she was seeing was not the diversified farming of her German immigrant ancestors; this was agribusiness boosted by tons of fertilizer and pesticides that caused the land to feel dense, oppressed, and claustrophobic.

The topographic map Lillian had given her revealed an ancient glacier's meltwater stream that had sent the Mississippi River to the east and the Missouri River to the west. Bordered by the two rivers, the landscape had remained basically unchanged over the millennia. The plat map indicated that Adam Reinhardt owned two hundred and forty acres—a sizable farm in those days. Purchased in the 1870's, the land was nestled snug against the western edge of the great divide between the two rivers.

Van wondered if the peaceable, acquiescent earth recalled its wild and forlorn beginnings. Can bedrock formed from layers of loose sediment accumulating and hardening over many millions of years ago remember its old life under the roiling shallow seas? Were the implacable ice, roaring winds, rivers and ancient seas still alive underneath this calm, cultivated crop cover? Does the land still recall its harsh beginning? How her father would have mocked such questions, as he had when she made her childhood book about loess. She had barely completed the thought when she heard her father's ridicule: "Don't be a dreamer, Vangie. You'll end up like your mother."

She jutted her chin out. Beneath the conventions of geology and history, between the loess and the cultivated cropland, between the Natives who once inhabited this land and the pioneers, between her deeply flawed parents, there must have been times and places where the earth's story and the human story met in a deep embrace. This was the story she secretly longed for, where everything was connected and memories were alive. Did her parents once love each other before they formed the great divide that separated them from each other and left her stranded between them? "Between a rock and a hard place," she informed the Reinhardt family portrait.

A white, two-story farmhouse surrounded by oak, hack-berry and silver maple trees shimmered like a mirage. "Okay, folks, here we are. I'm sure it didn't look like this when you first got here. Maybe the people who live in this house will remember something of your history." Did Letty's eyes just blink? As usual, too much coffee had jigged her up. Van pulled her car into the gravel drive, noting that the flower gardens were well tended, the house freshly painted, and various dependencies had been added to the original structure.

A knock on the door produced no response. A tied-up dog barked from its kennel behind the house. She headed for the barn calling, "Hello!" No answer. Of newer vintage, the barn was spotless, definitely not a working building, but rather a simulacrum with vinyl siding. The barn door was locked. She peered through a small window. It looked like the barn was used as a garage; it housed a truck and an RV, no tractor or other farm equipment. Whoever lived in the house apparently did not farm the land. Since no one was around, she backed out of the driveway and parked her car on a tractor road. Along the edge of the cornfield, a line of willow and cotton-woods beckoned. The map had indicated a stream of water named Sioux Creek that meandered through the land un-hindered. Instinctively, her feet found a pathway overgrown with weeds, giving her the peculiar sensation of following in someone else's footsteps. Van spied a smooth river rock at the grassy edge of the brook where she could sit without being visible to anyone on the road. Someone else had once found this spot inviting and sought it out as a refuge; she could feel it in her bones. She was not the first.

Once she had learned of such things, Van was convinced she had been born with a nictitating membrane. Eyes wide open, she saw the world around her like everyone else, but when the membrane came over, she could see against its screen a completely different reality. She had discovered this solitary entertainment as a child in Wisconsin when on warm summer days she packed a brown paper bag lunch and headed for the fields behind her parents' home. Pulling the top strand of barbed wire down and hooking it under the middle strand, she easily crossed the fence demarcating the house lots from the cow pastures. Boundary crossings never failed to give her the thrill of trespass.

An avenue of elm trees marked remnants of an old buggy trail that ran for miles through the far meadow. Van had once cut a long strand of her hair and tied it around one of the branches of a gnarled tree to claim it as her own. Underneath its gracious, leafy boughs she pictured horses and buggies filled with men, women, and children heading towards some happy destination. She remembered how she wanted to be kidnapped, be a part of their family, and in her imagining she did just that.

With her father's increasingly dire warnings, she learned that indulging in make-believe adventures was dangerous. Wasn't her mother afflicted with too much imagination? Was Mother really crazy? Wasn't that what her father implied when Van came home to a darkened house after a school activity and no dinner was on the table? With her heart pounding she would call out, "Dad, Dad, aren't we having supper tonight?"

From behind the closed door of his study he would reply, "There's a turkey TV dinner in the freezer, Vangie. Your mother lives in her own world. She's not fit for everyday life." Although it was true, Martin never explained why her mother was that way, where her mind had gone, or what she did all day.

Van had learned to fend off her daydreaming tendency. She trained her mind to anchor reality in verifiable facts, the agreed-upon evidence of dates and documents of history, and only then did she dare allow herself to bring her powers of intuition to bear. But imagination? Like a child held in cramped quarters, her mind clamored to run free. Now she was free to daydream as much as she wanted. She jutted her chin. No, she wasn't like her mother.

Sitting next to the stream, Van imagined how the uncultivated prairie must have looked to the Reinhardts on their arrival. She listened carefully to the voice of the wind, the crows in their caucuses, the buzzing beings going about their business, the trickling water of the brook, the earth beneath her green coverlet of corn and the deeper blanket of loess. The land may have been a fertile Eden as the boosters like to proclaim, but from her past studies Van knew that the first people to cultivate the prairie were often beset by plagues that were Biblical—prairie fires, grasshoppers, drought, snowstorms that sent stock flying.

It took a combination of luck and perseverance not to sell out after such disasters. In the family portrait, her grandfather Jacob did not project grit and determination. In fact, he looked a little dreamy. She pictured him seeking this refuge away from the unending demand of farm chores, finding a place to rest where his mind could loosen and fly. Wasn't it said that a grandparent's traits jumped a generation? Maybe Jacob wasn't a Reinhardt; maybe he was a dreamer, too.

The willow tree leaves shivered in a stiff breeze. A dark shadow flickered just outside her peripheral vision. She turned quickly but saw nothing. She felt suddenly vulnerable, exposed, unprotected—like she had stepped naked through the looking glass and landed in an alien country, somewhere she didn't belong.

The sky had darkened considerably; Lillian had predicted rain. Time to go. Big bruising blue and purplish clouds were lumbering toward her from the west, preceded by lower, faster moving, grayish white clouds, running like ghostly wolves in advance of what was coming. In the far distance lightning fractured the rim of the darkening skyline.

She pulled into the motel parking lot just as the storm hit full force with hard rain pelting on the roof of her car, followed by lightning and thunder in close proximity. She was not afraid of storms. Many times, as a small child she had sat outside and attended an approaching storm as if she were at a concert, counting the seconds between the flashing cymbals and tympani. No, it wasn't the storm that disturbed her. At the creek, she had felt almost threatened, as if someone had been watching her from a distance. There was danger; not physical danger, but something deeper.

She sat in the car until the storm moved past. She had picked Storm Lake as a place to stay because there was no motel or hotel in Maple Grove, but also because of its name, because she wanted to be near water, and because she thought her father would approve of its glacial origins. *Such a child, still trying to please.* Unlike Lake Mendota, Storm Lake was a bit eerie. Despite a tree buffer, the face of the lake was constantly exposed to the northwest wind. The water was never peaceful. Probably that's how it got its name, a big, roughed-up body of water stuck in the midst of cornfields.

Van propped the family portrait back up on the motel dresser. She gave Letty a stern and challenging look. Then she picked up the phone on the bedside table and dialed Em's number.

"Dr. Cooper here."

"Hi, Em. It's me."

"Where are you?"

"I'm staying at a Super 8 in Storm Lake."

"Sounds picturesque. I didn't think they had many lakes in western Iowa."

"The locals call them potholes. Leftovers from the glacier. Storm Lake isn't like our Wisconsin lakes. They get polluted and badly silted up from farm pesticides and soil run-off. It's actually a little weird, a big shallow lake stuck out in the midst of corn and soybean fields." Van was talking too much and too fast. Her voice was high, and her hands were trembling.

"Anyway, I decided to drive up here and get a motel room with a hot shower and air conditioner. I needed a good night's sleep and time to sort through some of the documents I copied at the town office. How's Mister?"

"He's fine. Were you able to settle your dad's stuff?"

"Not really. To tell the truth, he left me a map of Iowa with a vague note to do some family research. I wasn't going to do it, but was afraid it would bug me, and then, well, you know how I am about research. I did find some Reinhardts in the cemetery, but there's not a living soul in town with that name." Van took a breath. "The reason I called was that I think I might stay a few more days to sort through some of these documents. Do you mind taking care of Mister?"

"No problem with Mister. We always got along. He's a great cat."

Van relaxed and let go of a breath she didn't know she was holding. "Thanks, Em. I knew you would understand."

"As if I had a choice. I should know by now how you are when you get on the trail of something. You're positively forensic with your nose for trouble."

Van lowered her voice. "Listen, Em. There's something else."

"What? Did you go and fall in love with some big German farmer out there?"

"No, Em, I'm serious."

"What is it?"

"Well, I hope you don't think I'm crazy, you know it runs in my family."

"What? Your father was sane as a boulder!"

"No, no, it was my mother who was nuts. Or at least I think she was—maybe she wasn't. Maybe it's the Iowa heat, but I feel spooked."

"Do your research, Van. No spooks or ghosts, okay?"

"Well, it's not just Reinhardt ghosts. I'm afraid there are a few of my own."

Van could hear Em take a deep breath. "I suppose it's no surprise once you start digging into your ancestor's business. Believe me, when I studied Anne Hutchinson's life, those Puritans scared the bejesus out of me. Made me question a lot. You know, shunned for being a woman with unnatural desires, unfit for society, cast out, a leper. Sound familiar? Maybe we can talk more when you get back." Em paused. "I would like that."

"Okay, Em, I'll call you in a couple of days. Give Mister a big pet for me. And thanks again for being such a good friend."

Van hung up. Why hadn't she stuck it out with Em? *I'm such a chicken.* After Len, she had sworn off men. Women were always coming on to her as if she wore an "open for business" sign, but she wasn't up for relationship complications. At least that was her line. Truthfully, physical intimacy terrified her, sent her off kilter.

She and Emma had been cohorts—feminists who hung onto their positions as lone women in the history department, academic grinds, heads down, working toward tenure. Both single. Their male colleagues tolerated them, rolled their eyes, and called them the Van and Em show. The women worked in opposite areas of early American history. Emma's focus was

Anne Hutchinson of the Massachusetts Bay Colony, while Van studied Indian captivity narratives. There was one uncanny place where their scholarship overlapped; the Siwanoy had taken one of Hutchinson's daughters captive in the family massacre by the Siwanoy. Despite their different approaches, their mutual interests worked to inspire each other, and they often co-authored papers and co-taught courses.

Em was different than Van. She was blunt, didn't have the compulsion to be nice, didn't care about wearing make-up or fancy clothes, and didn't need to emphasize her femininity. Van had felt instantly comfortable around her, no shadowy female competition or jealousies. Em was a descendant of the Mayflower pilgrims. East Coast. WASP to the core. Brilliant. Older than Van. Straight as a stick. Or so she'd thought. Maiden lady. *Just like Katharina.* Was it good or bad? No way to weigh it out.

Tonight Van was just grateful that despite all that remained unspoken between them, she and Em had managed to remain friends.

She glanced at the family portrait. If Katharina was included in the census as a member of the family, why wasn't she included in the picture? Maybe she got married, which was a long shot, considering how old she would have been in 1900. Most likely she had died.

# MAPLE GROVE, IOWA

## New Year's Day, 1900

In the kitchen Letty handed Adam the vest she had finished late at the night. She watched her husband wince and ease his stiff right shoulder into the garment. It fit him perfectly. The children clapped their admiration. After breakfast, she pulled Adam's felted hat over his ears and double wrapped his muffler and let him out the back door to hitch Pet and Bucky to the sleigh for the four-mile run into Maple Grove. She bundled Lizzie, Margaret and Lena with neck scarves, woolen hats and fur muffs. George wore his Sunday woolen coat and hat with earflaps. She added an extra muffler and gave him his own lap rug to put over his legs. Letty did not want her boy to get a chill. In the sleigh, she adjusted the girls' heavy woolen robes for protection from the cold. Inside her gloves, her fingertips still smarted from last night's burn.

Pet and Bucky knew the road to town and were eager to move. Adam gave the horses a shout and the sleigh jolted ahead. Letty rarely left their farm. The commotion of the town disturbed her. But today, her objective—that precious family portrait—made her resolute. When she looked back,

Tante Kate was standing in the parlor window with her arms folded over her apron. Letty cast a fearful glance toward the copse of burr oaks and willow trees near the creek. In the early days, she had been convinced that these woods were a perfect hiding place for red men. Even last night a dark shadow was moving stealthily among the tree trunks toward the barn. She was sure that's what she had seen.

Twenty-four years had passed since Adam's decision to leave Illinois and pioneer in Iowa. She remembered it like yesterday. She was happily sitting in her mother's rocker, nursing her firstborn, the girl named Katherine, called Sister Kate, when Valentine Kroeber, a neighboring farmer, pounded on their door. Letty feared he was carrying bad news. In a panic, she covered the nursing babe and hurried into the next room. But Kroeber's loud voice could still be heard and what he had to say gave her such terrible fright that the babe spit up her milk.

"Adam, listen to this! Here's your big chance! The railroad company is selling off extra land!" He read aloud the announcement in the Illinois paper, translating into German, as he knew Adam was unsure of his grasp of English.

"The government wants 10,000 farmers," Valentine Kroeber read. "Can you imagine? The best farmland in the world. They are offering grants of land along the railroad lines in western Iowa, the best agricultural state of the Union, they say. 'Over a million acres will be sold at very good interest terms.' If you have the money, Adam, you would be a fool not to jump at this."

After Kroeber left, Adam sought out Tante Kate in the kitchen. Why did he not come to his wife first? But Letty knew he would never make such a big decision without securing his sister's approval. She always had the first and the last word. Later, Adam found Letty weeping.

"Adam, have mercy," she pleaded. "We have a small baby. I've heard such terrible stories—Hilda Broder told about Indians getting too much drink and capturing and scalping some German settlers. She said there was a Sioux uprising not so many years past. Can we not wait until the little one is older?"

Adam's jaw tightened. "We are not entering wilderness. As new purchasers, we've been promised that all the redskins have long since been removed, run away, or died off. The railroad company informs us that the Iowa frontier is closed and the opportunity for cheap land is closing with it. We cannot wait."

He snapped open his bankbook that registered all the deposits he had made while working for her father. "I have the money. With your father's death, your brothers no longer need us here. It is their farm now. The trip will not be long, and Tante Kate will see to it that you and the babe are comfortable."

Letty could plead no further. Owning land, not calming her womanish jitters, was topmost on her husband's mind. As the ruler of their household, his word was law, but behind him stood Tante Kate, and as usual, Letty was outflanked.

The next week, Adam and Valentine Kroeber drove the buggy into town. At supper that evening, he described how they had joined a long line of Germans, Swedes, and Yankees at the railroad company office. "We made it just in time," he said, swelling with pride. "I bought forty acres of well-laying ground in Iowa for nine dollars an acre." Tante Kate smiled her approval. Letty held her tongue. Each night her sleep had been ruined by nightmares of massacres, and red savages dancing with bloody blonde scalps in their hands.

A few weeks later, Adam bought another eighty acres from Frank Burns, an old Scottish bachelor who had put his money into an Iowa investment venture. "Burns is a paper farmer," he said. "He has never laid eyes on the land, and never had any intention to farm it. A suitcase farmer. He made a nice profit, but we have more land."

Wasn't this the hope every new immigrant to America carried in his heart? Hadn't Letty's own father done the same when he pioneered their farm in Illinois? The next day at breakfast Adam said he was taking young Jacob along to look at the land he bought. It pleased Letty to see young Jacob's eyes widen with excitement.

Before Adam left for Iowa, he built sturdy wooden trunks and Letty wore herself to tatters packing for the new farm. Furiously, she gathered quilts and feather beds, the rocking chair, a set of crockery, the teapot and pitchers, a tin door safe, pots and pans, china and silver, and other makings of a kitchen. She went over everything again and again while Tante Kate loaded the sundry trunks and chests to the brim with prepared cured beef and pork, sacks of flour, sugar, salt and coffee, potatoes and vegetable seeds. They put away jars of fruit, vegetables, and meat, not knowing what there would be for food on the far western prairie. At the last minute, Letty remembered to take some of her mother's things—the quilted coverlet, some good linens with Mama's cutwork and embroidery, her cameo brooch, and the blue velvet pouch decorated with German silver filigree. Letty packed in a frenzy, building a fortress of goods against the predations of savages.

Seated in the sleigh, Letty felt the weight of that blue velvet pouch against her leg. She had filled it with the coins she had saved to pay for the family portrait. It brought her comfort now as she recalled the frantic days before they left her family farm in Illinois. How each morning started out harmless enough as she pushed to get the extra bit done, but soon she could not stop. Although her sewing was prodigious, and the trunks full of provisions and their house cleaned to an inch, there was always more, more, more to do, and she would scurry and scamper about faster and faster until she collapsed from sheer exhaustion. Then it was as if the hornets in her head exploded from their nest and every little thing became a stinging insult and the smallest remark or inquiring look was a prick to incite her fury. The voices harangued—*you are not working fast enough, your stitching is ragged, the potatoes need peeling, the baby is crying, dinner is late, hurry, hurry*. To silence them, Letty burned her hand on the coal stove, stabbed herself with a needle, cut her finger with the big kitchen knife, decorating her apron front with red specks of blood.

"*Beruhige dich! Beruhige dich!* Settle down!" counseled Tante Kate. "Moderation! Can you not find the point of moderation?"

Even twenty-four years later, Letty cringed to recall Tante Kate's reproach. No matter how hard Letty looked for it, moderation was something she never found. As usual, Tante Kate was ever ready at hand with some darned potion or another. Letty drank so many of her wild weed teas she thought she would likely drown in them. They all tasted like dirt, but they must have done some good.

Kroeber had informed Adam it would take at least eight hundred dollars to work up a new farm from scratch. Before they left for Iowa, Adam opened his bankbook again and showed Letty he had withdrawn exactly that much money and had closed his account. Surely, she thought, he has turned out to be a good and provident husband, steady where she was not. Little Lizzie's bony body suddenly pressed hard against Letty, pulling her from her reveries. "I'm cold, Mama," she whimpered. "How much longer?"

Letty shook herself. Her mind was snarled as a yarn ball, so many threads, such an endless tangle to sort out. If she pulled one thread the rest knotted up. Lizzie was shivering, and Letty tucked her lap robe closer. "Soon, Lizzie. Soon."

"Will Sister Kate and Mary be there, Mama? I surely do miss them."

Letty put aside her usual aversion to this child whose presence in the world always reminded her of her lost Johnnie. She drew Lizzie closer. "Yes, yes, of course, everyone will be there for our family portrait."

"Ott, too?"

"Yes, Otto will come to town to join us."

"And Jacob?"

"Yes," Letty replied wearily. "Even Jacob."

The girl was so plaintive. Letty wondered how badly sorrow had damaged her daughter; she always hunched over as if under some invisible burden that gave her body an unbalanced look.


Heinrich von Schimmer's tight schedule was confirmed by the assortment of buggies and sleighs lined up along Main Street. Adam patted the horses, gave them some cut carrots from his pocket, and tied them to the hitch-rail. He turned to greet Josephus Kohler. The portly man sported a top hat and a thick fur-trimmed overcoat. His wife was adorned in a hat that looked to Letty like an exotic bird roost. Standing with them was Augustus Schmidtz, the president of the German Bank. His preening wife must have recently spent a fortune at Marshall Fields Department Store in Chicago. Letty shrank, certain her family looked handmade and homespun compared to these finely dressed citizens.

Without regular commerce in town, what little Letty knew about these fancy folks she had heard from Adam. He called Kohler "a businessman with clean hands who hired out his farm operation." Kohler owned properties—a hardware store in Maple Grove as well as his own dairy farm. Adam had bought their first milk cows from Kohler's dairy, and Schmidtz had mortgaged Adam's last purchase of land, despite the high interest rate on the loan. Farmers and businessmen. They needed each other. But just the other day she heard Adam grouse that Kohler and Schmidtz were in cahoots. At the moment, they were standing in the freezing cold disputing the recent local unionizing.

"I am all for the butchers organizing," Adam argued. "Even though it means they will charge more, we farmers will get a fair shake."

"You are wrong, Reinhardt," Kohler shot back. "The unions already proved themselves weak during the last depression. Once they start unionizing again, they'll want to get their mitts on everything—women telephone operators, retail clerks, even button workers. Right, Schmidtz?" The banker wagged his approval.

"But workers need protections—"

Letty had an attack of the fidgets and pulled at Adam's sleeve. "Please, Adam, can't this talk wait? We're allotted only fifteen minutes to get seated, posed, and photographed." She grasped his elbow and steered him down the wooden sidewalk toward the door.

Inside the studio, Letty handed the blue velvet pouch to a whey-faced young man who was von Schimmer's assistant—his son, she surmised, by the looks of him. She greeted her older children who were already there, dressed exactly as she had instructed. Nervously, she inspected each one, nodded her approval of Sister Kate's dress, plucked a piece of lint from Otto's jacket, straightened Mary's scarf. She put her hand to her throat and touched her mother's cameo brooch. Von Schimmer's assistant handed her the depleted coin purse and she tucked it into her side pocket.

The assistant arranged five chairs for seating and directed the others to stand behind them. Jacob's late arrival caused a trill of irregular heartbeats and Letty requested that the assistant find an extra for him chair in the front row. The only thing he could find was a swivel stool. Letty flushed to see how fine Jacob looked, all freshly shaven, his high cheekbones ruddy, his mustaches well-shaped, his hair neatly trimmed and combed. All the hurry of the morning had taxed her nerves to the limit. But Jacob always required something extra. She could never tell whether it was from her need or his. The ties between mother and child, and now middle-aged matron and young married man, were sticky webs, leaving both of them disquieted with so much left unsaid.

Letty was pleased to notice that Jacob had bothered to take the scrub brush to his hands, and his nails were freshly clipped. She had taught him this nicety as a young boy, telling him that even though he might be a farmer, his hands should always be kept neat and clean. Maybe it was a womanly thing to teach him, but he never forgot, even now when his hands were rough from hard manual labor. Probably his wife had instructed him, too, and Letty assumed his wife had gotten him into the suit and tie he had worn for his wedding six years earlier.

Her mind threw her this way and that, from present to past as if clock hands had lost their purpose. Hadn't she pitched an unholy fit when Jacob told her of his intentions to marry? To make matters worse, his wife had the very same name, Elizabeth. A common name, of course, with so many variations—Letty being special, given to her by Jacob when he was a small boy. His new Elizabeth, however, had insisted everyone use her full name.

How helplessly Letty had fumed. "Who does she think she is with my name, stealing my boy with her swanky attitudes and high falutin' ideas? How dare she? She is a thief, stealing him, not just from me, but from all of us. She is taking him away from the farm and into town. Nothing good can come of it."

Jealousy was a demon that picked a sore in her heart. It was the first time she had allowed herself such a furious protest. But it was to no avail; the wedding went on as scheduled.

In an attempt to console his wife, Adam had laid his hand on her arm. Letty brushed it off. "Didn't I teach him to speak good English, and raise him up? Even if he can't read or write."

"Letty, Letty, calm yourself." Adam shushed her. "I have long prepared for his departure, and if you had let yourself see what was right in front of your nose, you would have, too. We've done our best with Jacob, but he is no farmer, never was. The marriage will be good for him. Elizabeth is an educated lady."

Well, that had been six years ago and Jacob's wife has had him for better and for worse, as they say. In all that time, Letty rarely saw him. He stayed in town and kept away from the farm. Or was it she he wished to avoid? Her head hurt just thinking about it.

Von Schimmer gave them two chances to pose and look their best, and beyond that, it was up to each one not to make a sudden move or look cross-eyed by mistake. Letty sat still as a corpse and waited for the click and flash of the camera. The portrait was recording her living family on a glass plate during a rare moment when they were all together, freshly pressed, combed, brushed and shined to within an inch or two of their lives. She felt defiant, never considering she might be tempting fate.

Beyond tradition and social custom, in her private mind a darker motive for the portrait dwelt another. Pride was an obvious reason to capture her family on the glass plate negative on the first day of the new century. Pride in the fact that she and Adam had succeeded so far in fulfilling their pioneer dreams for almost twenty-five years and had managed to build a prosperous farm and produce a thriving family. They had survived many trials and obstacles, from the death of baby Johnnie to the dreaded hoppers, economic depression, drought, all of which caused great sorrow but were not of sufficient power to make them sell out.

Letty's secret motive, hers alone, was revenge. She conceived the photograph as a talisman, settling the score on those demon voices whose work it was to spoil her life. With this family portrait she could say, "Look! Here I am, right in the center of my family, age forty-four, a mother of eight healthy children, a good and faithful wife to my husband, even a good sister-in-law to Tante Kate. So let all the rest of you be damned!" She suppressed a smile as the flash went off.

# STORM LAKE, IOWA

## JUNE 2000

YET AGAIN, VAN STUDIED THE FAMILY PORTRAIT. Outside of the plat map and the census record, it was the only thing she had that made these Reinhardts seem like real people. She supposed she was lucky to have such an artifact, but it promised so much and told her so little.

She scrutinized the clothes the family wore. Of course, they wore their best, and like she had said to Letty's portrait, they were not too shabby. Prosperous. That's what it looked like. She considered the two younger girls. Margaret's arm rested casually on her father's thigh. Lena's hand was nestled in her mother's lap. Someone had taken the time to make them matching dresses, with fancy work at the bodice, neck, and cuff. Their hair was set in ringlets. They were obviously well cared for. Van could feel herself sinking. She felt a twinge of jealousy. Unlike these two little girls, she had been neglected. It had never occurred to her before.

Given that everyone was dressed in their finest, Van imagined they left the photographic studio and had a turn of the century celebration at the farmhouse. She pictured them at a large wooden table, enjoying their time together, a day free from farm labor. What did they eat? Probably their own farm products—ham, potatoes, kraut, homemade bread, preserves. Who did the cooking? She guessed the older girls. Why was she thinking about all this? Trying to insert herself into this family scene just made her miserable.

She felt frustrated and angry at what was missing, what was lost, disappeared, silenced. How was she supposed to fill out the lives of these people when she herself had so little to go on? And why did her father include her on his mission into the past? No answers there, either. After he shut her down as a curious, questioning child, she had given up any thought of pursuing the details of his family or where he came from. She never understood what compelled genealogists or why people were so enamored of their personal pedigrees. Outside of Em, most people she knew did not know their family lineages beyond their grandparents.

When she stared hard at the portrait, willing it to give up its secrets, Van thought she could discern shadows of missing people in the background. There were blurry smudges on the background curtain that, if she squinted, could resolve into ghosts. Spirit photographs had been popular in the nineteenth century. Maybe the Reinhardt photographer was one of those frauds who provided his customers with a photographic impression of their dearly departed fluttering inside their portraits. Van blinked. She thought she saw Katarina Reinhardt's figure in the blur. She didn't know who was standing next to her. She felt shivery. "No spooks or ghosts," Em had said.

Stick with what is known.

But knowing for Van was always more a matter of sensing rather than actually seeing or believing. That is what she had argued for in her scholarly work. This idea did not endear her to her colleagues. Imagination, speculation, fantasy, they grumbled, echoing her father. Van held out. In history there were obvious blank spots, silences, absences, something always left out in favor of a more acceptable narrative—the whitewashed heritage of colonization with heroic tales of explorers, pilgrims, Indian fighters, and doughty pioneers. Standard histories on the early lives of the new arrivals hardly mentioned any sense of the land and indigenous peoples beyond dramatizing the wilderness and its inhabitants as *inhospitable* and *menacing*. Wasn't that disconnection what drove her to study the Indian captivity narratives? That, and some barely conscious desire to be kidnapped herself, taken away to live with a tribe of others.

In the existing stories of women like Mary Jemison, Van had learned to tune her senses to the traces of truth flickering just out of sight. Within Jemison's published memoir, Van sensed a deeper voice, one that recalled the life experience of a complex, intelligent woman who had built and sustained a bridge between two irreconcilable cultures. Like Chief Blackhawk's a century later, her story held a fascination for Americans. Was it guilt that bonded the American psyche to those they tried to destroy by appropriation? Mary Jemison was claimed by the culture that recorded her story in the popular memoir. In that work, she was called by her white name, not Dehgewänis, her Native name. At least Mary Jemison felt impelled to leave a record of her unusual life, even if it was a redacted one. Van had no such thing for these Reinhardts, no scrap of paper written with their words, only the family portrait. Her father had dated it at the turn of the century.

This was all that Van knew: In 1900, the family had five girls and three boys. Certainly, the girls must have married, taken their husbands' names and moved off the family farmstead, which might explain the lack of Reinhardts in the Maple Grove cemetery. Nor was Otto, who looked constitutionally unfit to be a farmer, possibly consumptive, or the other boy, George, buried in the cemetery. That left her grandfather Jacob. In the portrait he was seated on some kind of stool in a position that made his figure appear larger than the others. Van sensed Jacob was a last-minute addition to the family group. He was a grown man. At some point he must have married, left the farm and moved into town. Besides her own father who was Jacob's youngest, there was no telling how many children Jacob and Elizabeth had had. None of them had stayed. A Reinhardt diaspora.

Was her aged father suddenly driven by guilt for abandoning his Iowa people? Did he want to repent for something by sending his only daughter back as his emissary? Too many unanswered questions gave Van a headache. All she had was the portrait with its hints, suggestions and portents. In a fit of pique, she turned the portrait to face the wall. She didn't want these people staring down at her in her sleep.

The motel room felt damp and unpleasant. *How did I end up here?* She felt adrift, even a little panicky. She missed Em but couldn't justify calling her at such a late hour. What would she say? *I'm scared?* She automatically jutted her chin. She needed to get a grip. She had let her mind go too far afield, her imaginary nictating eyelid again. Tomorrow she would go to the Carnegie Library and see if the Chronicle had printed obituaries back in its day. She needed facts.

# SIOUX CREEK FARM

## NEW YEAR'S DAY, 1900

ON THE BUCKBOARD JACOB SHARED the lap rug with Papa Adam. The rest of the family was snugged into the sleigh. The afternoon was brilliant, the air sparkled with fresh snow, a curl of smoke came from the farmhouse in the distance. Papa Adam gave the horses his familiar directions in German: *Huh! Ruhig! Brrr!* Pet and Bucky needed little coaxing. They knew the way back to the farm and were eager for their extra share of oats.

Jacob had not visited the farm since last haying season. What with his growing family and working on the road crew, there was neither time nor money for anything else. His sisters in town brought him news of the farm. But he could not refuse Mama Letty's invitation for the turn-of-the-century family portrait and the New Year's dinner. That morning Elizabeth had practically shoved him out the door.

"You must go, Jacob. She will never forgive you if you are not there."

Twenty-five years ago, Papa Adam had taken Jacob on his very first train ride on the Illinois Central that brought them to Dubuque. They crossed the Mississippi on a railway drawbridge into Iowa. The steam engine trains and the river steamboats were wondrous to behold. With such adventure, the prospect of building their very own farm on the far western prairie was a rushing thrill that over spilled like a spring stream breaching a dam. But when he laid eyes on the unbroken stretch of high grass prairie that Papa Adam was so proud of, Jacob was frightened. Could such empty land ever be made into a farm? There was nothing there.

"Where will we live?"

"First, my boy, we have to see about digging a well, then we can think about the rest. I have arranged in town for Hans Dieter Zweig to meet us here."

A man with a long white beard and slouchy felt soon arrived on an old swayback mare. In his hand he carried a forked willow stick. Jacob walked with Papa Adam through the tall yellow grass, while Hans Dieter followed the lead of the stick as if it was alive.

"Do you want to see how the stick works?" Mr. Zweig asked as he placed the forked stick in Jacob's eager hands. "Close your eyes, but not too tight, and the water will talk to you."

And it did. Jacob was struck with wonder. Mr. Zweig told Papa Adam that Jacob was a natural dowser.

"You found the water, Jacob; now I need to find a plow," Papa Adam said. "We can see Mr. Heim about renting a team and a sod-buster plow so we can plant the fields with wheat."

Mr. Heim's place was a chimney sticking out from a grassy mound. A scarecrow-looking man emerged from behind a curtained flap in the side of the hill followed by three small children with dirty shirts and bare bottoms. Jacob worried. Mama Letty would never abide living inside a dark badger hole. When they returned to Illinois, Jacob told Mama Letty that they had found water and the land was beautiful, which was the truth. But he did not tell her there was no house for them to live in.

When the family finally arrived in Iowa, an unpainted wooden house and lean-to stood in the clearing, and Papa Adam pointed out that their well had been bored right where the willow stick had told Jacob there was fresh water. He was ever so grateful for Mama Letty's sake that Papa Adam had arranged everything before they arrived and they did not have to live in a dirty old dugout soddie like the Heims.

That first fall, Papa Adam told Jacob he was past the age for book learning and that he would teach him all the makings of a good husbandman. Papa Adam counted on him as his most valued helper. This was their unspoken pact made on that first visit to Iowa—the natural bond forged between a father and son made ironclad through the daily pressures of duty and love.

There were happy times that first spring when he went with Papa Adam to buy grain from the big granary in the village of Maple Grove. Then they went to a neighboring ranch where they purchased their first six *milch* cows who would provide sweet milk and butter, enough for the family with left over to sell. Twenty laying hens and a rooster for the chicken coop were next. When a local farmer was selling out, Papa Adam bought a hay wagon and a team of horses for pulling and they rode home together one early evening in May. The air was filled with that smell of freshly opened earth and the sunset spread its warm glow across the far fields, evening birdsongs filled the air.

Mama Letty and Tante Kate came out of the house in their aprons as Adam pulled up in the new rig. The womenfolk admired the good-natured horses and the well-built hay wagon. They named the horses Pet and Bucky. That evening Jacob stayed outside in the balmy air still fragrant with the smell of the new meadow; the newly plowed fields were alive with the last lark songs. As a solemn questioning youth, he wondered if this piece of prairie farmland would be his life-long home. He neither longed for it to be so, nor rejected the idea in favor of some other more venturesome notion. That evening he was merely curious.

Always up by first light to prepare for the day's work, Jacob was diligent in his efforts. He took instruction whole-heart-edly, but shrank back when Papa Adam questioned, "Jacob, boy, how much seed do we need to get for next year's plant-ing? Can we use another *milch* cow? Should we start thinking about raising pigs?"

Jacob knew Papa Adam's efforts were meant to raise him up, to include him as a trusted partner, never an equal of course, since he was his father, but as someone he could count on, someone to share both his knowledge and his burdens. When Jacob faltered or was vague in his answers, his hesi-tancy brought a frown to Papa Adam's otherwise genial face. Jacob chided himself to pay more attention, to keep his mind alert, and not drift off into reading the skies or listening to the winds coming off the far distant plain.

Jacob knew how the water stick worked and he knew the weather. What he didn't know was who had taught him. One summer, after several successful years on the farm, Jacob could feel something was in the air. The crows were talking about it in the fields. He kept looking for the storms or the dry spell, but there was another feeling, one of dark forebod-ing that he did not know the name for—until they appeared. The black cloud in the sky did not hold rain but was com-posed of millions of hungry hoppers that fell to earth and gave ravage to their fields; within minutes they lifted off and went to land in some other poor farmer's crops.

The devastation the bugs left behind was worse than a tornado or prairie fire. People had to shovel them out of their doorways like drifts of black snow just to get outside. The

Reinhardts survived the plague of hoppers, but it marked Jacob with the dreadful knowledge of what a hellish thing nature can create for farmers. Surely nature had her ways of testing a man's spirit, but he thought the hoppers were the very worst thing ever known to happen on the prairie, and the damage they wrought was enough to make a man cry or lose his faith in God altogether. Some farmers packed up and moved their families to the town just to be done with those infernal creatures. But Papa Adam determined they would not let a bunch of insects chase them from their chances.

Jacob prayed he would never hear those crows talk of hoppers again. He always listened carefully to their messages when they were cawing in the fields, and wondered why no one else had heard them. That summer was imprinted on his mind as a terrible scripture like something Mama Letty had read to him from her Bible.

Jacob was still a boy when he discovered his secret spot next to the creek bed. They had just turned the sod over in that section one early spring, and he had found some arrowheads and small reddish shards of crude clay vessels. He put them into his overall pockets and later took them down to the brook to clean them so he could study their shapes. Their messages were indecipherable, some code he never could read. He spent hours imagining the lives of people who had lived there a hundred years before their family came to farm the land.

He had heard only bits of hearsay gathered from older farm hands with their tales of hostiles, the Sioux who camped on the creek with their women and children. On warm summer afternoons when the others were resting inside the house, Jacob hid from Papa Adam and the next set of loathsome chores; He laid on the grass by the creek with a smooth, rounded river rock for a pillow and listened to the bubbling sounds which murmured like women's voices in the distance. He watched great shreds of clouds grow into shapes he could name and then dissolve and grow again into other forms. He listened for the weather that was coming on the winds and again prayed he would not hear the crows talk of hoppers or chinch bugs. By the time he was twenty-one, not knowing any other life, Jacob stayed on the farm, though he had moved his sleeping quarters into the barn for the sake of peace and quiet.

One Sunday morning, a great inner restlessness drew him from a gray and dreamless sleep. Declining the family buggy ride to church services in Maple Grove, Jacob made his way through the backfield toward the stream. The dryness in the June air was an ill omen. He could taste fine particles of dust on his tongue and see spidery cracks forming in the earth between the rows of newly greening corn shoots. The water in the little brook had gotten so low he could barely hear its voice. As was his practice, he stretched his body full length on the earth, resting his head on his pillow of river stone, and closed his eyes.

The pictures racing past his mind's eye were unstoppable, as if time had suddenly gone haywire. A whole year flew by in an instant and he could see where it was headed—the stunted brown stalks dying of thirst, cows moaning, wells running thin and then dry, the farmers with their big hands stuffed deep in their overall pockets staring at the horizon for the plump, grey rainclouds that never appeared, their worried wives with pinched faces conserving what they could, the priest in his pulpit dedicating Sunday prayers to the Lord of rain, the bankers perched like predators waiting to see who would be the first to foreclose.

*Drought.* The word itself had the very sound of damnation. Being a reader of weather at that moment was a terrible curse. Jacob felt the violent pressure of the plow upon the land, the unnatural imposition of cultivated crops on prairie grasses. Like a raven circling the heavens, he viewed the earth cut into squares of desperately dry grain, besieged by insects, yearning for water. His gorge began to rise, and a wild revulsion took hold. His whole body trembled with terror at the thought of being forever and helplessly tied to the land in the way of a farmer: no escape from the relentless cycles of planting and harvesting, vulnerable to the whims of weather, continuously beseeching the God in heaven for benevolence, for mercy, for rain. Deeply confused and forsaken by this vision drained of water and his own empty future, he began to cry. His body shook with the choked sobs of a grown man and paltry droplets of salt tears seeped into the parched earth.

Desolate, he lay there without direction until music sounded from the wind in the prairie grasses. Then the whole living, earthly world began to hum and shimmer with life, and its beauty and brilliance overwhelmed, and he was instantly sucked backward in time. The land stretched out, fulsome and emergent, to the far horizon and beyond. His ears filled with the music of weather, the wind and rain and sun, as if old people, ancestors, were humming and teaching him their songs. He surrendered to the certainty that everything lived under the rule of water, how the earth could draw water away from the surface, pulling the moisture down into deep underground caverns carved by ancient seas.

The earth did this for her own secret reasons, her own thirst, not out of a Biblical wrath or punishment or revenge. The larger wheeling of the earth, the sun and moon and stars, dazzled and were awesome and magnificent, tender and terrifying. He understood that human beings could only survive on this earth if they knew these things, could hear this music, hear the sighs and whispers, sing the songs of water, wind and weather. The earth held him as if he were her child and a song welled up, pushing against his throat where it caught like a tumbleweed on a barbed fence. In keeping his silence,

Jacob had broken some deep bond with Papa Adam, formed so many years ago when he was still a child, when they had first seen the prairie land together.

Life inside the farmhouse was ruled by Tante Kate who had grown more taciturn with age. She ran the household as if she were a general to a small army. She kept pandemonium at bay by installing a firm routine of daily chores and duties that they all abided by. In the early days of building the farm, she labored alongside him in the fields, and he marveled at her endurance, which often outmatched his own. She was a strict and practical woman who always saw what needed doing next, giving direction in her stern German speech. Sometimes he caught her looking at him although he did not know what was being registered on her mind. "Don't be such a dreamer," Tante Kate always chided which added to his feelings of doubt and insecurity. All in all, he was neither fish nor fowl, neither the young farmer of Papa Adam's expectation nor the oldest son the women wanted, but something other, that went unnamed.

Surely, he was bred into the life of a farmer, but there was always that other place that went deeper than breeding, like an underground stream he sometimes got pulled into. It seemed real yet harder to name, like the way the black ravens held their caucus in a new mown field or the way the night breezes whispered to him about the weather, a different kind of speaking that murmured deep in his blood, another speech that whispered on the prairie wind—another tongue that sometimes sounded in his ear sweeping low across the prairie from a great distance, like the drum of his heartbeat, the sound so familiar yet full of dark mystery, this peculiar parlance that only he could hear— like his recurring dream of a cabin in the woods and a woman softly humming. This is what set him apart from the others.

In those days when Mama Letty's moods grew dark and

foreboding, and her look turned strange, he feared her peculiarities although the mother love she had so firmly planted in him from the beginning was as tenacious as wild prairie grass. He often made a special effort in her direction and he could still get a favorable look from her upon occasion. Sometimes he brought her a handful of prairie flowers, purple and white violets, or some wild strawberries, or cress he had found by the creek, and then he caught her smile just like in the old days.

But after the dream, the drought vision—From that morning on, his life fell into two distinct pieces—before and after. Jacob could not build a bridge between the people who raised him and all he had felt and remembered and sensed that morning. When he met Elizabeth in town or after church on Sundays, he was surprised that she was interested in speaking with him. He began to pay her secret court. When he finally revealed his plans to marry and move to town, Papa Adam didn't raise any of the expected objections, although Jacob knew his Papa was sorely disappointed.

"*Ja*, Jacob, my boy, Elizabeth is a *gudes Mädchen.* I do not believe you could find any better. I hope you will prosper in town.".

* * *

The table was set for ten. Letty's linen tablecloth and hand-edged linen napkins—that I made—were pressed, the durable china dishes washed and dried, the silver plate polished. The smoked ham was in the oven, the potatoes peeled, and while I waited to hear the bells of the sleigh, I looked out the parlor window onto the fields covered with fresh snow.

The harvest had been a good one. Everyone was well. The window reflected my face, and not for the first time, I questioned the importance people placed on photographing themselves. Since I was alone in the house, I allowed my mind to wonder how it would feel to have a small likeness of the people I lost. *Ach!* Didn't my memory book serve just as well as any high-priced photographer? Even if I had been able to will it otherwise, I could not rub out that small blink of time I had spent away. The truth of it was in my deepest marrow.

Jacob was my living testimonial to that brief season where I was unknown to everyone else, a small circle of time that enclosed the truest and best part of who I was. Was I keeping my book for him? Ridiculous. He couldn't read English, never mind French. Nor did I intend my words as a confessional. I had never had much use for the ear of a priest. Hadn't I suffered penance enough? I had written in my book because my heart was an unheated chamber and I meant to stir the embers someday by remembering. I retrieved the travel book from its home in my apron pocket and read the words I penciled so long ago.

\* \* \*

*Ah, Pascal! What a man he was! He had not much more height than me. He was smooth-faced; his coarse dark hair tied behind his head in a tail. A deeply creased, fringed leather jacket marked him as belonging to the fur-trade life. I was certain he had fewer years than I and although his figure was not so impressive, his words felt strangely powerful and I let myself be drawn toward him. His country French was intoxicating and foreign, so mixed with other phrases unfamiliar to my ears.*

*If he was looking hard at me, I stared back at him, this odd little man speaking in a compound of broken-up words that he mixed together in this prairie town. His appearance was as strange a mix as was his speech. I quickly observed that his body was tough*

and nimble and knew he would take me along because I had been forthright in my approach and had
made a good business deal. But to tell it true, I did
not care for my life. Half of it was over and I was
lost to my own knowing. I wanted nothing more than
to leave the wretched migrant town and when my
hand had reached out for help, what I grasped onto
was Pascal, and when I asked him again in my bit of
French if he would take me with him on his journey
north, he said, "Oui, Madame."

Back at the boarding house, I left a bit of money for Mrs. Smelzer, the widow woman who ran the
place, and penned a note for Adam to find when he
returned from the fall harvest.

"I have found someone to take me north. Will
write when I have news to tell. Your sister, Katharina."

I packed a small woven bag with a few necessities
and put most of my other belongings in the wooden
trunk we had brought from Germany for Adam to reclaim on his return. I did not stop to question my actions. They had been put into motion in such a way that
my very thoughts and movements did not seem to orig-
inate with me. I had the presence of mind to bring my
heavy woolen shawl for truly I did not believe I would
ever return from this journey into the country up north.
Nor did I care. I was propelled by something deep inside,
something fiercer than even the wilderness I was about
to enter, something whose nature I never knew existed.

Before I fully understood what had transpired, I
was straddling a prairie pony tethered to Pascal's pony,
looking at the back of his deerskin jacket, heading
into the unknown with a man I had just laid eyes
upon. My heart pounded hard in my breast, my mind

*spun like some child's toy top, and my mouth gulped*
*great draughts of prairie air....*

Why am I reading this now? I am old. Maybe my memory
is fading, and I don't want to forget. Maybe I am dying. Unable
to read any further today, I closed the book. Harking back to
that earlier time was always a perilous occupation. For years,
my daily life never afforded time for it, and then my plain
temperament ruled against it. I fear that giving heed to such
recollections might lead to a morbid turn of mind, a kind of
melancholia. Aside from rereading, what did I plan to do with
these scribblings? I climbed the stairs and tucked the book into
its other home under my mattress. Sitting at the edge of the bed
to catch my breath, I pressed my fingers to my eyes.

My thoughts turned to Jacob now sitting for the family
portrait. Six years ago, when he announced he was leaving
the farm to marry, I bristled with irritation. It was not the
natural order of things. As the eldest, he should have stayed
on the farm. But frankly, his departure was not a surprise. Jacob was always a dreamer, like an elf from the Old Country;
he had no predilection for the farming life, although he certainly put forth an effort. He was like the willow trees by the
creek, drawing life from the nearest available water source,
his own roots never reaching any deeper. Responsibility for
this deficiency in his character was mine alone.

Long ago, too long, I had relinquished my claim to him.
Maybe by doing so, I had deprived him of the very thing he
needed. I always told myself that withholding knowledge of
his origins protected him from uncertainty, confusion, and
potential shame. But in fleeting moments, I regretted not
keeping the little packet that contained his umbilicus.

"His memory cord," the old woman had called it, "so he
won't get lost." Now I was afraid his life had been sorely

compromised by my dereliction. It was hardly a wonder that when his wife Elizabeth set her cap for him, he was so easily taken. And Letty became fairly unthroned from her reason when she learned Jacob was marrying Elizabeth Konrad. Letty took to her bed with a sick headache that could not be relieved by any of my ministrations. That's the only time I had come within a hair's breadth of telling Letty everything, just to put an end to her nonsense. "Have some sense, Letty, he is not your natural child. He does not belong to you. He is mine." At the last moment, I sealed my lips and let Letty have her illusions and her tantrum, hoping she would tire of it and we could continue as we always had. Why had Letty not understood that he would leave the farmstead and move to Maple Grove with his new wife?

"*Konntest du dir das nicht denken*? Had you not seen this coming?" I asked in exasperation. She was a woman grown but she still thought like a child who'd lost her doll.

Over the years, Letty had purposely blinded herself. All she saw was Jacob, especially after Johnnie had passed, and I feared that her love was not completely wholesome. Perhaps the unnatural force of Letty's attention was what drove Jacob away from them and toward Elizabeth. Jacob's absence from the family made a strange ache in my heart, not in proportion to the simple fact of his marrying and moving off the farm. Though Letty had claimed him, I still bore concern for his welfare, and at a distance, which was much harder to abide. It was true I had yielded him, but deep in my innermost heart I never denied that his life would forever be inscribed in my own story.

This is why I keep my secret book. So I will not forget.

Adam never spoke about Jacob's leaving the farm, but I saw he was deeply affected. Once unmatched for vigor, he acquired a stoop, as if his shoulders had assumed additional weight, and the burden of it pressed him toward the earth.

Truly, Jacob's leave-taking presented a predicament for us all. Years ago, we had lost Johnnie, and Otto was too weak and ill-suited to take over the farm, and George was too young by far to show any promise as a farmer. The very thought of our future was like staring into a dark hole, impossible to say what lay inside it. Better not to dwell on it. Hadn't we had a good year? Wasn't everyone hale and thriving?

Adam surely had many good years left in him. Despite our many tribulations, he saw to it that we never gave up, never had to sell the farm, move into town or to the Dakotas or Nebraska like many of our neighbors when faced with a drought, a bank failure, a prairie fire or the plague of hoppers. Adam had been prudent in every choice he made about the farm. He had given studied thought to every acquisition of stock, each piece of new farm equipment, every decision for planting. His last big land purchase caused us to go into debt with Augustus Schmidtz at the German Bank, but those acres would pay back many times over in the coming years. Yes, as long as Adam was capable of governing our direction, we would have nothing to fear. The family would continue to flourish on the farmstead, in spite of the vacancy that Jacob left behind.

The sleigh bells jingled in the distance and when I squinted out the upstairs window, I could not believe my eyes. There was Jacob sitting tall on the buckboard next to Adam. None of his family was with him. I hurried downstairs and set another place at the table. There would be eleven at the table. Our original family complete once again.

\* \* \*

The sleigh pulled into the barnyard and Jacob jumped off to unhitch Pet and Bucky as if he had never left the farm. While the family went into the house, he stayed in the barn, brushed the horses and gave them their extra oats. He cracked the skin of ice on their water trough and put fresh hay in their stall.

Jacob put off going into the house as long as he could. If laboring in the fields and barnyard were a source of anxiety in those years, the interior of the farmhouse had proved ever more stifling. The smell inside the house sickened his senses. Coming into the kitchen with the sweet smell of the open fields and meadow still fresh, he encountered an odor that he recalled vividly from before, when Letty had turned on him at the announcement of his wedding plans. It was not that the house itself was ever untidy or disorderly. Hardly. Tante Kate promoted the virtues of cleanliness and under her guiding hand systematic order always prevailed. But Letty's presence was like an invisible blight silently browning the edges of their life that gave Jacob a queasy feeling of something spoiled and unwholesome.

* * *

Letty lowered her eyes but did not close them when Adam pulled the sleigh into the yard.. Right before Jacob jumped off the buckboard, she saw that woman standing next to the cow barn in a frayed blanket shawl, closer than she had been last night. She had been lurking there since last night. Letty was sure of it. She must have hidden in the shadows, for when Letty blinked the woman was gone and in her place was an old horse blanket hanging on the barn door hook.

This was not the first time Letty had seen the strange woman. One morning soon after their arrival in Iowa, Letty's body dropped a ruined baby. She never knew if it was a boy or girl as it was not yet fully formed, and Tante Kate never said. Still, this failure to hold life created a considerable mess in the sheets and in her drawers and caused Letty no small amount of pain. Letty tried to do her chores despite the bleeding and the cramps, and down by the creek she thought she saw a woman—but the figure disappeared, whether a ghost or a shadow. She was real, though, Letty was certain. Even worse than seeing a phantom was the dark shame that crept in for not being able to carry that baby. How the voices rebuked her! Was it the woman at the creek whispering? Did she snarl and smirk, call her an unfit vessel, a sinner, a body unworthy of carrying a new life? Or was that the priest at Mass, or her own father dead in Illinois? They never said what her sin was, so she never could confess it. Did Tante Kate secretly bury the slipped tissue? Was there anything to bury? No one ever spoke of it.

Days later, Letty looked westward from the bedroom window, beyond the newly plowed fields where the willow and cottonwood trees grew by the brook. She glimpsed a dark shadow. Just a cloud passing overhead. But the sky was clear and cloudless. She blinked to clear her vision and made out a figure standing quite still, a lone woman in the distance wrapped in a blanket shawl that made her resemble an ancient tree stump.

When they brought in the new team, the cows and chickens, when the new little shoats arrived, the woman stood in the far field near the creek. She was sometimes absent for seasons at a time, only to reappear when some change was happening. Any new event drew the woman to that spot—the morning they took little Johnnie away to be buried, Letty saw her quite clearly.

On a warm spring day when she and Tante Kate were planting the kitchen garden, Letty stood and stretched her back, and looked past the far field and, sure enough, there was the blanket woman.

"Have you ever seen a stranger around in the fields, maybe an old woman in a blanket shawl?"

Tante Kate reared back as if she had been snakebit. She wiped her big red hands on her apron and said, "*Da stimmt doch was nicht!* You are mad! Seeing things that aren't there is a sign of *Wahnsinn*! Madness!"

Tannte Kate frightened Letty deeply with that outburst, warning her never to speak that way again. *Madness!* Letty's tongue fairly froze as if she had stuck it onto iron in winter.

But there she was again, Letty acknowledged, on the first day of the new century. Whatever her more brazen appearance portended, it could be nothing good. The blanket woman's presence made an indelible impression on the dark glass of Letty's mind, as surely as if she had made a photograph of her. Letty willed the image away. Her family was together; they were celebrating the new century, almost a quarter century on their farm *and* her forty-fourth birthday. Real or not, there was no place for anyone such as this specter. Letty would not notice her presence. But it frightened her that the woman had come so close to the house.

Adam gave Letty his hand and helped her out of the sleigh.

The house was filled with delicious smells. Jacob came in and they settled in their chairs around the table. Adam bowed his head to say table grace. "*Komm, Herr Jesu, sei unser Gast und segne, was Du uns bescheret hast.* Bless our family and bless our years on this farm. May we be granted many more. Amen."

Pride was known to be a sin, but Letty could not suppress a smile. Her mouth twitched from the effort. She felt triumphant. On her own she had accomplished the task of saving for, arranging and completing the family photograph.

Seated across from her eldest daughter, Letty glanced at Sister Kate for confirmation. Such a fine young woman, a bit somber and lacking in gaiety, but maybe that is just how it was being the oldest and most responsible girl. Or maybe it was because Sister Kate hadn't made a baby yet. Was it a curse to have named her first girl after childless Tante Kate?

After everyone ate their fill, the older girls cleared the table. Tante Kate brought in the pies and lightly touched Letty's shoulder. Every wicked thought she had about Tante Kate was quickly followed by its opposite. As much as Letty hated to admit, she could never have accomplished this life without her sister-in-law, especially in the early days. Tante Kate had helped her through the hazardous birthing times, and when the wheedling demons of doubt and damnation plagued her mind, Tante Kate's medicinals set her to rights. With Tante Kate's care and potions, the wicked voices faded into the distance, their worst messages unfulfilled, and truly, Letty was grateful.

At the best of times, her fine children took hold of life and thrived upon their farm, and Letty always tried to do her best with Adam for affection's sake. She felt nothing but warmth and pride that he was her good husband and that they had survived. Letty caught Jacob's eye and gave him a wink.

\* \* \*

I shot Adam a look. His loaded fork was suspended in midair. We had both seen Letty wink at Jacob. *Mein Gott!* What devilish thought prompted her to make such a gesture to a man she considered her son? Jacob was no longer a child, he was a married man of thirty-one, a father with children of his own. She has lost her reason! Adam and I discussed almost everything, but we had never spoken about Letty's outlandish feelings for Jacob. What could we say? I was gratified to see Adam's plate piled high with my smoked ham and potatoes. He relished his food. Letty's wink did not dent his appetite.

Adam raised his glass. "*Prost!*"

I lifted my mug of homemade beer with everyone else. Their beer had never been under scrutiny during the 1855 year of prohibition, nor was it now. I certainly had no use for drunkards, but I had never understood why or how beer drinking came to be a crime. Iowa was full of German breweries and beer gardens, just like the Old Country.

"Let us praise the Lord for this bounty and to all those at this table, and those others who have gone before, who have provided our family with the grace and endurance to build and keep our family farm." Adam slurped his brew.

"Amen." We all replied.

Over my raised mug, I studied Adam. I had always been able to read his thoughts and feelings as if they were my own. I was certain Adam had directed his toast to Letty's father, old man Bauer. The memory of his death jolted me still. We had never informed Letty of the true circumstances of her father's death. Don't put a stick in a beehive. I took a large swallow of beer.

It was not hard to explain Adam's feelings for the old man. Bauer had bestowed upon Adam what he had not seen fit to pass on to his own two feckless sons, the knowledge that can only come to a man from working with the land and animals for all his grown years. In truth, Bauer had been more father to Adam than our own. How odd to think that the old man's death had helped Adam become the man he was now. How I wished Bauer could see Adam now, and all he had accomplished. He would have been proud.

I excused myself from the table and went towards the kitchen. For a moment, I turned and stood in the doorway while the family visited and finished my pies. The older ones did not have time for the farm, so I had not seen them recently. Sister Kate was a married woman, and I could see she was obviously a dab hand at the sewing machine. She had fashioned her dress on the same pattern as Letty's, a sedate design of black serge trimmed with store-bought decorative braid in shades of blue and violet that matched their eyes. She and Letty could have been sisters. On the other hand, Mary had clearly squandered her husband's bank account on a store-bought under blouse with a tasseled scarf tied to one side, a smart touch that declared her vanity and eagerness to be fashionably up-to-date.

Otto worked in some kind of gentlemen's establishment in Early. He owned a black wool suit, and wore a white bow tie that looked a little foppish to my mind. He had never shown interest in farming or anything that required sweat. His world was indoors, preferably in the dark, cavernous halls where liquor, pool, and cards were the work of the day. I did not like the smell of alcohol that greeted me when he came in the door. Turning last to Jacob, the afternoon sun catching his profile, I was startled to see in Jacob's visage the man who was his true father. Had I never noticed that before? I held the doorframe to steady myself, but no one noticed my chagrin.

When the family portrait finally arrived at the end of January, I helped Letty hang the ornate, gold-painted, plaster frame above the davenport. Jacob was seated at the end of the first row. As a grown man, he was easily the handsomest of the lot. That was my prejudice and wasn't what unnerved me. Again, I saw another presence visible in Jacob's face. Was it not plain for all to see that Jacob's size and features did not favor anyone else in the family?

I thought again of my travel book, that held so many secrets.

PART TWO

# Gone

# MAPLE GROVE, IOWA

## JUNE 15, 2000

VAN ROSE EARLY THE NEXT MORNING. As Lillian predicted, the storm had merely made the air more humid. She headed straight to Dee Dee's where the air conditioner was running full blast. She ordered toast and black coffee. Dee Dee shook her head in disapproval.

"Breakfast is important."

"I know," Van replied, "but I want to get to the library first thing."

She didn't mind Dee Dee taking a maternal tone. She couldn't remember the last time someone had actually looked out for her welfare in such a simple way. Is this what she had missed by not having a normal mother? Van had built her idea of *mother* around a vacancy. An endless parade of frozen TV dinners pained her heart.

"You can always come back this afternoon," Dee Dee said. She put a mug of black coffee and a plate of heavily buttered toast with a large jar of homemade strawberry jam on the table. "You may have noticed, breakfast goes on until two around here."

"Thanks," Van replied. "Depending on what I find at the library, I just might do that."

Van sipped the coffee. It was surprisingly good, rich and dark. She had her prejudices. What had she expected? The brown water that her father made in that horrible aluminum percolator? Absently, she slathered the toast with jam. She hoped the coffee would clear her head. Sleep had been fitful, full of dark dreams she couldn't remember, except for the lingering sense of foreboding that left her exhausted. From her backpack, she fished out the file folders and notes. She took a quick glance of the portrait and was relieved to see that, in the daylight, the ghostly smudges she had seen last night were probably a slight flaw in the photographic plate. With breakfast and coffee, Van felt more rational.

Her journal notes from the cemetery stone listed Adam Reinhardt's death date as 1901. He had died a year after the family portrait was taken. "What happened to you?" she asked Adam in the photograph. "You look so hale and hearty. Let's go see what your obituary has to say."

She left Dee Dee an embarrassingly large tip.

"No need to pay me in advance," Dee Dee teased. "If you insist, you now have a ten-dollar credit."

Van blushed. Overheated, she hoisted her backpack, put on her dark glasses, pulled her visor down and was instantly hit by the wave of warm humid air as she walked out the door and down to the library.

Lillian had shown her a photograph of the original Carnegie Library. The building had hardly undergone remodeling since the turn of the twentieth century. Inside, however, it had all the trappings of a modern institution complete with computers and electronic devices for checking out books. And there was Marion, the librarian. Not a joke, but her real name, on a nameplate on the desk—Marion Grob, smartly dressed in a tailored shirtwaist dress.

"You must be Ms. Reinhardt. Lillian said you would be stopping by. What are you looking for, dear?"

"My name's Van. I'm in town for a couple of days doing some ancestor research. Lillian said you had back copies of *The Chronicle*."

"We do. And I can tell you it was a sad day when that newspaper closed down. What years are you looking for?"

"Let's start with 1901. I'm looking for Adam Reinhardt's obituary." Van hesitated and then asked, "Are you Lillian's sister?"

"No, dear, I'm her sister-in-law, married to her younger brother."

Was everyone in this town called "dear"? It made her feel young although she was probably the same age as these women. Ordinarily it would have grated on her nerves. But Van felt cheered by how these locals addressed her. It did make her wonder, though, if Martin had needed to escape the small town where everyone knew everyone's business. The grapevine could be an informal safety net, but also a vicious rumor mill. Was that enough reason to run? Because Van was convinced that he did run, as fast and far away as he could manage. She still had no idea what propelled him out. Aspirations to become something other than a small-town boy didn't seem to have enough power to force such a radical severance.

Marion directed her toward the section on Iowa history. A few patrons, elderly folks reading newspapers and periodicals, gave the place a comfy, lived-in feel. Martin must have frequented this very building many times as a child. There was something about a library's atmosphere that was deeply reassuring. Ever since she was young, Van had felt safe in a library. As soon as she could read, she had begged her father for a library card.

She inhaled the familiar and not unpleasant odor a library gave off, a certain dry aroma conducive to studious endeavors. Or maybe it worked in reverse—all that focus and study gave the air its particular fragrance. The atmosphere was timeless: a certain monastic quality of muffled quiet surrounded the long wooden tables, the lazy dust motes floated in the slant of sunlight, the rows of books stood in orderly formations. Van recollected other libraries, more famous and elaborate ones, which had served as a kind of burrow for her studies over the years. The Wisconsin Historical Society Library with its grand marble entrance and large oil paintings of 19th century dignitaries had been her home when she was writing her thesis on Indian captivity narratives.

Van had been unaccountably drawn to the story of Mary Jemison, the white woman who had been captured as a child by the Seneca and chose to stay in their company for the rest of her long life. There were others like her, women who had voluntarily stayed with their captors, learned their ways, married Natives, and bore biracial children by their own choice. Only when she was in her eighties did Jemison venture forth on foot to tell her story to white people who had the power to publish her words. Van had analyzed these documents looking for the living thread of a woman's life covered by the religious and political agendas of early male editors and publishers. She probed underneath the shapers and censors and let herself imagine these women—never enough to make it look like she was making things up, even though she considered most historical narratives to be a form of fiction.

Outside of a childish fantasy of being kidnapped, Van never fully understood the driving force behind her desire to know these captive women, a draw strong enough to sustain her through years of research and writing despite disinterest from colleagues in the history department. Even Len had mocked the project, calling her a wannabe. Her father had refused to discuss her topic, calling it romantic fantasy, female trivia. Van stubbornly dug in and stayed true to what mysteriously compelled her. She'd had only one ally, an important one—Harry Turnbull, her thesis adviser at the time. She thought about Turnbull with affection.

An aging, toothless lion of the old school, Turnbull, too, had cast a long, jaundiced eye on her project, but he admired Van's determination. "History is a commitment to the Truth," he declaimed in his stentorian voice. "No matter how difficult it is to achieve, or how contradictory it may appear to our precious inherited beliefs or acquired convictions about how the world should be, we must be dedicated to the Truth." And in that spirit, years before anyone used the term political correctness, Professor Turnbull had given Van the encouragement she needed to pursue her unorthodox subject. She could sure use his support now, but he was long since dead. She drew the line at calling up his spirit. He had trained her mind for research, but the instinctual drive for exposing buried truth was hers. *I should have been a detective.*

Van found an unoccupied wooden table and pulled out the folder that held the family portrait. Leaning back in her chair, she studied Jacob. He was handsome, with a long narrow face marked by high cheekbones and the same shaped nose as she had, although his chin did not jut out. His gaze went to the middle distance, not to the man behind the camera, but his look was enigmatic. What was going on in his mind? He was claimed as Letty and Adam's son in the census record but that seemed unlikely, given his and Letty's closeness in age. Martin had never alluded to anything about this. Maybe Jacob never knew his parentage; perhaps no one ever spoke of it. Maybe there was a shadow of shame, an illegitimacy that no one wanted to claim. That was often the case when a woman got pregnant outside of marriage—especially in the early days of settlement. A widow with a child had status, even pity, but a single woman left with a child to raise by herself was the very definition of impossible. At her high school in the 1960s, Van had heard rumors about girls who had "gone away" for a year. If and when they ever came back, they were never the same. They were lost, damaged somehow by something unspeakable. Nobody ever gave a thought about what happened to their children, where they went, or who took them.

A memory flickered briefly, a firefly whose light she quickly extinguished.

Van's mind boggled at what it must have taken to build the Reinhardt farm from scratch, all that labor and joint effort on everybody's part. It was not difficult to understand how a pioneering family living isolated on a prairie farm could keep things hidden. Perhaps the definition of family was more inclusive and everyone, from young to old, was preoccupied with sheer survival and little time or energy to put a fine point on the niceties of lineage. She registered the irony. Here I am, 125 years later, a Reinhardt orphan sitting in the Maple Grove library stringing together the past, tracking these ancestors back, searching for the missing pieces of their lines. Their untold stories lured her, but their secrets seduced her.

Van knew all about secrets. She had kept more than a few of her own. From the first day of this Iowa trip, shades of Len and her mother pursued her like abandoned waifs clamoring for attention. Van was losing her ability to shove them aside. Her only known remedy was to stay focused on the task at hand as a historian. She was there to do research into a more distant past, which had nothing to do with her personal past. She was constructing a narrative of the Reinhardts, just like she constructed a fuller narrative of Mary Jemison. *Period.*

Van pulled out her journal. This time she addressed her father directly. Although he was definitely dead and buried, maybe some part of him was still available—a weird thought. But worth a try.

*June 15*
*Thursday*
*Day Four*

*Dad,*

*I am in your childhood library in Maple Grove. Can you imagine that? I remember when you got my first library card. You told me how important it was to read. I guess I really took your words to heart, since I have spent most of my adult life in libraries. I vaguely recall you saying it was a shame that your own father couldn't read, though he had worked in town as a road laborer. He had been raised on the family farm. He must have known every inch of it. Maybe farming wasn't in his blood. Whatever that means. Well, what does it mean, Dad? I think there was a lot more to this family story than you ever said. You left out a lot, Dad—in more ways than one. You left me with a phantom lineage—people are missing. Stories have been censored.*

She shut the journal and loosened the tension in her neck and shoulders. She was angry. Why hadn't he told her about these people? How was she supposed to figure all this out? Why was she kept in the dark? Maybe this was how her grandfather Jacob had felt, out of place, loosely tied to a family who claimed him but never gave him the truth of his origins. Did he ever find out, she wondered. More to the point, would she?

"Excuse me, dear," Marion Grob, interrupted. "You might want to have a look at our Iowa history collection. We have a pretty good selection. It might take me some time to search *The Chronicle* for Adam Reinhardt's obituary."

"Thanks, Marion. Take your time. I'm in no rush today. Your library is great."

Van pulled several books from the shelf, made a small stack on the table, and settled in. Research was an old and comforting habit. She found an article on the origins of the Maple Grove Carnegie Library where she was now seated. No surprise that its birthplace was The Women's Reading Circle, in the late 1890s. A handful of civic-minded women from Maple Grove organized and raised money for the first Free Library for "mental improvement." After many of their petitions to the philanthropist, Andrew Carnegie, were declined, these determined women finally got his agreement to give $4000 for the building if the town would furnish a site. This was the first time that Carnegie gave money for a library to a town with a population of fewer than five thousand.

Leave it to a small group of determined women, Van thought. There was no listing of the original members of The Women's Reading Circle. Virginia Woolf had it right: For most of history, Anonymous was a woman. Maybe the Maple Grove women helping Van were their descendants.

Van was a trained scholar, yet pawing through archives and documents, exhuming stories about dead people, was never a simple intellectual exercise; it was hot, visceral, and tantalizing. Uncovering buried truths was a thrill akin to revelation. There were dangers, too. The past could enchant and bewitch—entice you deeper into the woods until you were lost. Or the restless dead could slip through the veil and start a ruckus, like what happened to her at the creek bed, or last night when she stared too hard at the family portrait and thought she saw ghosts. For the first time, Van worried about poking her nose into a history that had been purposely hidden and denied her, maybe for good reasons. She had given her late father a week of her sabbatical to do the research. Seven days. A Biblical number. She checked her watch—a nervous habit. How long had Marion been looking through the back issues of *The Chronicle*?

Van sorted through her stack of books. Her years of research on French fur traders who intermarried with Native women made her curious about Iowa Indian removal and resettlement. She still owed the academic journal a paper she had delivered at the American History Conference last Spring. Maybe she could recover her motivation. Several textbooks proved deeply disappointing, perpetuating tired old prejudices—hostile and degenerate Natives who refused to farm, Indians who demanded annuities, and went on the warpath. She looked to see when these books were last checked out. More than twenty years ago. She hoped they were no longer used in a classroom.

Van slammed the book shut with such a sharp snap that a frowning elder turned her way and put his finger to his lips. There were things she did not want to think about—in fact, for years she had managed to shove them into the deepest darkest hole she could find. Now memories streamed as if a documentary filmmaker with an unsteady camera were at work.

She had just turned twenty and was writing her senior thesis. She and Len were planning a journey back in history, canoeing the Fox River to Green Bay and Glory of the Morning's land. Present-day dams, locks and arduous portages had made the trip impossible. Instead, they made a trip to the Boundary Waters. She had just been offered a good scholarship for graduate school in the fall. Then her mother died, and then—.

Her body tingled, jagged energy coursing through long unused circuits. Why did Len have to show up now? His presence was like an invasive species. It had been almost thirty years since she had last talked with him. That conversation had set her life on a path of no return.

She had called him from the pay phone in the student union. The phone rang and rang. She imagined his dark eyes snapping in irritation at the intrusion. The only time she had ever visited his apartment, she thought it had resembled nothing so much as a raven's nest, filled with all the bright and shiny bits accumulated over the years. She stepped carefully around an eclectic mix of new and old artifacts, a typewriter, a black wall telephone, a black and white television set, an aging pair of wooden snowshoes with gut lacing, a handmade birch canoe paddle, old treaty maps stuck on the walls with thumbtacks, a threadbare red-striped blanket with a ratty beaver pelt sewn into the center that he used as a throw over the sofa, the latter a kind of strange family heirloom passed down from his father's side of the family, the French trapper, the *voyageur*.

He finally picked up.

"Hi, Len, it's me. Can I come over? I have something important I need to talk about—in person."

"I'm not sure I'll be here. Can it wait? I'm going up north for a while."

She had flinched hearing his cool, detached voice. How could she have set that little snare and put her own big foot right into it? Why did she always forget the most important thing about him? Only twenty, Len was already an escape artist.

"I'll let you know when I get back." Len hung up.

Van looked at the dead phone in her hand and whispered, "I'm pregnant."

Marion Grob startled her. "I have the information you wanted on Adam Reinhardt."

Van placed the books back in the stacks. She was a historian. She needed facts.

"Don't be a dreamer," her father had warned.

"Stick to your documents," Em had said. "No ghosts."

# SIOUX CREEK FARM

## AUGUST 1901

FOR THREE DAYS RUNNING, Letty and Kate donned clean aprons, rolled up their sleeves, and prepared plates of food—roast chickens, sliced hams, ring baloney, potato salad with bacon, cabbage kraut, bread and pies, and shot glasses for schnapps. They set up long tables near the house and feed the haying crew in two sittings—dinner at midday and supper in the evening. All able-bodied neighbors had gathered for the seasonal ritual including young George, who joined the men for the first time. Even Lizzie, Margaret and Lena had their chores, dashing back and forth to the kitchen with platters of food. When the work in the fields was finished the crew toasted the harvest with schnapps while the girls cleared the tables.

As usual, I noticed, Letty had worked herself into a nervous tizzy, mumbling and griping, scurrying in and out of the house in a dither. I sent her to bed with a steaming cup of valerian tea and promised to check on her later, always a thin line between hard work and her collapse.

After the crew left, I retreated to the rocking chair on the porch. The early evening spared its light. Windrows of sweet-smelling hay ran in heaped up mounds as far as the eye could see—a picture worth painting. The end of summer was a time when farmers knew how they had fared throughout the growing season, knew what they could put in the barn and in the bank. Haying in times of plenty was a joyful thing, the best of times for all concerned, and this late August with hot, dry days and balmy evenings was truly a boon.

Adam hitched Pet and Bucky to the loaded hay wagon and headed to Hoeffelder's farm three miles to the south. How generous my brother is, I thought. The neighbor, a childless widower, had helped in the fields and Adam bartered surplus hay for his labor. As if it were yesterday, I recalled the May afternoon Adam and Jacob returned from an auction with the hay wagon and a pair of young horses for pulling and plowing. A local farmer was selling out and moving to Nebraska. One farmer's loss was another farmer's gain. Pet and Bucky were now more than twenty years old, still a steady and reliable team. And Adam would soon be sixty. What troubled me more than my brother's age was the fact that he sat alone on the hay wagon.

Twenty-five years ago, young Jacob had accompanied Adam on the train from Illinois to Iowa to view the uncultivated prairie land my brother had purchased sight unseen. When they returned, my usually reserved brother simply overflowed with gladness. At the Bauer dinner table, he extolled the purchase of land and proclaimed Jacob's skill with the water stick. Yes, along with knowing the weather Jacob had inherited certain skills, but not from me. At that moment, I foresaw how Adam and Jacob would build the new farm together, and how Jacob would be the one to carry it into the next generation. He was almost nine years old.

"Old enough to begin," Adam had told me. We never spoke of the fact that the boy was not of his seed. Hadn't

Adam bonded to him as a true father? I had felt certain Adam would teach Jacob all he knew; just as old man Bauer had done for him.

Jacob's marriage and move to Maple Grove was a deep reproach of Adam's patrimony, a turning away from all they had achieved. Shortly after Jacob left, we suffered the worst drought in memory. Those two events coming hand in hand almost broke Adam. Bad enough was the drought and its devastation—we would recover—but the loss of Jacob, someone with whom to bear the hardship, that was irreplaceable.

At least Jacob had made time to help Adam with the haying. A man in his prime, Jacob pitched hay onto the wagon, his pace steady like that of a good animal, strong and uncomplaining, without need of rest, no work too difficult. How Adam must covet the young man's strength. He had once been able to work like that. But unlike Adam at his age, Jacob had no forward-seeking vision that I could ascertain. Maybe young George will take over the farm one day. In truth, none of us had really stopped to take the boy's measure or his suitability.

Ordinarily, I did not indulge in the dismals, but this particular evening, because of its sweetness, because I saw the burden in my brother's sagging body, I yielded to an old lamentation. Wasn't it Adam's right to reap the rewards from the labor of his middle years? The farm could easily have been Jacob's, the handing over as natural as day following night. What part did I have in steering this course? Since the day I had returned with Jacob in my arms, I was convinced that Adam would benefit from having Jacob as his son. Over the years I had trained myself to say nothing other than what was necessary for practical day-to-day living, and that became my habit and how I was known. There was no calculus for measuring the weight of my silence nor on whom it would fall hardest.

I watched until Adam and the loaded wagon were a small cloud of road dust on the horizon. The sunset spread its fine red line of glowing fire across the far west, whippoorwills and meadowlarks struck up their twilight song, and farm dogs barked in the distance.

\* \* \*

Josephus Kohler had just finished his dinner—a fine repast of freshly slaughtered roast beef and hot potato salad with bacon drippings, and a dish of sliced garden cucumbers and onions in a dressing of dill, vinegar and thick milk. He had topped it off with a small bit of *Apfelkuchen* and black coffee and had a filled pipe in hand in anticipation of extending an already enjoyable evening. He went into the room he used as an office to attend to the account books for his hardware store. Settling into the swivel chair at his desk, he lit the pipe, turned on the lamp with a green shade, bent over the large ledger and entered a column of numbers, admiring his crisply legible script and his profits.

He was about to list out the hardware store's iron nail inventory when he was distracted by anxious, excited voices in the kitchen—a man's distraught voice, his wife's soft mewling, another man's guttural moan.

His wife came to the doorway of the office, her face pinched and pale. "Josephus, there has been an accident! It is Adam Reinhardt: I am afraid he is fearfully wounded. Hoeffelder brought him here and he's laid him out on the kitchen table. Please! Come and see to him!"

Kohler's first response was not charitable. Farmers were always getting themselves into terrible mishaps, especially during haying season—chopped-off fingers, broken bones, and severed limbs. He read the grisly stories every week in

*The Chronicle*. He did not relish the idea of what he might see on the very table where he had just eaten such a fine and satisfying meal.

"Couldn't he have found some other place to do his dying?"

"Have some mercy, Josephus."

"Yes, yes, of course, I will come right away." He slowly tamped his pipe and meticulously blotted his books, put the pens aside, and stoppered the inkbottle.

Kohler did not consider himself a do-gooder or a bleeding heart. He did not generally involve himself with other people's miseries, large or small. He just wanted folks to buy his goods and be timely in paying their bills. He did not care to know the petty dramas of their daily lives. He took comfort in the tidy discipline of accounting and the neat tabulation of numbers, not in the inevitable and unruly messes people made of their lives. He refused to be rushed towards this disagreeable intrusion into his pleasant evening.

Adam Reinhardt's body took up the whole kitchen table. Bits of hay stuck in his beard, a dark blotch of blood oozed from his gut, and the right leg of his overalls was skewed at a bad angle. His wife had managed to dribble some of his best one hundred proof whiskey into the man to dull the pain. With a sweep of his arm, Kohler brushed his two gaping children aside, and ordered his older boy to hitch the surrey.

"Go fetch Dr. Wiedersheim. Tell him to hurry."

Hoeffelder stood in the kitchen, clutching his straw hat, and moving from one foot to the other. His face was gray.

"How did this happen?"

"He was bringing a hay load to my farm," Hoeffelder stammered. "I came out to the road when I heard the dogs. They must have got loose from Axel's farm. Just the other day I told that *Dummkopf* his *scheiss Hunde* should be shot. I yelled for Adam to drop the reins. Too late. The horses bolted

into the ditch. They are banged up, but *danke Gott* I didn't
have to shoot them. They're stabled in my barn. Took some
time to get Reinhardt out from under the wagon. I thought it
best to bring him here." Hoeffelder was panting. "Is it dire?"

"Easy, man," Kohler said. "Wiedersheim will be here soon.
Go back home. I'll send my boy over later to get the horses."

His wife handed Hoeffelder a glass of whiskey. He tossed
it off in one gulp. The man was clearly beside himself. No
wonder. Reinhardt's wretched state elicited strong revulsion
and Kohler swallowed hard to keep his dinner down.

Kohler had never needed Wiedersheim as a personal physician, but he had witnessed the doctor's prowess when he was
called to treat a dairy cow's difficult birth or dispatch a calf
with a broken leg. He watched as the man hopped from the
surrey and rushed into the kitchen, gripping his scuffed black
doctoring bag. With one continuous graceful motion, Wiedersheim loosed his jacket, rolled up his shirtsleeves, pulled a
rubber apron over his vest and trousers, and prepared himself
to confront whatever bone, blood and gristle was presented.

Kohler tilted his head in awe of the delicacy with which
the doctor wielded a large pair of shears and carefully snipped
the length of Adam's heavy denim overalls. When a sharp
stick of bone protruded from Adam's great white leg, Kohler
hurried outdoors and promptly spewed his dinner.

Wiedersheim suggested they set up a makeshift cot in
Kohler's office. Kohler grimaced. His emptied belly was still in
rebellion. He did not relish using his office as a hospital ward.
He stood aside while his son and wife helped Wiedersheim fit a
blanket litter under Adam's body. Adam, a giant of a man, in a
shock-induced state made his dead weight awkward and hard
to handle. Wiedersheim gave Kohler a grave sideways glance
and in a heavy-hearted voice, said, "I administered morphine
for his pain. I'll see that Father Storch comes out right away."

Kohler sent his boy in the good carriage to fetch Mrs. Reinhardt. He instructed his wife to handle the situation with the priest who would give Adam Reinhardt the last rites. Once the doctor and the priest finished their ministrations to body and soul, it would be up to Kohler and Augustus Schmidtz to deal with the cleaner business and logic of the law. He hurried in his single rig to the banker's home in Maple Grove.

A late summer cold made Schmidtz testy. A staunch Lutheran, he agreed to come to Kohler's house only after Father Storch had concluded his churchly rites. On the way, Schmidtz confirmed, as Kohler suspected, that Reinhardt had bank loans outstanding and that there was probably no will. They agreed that finalizing the details of Reinhardt's last wishes was of the utmost importance for all concerned and would be a difficult process with a drugged and dying man. They hurried back to Kohler's office where Adam lay on the cot.

"Adam! Adam! Wake up, man!" Kohler rasped. "We have business to attend to. You must wake up!"

"Is the haying not done? Did Hoeffelder not get his promised load of hay?" Adam croaked in his delirium.

"Adam! Adam! *Du musst aufwachen*! We need you to be awake!"

Kohler bent his head so close to Adam's mumbling mouth he could smell what the man had just eaten—kraut and ring baloney with dark mustard, washed down with a draught of beer. Repulsed by the intimacy of this odor, he closed his eyes and pulled away from the smell of recently consumed food on a dying man.

"Adam, this is urgent! *Du musst dich anstrengen*! Make an effort, man!" Schmidtz implored.

"Augustus Schmidtz and I are writing up your last will and testament. For your family's sake." Kohler shouted as if to a deaf person.

"*Gott in Himmel! Ich liege im Sterben*!" Adam whispered. "Am I dying?"

Kohler did not answer. Instead, he read from the document. "I, the undersigned, Adam Reinhardt, of the county of Ida Grove and the State of Iowa, of the age of—How old are you, Adam?"

"*Sechzig Jahre*." English words escaped his grasp.

"—of the age of sixty years," Kohler continued, "being of sound mind and memory and understanding do make, publish and declare this to be my last will and testament—"

Kohler hoped all this was true—that a man in Adam's condition knew what he was doing.

"Now your debts, Adam," wheezed Schmidtz. "You will have to sell some of your land to pay off the recent land purchase debt at the German Bank."

"Only eighty acres—" he gurgled.

Schmidtz coughed into a white linen handkerchief and continued:

"First, I direct that all my just debts be paid by the executor hereinafter named, including the expenses of my last sickness and funeral expenses, and at the death of my wife, my estate is likewise to pay her funeral expenses, and I direct that a suitable tombstone be erected over my and my wife's graves in due season. Moneys will be set aside for Masses."

"*Ja, ja,*" Adam nodded his assent. "*Ja,* I am dying. But am I burying Letty, too? *Mein Gott!* The priest from St. Bernard's? He was already here to get his cut?"

"You are all set with God," Kohler said. "Father Storch gave you your last rites. Schmidtz and I want to put your earthly affairs in order."

Kohler read from a document. "I give, devise, and bequeath to my beloved wife, Letty—"

A sob crawled from Adam's chest and almost choked him. "*Meine liebe Frau,* my beloved wife." Kohler turned away, clenched his jaw, took a breath, and continued, "—in the event of my wife's decease, the rest and residue of my estate shall be divided among my living children, share and share alike."

"*Ja, ja,* that is good. But the farm? And Katharina? They cannot make do without her." His words were garbled with moans and rattled breath.

Kohler and Schmidtz put their heads together and conferred in whispers. Kohler read the provision.

"Thirdly, I provide that my sister, Katharina Reinhardt, shall be reserved a place in my homestead and be taken care of during her remaining years as a member of my family but, should she elect otherwise, she shall receive the sum of one thousand dollars in cash out of my estate and all obligations on the part of my estate to said Katharina shall cease."

Adam made a strangled laugh. "She will never leave the farm or the family."

Kohler ignored his comment and plowed on. "Now, Adam, an executor to carry out your will. Who will you appoint?" Kohler leaned close; the smell of Adam's breath churned his stomach.

"*Sie!* You!" he whispered. "*Tun Sie es.* You do it."

Kohler took a sharp inhale, as if breathing in Adam's last breath. "Yes, Adam, if that is how you want it," Kohler exhaled. "I will agree to see to your wishes."

Only when Reinhardt looked squarely into Kohler's face and requested that he be the administrator of his wishes did Kohler feel the overwhelming import in his lower back, as if he had attempted to lift something far beyond his capability. Desperate to retract the offer, Kohler remembered the eldest son, Jacob, but quickly recalled that he had married some years previous and had left the family farm for a life in town. Probably some kind of falling out between father and son. It was not uncommon. Kohler did not want to trouble the dying man with such a line of questioning. He could not refuse this poor farmer who was breathing his last. He was not an unfeeling monster.

Schmidtz covered his nose with his damp handkerchief and handed Kohler the typed and signed document, who read it aloud to Adam ending with the clause: *"I hereby appoint Josephus Kohler of Maple Grove as my executor of this my last will and testament and he shall give such bond as the court may direct."* Kohler affixed his signature in his finest cursive script. He relied on the wisdom of Augustus Schmidtz, who was familiar with farm tragedies and foreclosures and hardened to the disassembling of lives and property.

The clacking of typewriter keys filled the room like locusts in a dry summer.

"One more thing, Adam, and then you can rest. You must sign, sign your name here."

Kohler put the pen in Adam's trembling hand. Schmidtz held the paper as Adam scrawled his signature for the last time. "Adam Reinhardt."

Overtaken with a prolonged coughing fit, Schmidtz requested that Kohler's wife drive him back to Maple Grove. Between barking coughs, he promised to file the documents in the town office first thing in the morning.

No sooner had Schmidtz left than the surrey arrived with Mrs. Reinhardt who was accompanied by Adam's elderly sister, Katharina. Kohler vaguely recalled hearing that the old woman had a grim streak, and gossip gleaned from his wife and the local churchwomen said Reinhardt's wife was strange and overly excitable. He recalled seeing her a year ago at von Schimmer's photography studio, a mousy, skittish woman.

With murmured sympathy, he ushered the two women into the dimly lit office where Adam lay with a blanket pulled up to his dark beard, hiding his crushed and irreparable body. The room was filled with the dying man's unpleasant exhalations; his face glistened with a greenish cast from the desk lamplight. He informed the women that Father Storch had given Adam the last rites.

"Letty, *mein liebe Frau,* my beloved wife." Adam's words broke through his tortured breathing. "Letty, mein Letty, *Ja, ja, Ich komme nach Hause.* Wait for me! I am coming home."

The hallway clock chimed midnight. Kohler slipped into the hallway, granting the women their moments of privacy with the dying man. He dreaded nothing more than female hysterics. Reentering his office prepared for the worst, he was made more fearful by what came in its place.

Mrs. Reinhardt sat perfectly still in Kohler's desk chair, while Katharina's imposing figure shielded her against the harsh vision of the broken man on the cot. The women were silent and pale as ghosts, Katharina's large frame bent as if she had been poleaxed. But it was Mrs. Reinhardt who gave him the fright. She managed to lock him into her gaze and try as he might, he could not pull away. Her hard blue eyes dilated, then rolled in their sockets as if some central device had gone haywire. Kohler fought off a sensation of vertigo, and in an unlikely fit of pity he said in an unctuous tone more befitting of an undertaker, "Don't worry, I will take care of everything."

Three days later, Kohler's wife placed *The Chronicle* on the table next to his breakfast plate, the page opened to Adam's obituary. He had let his breakfast go cold, the eggs congealed in bacon fat, and his favorite raspberry jam bled into the toast.

\* \* \*

Like some exotic displaced bird, a spray of orange gladiolas sent by Josephus Kohler perched on top of Adam's closed casket. Two ushers grasped Letty by the elbows and led her toward the sanctuary, the guest of honor, so to speak. I followed close behind and took my seat next to her in the front pew along with the five children, the three younger girls mercifully kept at home with Jacob's wife. I was never in regular attendance at Sunday Mass, and the church was filled with people I did not care to know. I abhorred this much exposure put on the family in our time of loss.

"*Introibo ad altare Dei.*" Father Storch's tuneless voice barely penetrated the woozy odors of beeswax and incense and layers of cotton wool that gave me a heavy brain. Adam's death had come upon us from out of nowhere, maybe from hell itself, shaking the family like trees in a cyclone. Encased in our blacks, still in shock, we were bent under an ungodly and ferocious storm of grief.

My arthritic hands grasped the back of the pew and I forced my aching knees toward the kneeler. I bowed my head, but not in prayer. Instead, I went over the events of the last few days. After Letty and I returned from Kohler's the night of Adam's accident, it took a great panting effort to get her up the stairs, undressed, and into her nightclothes—she was stupefied, her mouth hung open like a bell that had lost its clapper. I crawled into bed next to her, in the very place where Adam had slept the previous night. The old mattress had given in to his weight over the years, and I felt the contours of his absent body against my own. I held Letty in my arms and stroked her hair and spoke comforting words like a mother with an injured child: "*So, so, sei still, ist schon gut, Letty.*"

The hardened shell enclosing my heart softened and I made a silent vow to devote myself to Letty, to midwife her through this grievous time. It was one way of ensuring my place within the family, and the only way of fulfilling the promise I had made in my heart as Adam lay dying. With

Letty sleeping in my arms, I dreamed again of the man from my long ago:

I do not know where I am headed. Straddling a prairie pony, hair loosened, plain-spun dress hitched up to show my blue woolen stockings and black leather lace-ups. Wrapped in a heavy shawl, clutching the reins, staring at the back of a man's rude country jacket—

The next day I came upon Adam's barn coat on the hook by the door, his muddied boots, and hay-speckled shirt, clothes he had so recently worn. They stabbed at me like vulture beaks, opening fresh wounds around my newly tender heart. Out of sheer will, I forced myself to forgo grief and tethered myself to the immediate needs of the family. Letty had stopped speaking and had to be dressed and undressed, her body rigid and unbending like a wooden doll. Given Letty's incapacity, I appealed to the older girls. Despite their own sorrow, they agreed to care for the younger children. Little Lena and Margaret left the house holding hands as if they could make their way through this disaster only if they stuck together.

Lizzie, just twelve, clung to Letty's lifeless skirts thinking her mother's lack of movement meant safety and not the frozen kind of danger I knew it to be. George pretended that all at once he was a man, and insisted on wearing long pants. And where were the men? Otto had skulked about like a shadow, appearing and disappearing. And Jacob? When he came to pick up the children, he looked like a recently slaughtered steer, the blood drained from him, his eyes fixed on his shoes as if he could fathom this disaster only by staring at them.

Augustus Schmidtz sent a post informing them that Josephus Koehler had been appointed executor of Adam's will. I wondered how Adam could have agreed to this in his delirium. As the oldest male in the family, wasn't Jacob the next in line, even though he was no longer living on the farm? I doubted Kohler was up to the task. That wretched evening in his office, he did not look well and outside of the outlandish gladiolas, he hadn't made an appearance at the funeral, although his wife was in attendance. The older girls assured me that Kohler had a good head for business, given his successful hardware store and dairy farm, but whether he had what it would take to manage the Reinhardt family's affairs remained to be seen. Kohler had requested a meeting three days from the funeral service, where he would read out the will. I was not optimistic about the meeting.

Father Storch's voice broke into my thoughts as he implored us to attend to the Gospel. I sat back in the pew and picked up my ancient German missal, its covers worn from age but not from use, and found the passage but did not read it. The priest peered down from his perch on the pulpit. His black vestments hung from his scrawny body, and he appeared like an ill-fed crow contemplating a fresh carcass. The sight of him provoked such a fury I gripped the pew until my knobby knuckles went white. The cotton wool burned off my head in a flash of searing heat. What kind of God is this? The God of Disaster who loosed his evil hounds from hell? And this priest with his pious voice who was trying to convince us of the great wisdom of God's will, who offers his sympathies like so much treacle. What does he see when he looks down at us—a family broken like Adam's poor body? Surely, he must know he is handing us an empty cup.

"*Hoc est corpus meum, quod pro vobis tradetur.*"

Like one body the congregation went down on the wooden kneelers, and the pain in my knees brought me back to my senses. "Yes," I reprimanded myself, "You have to take the damn wafer." To refuse it would be unseemly and draw unnecessary notice and later, gossip.

But I would not draw comfort from that dry circle of bread said to be Jesus Christ's crucified body. I refused to place myself in the bosom of the Lord of Destruction. I could not delude myself with the notion of God's beneficence like so much money in the bank. I did not want to draw on a bankrupt account. For sure I was getting old, but I would muster the strength for what lay ahead, certain I could only find it within myself, not in fraudulent words from a dried up cleric. With blasphemy running in my veins, I joined the line of communicants heading toward the altar rail, guiding Letty as if she were a sleepwalker. I doubted Letty even knew where she was, but the ritual was so deeply embedded and familiar she went through the gestures by rote.

"*Ego sum resurrectio et vita.*"

We emerged from the cool darkness of the church. The heat of late August assaulted and sucked my breath away. We were not done with this sorry business yet. The Reinhardt family had three buggies in the cortege to accommodate them to the cemetery. I made sure not to sit near the priest, as I did not trust myself in his proximity. The mourners—farmers, their wives, village neighbors—dressed in their funeral blacks, fanned their flushed faces as they clambered into waiting buggies, and headed for the outskirts of town.

It was a simple truth. Tragedy brings out the unexpected in people, both the best and the worst. The older farmers would take Adam's death the hardest. Only they could calculate the cost of his untimely passing, add up the sum of a lifetime of labor, and reckon the potential loss of the farm. I was grateful for their genuine sorrow even though they would be first in line to take advantage at a farm auction. Life was meant for the living, the harvest was completed; the neighbors could surely use the bushels of corn and oats, the stacks of hay and straw. I did not begrudge them their needs.

)nce they were assembled at the gravesite, the eyes of the modest farm wives fixed on Letty, measuring her grief like so much yardage, curious to see what she was made of, if she would come apart at the seams, an eager glint revealing their desire for a grand display. *Schadenfreude.* The Germans knew to put a name on it, that strange welling up of happiness in the face of your neighbor's misfortune, the feeling of having been spared and glad of it—a sense of being a bit superior that you had been bypassed and maybe because you were more wholesome and worthy. Seeing those ordinarily God-fearing and good-hearted women made me want to spit. I closed my eyes to take them out of sight and there was Adam, my beautiful brother as he was when we had left Germany almost thirty-five years ago, so full of hope and the confidence of youth, so strong and vital and full of promise, so eager to sail off to the land of America.

"Adam, Adam, where are you now? I cannot go with you on this journey as I did when we first came to this country. I must stay behind. You can be certain I will do as much as I can. In your place, I will watch over Letty and the children. I only hope it is enough and not beyond my strength."

"*Requiescat in pace,*" Storch intoned. Young George joined Jacob, Otto, and Hoeffelder as they lowered the coffin into the newly dug grave next to baby Johnnie's flat marker. Tiny tongues of green moss and orange lichens licked the edges of his little stone. Letty's arm made a violent twitch, and I quickly grabbed her as she lurched toward the open grave.

# MAPLE GROVE, IOWA

## JUNE 16, 2000

MARION GROB HANDED VAN a copy of Adam Reinhardt's obituary. She wasn't smiling.

### August 28, 1901

Adam Reinhardt of Sioux Creek Township was injured in a runaway accident near John Hoeffelder's place. He died from his injuries at the home of J. Kohler last Wednesday evening at 12 o'clock.

The deceased was born in Heidesheim, Germany, in 1841 and came with his sister, Katharina, to America in 1866, locating in Dixon County, Illinois where he met and married Elizabeth Bauer. In 1877 he purchased a farm in Sioux Creek, Ida Grove township, where he settled the following spring and pioneered a farm where he resided until the time of his death. He leaves a widow, eight children, and an elder sister to mourn his loss. The funeral will be held at St. Bernard's Catholic Church on August 31st. The sorrowing ones have the sympathy of all in their hour of affliction.

Brief and devastating. Van's throat clenched against the pain of loss. Two months ago, as one of a handful attending her father's graveside, she had only felt numb. But this was more than a single tragic death.

"I'm sorry, dear. How unfortunate."

"It's rather shocking. I have their family portrait, taken just the year before, where the family is whole and Adam looks so strong and healthy. There are still young children, too. Hard to imagine what happened after his death."

"You might want to go to the Ida County Courthouse to get the probated will. That is, if there was one. I know you aren't the average tourist, but the Courthouse is worth a visit. It's on the National Registry of Historic Places. My neighbor Shirley works in Records. I can give her a call and see what she can find for you. Where are you staying, dear?"

"In Storm Lake, at the Super Eight."

"Well, Ida Grove is right between Maple Grove and Storm Lake, close to the town of Early. You can get there in about twenty minutes if you take Hwy 59 and don't speed. I'll draw you a map."

Marion rummaged in her desk for paper and a pencil, and Van wondered if Marion was a member of the clan of motherly women who all knew each other and secretly ran the whole town. Or maybe she was just lucky. Maybe sisterhood wasn't just a fancy idea, but a deeply comforting practice. Maybe they came from generations of pioneering women like The Women's Reading Circle, where mental improvement and helping others was cultivated as a virtue as well as a necessity. There was probably a dark side to everyone knowing everyone else's business, but Van welcomed their help. It was like being in a fairytale, following a trail of breadcrumbs, which reminded her that she was hungry.

She stopped at Dee Dee's for an egg salad on whole wheat and coffee to go for the road.

Van propped the family portrait on the passenger seat of her car. She made a quick study of Adam—the deep-set eyes, dark hair combed back, a full brush mustache and beard that covered his necktie, shapely hands that rested lightly on his knees—a vital man, a real patriarch. He was sixty years old when the accident occurred, just a year and a half after the portrait had been made. What a horrible way to die. What a sad and calamitous death. She thought of the young children, the women. How did they manage? They must have been shattered by the loss of their paterfamilias. Who took over the farm?

She put the lidded cup of coffee in the holder and placed the sandwich bag on the passenger side. Eating while driving was a terrible habit. But she was on the hunt now. She checked the map Marion had made. After she got on Hwy 59, she opened the wax paper and took a bite of pickle. Why hadn't she ever liked dill pickles? These were delicious—homemade with just the right blend of sour, salt and spice.

The Ida Grove courthouse was a stately two-and-a-half-story brick building with a tall tower, Italianate style. Like the old Carnegie Library, it had undergone some remodeling, but retained its original elegance. However many jokes there were about Iowans they certainly demonstrated taste in their public buildings.

Just as Marion had promised, Van found Shirley waiting for her in the Records department. Shirley's brown eyes blinked like a bird's behind a pair of black frame glasses. A thin woman, maybe in her late fifties, her brown cardigan was buttoned to the neck against the air conditioning. No wedding ring. Another spinster?

"I am guessing you're Ms. Reinhardt? Marion just called and said you were on your way, said you're looking for documents. If so, I'm your girl." She batted her eyes.

"It was so kind of her to call ahead. She probably told you I'm on a bit of a family search. My great-grandfather Adam

Reinhardt died in late August of 1901. I have his obituary from *The Chronicle*. I'm wondering if you have a record of his will, or probate documents?"

"I'm sure if there was a will, I can locate it for you. It may take a half hour or more. You might want to go down the street to the coffee shop while I look through the records. My friend Laureen makes a damn good cup of coffee."

Shirley's spunk made her smile. So unexpected from a little brown wren. Van checked her watch. "Thanks, I'll be back around 3. Will that give you enough time?"

"Sounds about right."

"By the way, my name's Van."

Midafternoon and the coffee shop was quiet. She ordered black coffee. Not as good as Dee Dee's, but adequate. She added to her odd quartet of helpers—Dee Dee, Lillian, Marion, and now Shirley. Whatever she needed, it seemed these women had her covered. Shirley had reminded her of Em. Maybe Shirley was gay. They shared the same preference for brown-bird colors, the same bright-eyed efficiency, and the same spark of conspiratorial heat, underneath the camouflage.

She pulled out her journal. Even if he was dead, she addressed her father directly.

*Ida Grove, Iowa*
*Friday, June 16*
*Day Five*

*The only reason I am here is to do the research you requested. I have located your grandfather Adam's obituary. So tragic. Surely you must have known how he died. You never spoke of it. Truthfully, you never spoke of much. I'm in Ida Grove waiting to get a copy of the will, so I have some time on my hands.*

*Well, I hope you don't turn over in your grave, as they say, but I think it's only fair that if I have to find things out for you, you need to know about me—things I never dared tell you.*

*For one thing, I had a very passionate affair with my colleague, Emma Cooper. You met her once. I am sure you don't remember. She is a very plain-looking woman—*

She pictured her father's outrage as she wrote the words that were once unspeakable. She pushed her chin forward.

\* \* \*

Two years ago on Christmas vacation, Em phoned her apartment out of the blue. Most of their colleagues had left for family visits, for Florida or some warm Caribbean island. She assumed Em had gone back East.

"If you're not busy, come over to my house this afternoon."

"Okay, I'll bring the paper I'm working on for the conference ..."

"Forget your paper. Bring your skates. The ice is perfect," Em commanded.

"I'll be right over!"

Van dug through old camping gear, boxes and boots stuffed in the back of her closet and finally unearthed her figure skates. She ran her finger against the blade. How many years had it been since she used them? It was once a solo delight. When the ice was frozen solid on Lake Mendota she would skate as far out as she wished, clambering over ice heaves. Sometimes she skated all the way to Picnic Point. On the way she greeted ice fisherman who sat on buckets like frozen statues with their lines sunk in a hole, and a bottle of whiskey nearby to keep them fortified—such a hope-filled male ritual. Such a male pursuit. She never saw women ice-fishing.

Em's house was in a residential area five miles from the university campus and on the east side of Madison on Lake Monona—private, anonymous. She had never visited Em at home. They always worked out of their department office.

Van pulled her car up to the spacious bungalow with front porch columns and parked on the street. Em once told her she bought the place because it was one of those Sears Roebuck kit houses, built in the early 1900s and shipped by rail to Madison from Chicago. Em was a great fan of history. They had never talked about money, but Van was sure Emma drew on a sizable trust fund, all those East Coast private schools, and her alma mater, Vassar College, the Ivy Leagues. Despite its scholarly reputation, the University of Wisconsin was a land grant university, a peasant next to those aristocrats. But class hardly mattered in academia. She and Em were intellectual equals. As feminists working in obscure areas of early American history, they had created a redoubt that buffered them from the Department's young turks and internecine battles.

Inside, the house was spare—solid, dark wood panels and beams. Form follows function. That perfectly described Em—efficient, utilitarian, without ornament or frills—everything as it seems, everything with a purpose, no hidden nooks or closet crannies. Skates in hand, they went down the outside stone steps to the lake. The ice was clean, clear, blue-black. It had been an unusually cold December without much snow. Van estimated the ice to be at least a foot thick. Beneath the frozen surface there was moving water, where the fish were living down there somewhere in their secret world. The ice fisherman with their lines sunk in a hole knew that.

Compared to Em's black hockey skates, Van's white figure skates felt girlish. But the women kept up with each other in long graceful sweeps. They took off for the middle of the lake.

As the temperature dropped, the ice talked in pops and pings. Van executed a few turns, and Em skated backwards as fast as she could. Away from the safety of the edge, the lake moaned as if a leviathan had awakened from the deeps. They laughed like kids when Van landed on her backside. Em pulled her up and then into her arms. That was her first move. The rest happened inside the house, on the couch, a glass of rye whiskey apiece, and then the upstairs bedroom. Their bodies melded together. Em knew how a woman's body worked.

This was her secret. Van surrendered without resistance. It was shocking, like falling through ice only to find the water underneath was warm, as if in a dream, and Van rode wave after wave of sensation, coming up for air and going back under.

Early the next morning Van woke Em.

"Now what?" Van asked her.

"What do you mean? Nothing has changed. We continue on like always. Only now we can spend the weekends together. Hey, it's still early. Come here." Em tried to pull her back under the covers.

"I have to go home and feed Mister. He'll wonder what happened to me."

"You can bring Mister over here. I like cats and he might appreciate a change of scenery."

"I have to think about things, Em. Last night might not mean much to you, but it does change everything for me."

Em flinched.

"Sorry, I didn't mean it that way," Van whispered as she nuzzled the warmth of Em's neck and slid back under the covers.

Their affair was incandescent and clandestine—steamy mornings in Em's bed before running to campus to teach a class, panting kisses behind the closed door of their shared office, sharing a room with a king size bed at conference hotels and making love all night. The thought of being discovered was risky. Maybe they would lose their jobs. That wasn't the real problem. Despite her early years as queen of the one-night stands, Van wasn't built for such ferocious intimacy. Especially not with a woman, especially not long term.

Em's passion scared her—left her breathless and destabilized. She could never linger. She was claustrophobic. Unraveled. Always on the verge of falling apart. Often, she pushed Em away, made some excuse—her cat, a paper to write, a class to prep for—the real reason left unsaid, because of—what? No words for it. The one time she confided in her colleague, Pam had suggested a therapist. She probably had attachment problems. No surprise there, Van thought, considering her parents.

Or, Pam offered, maybe she was afflicted with lesbian bed death. "You know, when a relationship between women asphyxiates due to lack of oxygen."

"Is that really a thing?" Van asked. It sounded bad. Anyway, the sad and simple truth was, she had crushed Em by shutting down their sex life. She frequently saw Em with younger women—never the same one twice. Van limited her relationships to Mister.

Laureen had refilled her coffee cup twice. Van checked her watch. She had been sitting there for almost an hour. Shirley must be wondering. She finished the journal entry she had started.

*Okay, Dad, I am going to switch the subject. Not much more to tell anyway. Em and I are still good friends and colleagues. She is cat-sitting Mister. Now there's a definition of a real friend—one who will clean out a cat's litter box for you. I know you always hated cats.*

*Your daughter, Van Reinhardt*

*P.S. By the way, I thought you should know, years ago I legally changed my name to Van.*

She closed the journal.

Back at the county courthouse, Shirley handed Van a folder with papers.

"I made copies of the probated Will and Inventory submitted to the court by the estate executor, a man named Josephus Kohler."

"Thanks, Shirley. This will be a great help."

"If you need anything else, just give me a holler. Glad to be of help. Say hi to Marion when you see her. Tell her I'll see her in a couple of weeks at the Maple Grove Fourth of July Parade." Shirley winked, or maybe it was just a nervous tic, probably an occupational hazard from staring at documents for years.

Van took the papers. It was too late for Dee Dee's and the library was closed. She pulled several bottles of water from the cooler in her trunk along with a bag of trail mix, drove back to the motel and signed up for another night. She had checked the campsite near Storm Lake, but it was much too civilized and booked up with summer RV campers. Not her idea of camping. She laid the courthouse documents on the polyester spread and began systematically putting the known pieces together. At least it was a place to start. Formal documents calmed her.

In the journal entry to her father, she added another PS:

*Josephus Kohler was Adam's Estate Executor, though so far there is no sign of any wrongdoing on his part. He had to file a yearly report so I will see how he managed their affairs. It looks like a considerable job. Your dad is listed as an heir, living in Maple Grove—and he had a large outstanding loan that went unpaid. He did not take over the farm and was not appointed executor. Maybe he wasn't good with money. Was that why you were such a*

*fanatic about paying bills on time? It always confused me
as a child. I was always afraid we were one step from the
poor house. Scared me so much that I have never once
been late paying my bills.*

Josephus Kohler, Executor and Administrator, had filed
the papers. The Statement of Heirs named the widow and the
eight Reinhardt children and their ages along with Katharina
Reinhardt who was listed as "sister to deceased" and "condi-
tional heir."

So, Katharina, the maiden aunt, the older sister of Adam,
was not married or dead but still living with the family at age
seventy-five. And Josephus Kohler was, in fact, the Executor. But why had Jacob been bypassed? Primogeniture was a
very powerful factor in how land was passed down, especially
among those of German heritage. As the oldest, Jacob would
have been first choice for executor and first in line for inher-
iting the farm. The obituary listed him as a son, although anyone who bothered to count could see that Letty would have
been too young, and if he was Adam's son he would have
been named. Something fishy here. No census or obituary
clarified or challenged the fact, but an oldest son bypassed as
executor signified something.

Van had a hazy recollection of her father mentioning the
name of the man appointed executor for the family. He had
embezzled the Reinhardt land and money. Did she remember this right? Her father had talked more before her mother's problems shut him down, but she had been very young
and didn't know what embezzled meant or who these people
were, so his observations had held little importance for her.
Adam had died in 1901. Martin was born eleven years later.
He was probably repeating family hearsay. Families are like
that; stories get told and passed on and no one bothers to

verify the facts. They gather weight and become the stuff of family lore and legend.

A description of real estate followed: Three purchases of land—the original 160 and 40 acres and the later 80 acres—that constituted the whole of the family farm as she had seen on the plat map. Van recalled reading somewhere that German farmers never acquired land beyond their capacity to farm. 280 acres represented a sizable acquisition and testified to Adam's ambition and successful husbandry. Listed on the real estate page was an outstanding loan of $2000 for the recent purchase of additional acreage. There was no record of the net worth of the farmland, whether it had been sold, or who took it over.

Under "Notes and Accounts and By Whom Owning" was an outstanding loan of $800. The entry showed that Adam Reinhardt had lent the money to Jacob Reinhardt in 1894 at a rate of 8 percent interest. A note on the page said this money was advanced to Jacob Reinhardt for a house mortgage. Under the likelihood of payment Kohler had penned, "Doubtful," and beside the current state of the debt, he wrote, "Bad."

Okay, so Jacob had an outstanding loan to the estate. He had not made a payment in seven years. This did not sound good. $800 in those days must have been a lot of money. At 8 percent, the interest would have accumulated to a sizable amount. From his comments, Kohler obviously considered Jacob a financial risk and maybe that was why he had not been appointed executor. Van smelled trouble. Tomorrow she would go back to Ida Grove and ask Shirley for more records.

Meeting Shirley made Van lonesome for Em. She wanted to hear her voice, get her practical, no-nonsense reassurance. She picked up the phone to call and then put it back down. She hated feeling needy; it was so unlike her. She would call her tomorrow when she was rested. No chance of sniffling on the telephone, especially when she didn't know why she felt so sad and frightened. She needed sleep.

In the morning Dee Dee would make her a big farm breakfast. Van would ask around for other campsite recommendations. She had a few days to go and then she could be done with these Reinhardts. They were proving to be nothing but heartache and trouble.

# SIOUX CREEK FARM

## September 1901

My mind is full of holes, Letty thought. *I must have been at the funeral and the cemetery where they buried my husband next to baby Johnnie.* Was it days ago? Ever since, she had forgotten how to take a step or bend an elbow. When Tante Kate struggled to get her upstairs, undressed, and into the bed, she tried to make it easier, but could not locate the hinge that joined wanting with her limbs. Tante Kate climbed into Adam's side of the bed and held her. Letty was shocked but could not protest. Tante Kate's body was big like Adam's, but softer, so much softer.

A few days later, Letty watched Josephus Kohler from her bedroom window as he drove up to the farmhouse in his pretty rig. From her bed, his low, patronizing voice was audible. He was in the kitchen speaking to Tante Kate in German, believing wrongly that she did not understand English. For reasons Letty never understood, Tante Kate purposely nurtured that misperception. Kohler made inquiries after "the widow Reinhardt," and questioned Tante Kate about the family's plans. Where was Jacob? Shouldn't he hear what Kohler had to say? Didn't they need a man to stand up for the family?

"I strongly advise that you move off the farm, Miss Reinhardt. You will be much better off in town, closer to the older girls. It is not possible for two women to run such a big farm operation, especially given your age and Mrs. Reinhardt's indisposition. It is a shame the older boys have not shown an interest in farming. In any case, I will have to sell off eighty acres in order to balance up your accounts. Adam Reinhardt agreed to this provision. The will reads as such: *'The Court finds that the personal property of said estate is not sufficient to pay the debts of said estate. And of the real estate belonging to said estate the Court orders the following sold, by said executor, Josephus Kohler, to wit: the West Half of the Southwest Quarter of Section Two, Township Eighty-four, North, Range Thirty -two, West of the 5th P.M. for the purpose of paying the debts of said estate.'*

"I am truly sorry."

After he left, Tante Kate banged pots in the sink and muttered to herself in German. The next morning, she was grumbling, grumbling, grumbling. "Kohler says we cannot stay here at the farm. We have to move into town."

She parked Letty on a kitchen chair while she sorted through things and packed what we needed for the move to town.

Letty's mind was in a swivet. Leave the farm? When? Where would they go? Was the move for a short while or forever? The same force that froze her body had sealed her mouth, and all her questions went unasked.

The minute they got into bed that night, Tante Kate set up a whistling snore. How Letty marveled at the old woman. Letty never knew her to start at a shadow, or shriek at a mouse, or blush or faint, or cry at Adam's funeral. Neither Tante's teas and tinctures nor sedatives from Dr. Wiedersheim helped Letty find sleep. She worked her thoughts threadbare. If she closed her eyes, all she saw was Adam broken and dying on that rickety bed in Kohler's office. If she kept her eyes open, maybe it wouldn't be true.

*Psst!*

Letty shifted her eyes to the darkened doorway thinking one of her girls had a bad dream. Then she remembered the girls were not at the farm. Tante Kate had sent them to stay with Sister Kate in town.

*Psst!*

Her scalp tingled. A cold draft from the open door blew in a smell of wood smoke mixed with another musky odor. Letty jammed her fist to her mouth to keep from crying out. A form in a tattered blanket shawl lurked in the doorway. How had she gotten into the house and up the stairs without waking Tante Kate, who was more vigilant than a guard dog?

"*Mrs. Elizabeth!*"

The woman's voice was rusty and harsh. How did she know her name? This was not one of the wicked voices in her head. No. This was different. Something outside of her, someone with substance.

"*Mrs. Elizabeth, they are stealing your land. Not like thieves in the night but in the broad daylight, in front of you and everyone else. Stealing land with their quill pens and parchments, their promises of help and money. Stealing from you while telling you they are doing everything in your favor. Don't believe them, Mrs. Elizabeth.*"

However did she come to know of this? Was she referring to Kohler's visit?

"*Do not listen to them, Mrs. Elizabeth. They talk with a tongue split at its root, making their messages divided and meant to confuse. Our children were starving, sickly, dying, and they drove us off our land with their pens and papers, their double-tongued talk and their courts of law.*"

Letty's body went rigid under her mother's old quilt. She

wanted to prod Tante Kate but feared a scolding for seeing phantoms that weren't there.

"*Mrs. Elizabeth, they are doing the same to you, driving you off your land. They say it is for your own good, sending you to live in town, cutting you off from what feeds your body and your spirit. Yes, they did that to us and our children and old people quickly took sick and died or froze or starved to death. And your children will starve, too. Maybe not from want of food, but in their spirits they will go hungry. Look how they sent those black hounds chasing your husband's hay wagon. Our men were pursued and came back bleeding and broken, just like your good husband.*"

Letty could not abide that woman speaking about Adam and how he died. She never let herself picture what happened to her dear husband. She felt badgered, clenched and un-clenched her fists, opened her mouth, but no words came to her defense.

"*Did you see, Mrs. Elizabeth, how they made your husband sign his name on the paper giving all power over your family to a man not of your kin? Our men were told to put their X mark on the parchment paper with a quill. They called them chiefs and braves and principal men, when they were just tired and defeated men with starving families.*"

Her speeches made Letty's heart clatter. Was this something she had heard about? Her mind crashed like a trapped bird flying against window glass looking to escape. Just today Josephus Kohler read aloud from a document in his high and important voice. "The Court finds that the personal property of said estate is not sufficient to pay the debts of said estate." Yes, yes, the woman is right! They intend to steal the land right out from under us. The woman has come to warn me.

"*Mrs. Elizabeth, our babies are crying, they are hungry, they have nothing to eat, my own breasts have withered, our*

*men can no longer hunt for food, we are lost in the strange*
*land they sent us to, they have taken everything, all the food*
*animals have fled their homes, we cannot find them. Can you*
*not hear the thin cries of the little ones, whose stomachs are*
*hard like stones?"*

The terrible voices chimed in with their familiar clamoring. They poked and prodded, taunted and jeered, picking at her skin with their sharp barbs. *Useless woman, unfit, your life is over, better off dead.* But even they couldn't stop the woman's pleas.

*"They are taking your land like they did ours, they will*
*send you into a village where you will have to beg for your*
*children. Maybe you will watch their little bodies shrink in-*
*stead of growing stronger. Their evil is like a poison that kills*
*slowly. You must stop their killing. You must fight them be-*
*fore your family falls into ruins. I cannot rest while our ba-*
*bies are crying for food, for life, Mrs. Elizabeth."*

The tornado in Letty's head took the shape of a funnel. Using all her might, she could not hold it back or stop its force and the pressure darkened and gathered until it found the weak opening of her mouth and pushed it wide open, releasing a ferocious howl that filled the house.

\* \* \*

Letty's wail shattered my sleep as if I had been laying on train tracks with an engine bearing down. I bolted upright, clutching my heart to keep it from breaking through the cage of my ribs. Letty's rigid body had unloosened. She moved back and forth like a rocking-chair gone mad, grabbing fistfuls of hair, and making sounds that were not quite human. Although I did not believe in the devil, I thought with a chill that this might indeed be his work. But as soon as I touched

Letty's arm and spoke her name, she began to cry like a child, and I enfolded her trembling body in my arms.

All those years I had spent keeping Letty on a steady course, keeping her moods in check, keeping her body well, her mind in order, could not withstand this shock. The loss of Adam and now the farm might well prove to be her undoing. In the shelter of my arms, I allowed Letty to rave. Wasn't it better than turning dumb? Let her cry and talk herself out. In any case, there was no stopping the torrent of words that poured from her unbuttoned mouth. Desperately, urgently, her tongue untied itself.

"The woman—she was here—they are stealing our land—we have to stop them—the children are starving—stop them." Panting words pushed against each other without pause. Her voice a strangled cry against my chest. Much of her jibber was unintelligible.

Although I did not believe in childhood fairytales, I thought this might be a *Drudenfluch*, a part of Letty that had separated itself and was now terrorizing her. When she claimed the woman was a redskin savage, I feared Letty's night terrors might have to do with my own past. But common sense quickly laid hold. My travel memory book was hidden far under my mattress and Letty could not possibly have broken into it.

I soothed Letty like a child with a bad dream. "*Da, Letty, sei ruhig, es war nur ein Traum, mein Kind.* There, there, Letty, it was only a dream, my child."

But she was not easily consoled. "We have to stop them!"

"*Ja, ja,*" I assured, "*Wir weden sie davon abhalten.* We will keep them from it."

With my continual reassurance Letty's body softened, and after a few hiccupping breaths, she passed into a fitful sleep.

Adam's death, our pending move off the farm, and

Kohler's plan to sell off land was enough to drive anyone over the brink into madness. I prided myself on being commonsensical, but hadn't I, too, lost my bearings? Hard enough for my dear brother Adam to die in that hideous way, but to lose all that he had dreamed about, all that we had built together, it was more than any of us could rightfully bear. Adam's death chained itself to all my past losses and they rattled through my mind like some ghost train, each car carrying its heavy load of sorrow—sweet Maman and Papa, Pascal, the people from my brief long ago life, baby Johnnie, and now Adam. I was determined not to add Letty to that long list. Let her rant, but only with me. No one else, especially not the children, need be privy to their mother's derangement. I vowed to keep my place within the family, to keep Letty safe.

The next morning, I promised Letty, "We will keep our plan to stop them—a secret just between the two of us—no one else is to know. It must be our secret, Letty, only ours."

With constant promises, I convinced Letty I would help with whatever frantic errand she felt compelled to run. I entered into this harmless conspiracy as succor for the moment. Surely, I did not intend to put myself in league with the Prince of Darkness.

"God forgive me, if I am wrong," I prayed to whatever god would listen. "I only seek to give her comfort and give us peace."

Before we were forced to close the door on the farmstead, I asked Jacob to arrange a meeting with Josephus Kohler. I wanted Kohler to spell out, in Letty's presence and in careful detail, the terms of Adam's will—what we would have to live on, how the money would come to us, and what he planned to do with the farmland. I hoped Kohler's businessman's logic would settle Letty's overheated suspicions about stolen land and starving children. There was no doubt, as two women we needed Jacob's presence. He should have been at the farm when Kohler first came to visit them. Even though he carried his grief like an unopened package, burdened by its weight and afraid of its contents, I wanted a man to represent us.

Grudgingly, Jacob obliged. I had little patience for his trepidation. Timidity was not in his blood; certainly, I never had any earthly use for it. There was nothing to do but forge ahead. What was done was done. I had Letty to think about. We had the younger children to care for. I had my vow to Adam to keep.

* * *

For a man so polished in his business affairs, Kohler's awkward manner made me feel odd, as if I had dragged something unsightly into his tidy office. Other than that horrible green lampshade that cast its peevish glow, there was no other trace of the room's former use as Adam's last quarters. I shoved those thoughts away, while Kohler busied himself, arranging three wooden, straight-backed chairs for our family trio.

Seated at his large oaken desk, Kohler's foot jiggled as he politely inquired as to our needs. I had instructed Jacob to speak in English so I could observe their interactions. Kohler nervously tamped his pipe and fidgeted with his desk implements as Jacob stuttered out their concerns and attempted to interrogate the man who had taken his place as executor of Adam's wishes. When Kohler brought out the signed documents and handed them to Jacob, my heart sank, for I knew he could not read them. Jacob did not even look at the papers but kept urging Kohler toward his line of questioning. "We need to know the terms of the will."

"Here," Kohler said, pointing and tapping the papers with his well-chewed pipestem. "It is all right here. The whole of

Adam Reinhardt's estate is bequeathed to his wife, Elizabeth."
He nodded towards Letty, gave her a tight smile, and addressed
her. "As executor, Mrs. Reinhardt, I am authorized to sell some
acreage to pay off the outstanding debts. Your husband spec-
ified which acres to sell off. As soon as you move to town, we
will arrange an auction at the farm. You will receive the pro-
ceeds—minus expenses, of course. All other debts and assets
are listed here." He pointed again with the pipestem to another
page with a column of carefully scripted numbers running the
length of the ledger sheet. "Everything is in order. I will make
my yearly accounting to the court, as required. As I said, you
will also have the assets from the auction at your disposal."

Kohler had barely finished his report when Letty shot upright in her chair and in a shrill voice proclaimed, "The children are starving while you sit here and tell us lies with your
pen and paper." She jabbed her forefinger at him. "You made
my husband sign those papers so you could steal our land. I
have been informed by a reliable source that you and men like
you have done this before. Many times. You say it is for our
own good, sending us to live in town, cutting us off from what
feeds us. We won't stand for it. We will do everything we can to
stop you from committing these outrages against us!"

I was aghast. I swiftly grabbed her arm, and chastised her
in German, saying they would discuss the matter later. Letty
sank back into silence. Kohler stared at her as if she had just
grown two heads. Jacob studied his shoes that were covered
with a thick layer of mud from his work on the road crew;
bits of dirt had dribbled onto the office floor.

I quickly ushered Letty and Jacob out the door and extended my hand to Kohler, saying, "*Danke, danke. Auf Wied-
ersehen.*" His hand was soft and moist, an anxious woman's
hand. We left Kohler pale-faced, holding onto the doorframe
of his office.

In the buggy, despite the chill of the fall day, a fine line of mist beaded on my upper lip and brow, my armpits damp. None of us spoke as Jacob drove the team back to the farm. Despite all appearances, I wondered if Letty's outlandish speech might carry some truth. Did Kohler pose a threat to their livelihood? He was impatient, jittery, and had clearly been testing Jacob's abilities. I did not know what he was hiding or what trouble he was capable of making and wanted to risk nothing. Then again, how could Letty turn so reckless, threatening Kohler, after all the promises she had made? I would have to keep Letty sheltered until such time as she was more stable. With Adam gone, my still considerable strength would be a shield against Kohler and his designs, whatever they may be, and I vowed yet again to safeguard the family from further such confrontations.

Early the next morning, Letty was hunched up in the corner chair at the kitchen table, her nervous fingers balling pieces of bread into tiny rice-sized pellets that she had lined up in rows. When I raised my eyebrows in question, Letty smiled. "I am making bread so the people will not starve."

* * *

The pickled herring had a bit too much vinegar, which Kohler remedied with a pinch of sugar, and the *graubrot* tasted stale, although his wife had baked it that very morning. Ever since Adam Reinhardt died in his office and he became executor of the estate, his appetite was not what it used to be. He no longer counted on his usual pleasure in daily meals, preferring to eat only what was necessary to keep himself going. He had lost his fondness for the finely prepared dishes, the specialty meats and smooth gravies and sauces his wife unceasingly pressed upon him lately. With worry and concern for his lack of appetite, she admonished him. "Your vest and trousers need to be taken in again as they are becoming too loose on your frame. You must eat more, Josephus. You must keep up your strength," she counseled.

He had always been a portly man and his relish for the delights of the table was as much a part of his reputation as was his appreciation for fine aromatic tobacco and good Scotch whiskey. He was never a glutton nor did he over-imbibe. Rather, he took pride in being a discriminating connoisseur of the finer things life had to offer a prosperous man, and he congratulated himself on the fact that he could afford them. One winter, before the Reinhardt tragedy, he had sent all the way to the New England coast for fresh, succulent oysters in a shell packed in ice that came by train to western Iowa. That caused quite a stir and even made headlines in *The Chronicle*. With the executor appointment, his once lively palate had deserted him, leaving his appetite in a dull and savorless state. The whole executor affair was a highly disagreeable business on all accounts.

Kohler had not looked forward to the meeting with the widow and her son Jacob. For one thing, while making up the list of estate heirs, he was struck by the discrepancy in the ages between Mrs. Reinhardt and Jacob, and it hit like a thunderbolt that Jacob could not possibly be her son as they were barely years apart in age. He deduced that the reason Adam Reinhardt had not assigned Jacob as executor of his will was that Jacob was not his true son either, although he was duly listed as an heir along with the rest of the children.

The prevailing predicament that Jacob Reinhardt posed for Kohler was not a question of his legitimacy, however; it was the outstanding loan of eight hundred dollars, which he now owed the estate plus accrued interest at eight percent. When Kohler consulted Augustus Schmidtz, the banker confided that the debt was long overdue and likely would never be made good. Kohler dutifully noted the facts in his report to the Court of estate inventory:

"Notes and Accounts: By Whom Owing: Jacob Reinhardt. Date of loan: 1894. Interest: 8%. Secured by mortgage. Doubtful? Yes. Bad?

He added a check mark and a clarifying comment: *"This mortgage was given to secure cash money advances, Adam Reinhardt's signing as security for Jacob Reinhardt."*

The way Kohler figured, Jacob Reinhardt's debt was a loss on the Reinhardt family's balance sheet. He was loath to bring it up. He hated knowing these intimate family complications, much less becoming entangled in them.

He had made a report to the Court, petitioning that a portion of Reinhardt's farmland be sold to satisfy the remaining claims and debts on the estate. To do so he was required to post a bond of $4,000. Hardly a small amount. He could afford it, but it did tie up his capital and no interest accrued. The pending land sale must have prompted that unsettling visit from Adam's widow, the old aunt, and Jacob Reinhardt.

Initially Kohler meant to extend himself kindly towards the two bereaved women when they entered his office dressed in their funeral blacks and widow's weeds. In going over the accounts, he had noticed that Mrs. Reinhardt was running up a sizable bill with Dr. Wiedersheim for house calls and prescriptions for nerve tonics and sedatives. That the widow suffered dejection since her husband's untimely death was understandable, but conventional bromides were as far as Kohler's sympathy stretched. He hoped Wiedersheim had better luck with her. During the meeting, the widow was taciturn and the old *Jungfer* spoke no English. Kohler patronized the family's condition and patiently clarified the details of their arrangement. He reassured Mrs. Reinhardt, who had remained silent and distractible, that she would have a sufficient amount of money left from the auction to satisfy her family's immediate needs and to pay some of their outstanding bills.

He had surmised correctly that the women had brought Jacob to be their spokesperson. But Jacob never looked at the documents handed to him, although the answers to his questions were written right there in black and white in a very legible hand. It had occurred to Kohler that the man might be illiterate, but he was not inclined to pursue these matters any further. Jacob's position had not been contested by anyone, so he thought it best to keep his suppositions out of it. But he could not help looking upon the young man with some misgiving. He feared Jacob's resentment of the executor role he was forced to play in their lives, a role that maybe should have been his. That was bad enough.

What really served to put Kohler off his feed was not the old woman or Jacob; it was Adam's widow. He was totally unprepared for her attack. No sooner had he mentioned the sale of eighty acres than she lambasted him. Her imperious tone and manner, unlike anything he had previously witnessed, sent a sickening shudder through his system. An instant rush of fury and fear collided mightily in the region of his gut. He was determined not to lose his lunch in front of them.

Possibly it was Katharina Reinhardt who filled the widow's head with such rubbish. Kohler judged the old woman to be a bitter old *Jungfer* from the old country, as dour and balky as an ill-tempered mule. The old woman was quick to scold the widow in German and without further ado, the three of them were out the door, leaving him a shaken man. Feeling dizzy, he had forced himself to rise and show them out, holding onto the doorframe as he watched their black buggy jounce down the road. Kohler was splenetic. Despite Mrs. Reinhardt's ludicrous accusations, her family had not slipped into poverty, her children were not starving, and he had not stolen their land or their money.

A few days later, Augustus Schmidtz informed him that payments on several of Adam Reinhardt's bank notes were heading into arrears and the mortgage and taxes on the farmland would soon be overdue. Kohler never looked kindly on unpaid debt, seeing it as a sign of personal dereliction, not financial. He needed to attend to those bills.

Ever solicitous, his wife had taken special pains to prepare his favorite meals. Tonight it was sauerbraten roast with her delicate potato dumplings flecked with green parsley, but he could not eat. She brought him a steaming cup of strong peppermint tea and some potion Dr. Wiedersheim had given him for dyspepsia. Kohler turned on the lamp, took out the ledger book and continued his annual report to the Court.

He took his time listing the items and adding the sums. The sheets of paper with their orderly column of accounts received and accounts payable served to pacify his mind. Then he wrote the petition to the Court for the sale of eighty acres. By the end of the evening, his tea was cold, his filled pipe unsmoked, and his stomach soured. In the morning he would return to his office and prepare the papers for presentation to the Court. He still had obligations to lease the remaining farm fields, but that was an inconsequential matter, merely one of finding the farmer who would pay the best price. He had fulfilled his duties and fervently hoped he would not lay eyes on these Reinhardts anytime soon.

Kohler reached to turn off his desk lamp and sensed the uncanny presence of Adam Reinhardt in the room. Kohler shook his head to clear his mind. He attributed his dreadful thoughts to the late hour, mental exhaustion, and lack of food. When he left the office, the rest of his household was in complete darkness. The clock in the hallway chimed twice. His stomach grumbled from the lack of provisions, and he prayed for a few hours of undisturbed sleep.

# MAPLE GROVE, IOWA

## JUNE 17, 2000

SATURDAY MORNING AND DEE DEE'S was a clatter of plates, cutlery and the congenial chit-chat of old folks waiting for breakfast. Dee Dee was working at a pace from grill to table to counter. Lillian from the town office was in line for a take-out lunch. She gave Van a wide smile. "Maybe see you later, dear, but first, you get yourself a hearty breakfast."

Van stepped aside as Dee Dee squeezed past juggling a foot-high stack of pancakes destined for a crowded table. "Folks here prefer to eat home-style," she explained, spelling out the obvious.

Back at her post behind the counter, she asked, "Now what can I get for you this morning, hon?"

"Give me the whole shebang. I need nourishment. Between the town office, the library and the Ida County courthouse, I've got my work cut out. Research burns calories like you wouldn't believe."

Dee Dee cracked eggs with one hand, laid slabs of bacon and hash browns on the sizzling griddle and popped two slices of wheat bread into the toaster. "Those girls helping you out?"

"Best research assistants I've ever had, bar none."

Van settled into her back table. No one else ever ate alone; even the old-timers perched side by side on the red stools kept up a continual banter. Dee Dee brought her coffee.

"Helen was in the other day asking about you. She's on her way up to South Dakota to visit her ninety-five-year-old sister who's in a nursing home. She seems to have taken an interest in you. Hopes you'll be here when she gets back."

"I guess it depends on when she's coming back. I gave myself a week for this project, but the more I get into it, the longer it takes to sort out. It's already day six. Which reminds me, are you open on Sundays?"

"Even God took a day off, hon. But there are a few other places to get some eats. Chinese. It'll get you by for a day."

Dee Dee brought a breakfast fit for a giantess. Between fork-fuls of eggs and hash browns doused in ketchup, Van listed out her next steps—back to Marion and the library, and then to Shirley in Ida Grove to see if there were more Kohler documents.

Fully fortified, Van walked to the library and found Marion minding the front desk. "Not many patrons here this morning. People getting ready for the weekend I suppose. What can I help you with today, dear?"

"I thought as long as I'm doing research about early pioneer days, it might be a good idea to explore Iowa's Native history. You know, the tribes that were here before the land was sold to farmers."

"I see." Marion frowned. "Well, there are a few textbooks. But I guess they are pretty outdated, if you know what I mean."

"I do know. I took a look at a few of them the other day. Isn't there anything more recent? Maybe something from the university?"

"I'll check the catalogue for you, dear. Maybe something has come in. Most folks here don't bother with university acquisitions."

Van took a seat at the empty library table, closed her eyes and almost fell asleep.

"Ms. Reinhardt?" Marion Grob took her by surprise. "Sorry to interrupt. I've found a few monographs documenting the U.S. Government Treaties in the early 1800s, and of course, there is a history on the Black Hawk War and we have a copy of Black Hawk's edited memoir. Is that the kind of thing you are looking for?"

"Thanks, Marion. I'll take a look at them."

"How long do you plan on being in the area?"

"That's anybody's guess right now," Van laughed. "Research is like hunting—you have to follow the tracks where they lead you."

"Take your time, dear. No use rushing what can't be rushed."

Van took the books from Marion and checked her watch. She still had an hour before heading up to Ida Grove. She put the government monographs on the table.She wasn't interested in government documents. She wanted stories.

Van's early work on Indian Captivity narratives had been aiming in that direction, before the idea of women's studies was a glint in anyone's eye. In the late '70s, she was one of a handful of feminists who asked pointed questions about the role of women in American history. It had been a radical move. What was known about women's intimate domains—their sex lives, private sentiments, their fears and foibles, their domestic arrangements and child-rearing practices, in other words their life experience—was silenced, held hostage by Jackson Turner's irrefutable paradigm of Manifest Destiny. Rugged, indomitable American men had secured and settled the West and women, much less Native women, had no part in it. Van's efforts to bring women into that history did not endear her to her male colleagues who heartily dismissed her with faint praise—yes, all very interesting, *women's work*, of course, but so few sources, so little evidence, no real scholarship.

Then she had met Len, who prodded and provoked her until she dared to dig deeper and study the fur trade in America, a minor and even lesser-known aspect of American history, one dominated by white male concepts of progress and economics. But as she researched the early days of Prairie du Chien, she discovered inter-marriages of Native women to French fur traders, noting their crucial role in the trade, and the subsequent creation of a whole class of *métis* offspring. She had often wondered what their lives were like, what they thought about.

Her father's reaction when she had deigned to mention her academic pursuits felt over-sized. "Is this absurdity what I've been paying for all these years?" "You will never get tenure with these half-baked notions." "How did Turnbull let you get on with this nonsense?" "Who the hell is this Leonard LaChance?" There was too much bluster, too much contempt.

Martin's ferocity took them both by surprise. He retreated into his hole, and she never spoke to him again about her work. Years after Len disappeared and she received her position at the university, Em came on the scene and together they had eked out a niche, a rickety platform that eventually grew into a solid women's studies program.

Van jutted her chin. Silencing women's histories was one thing, but her own past history was another— so much of her early life had gone unexamined and unspoken that it was impossible to imagine it otherwise. Ironic. Maybe she was like her dad after all. Is that what he wanted her to know by sending her on this cockeyed trip—that she ran away from trouble just like he had? What a legacy. It was too late for him, but maybe it wasn't for her. In their last phone call, Em sounded interested, even eager to hear what she had to say.

UNSETTLED | 183

Like a feral cat warily inching toward a warm hand that offered food, Van feared being trapped.

The government monograph on the fur trade had an image on the cover. A beaver pelt. Van stopped. If she believed in such things, she could feel Len's spirit elbowing her. There were too many coincidences that led back to him. She had seen a beaver pelt blanket in Len's apartment and been put off by the animal skin. But when she touched it she could not believe its luscious, silky softness. Spontaneously, she had pressed her face right into the center of that dark fur and knew instantly why the great beaver nation had been hunted to near extinction in the last century, why the animals who carried this level of rich beauty were so vulnerable to human desire.

She never asked where Len had gotten the blanket, just assumed he had inherited it. She would never know. He had vanished. Sort of. Maybe he was dead. Years ago she had searched for him and when she didn't find him, she sealed him in a mental time capsule and buried it along with their year together. She was an expert at deep-sixing anything she didn't want to think about, as the cemetery of skates and camping gear in the back of her closet attested. Len was dogging her on this trip. He was a Houdini, and she wouldn't be at all surprised if he showed up at Dee Dee's one morning. Then what?

It wasn't just about Len. It was much more than that. Some longing deep in her heart roared past the old stop signs. *Don't be a dreamer like your mother*, her father always admonished. But he was no longer alive except as a scratchy record in her head—always saying the same old tired things. Back in her car, she turned on the air conditioner, and drove north for Ida Grove and Shirley.

The road bisected fields of corn and soybeans. Van pictured Iowa before the settlers arrived, tribal lands held between the two powerful arms of the Mississippi and the

Missouri. In that earlier time, people of mixed blood ancestry lived together, before Indian-Anglo encounters degraded into histories of displacement, deceit and alienation. She had glanced at one of the government monographs Marion had given her. The 1830 treaty signed at Prairie du Chien listed the tribes who signed the doomed document. It was a crushing account.

Twenty-nine men of the Sacs and twenty-six of the Sioux of the Mississippi, and Mdewakanton band put their X on the big paper. And a great number of Wahpahcoota, almost sixty men in all, put their mark down. Later twenty-three men of the Yankton and Santie Bands signed.

Outside of sensational tales of murder and mayhem, misrepresented history, and place names like Black Hawk, Sioux Creek, Pocahontas and Keokuk, Van wondered if the Reinhardts ever gave thought to the people who had populated the prairies before them. By the time they pioneered their farm, there was not a Native in sight. Didn't the family dream of those who had lived there before? Didn't they ever wonder where the tribes had gone? Len once told her that his ancestors slept in their graves on the bluffs above the Mississippi river. He believed that if their hallowed burial sites were disrupted, the spirits of the dead were destined to wander. There was a time when Van might have registered this as truth.

"I thought I'd see you again, sooner or later," Shirley said, batting her eyes. Was this a nervous habit or was she flirting?

"You guessed right. Now I'm looking for anything you might have on Josephus Kohler from 1901 on. He was the executor of Adam Reinhardt's estate and was required to make yearly reports. I was hoping you might have them."

"You're a regular Sherlock Holmes, my dear. Are you trying to solve a murder mystery?"

"Actually, I'm a professor of history, but maybe that's just another way of saying the same thing. I really don't know what I'm looking for at this point, Shirley, I'm just looking."

"I'm happy to be your Watson then. Come back in a half hour. You know where the coffee shop is. Say hi to Laureen for me." Shirley flitted off into the back room.

Van walked down the street to the coffee shop. Her braid felt heavy and damp under her visor. She had let her hair grow for years, never attending to fashions in women's hair, just trimming the ends when they got too ragged. For the classroom, she gathered her hair into a twist that looked somewhat professional. She preferred the braid, but not in this weather.

She greeted Laureen, sat at a far table, ordered coffee and checked her watch. Something was trying to get her attention. A lump lodged between her heart and her throat. She wanted to sob, but kept swallowing back. She felt young. What was her problem?

She pulled the journal out and began.

*Ida Grove*
*Saturday, July 17*
*Day Six*

*Why did you make me feel ashamed of the way my mind worked? You always said, Don't be a dreamer. Were you afraid I might turn out like Mother? Was she really crazy? Or was she trying to find a poetic voice in the midst of soulless suburbia—*

These thoughts were not new—they had always hovered beneath the surface where they occasionally bobbed up—but she had never spoken, much less written them. There was nothing but a hollow ache where her mother should have been. Van had understood as a young child that her mother was not like other mothers, that she lived in a world of her own making, sleeping during the day, pacing the house at night, reciting words she scribbled on scraps of paper.

"What are you writing?" she once asked in a shy voice, hoping for a way to talk to her.

"Poems," her mother said. "Words have power and magic in them, Ev. You can feel their vibrations."

"Can I see?"

"You're too young to understand."

Van didn't understand. What she did know was that you couldn't eat poems for dinner or expect a cake on your birthday.

"You mother is not well. She needs to rest," her father had said.

Van crossed out the words she had written. She opened the paper napkin at her table and, using the blade of the plastic cutlery knife, sliced the page out of the journal and crumpled it up.

Laureen brought her a second refill on the coffee. "No charge," she said.

Van turned her attention to the farm auction list Shirley had given her. It read like a litany of the martyrs. After each entry, Van whispered "Lord have mercy."

Kohler's list of farm equipment and its worth in dollars and cents was grievous, but the animals, the livestock—the *milch* cows, steers and heifers, the workhorses, chickens and geese, the spring shoats—made her teary. Van blew her nose in the paper napkin. Dispersing her father's lifetime of work—the lectures, books, papers, and desk—even putting her childhood home on the market had only produced occasional heavy sighs. Why was she getting emotional over losses that happened a century ago to people she never knew, even if they happened to be her ancestors? Perhaps grief, like an underground stream, ran silently down a lineage. Could unnamed sorrow be strong enough to bind her to these people?

The total gain from the farm auction was $2205.20. If she

asked Shirley to help, she could calculate the relative worth of that money in 1901. But she figured it was quite a good sum. Even given the debts, the family was hardly in dire straits.

The next set of papers Kohler had filed showed additional money added, along with deductions. Kohler was very fastidious in his accounting.

*"In the matter of the Estate of Adam Reinhardt, Deceased. Josephus Kohler Executor.*

*Comes now the above-named executor and shows to the Court that he is the duly appointed and legally qualified executor of the above entitled estate. That in this report he has paid and received the following sums and property, to wit: As executor, he caused to be sold the personal property belonging to said estate. The total amount: $2936.13 and amount received from sale of corn $63.75.*

*Total amount received $2,999.88*

*That he has paid out and dispersed as legitimate claims and debts against said estate the following items, to wit:*

*Silas Chesterfield, auctioneer, $2,*

*Mr. Martin Beeber, note secured by mortgage $2,180*

*Deering Harvester $109.76*

*Dr. Wiedersheim account 5.50*

*Release of mortgage and account of Silver Creek County Pioneer 1.50*

*One half taxes for $36.15*

*Total amount disbursed $2,352.91*

*There are no further claims filed against said estate to be adjusted or paid at this time.*

With Adam's death, the Reinhardts had lost their prosperous farm built out of uncultivated prairie land. To Van's knowledge, none of their three sons, including her grandfather Jacob, had taken up farming. Come to think of it, her own father had never even planted a flower.

The auction list was pure tragedy, not to mention what it meant to the remaining family members. Was any one of them present for the auction? Certainly not Letty or Tante Kate, or the other children. It would have to be Jacob. What could he be feeling to see the family's life's work scattered to the winds? Loss upon loss? Was this why everyone lost their taste for farming? She contemplated the fragility of family history, how it was always teetering on the brink of extinction from one generation to the next. The dark and forbidden stories fell into holes like abandoned wells, never appearing in the official records. Without a fuller telling, a family's history becomes enervated, loses its vitality and vigor; grows dull and wooden, and is easily forgotten. Van added the piece of paper she had knifed out of her journal and tossed it along with her used napkin into the trash basket by the front door. She paid Laureen for the coffee, left her a good tip, and headed back to Shirley to see if there were more documents to be had.

# SIOUX CREEK FARM, IOWA

## AUTUMN, 1901

---

JACOB CAME LATE TO THE FARM AUCTION on Saturday morning. He had no need to come earlier to inspect the goods. He knew them all too well, right down to the last hay rake, and he certainly was not there to bid or buy. He came with the same intent he went to the burying: to pay his last respects to Papa Adam. The morning was brilliant, the wide-open sky a deep autumn blue, free of clouds, the maple trees in front of the homestead a final flame of rusty orange. He smelled winter in the air and knew it would be a hard one.

The haying season and the harvest were well past, and the fields were stripped of their grain and corn, the rolling acres of spent yellow stubble stretched out to the far horizon. The abandoned kitchen garden held the last twisted tomato vines with their fat, rotted-out fruit laying on the ground alongside some oversized cucumbers big as logs. The unpicked squash and pumpkins were bruised and split and the overgrown cabbages had gone bad, their greenish white leaves splayed open, revealing pale empty heads. Nobody had the heart to come and pick anything after the family had moved off the farm and into town. People probably reckoned it would make for bad luck to take a dead man's food. On the day of Adam's funeral Otto had put a flask in Jacob's pocket. Jacob had refilled it many times. He reached for it and took a long pull now.

He stood off to one side, away from a thick clot of men standing near the barn in their straw hats, bib overalls, and barn coats. They were good neighbors; some had been at the funeral where they offered their condolences, and a few nodded sympathetically in his direction. Sun-bonneted wives with their little girls clinging to their skirts milled about their bidding men while the boys horsed around in the yard oblivious to the business at hand.

Farm auctions were like funerals, Jacob thought, the only difference being that at auction worldly remains do not go into the ground, but into the hands of others. He had been to auctions where a certain breed of vulture, men who smelled death on the wind, ran to it for what they might lay their hands on. These men were not farmers who would put to good use what they bought, but brokers who turned around and sold at maximum profit what they grabbed at a bargain price. Jacob could not quell a sudden surge of resentment. Other scavengers came to pick through the spoils, the leftovers from a family's adversity—their gain from another's loss. He knew it well; hadn't he and Papa Adam bought Pet and Bucky and the hay wagon from just such an auction? Jacob reached into his pocket and took another draw from the flask. Otto frequently left bottles for Jacob in the cob house whenever he came to town. Jacob had appreciated the brotherly sentiment.

Silas Chesterfield stood on a wooden platform so he could look out onto the bidders and see their flashing hands. He was known throughout the region as a premier farm auctioneer. A lanky man with a long, narrow leathery face and a wide prominent mouth, he extolled the merchandise, urged and harangued his buyers into making, then raising, their bids. In a high-pitched rhythmic gabble, he began his call. "Whata-mIbid, whatamIbid?"

The stock went first, the cows wide-eyed and bellering as they were separated from calves who cried back like lost children.

"Fourteen prime *milch* cows. WhatamIbid, whatamIbid? Fifteen each? Do I hear eighteen? These healthy animals are all fine producers, eighteen? Do I hear twenty? Twenty-two, twenty-two? Do I hear twenty-five? Twenty-five? No? Going, going at twenty-two. All sold to the gentleman in the front, Mr. Hjelmer Olafson, I believe."

Next came a group of year-old heifers with their large, terrified eyes showing white, their hooves dug into the dirt as they resisted being shoved apart from their mothers. They sold for ten dollars each to the man representing the big Cookson Ranch south of the farm. How many times had he helped Papa Adam at calving time, awake throughout the night coaxing those little beasts from their mothers' warm bodies, greeting the live ones and grieving the ones who came disabled or stillborn?

Almost a month had passed since they had buried Papa Adam. Jacob was still stunned by the fact of his death. Everything went helter-skelter—Mama Letty, Tante Kate, and the younger children took flight into town, where they lived like fugitives in a small, rented house across the alleyway from his family. Tante Kate had led the charge, saying Mama Letty could not bear living in the farmhouse after Adam's death. The close proximity of those two grief-stricken women and the younger children was more than Jacob could bear at times. He could not get his footing, especially with Mama Letty, who had grown stranger than usual in her bereavement. The visit to Kohler's office had been humiliating. Tante Kate had requested his presence as the only able male in the family.

Kohler had intentionally challenged his competency, leaving Jacob feeling exposed and disrespected in front of everyone. Then Mama Letty thrashed Kohler with her accusations.

The notion that maybe all this devastation would not have happened if he had stayed on the farm would not leave him, and he sank under its weight. No one ever blamed him outright. But no argument he could muster in his own mind could budge that awful truth from his chest. He felt trapped and wearied by it all. He was angry, the smoldering kind that left him half-dead inside. No one had ever really understood why he'd had to leave the farm. They all judged it a weakness in his character, like Otto who owned a saloon. Mama Letty had blamed his wife and her so-called elevated opinions and ambitions, which was just another way of saying he did not know his own mind. Well, that was true. He could hardly explain himself. He was not built for the farming life. It was like asking a horse to be a cow. A man could not make himself into something he was not.

"Sixty spring shoats, whatamIbid? WhatamIbid? Not a runt in the bunch, take 'em all together. Two hundred. Do I hear two twenty-five? Two twenty-five, going, going, two forty now, two forty. Do I hear two fifty, two fifty? Going, going at two hundred and forty dollars. Sold."

The pigs were a later addition to the farm. They had never appealed to Jacob, neither the animals nor their meat. Like cow's milk, he had a true aversion to it. Everyone thought it abnormal that a good, strong German man would refuse to partake of pork *wienerschnitzel* and sauerbraten or to pass up thick pink slabs of ham and rashers of bacon. But there was nothing of those creatures he cared to put in his mouth, especially not the so-called delicacies of pig knuckles, souse, and headcheese.

"All right, gentlemen, a Poland China boar, a bit tired but a goodly fellow, still able to be of service. Do I hear ten? Then it is. Do I hear fifteen? Fifteen, do I hear eighteen? Eighteen? No? Going, going, Sold! The old Poland China boar sold at fifteen to Mr. Kurt Rodenschmidt from Early."

Papa Adam had showed a real affection for his pigs. That old boar had recognized him as a friend, making soft soughing murmurs like a woman in love when Papa Adam came by with extra slops. And each spring he held the little shoats in his arms like so many pink babies, as if they were his very own children. There were no farm animals that did not please Papa Adam. He knew them so well, their habits and their needs. They were simple and understandable to him, unlike the complicated people he lived with. And now these creatures, taken off by other men to other farms, would live out whatever days they had left before landing on someone's dinner plate. Jacob felt as sorry for that old boar as he did for anybody, losing his long-time good friend.

The six workhorses went at a nice price of thirty-two dollars each while the pair of horses went for forty-eight. Again the buyer for the Cookson ranch took away the best bargains. This was the hardest to bear. He recalled how Pet and Bucky responded to Papa Adam's voice and commands to go, steady, and stop, given in a calm but strict no-nonsense manner, and in German: *Huh! Ruhig! Brrr!* As a boy, Jacob had tried to imitate the calls but the horses always knew the difference. Pet and Bucky had recovered from the accident, but Jacob could not imagine their confusion to lose Papa Adam's steady direction and how they might be whipped or prodded because of their bewilderment. A sharp prickle of hatred ran up Jacob's spine and down his arms.

Mama Letty was right. Josephus Kohler was a crook. What does he care about the horses, the farm, about what has happened to our family, as long as his list of numbers balances out and he makes a little money on the side? He will surely steal from us and we will get nothing back from a lifetime of labor. Who is he to us? He is not our kin. Why was he put in the place where I should have been? Jacob took a long pull from the flask.

The stock-buyers moved away from the barn and helped each other load their purchases. It took a small group of men and boys to convince the shorthorn bull that he was not headed to perdition. They forced his massive body up the wooden ramp to the hay wagon, where he was firmly secured with ropes and a chain. The hellish racket of the displaced livestock—the chickens, geese, squealing pigs, and bellowing cows—nearly drowned out Silas Chesterfield's continuing spiel.

The crowd thinned after the stock sold. Next came the farm equipment and a different kind of bidder. The lumber wagons and shoveling boards, the tongueless cultivator, the riding cultivator, and the new Deering mower, the disc harrow and the corn planter, and the bobsled went to men who were already established farmers and wanted to add to their productivity. Jacob recognized the old walking plow from the early days on the farm. It sold for fifty cents to an elderly farmer who must have been nostalgic for his past days of hard labor. Jacob's throat constricted as the old hay wagon that he and Papa Adam bought at their first auction, the very one that had turned over on top of him, was auctioned off. In need of an axle repair, it went for three dollars to some farmer he did not recognize—a man in a patched overall who looked down on his luck.

By now, the women had moved forward as the household items were auctioned. Verbena Rausch, newly married, was flushed to a high color as she made off with the iron cookstove, two bedsprings, and a chair. The rest was picked through, and the last to go was the old couch with fabric worn so thin black horsehair peeked through bare spots on the arms. It seemed hardly worth the effort to load it, but a stout woman in a stained apron seemed pleased and proud to pay two dollars to be its new owner.

The crowd dispersed and then it was over. Jacob could not grasp the fact that it took a little over half a day to dispose of what had taken twenty-four years of sweat, worry, and continuous hard toil to build. Everything was gone. Kohler had sold the farmhouse, and leased the fields out to a neighboring farmer. Jacob looked around at the dismembered farmstead and felt numb and helpless. Stumbling over dirt clods, his feet sought the familiar path to his old refuge. The creek bed was overgrown, but through the weeds he could see the smooth stone pillow was still there. He took the flask from his pocket and drained it.

The hubbub from the auction had quieted and the late afternoon sun sunk below the horizon chilling the air. There would be a killing frost tonight.

"Papa Adam, Papa Adam," he cried, "I am heartfelt sorry I could not accept what you had to offer, but I did not mean for us to lose everything. I only meant that I could not be a farmer like you. I did not mean to abandon you in the midst of the drought. I just could not abandon myself, although God knows the only plan I had was to marry Elizabeth and make my own family. But still, I was your eldest son. With your last breath you put a thief in charge of our lives and took your disappointment in me to the grave." With the emptied flask in his hand, hot angry tears ran down Jacob's face.

# MAPLE GROVE

## 1902

BEFORE THE AUCTION TOOK PLACE, our family moved to a small rental house in town. I had my hands full managing the household. Instead of milking cows and feeding chickens in the morning, I made breakfast on weekdays and got the children off to school. I fed them at noontime and then prepared a simple supper. The day's chores were laid out in much the same manner as I had done at the farm. Monday was wash-day. Tuesday was for ironing and mending. Wednesday was set aside for house-cleaning. Thursday was shopping day. Friday was occupied with baking bread and cooking non-meat meals. Saturday, the children had their various needs, and I often sent them to Jacob's, or Sister Kate's house. Sunday, the children joined Jacob's family, Sister Kate and Mary for Mass at St. Bernard's, while I stayed home with Letty, who was unfit to go out in public.

Since her outburst at Kohler's, Letty was obsessed with the belief that Kohler had instigated Adam's death to get the farm, that he had stolen our land and was keeping our money so the children would starve. During the day she was silent as a stillborn, but in the dark of night she roamed the house with her laments. She had lost weight and hardly slept.

Jacob's family lived around the corner, but he came over to our house only out of duty and obligation born of guilt. Always alone, he never brought his little girls to see their grandmother and great aunt. I assumed his wife did not want them exposed to us—these strange relatives.

When I informed Jacob that Letty had been spending days in her room writing letters to Kohler he responded by saying, "Maybe there is some truth in what Mama Letty is thinking."

I shrugged.

"I do not think Mama Letty can do much good or ill by writing letters in her room. I do not think it is a cause for worry and if it occupies her overmuch, there can be no real harm in it," he said.

How could I argue with that? Writing a letter was far outside of Jacob's reach. And hadn't I once used writing as a way to keep my secret life alive?

One Sunday, while the house was quiet and Letty was preoccupied in the bedroom room with her letters, I sat in the rocking chair and put another patch on Letty's old quilt, the one she had brought from Illinois. The new patch was a piece of russet silk lining, a scrap left over from Adam's vest. The gentle rocking motion put me in mind of being on a prairie pony. I reached into my apron pocket and retrieved my travel memory book and a stub of pencil I had filched from Lizzie's book bag. In the margins I wrote my current thoughts in German.

*This pencil is down to a nub and needs sharpening. The kitchen knife will do for it. Again, I question why I wrote these words that only I will ever read. I polished them like precious gems. I was careful to be true and faithful, to neither exaggerate or diminish, to give everything its proper weight, to write of myself as I was, not as I have become. My secret treasure of time. Surprising how these old matters still live inside me.*

Although it took an effort to read the words I had written so many years ago, I found the French consoling and was easily pulled into that time of my life.

*I had made it plain to Pascal where I wished to go. And he had been agreeable but said he had to stop to see his mère and grand-mère who lived in a cabin. I had no argument with his plan and believed he would be true to his word. I possessed the presence of mind to check with the merchant Selby who thought it highly improper for a lady of my age and breeding to travel in such a rough manner, but he did reassure me that Pascal would do me no hurt or harm. To show I had placed my trust, I gave Pascal my roll of cash money and watched as he stuffed it into a leather pouch tied around his neck.*

*Along the river valley we took shelter in abandoned shacks or trapper's huts set off the trail, and occasionally a homesteader gave us lodging. When no other accommodation was found, we slept on pine boughs, close by a twig fire for warmth, and I heard wolves howl in the distant hills, and this set the ponies to nickering and my teeth to chattering. My nature was not prone to fearfulness, I was not lily-livered, but still I trembled. "Might we not get lost forever in such uninhabited open land without the safety of farms or village?" I asked.*

*"Oui, Madame, some say immigrant women go mad with fear. They call it prairie fever. But you are with me, and I know every inch of this wilderness by heart, like some people can recite the Bible." Pascal moved closer and pulled my woolen shawl and the rough horse blanket over me. I had never been that close to a grown man's body, never before felt the kind of warmth and smell that a man's body offered and, without shame, I took comfort from him, but not in any way that he might notice.*

I had to shake my head. How naïve I had been. Of course, Pascal must have known exactly what was happening. But I had been in thrall to the adventure. Excitement and fear in equal measure. It warmed me to remember how it was.

*The water crossings posed a hazard. Pascal removed his heavy leather boots and put on buckskin moccasins and leggings. "Indians believe these are better for long travel, their wetness easily dried by a fire," he said. When we crossed one particularly full stream, I stayed astride my pony as Pascal led us through the frightening water. He spoke softly to the horses and addressed someone. Toussaint? A saint? A prayer for safety?*

*One time we took shelter at a remote two-room log cabin where Pascal was a welcomed visitor. Coming from a long line of farming people, I had never seen a man who conducted himself as he did, like a living newspaper, gathering stories, reporting the noteworthy accounts to these isolated folks hungry to hear his tales, his bits of news and precious information.*

*"Eh! Petit Pascal!" They clapped him on the back as an old friend. They called him by that name, not because of his height which was not great but, he told me later, because they knew of le Grand Pascal, his French fur-trading grand-père.*

*Our hosts assumed that Pascal had finally taken a wife and gave us their good ticking bed under the rafters. Pascal palavered with them far into the night in what I surmised to be a mix of Indian and French. It occurred to me then that they were a family of mixed blood, and I figured Pascal was one of these, too, although the French and Indian seemed in equal measure and not in any open quarrel with each other.*

I considered the facts and feelings of what I had written. How vivid my memory was for the details, no embroidery or exaggerations. I must have made a record of everything at a time when the French was still fresh in my mind. I could never have written such recollections in German.

*Over the weeks, our minds grew attuned to what the other needed and gratitude blossomed in my heart for this little man who lived off his words, and who had agreed to my mad request to travel with him I knew not where, with so little spoken between us.*

I could hear myself snoring. The travel memory book lay open in my lap. The pencil dropped to the floor and roused me. I must not let anyone see me nodding off like this. This rare bit of privacy before the children returned is all I had, and my memories were in full flood. I pressed my crooked fingers to my eyes. The work of memory was a labor more difficult than fancy needlework. A wrong stitch and the whole thing could be thrown off. My poor fingers were incapable now of such beautiful penmanship. I had never crossed out a single word. My recollection of French, although tarnished like an old silver spoon, gained polish the more I read.

*We had left the open prairie for a place that was more wooded. The trees were leafed in tender greens and buds showed pinkish red, and the daytime air was fragrant with the smell of newly moistened springtime earth. We had encountered no terrible storms, although one night winds blew wild around us. "They are sent by Old Grand-père Tate," Pascal said. I did not fathom how an old man, even a grandfather, could send such a wind. During our few exchanges, I understood we were headed for an old trading post near the big river. Pascal's maman, Marie, lived there with his grand-mère, Lucy, on a tract of land set aside by the government.*

*Stories of Pascal's French fur-trading grand-père and his Indian grand-mère tumbled from his mouth like a spring river and I could feel how the two streams met and made in their joining a more forceful river way. I pictured how this land called America was formed of many such mixtures, such join-ings, and I felt a sharp sorrow knowing the land was cleaved into pieces by settlers. As far as I could tell, the two old wom-en he spoke of were the closest thing he knew to call home.*

*I pondered my own mixed blood, the French of dear Maman and the German of Papa, and I began to know myself as neither one nor the other. German, which Pascal had a true distaste for and would seldom speak, was the language that governed the thoughts of my practical mind, while French, the private tongue of Maman, held the key to my heart's truer feeling. Only in that tongue, the language of love and lullaby, did I become close to something tender. From Pascal's style of French, I learned the words and phrases that were of impor-tance for conversing, and the German words faded and lost their meaning and I was no longer lonely.*

*One day Pascal began talking as if he had never before had another to speak with while on the trail. I was uncertain he was addressing me, until he launched into the topic of women.*

*"Eh, I am a great grandson of Toussaint, a famous voya-geur. It is his jacket I wear, and traveling is my way of life and livelihood. I know all the territories, the rivers, wagon trails, the old woods trails and encampments of my grand-mère's people, and their ancient hunting grounds now sparse of all forest food and fur-bearers. I know the forts and agencies and I know all the kinds of human beings that are trying to grab a living from this land. And I know how to speak their words. I travel in and amongst them like the wind, I am part of them all—and I belong to none of them. Non, Madame, no decent woman would ever want this for a way of life."*

*With his speech ringing in my ears, I asked, "And what will your mère and grand-mère say when they see you have brought a woman along with you this time? I want to be prepared for any unpleasantness."*

Pascal laughed. "At first, old grand-mère Lucy, my unci, will make jokes. 'Where did I find this old aisaca?' she will ask in Dakota with a serious face. 'Have you become so desperate for a wife?' She will pity me for my loneliness. 'How is she in bed?' She will roll over herself in laughter, covering her toothless mouth with her soft wrinkled, brown hand, while tears run down her face. I will bow under these hailstorms of love that she will most certainly dispense upon my head. I can only hope it will be of short duration. Aiii, it is not easy for a grown man to be poked and pounded with this brand of old woman's humor and not feel beaten down like new hay in a storm."

I was shocked by how freely he spoke of such matters, and was about to take offense when Pascal laughed. "You may think it unseemly for an old woman to be so shameless, so full of impropriety, but grand-mère Lucy is loving me like a wolf mother loves her pups, pawing, growling and boxing their ears. You have nothing to worry about; they will take you in and ask no further questions. They will do so because they are generous in their hearts and their love for me knows no limits."

Pascal's bright smile clouded over. "Still, it will be strange for them having a white woman in their little cabin. Once she has had her laugh my ancienne grand-mère will probably go quiet. She will not say her name, nor speak anything but Indian; although I know full well she understands our French patois. Ma mère will only give her Christian name, Marie, and she will show how well she learned to speak and behave in missionary school. She will show only her French side and hide her Indian face as she was trained to do." Pascal looked away and his mood turned dark and for the first time I was truly afraid.

Yes, I was afraid. I was entering a world I knew nothing about. How bold I was. But I was alive. And that is what mattered. I was willing to enter whatever mysterious world Pascal brought me to because I trusted him.

*"You must not speak any German while we are there. Ma mère only understands French and English and grand-mère, Lucy, will take it badly. Aisaca, she calls foreigners, the 'bad speakers.' Eh! How can I tell you what happened to grand-mère's people? As a girl she saw her entire village destroyed, children dying of disease and starving, everyone sent away to live in places where they could not survive. Her people have names for the Indians who stayed and submitted to the white man's plan for turning them away from the hunt by giving them cows and a shovel. 'Cuthairs!' they call those Indians who cut off their braids and put on pantaloons. 'Dutchmen!' they call the ones who take up farming. They spit those words out of their lips like a curse and, in an Indian way, it is.*

*Mon père, Joseph Pascal, was one of those who took the cows and tried to work the land and his curse was that he lost his Indian spirit. He became possessed by another spirit that meant to do him harm and it did. His mind was one filled with such a great confusion of Catholic saints and martyrs and Indian ghosts, bad spirits, and witches and truly his character was not built strong enough to withstand those forces that went to war inside him. Aiiii! Mon Dieu! Wars are not only fought by people on the land; they are fought inside the minds of those who carry the double blood of the half-breed. For mon père, the drink came only at the end, but it was the final blow that knocked him down, like a white man's shack in a prairie storm. He was a man not built to bear the full force of those fierce crosswinds. Ah, ma cherie, I did not mean to tell you so many hard things."*

*His affectionate address took me by surprise. I did not press him with further questions and Pascal remained quiet for the rest of the day. When the sun was almost gone and the trees made long shadows in the golden light, Pascal broke his silence.*

*"On arrive. We are almost there," he whispered. "I can sense it in my body and the ponies feel it, too. See these out-lying, shabby cabins with their empty racks for drying meat and the thin, gray smoke rising from the chimneys like ghosts?" Scrawny dogs barked at us from the yards.*

*"A welcome would not be had for us here," Pascal said in a quiet tone. "These are people who have lost their path, dying from the white man's ways and the whiskey bottle." In a voice so low he whispered, as if to himself. "These lost mixed-bloods haunt my dreams because they are like me—and surely I could have been one of them."*

The children came rushing through the door from Mass demanding Sunday pancakes. I quickly stashed the pencil and notebook deep into my apron pocket. I searched for the needle I had used to patch Letty's quilt and found it stabbed into a piece of russet silk fabric.

\* \* \*

The household was dark and hushed except for Tante Kate's rhythmic snore. Letty hardly ever slept. Always on alert. Wood smoke and something wildish wafted into the closed air of the bedroom. The blanket woman had followed her to the house in town. Letty had taken to plugging her ears with candle wax, but the woman's voice, harsh and pleading, was still audible.

Psst! Psst!

"Mrs. Elizabeth, you will have to go to that man for everything like we did. You will have to beg for food for your children, for clothing and all the necessities that are rightfully yours. The dark clouds came over us and pressed down on our heads. Can you not feel that same pressure? We had to sell our lands because we were dying from the poverty. They called our children half-breeds. We sold the land to them and then they locked us up on small pieces of rocky earth and told us to start farming if we wanted to live".

Had not Kohler already sold eighty acres of their land? Were they not forced to move off their farm? What more was he capable of? Were they not living with scarce provisions? If the blanket woman's visitations were not enough, the voices in Letty's head continued to shout their indictments—*stupid woman, useless eater.* Letty ate less and less so her four younger children could have more. She flouted the extra food Tante Kate piled on her plate. She spit unchewed food into her cup, along with the decoctions she'd been given to help her sleep. Her refusals bucked up against Tante Kate's unbreakable resolve. But when it came to her suspicions of Kohler, when she told Tante Kate she knew for certain he stole what belonged by rights to them, making a profit off what was not his, forcing them to account for every penny spent, Tante Kate never rebuked or asked where she got such ideas. Since Tante Kate had laid into her at Kohler's as if she were a wicked child, Letty's lips were sealed against disclosing her nighttime informant.

Each time the blanket woman paid her a visit, Letty promised to do everything in her power to correct the wrongs that were being perpetrated. "Yes, yes, I must do more," she promised. But the woman found more horrible things to fill Letty's wax-plugged ears.

"Mrs. Elizabeth, my people are so sick and weary. We have become so poor I do not think we will survive. We have become a wandering nation shoved out of our home-lands, moved away from our sacred burial grounds. Our ancestors' bones cannot rest. You must help us or the same will happen to you. They will send you away, too, away from your home and family. Do not forget about us."

A shivery chill ran down her arms; the woman's desperate supplications were mind-numbing. Despite her stupefying fatigue and Tante Kate's potions, Letty could not sleep. She grew clumsy, dropped things, slipped on the stairs, banged into walls. There was no peace to be had while the woman filled her ears with misery, while such devastation was proceeding, and her family and others were so threatened.

The following afternoon, when Tante Kate was in the basement at the washtub, Letty slipped out of the house. In her pocket was the blue velvet change purse filled with coins she pilfered from their grocery fund. At the Main Street post office, she purchased a pad of pale blue paper, a stack of envelopes, and a sheet of stamps. During the day, she commenced to write letters, whispering the words aloud to make sure her thoughts were convincing and persuasive. She wrote and then re-wrote until everything met with her satisfaction. The more she wrote, the more formidable she felt. For the first time in her life, she was determined to make her accusations and declare her dissent. She was certain she could win their farm back. Certainly, Kohler could see from the words she chose that she meant business. He would take her seriously. She knew he was that kind of man.

*Dear Josephus Kohler,*

*It has been some time since I spoke with you in person in your office, and still you have done nothing to address my complaints and the evidence is piling up against you.*

*I hereby issue a formal complaint on behalf of myself and others who have suffered from your doings. We know that you have sold off land that does not belong to you. We know that you have enlisted the Courts of Law in your fraudulent practices, so everything appears to be authorized and proper when you know it is not. People are sick and weary and despairing, and children are dying from starvation. Everyone has been moved off their land, forced to beg for their few necessities. I have heard testimony to this effect and add my own claims. This policy of greed and graft must be stopped immediately, or we will take action against you.*

*I hereby request that you return our farm to the Reinhardt family and I also wish an additional payment of $30 for my family's monthly expenses and an additional $10 for more groceries for the children. We owe Everson's mercantile $6 for shoes for my two youngest and approximately another $2 for thread and some cloth.*

*Sincerely yours,*
*Mrs. Elizabeth Reinhardt*

Some days even breathing required too much exertion, and Letty could not muster the strength for writing. Tante Kate sent George, Lizzie, Margaret, and Lena to stay with Mary and Sister Kate so Letty could rest. Letty rarely saw her boy, Otto. She was told his time was taken up running his restaurant in Early. Or was it a pool hall, or a tavern? She couldn't recall. He would not be of any use in any case. Her youngest boy, George, although wearing long pants and due to begin high school, was too young and innocent of the world's wickedness to be brought into her confidence. He was planning to work the fields at their old farmstead in the summertime. That he wanted to work for money made Letty proud, even though Hoeffelder would take advantage and probably pay him just pennies,. At least one of her children would have a foothold on their old farm until she could get it back into their hands.

On a Saturday in late spring Jacob came to fix the steps on the porch. Letty told him she had been writing to Kohler about his crooked doings. He seemed pleased to hear that she was calling the executor to account. She knew he had no regard for the man. Letty refrained from telling him she was aiming to get the farm back. She never showed him the letters because he could not read, and again she regretted that she had not pressed him harder when he was a boy. She could surely use his help in her claims against Kohler and his corrupt cronies. When she whispered about the blanket woman who visited her with frightful stories, Jacob had put his hands up and shook his head. Afterwards, Letty proceeded in secret without anyone's support. She waited for Tante Kate's morning visits to the outhouse and rushed the two blocks to the post office to mail her letters. Writing had emboldened her; getting the farm back in their possession had given her purpose and direction.

After a reasonable amount of time with no replies from Kohler, Letty stepped up her campaign. She made one final attempt, gave him one last chance to answer for all the unspeakable losses. If he did not respond she was prepared to bring her case to Judge Mallett at the Ida Grove County Seat and present the evidence in the Court of Law herself.

*Dear Josephus Kohler,*

*Sir, as you are well aware I have written to you many times listing out our grievances. You have moved us off our land and have caused us to beg to you for money that is rightfully ours. I have told you many times how the children are starving. We are being shunned and persecuted for our ragged and destitute appearance, which we cannot help. Our clothes are all in tatters. How is it that I have never heard a word from you on our behalf?*

*I must assume that these matters do not concern you. I warn you that the consequences of your dereliction will be severe and long lasting.*

*Yours truly,*
*Mrs. Elizabeth Reinhardt*


Still no answer.

Letty did not consider herself practiced in deception, but she soon became adept at it. She had been sneaking pennies, nickels, and dimes, nothing larger, from the old glass jar Tante Kate now kept for petty cash. The clasp on her blue velvet purse could barely snap shut. In preparation for her appearance in court, she wrote lengthy briefs, lists of grievances and complaints, of injustices and violations, of accounts and the little recompense received. She recorded everything the woman whispered to her at night. She demanded that the farm she and Adam had pioneered be turned back over to their family. By the time she finished, she had accumulated a thick stack of pages written in tiny script. She was certain this information was not known to the Court and that they could not help but be persuaded by her thorough inventory and her conclusion that Josephus Kohler was a thief and should be charged with grand larceny and put behind bars. This was a small charge to be laid against him considering the grave damage he had done and was doing to so many. It had taken Letty months to pilfer the price of a round trip train ticket.

When the day finally arrived, she dressed in her black

serge dress, the widow's weeds she had worn since Adam's funeral. She had never noticed how ill-fitting the dress had become. It hung off her body like rags pinned on a clothes-line. Despite the hot July weather, she added three additional sweaters to fill out the dress. She was not of a mind to worry about appearances. There were more important matters to attend to. Early in the morning, when Tante Kate headed to the backyard outhouse, Letty dashed out the front door and made straight for the train station, clutching a large cloth handbag that held her sheaf of papers.

At the courthouse, people rudely rebuffed her efforts to get a hearing. They pushed and shoved her away from the judge's chambers, telling her to go back home. When they would not allow her to enlist Judge Mallett in her cause, she vehemently protested and rushed into his chambers and hit the judge with her handbag. They called the police. Letty showed them she had a return ticket to Maple Grove. Two burly men with badges escorted her back to the train station and waited until she boarded the train.

Once the train got going, she smelled the woman's scent and heard her voice.

"*Now you know. White men put sticks in their ears so they cannot hear our suffering.*" She was right on that score. But the blanket woman was not finished.

"*You did not fight hard enough. You are a weak woman like all the rest of them. Listen to me, Mrs. Elizabeth. They are stealing our children from us, putting them in schools where they will forget where they came from. Just like Jacob was stolen. Watch out, Mrs. Elizabeth or they will snatch all your children, and they will become lost to you forever.*"

This was a stunning blow! Was it true? Her younger chil-dren had grown away from her since Adam died and they had moved to town. The children went to school, played with their friends and cousins, but they never wanted to sit or talk with her. Surely the woman was right—Letty was losing them. Had this slander been planned behind her back, too? But Jacob? He was her son. She did not steal him from anybody. She raised him up from when he was small, taught him everything she could. He belonged to her, of that much she was certain. Anyone could see it was recorded right there in the census and Adam's obituary.

Maybe the blanket woman was lying to her. Maybe everyone was lying to her. No one wanted to hear her. The train heading back to Maple Grove had picked up speed and she stepped into the space between the cars to seek some relief from the heat. A hand like a sharp gust of wind struck her back and sent her into the air. She hit the ground. The emptied velvet change purse and her handbag with all the carefully compiled documents flew from her hands. The pages fluttered like so many frightened pigeons, the pale blue paper scattered to the winds across the fields of summer corn.

* * *

The minute I returned from the privy, the house was silent, and I knew instantly Letty was gone. Where was she? I hung my apron on the hook and briskly walked over to Jacob's place through the back alley. Jacob was not home, and I spoke briefly with Elizabeth who held a squalling infant in her arms. No, she had not seen Letty. The streets of Maple Grove were sweltering, and I was panting. Maybe Letty had wandered off in a delirium like a lost child. I had to find her before she created a disturbance. The cemetery was miles away. She had no money, so she probably didn't venture into the Mercantile. I peeked inside St. Bernard's church hoping to find Letty in their family pew. But she was nowhere to be found. When the children returned from school, I sent them over to Sister Kate's. There was nothing more to be done but wait for word of Letty's whereabouts to arrive.

And finally, it did.

Dr. Wiedersheim appeared at our door in the early evening to inform me that Letty was in the Ida Grove County Hospital recovering from injuries incurred when she jumped from the train as it was leaving the county seat. My hand flew to my mouth. He immediately reassured me she was not dead. The train had not gathered full speed and her injuries were not severe, mostly bruises and lacerations.

"But this is a very serious matter," he warned, as if I did not know it. "She has attempted to take her own life. Her sanity is completely gone."

My heart set up a dreadful flutter as I strove for some explanation of what Letty might have been doing, escaping from the house, running off to Ida Grove on some bootless errand.

I thanked the good doctor profusely and requested that he release Letty back into my care, offering round-the-clock nursing as a ransom. From the way he arched his right eyebrow, it was clear Wiedersheim questioned my abilities, if not my own mental capacity.

"I am keeping her under heavy sedation, and it is not possible to bring her home for several days. Something must be done. She needs more than constant watching. Furthermore, you must understand, Mrs. Reinhardt broke into the judge's chambers in Ida Grove County talking some gibberish about stolen land and starving children and demanding justice be done. When she could not get a hearing she physically attacked Judge Mallett, and the judge ordered her taken away." He paused. "I am sorry to tell you that she was led out of the courts by the deputy sheriff who put her back on the train. Thankfully, they won't press charges." Dr. Wiedersheim shook his head in disbelief at what he was telling me.

With a heavy heart I pictured Letty, who probably weighed no more than one hundred pounds, soaking wet, going after the portly figure of Judge Mallett. I easily imagined what she had been raving about as I had witnessed her string of accusations during the meeting with Kohler.

"The police escorted her to the train and helped her find a seat. And then, as the train headed out of town, she jumped off." The creases between Wiedersheim's eyes were crimped into a frown. "*The Chronicle* has gotten wind of the story and it will be in the papers."

How wretched. *The Chronicle* would surely make a spectacle of Letty. Her derangement would become public scandal and fodder for gossip. Worse for me was that Letty had undertaken her mission to the county seat completely behind my back. Hadn't I sheltered her for months since Adam's death? She had not been well, but I never realized she had gotten so much worse. Caring for Letty had given my life a purpose, and now that purpose was going to be wrenched away by men who had the power to do such a thing. With her actions, she was bound to pass into the keeping of others, and I was helpless to fight against it.

Frantically, I went over it. No one had taken Letty seriously. Jacob thought her letters were harmless pastimes. If Letty had stuck to our secret conspiracy, we would have been all right. But, no, she had sneaked past me. Maybe it had been a mistake to let her write everything out. Maybe the writing had caused her to become more deluded. For a moment I feared I would be held to blame. I went no further with that thought because Wiedersheim came close to declaring me insane to boot. Suddenly, I felt diminished, useless, and old, very old.

Two days later, they brought Letty home. She had been

wearing layers of extra clothes when she jumped from the train, and the extra padding had protected her upper body from the full impact of the fall. Still, she was a sorry sight, all black and blue, with deep cuts and scratches on her face and hands where she had hit the cornfield by the side of the train tracks. Because of the medicine Wiedersheim had adminis-tered, the light had gone out of her eyes. Her body was like a wooden doll with its limbs unstrung, the same as the night Adam died. With the help of the older girls, I got her upstairs and into her room. Wiedersheim left bottles of medicine with strict instructions as to dosage. I silently refused to obey. His medicine was surely meant to keep Letty in a dull stupor, not help her get well. After he left, I decocted a strong herbal infusion that would release Letty from the ill effects of Wied-ersheim's poisonous brew of opiates and whiskey that made her act and smell like a sodden drunk.

* * *

Kohler had just finished a breakfast of poached egg and dry toast, the bland diet prescribed by Dr. Wiedersheim to offset his chronic indigestion. When his wife came rushing in with the newspaper article stating that Mrs. Reinhardt had thrown herself from the train, Kohler's stomach lurched and his throat burned with a reflux of acid.

"That woman will be the death of me!" His next thought was that as soon as the widow recovered from her injuries, which *The Chronicle* reported were mercifully not severe, he would arrange for her confinement, as she surely was a lunatic.

For months he had received Mrs. Reinhardt's scathing, inflammatory letters that threatened him and his family's rep-utation if she could not reclaim the family farm. He could have pressed charges against her for sending threats through the mail, but he had no appetite for a further ruckus with the widow. The letters were written in a tiny chicken scratch scrawl, the rantings of a demented woman, yet he could not see fit to destroy them. He had stopped opening the pale blue envelopes and stuffed them and their malevolent contents into a hidden drawer in the back corner of his desk.

He refused to let himself be intimidated by this woman's unfair accusations and was infuriated by her insinuations and demands. What right did she have to question his morals by implying that he was devious and double-dealing in handling her affairs? She even wanted her farm back. His blood boiled to bad effect on his stomach. Had he not acted in a prudent manner in this thankless task? She had recently petitioned the court claiming her inability to handle her own matters and turned all of bill-paying over to him by court order. As executor, he had her last petition.

Kohler saw she had managed to pay off some debts incurred after her husband's death, with probable help from her oldest daughters. Then, claiming serious illness, she had petitioned the court to direct Kohler as the executor to pay her bills. This he had dutifully undertaken, despite his great distaste for the imposition of yet another task from that quarter. The extra burden of managing her personal money was not something he relished doing. None of her people showed the slightest bit of gratitude for his efforts. In fact, they continued to view him with varying degrees of suspicion. He was certainly not in Jacob's favor—nor old Katharina's for that matter.

Kohler wondered how the widow had managed to slip past that ancient German watchdog. This new development did not bode well for the family's welfare. That woman could not be allowed to run loose on the streets. And what was she doing traveling to the Ida Grove county seat? Attacking Judge Mallett? What further manner of mayhem was she capable of perpetrating? With this latest situation she had proved dangerous to herself and beyond that he did not wish to contemplate. Obviously, she was hopelessly insane.

His wife complained he was a mere shadow of his former self, always cross with her and the children. "Josephus, you never seem to know a moment's peace!" she admonished. Dr. Wiedersheim was also well aware of the toll this Reinhardt business was taking on his condition. Sending the widow away would be the best possible solution for all concerned.

Dr. Wiedersheim quickly confirmed Kohler's assessment of insanity. He was familiar with an asylum in Dubuque, and believed it to be a reputable place for the care of the insane. Kohler could see no other possible course of action. Surely this was in the best interest for her safety and that of the others, including himself. Judge Mallett was a personal friend. After his altercation with the widow, Mallett would understand the unpleasant nature of Kohler's obligations to the Reinhardt family and would be sympathetic to the case. He and Wiedersheim would have no problem enlisting his help to prepare the documents and issue the court order mandating her committal. And just in case they needed further documentation of her delusional state, Kohler had the unopened stack of letters, clearly the ravings of a madwoman, as evidence.

The heat of August made the meeting with the Reinhardt family especially disagreeable. Cramped into their small living room with barely enough seating, Kohler's face was flushed with perspiration and embarrassing sweat had pooled under his arms and groin. A miasmic odor floated like a vaporous cloud into where they were seated. He could not identify the smell although he had always prided himself on having a most discerning nose. He believed the odor to be emanating from the kitchen and assumed it was probably some herbal preparation stewing on the stove. The unsavory reek did not sit well on his soured stomach.

Kohler was offered a hard straight-backed chair directly facing a large family portrait that hung in a prominent place over a dingy sofa. The picture loomed as a bad omen. He recognized Adam Reinhardt and his wife and children and was seized by what a dreadful loss the family had suffered since the man's death. Immediately it put him in mind of his own plight. One never realizes how losing paternal protection can destroy a seemingly prosperous family. Convinced that the Reinhardts would never recover to their previously sound condition, he deplored his entanglement in their ill fortune and resented the toll it was taking on him.

The meeting included the two older Reinhardt daughters who had been caring for the widow's younger children. They bickered among themselves about the best course of action for their ailing mother, though they agreed that, "No, she was not in her right mind," and, "Yes, her latest behavior had caused everyone, especially the younger children, a great fright."

The old aunt growled her objections in German. "But do they have to remove her to an insane asylum? Especially one so far away from home?" She was adamantly opposed to having the widow taken away. Katherina was positively unbending in her conviction that she could still care for her. She promised the older daughters that she would not allow Mrs. Reinhardt to escape her custody again.

The eldest son, Jacob, did not offer any resistance and Kohler took his silence as tacit acceptance of the proposed plan. The other son, Otto, was nowhere in sight. In the end, the grown daughters acquiesced, leaving the old aunt bitterly opposed and decamping in a huff.

Judge Mallett had papers written up for the committal ahead of time and Kohler petitioned the Court for temporary guardianship for Mrs. Reinhardt. In hopes of extricating himself from this increasingly hellish mire, Kohler signed his name to yet another document, one that further bound him to the Reinhardts. After meeting with the judge, he went straight to Wiedersheim's office for further consultation on his deteriorating digestion.

# IDA GROVE, IOWA

## JUNE 17, 2000

SHIRLEY'S MOUTH WAS PURSED as if she had just tasted something sour. "Glad you're back, Sherlock. I did some digging and found some Kohler documents. I'm sure they will interest you."

Van took the copied documents from Shirley.

"You might want to take a seat and read these here," Shirley said and pulled a chair over to where Van was standing.

Van raised her eyebrow.

"I'm just warning you," Shirley said, "It's written in legalese, but it's quite chilling."

The first page was a petition to the court.

*"Comes now Elizabeth Letty Reinhardt and for cause of action, and as grounds for relief states:*

*1) she is the widow of Adam Reinhardt.*

*2) on August 31, 1901, Adam Died.*

*3) that Josephus Kohler was appointed and qualified as executor of said estate.*

*4) Less than one year has elapsed.*

5) *"That shortly after the payment of said claims she had become seriously ill, physically, and for the greater portion of the time since has been under the care of a physician. That during the greater portion of the time petitioner's mind was in no condition to comprehend her business or to attend to business details and that by reason of the foregoing facts etc. she petitions the court to direct the executor to pay her bills."*

"Sounds like she was still grieving the loss of her husband," Van said. "I suppose a widow's grief could be incapacitating, could qualify as a serious illness. Her husband died unexpectedly, the family left the farm and moved to town so quickly. Everything auctioned off. Overwhelming losses for anyone in her position I would imagine. Looks like Kohler assumed extra responsibilities for the family."

Van felt detached. Which was perplexing. She had felt more for the women she had studied and written about—Mary Jemison, Susan Rowland, the women captured as children by Natives. Her sense of Letty was distant, removed, her feelings about her theoretical. Letty was listed as her father's grandmother, her great grandmother. When Van stared at Letty in the family portrait, she had felt her eyes watching but there was no kindred connection. Her story was sad, even tragic, but not uncommon—bereavement, a widow with young children to care for—nothing to stir the heart beyond the ordinary woes. Women have suffered worse. *Maybe I'm just getting cynical.*

"Read the next petition," Shirley directed.

*J. Kohler vs. Elizabeth (Letty) Reinhardt:*

*Comes now your petitioner and represents to the Court that Said Elizabeth (Letty) Reinhardt while upon the train between Maple Grove, Iowa and Ida Grove, Iowa, and laboring under an insane delusion attacked the sitting judge and then on return to Maple Grove threw herself from the train in an endeavor to suicide.*

*Your petitioner shows to the Court that he is now administrator of the estate of Adam Reinhardt, deceased, husband of Elizabeth (Letty) Reinhardt, and that the same needs constant attention.*

*Elizabeth (Letty) Reinhardt is now insane and has personal property to the value of about Three thousand dollars ($3000.00) which is liable to waste and diminish in value if speedy care be not taken of the same. To that end therefore the said property may be taken care of until a permanent guardian may be appointed, your petitioner asks the Court to appoint J. Kohler guardian of said Elizabeth Reinhardt, insane, and that she be committed to a suitable hospital for her care.*

"Oh. *Oh,* now this is—this is really hard." Van shivered, her scalp prickled, her hands went cold although moments ago she was bemoaning the heat. "This on top of everything else, those poor children. Such a terrible word—*insane.*"

"I found it pretty shocking myself. She must have lost her mind. Sounds like Kohler shipped her off to an asylum. I believe the closest one is in Dubuque. You might want to check with Marion at the library. *The Chronicle* probably had a field day with this event. Stories of such calamities were their bread and butter. Are you all right? Do you want a glass of water? You look awfully pale."

"Thanks, Shirley, I feel really—honestly, I had not expected to find this—Letty going crazy, Kohler committing her, taking over her guardianship, gaining more power over the family."

Van's breath was shallow; she felt faint. She needed to get back to her car, she needed to drive fast, her legs twitched, and she wanted to run, run, run.

Shirley brought a glass of water. She put her hand on Van's shoulder. "Maybe being a detective is best left to crime novels."

"I'm okay, Shirley, just a little woozy. It's probably the heat. Thanks. I know things like this happened. I'm a historian, remember? You might not have guessed it, but I have a reputation. Once I get on a project I'm like a dog on a bone; I won't put it down. Can you go back into the files and see what else you can find on Kohler? I'll come back tomorrow."

"I won't be working tomorrow. It's Sunday."

"Oh, right. I guess I lost track of time. Monday afternoon then?"

Shirley gave her one of those winks. "That's my girl," she said, patting Van like a dog. "I'm still your Watson, no problem."

Van sat in the car and waited for the ringing in her ears to stop. Her hands were shaking. She started the car and turned off the air conditioner. The copied pages sat on the passenger seat. Images of her mother flashed like a grade B movie trailer—a middle-aged woman, hair uncombed, in her nightgown, bottles of prescriptions on her night table, unable to get out of bed until the middle of the night when she wandered the house where she smoked, wrote on scraps of paper, and sat in front of the blue flickering light of the television set.

"She's just having a few bad days," her father said. "She'll be right as rain by tomorrow." Something about her period. Doctor's visits. Psychiatrists. "It's mid-life," her father said, "menopause. It happens to women." Martin stayed later and later in his office on campus. Except for mysterious comments about the magnetic energy in words and poetry, Van's mother rarely spoke to her. The house was like being shut up in solitary confinement—with the blue haze of television on.

Then her father had her mother put in the hospital. Not just any hospital, but Mendota State Hospital for the Mentally Ill. Simply "Mendota," they called it, and everyone knew what that shorthand meant—the asylum, the nut house, the loony bin. Unfathomable darkness surrounded the place and its inhabitants. Van had just started high school and could hardly bear the shame. She had never brought friends home. She made the honor roll that year and every year after, aced her exams, top of her class, a model student. No one would guess.

The state hospital was at the northern end of Lake Mendota. She would stare across the lake and almost make out the two-story brick building where her mother was incarcerated. She thought about it like that, as if her mother was in prison. But what was her crime? The first time Mother was gone for a month. A year later she was sent back. Had she been there four times? Van could not recall her mother resisting. It was not like the movies. There was no straitjacket. Her mother just would be absent from her room when Van came home from school. Gone. TV dinners and studying was her routine, that and saying the obligatory good night to her dad through the door to his study.

She made a plan one winter of skating across the lake to visit her mother, but the lake ice was covered in snow, and it never happened. Nor did her father take her there. She wondered if he had ever visited. The hospital stays became shorter. No one told her what kind of treatment her mother received. Mother came home foggy and disoriented, blank behind her deep blue eyes. And always there were the drugs. Her mother was an invalid. None of what was happening made sense. Van couldn't wait to get out of the house to escape the gloominess. As soon as she graduated high school, she used her small savings to rent a room on the university campus. She never lived in her parents' house again.

Van met Len in an American history class where they had taken up the contentious question of Native American collusion with the French and British fur traders. They became lovers, crashing into each other's bodies with a fierce and reckless hunger, reaching into each other's secrets, reading each other's bones like blind people reading Braille. Their minds were tuned differently but they felt like kindred spirits, both of them stubborn loners, glad to have found each other. Len was a scholarship student from northern Wisconsin, two years older than she, energetic, bright; he was hard on Van, teasing her about her braid and her long nose, calling her Pocahontas. In late summer, they had just returned from the canoe trip in the Boundary Waters, and she was unloading gear from her car when the phone rang in the kitchen of her apartment.

"You better come home, Vangie. Your mother has died." His voice was like a chained dog that had barked himself hoarse.

"I have to go," she told Len. "It's my mother." She couldn't say the rest of it. "I'll give you a call later."

An accidental overdose is what she was told. Van never believed it.

A week later when she called Len from the student union, he told her he was going up north. It was the last time she saw him. Two big losses, one right after the other. Well, three, if she counted the loss of her father to the bottle, and four if she included the pregnancy, and five if she added losing her ability to trust that others would ever care for her.

Van drove back to Maple Grove. She couldn't decide where to go. The motel felt too isolated, Dee Dee's too exposed. The library was her best option, still open on Saturday. She needed to pull herself together. Her mother had been dead for more than thirty years. For all that time Van had locked her mother's illness and her death in a vault. No one had the key. Not even Van. She had lived without a mother for years before she actually died. After Mother's death, a few mothers of friends tried to take her under their wing, but Van had already grown a thick skin, developed an attitude of fierce independence, and shoved any need for maternal care as far away as she could. Maybe that was what drove her and Em apart. Em had opened the possibility of female warmth, love, and companionship. The closer Em got, the colder Van became. The women she encountered in Maple Grove, her team, she thought with affection, had managed to pry open her heart. Their kindness was simple, uncomplicated, natural—and devastating.

Marion was presiding behind the front desk. She gave Van a welcoming smile.

"How's the research going, dear?"

"I guess you could say it's taken a turn for the gothic. I was hoping you could go into *The Chronicle* back issues and check the week of July 15- 20, 1901. See if you can find an article about Elizabeth Letty Reinhardt."

Marion frowned. "Sounds serious, dear. I'll see what I can find. Looks like the table is all yours for the afternoon. You can make yourself right at home."

Marion retreated and Van pulled out her journal. She wrote directly to her father.

*Maple Grove,*
*Saturday, June 17*
*Day Seven*

*I don't even know how to begin this. I just got Kohler's 1902 reports to the court. He had Letty Reinhardt declared insane, committed to an asylum, and then he took over as her guardian. I wonder what drove her crazy? I don't know if you ever knew any of this. It happened before you were born. All the documents say Letty was your grandmother and it would seem you would have known or been told about it at some point. But that isn't what is important now.*

*What I want to know is what happened to Mother?*

*Was she going crazy herself? She was writing to someone who was dead. What did she expect? A voice from the grave? Twilight Zone? She couldn't help herself. The vault she had locked years ago had been cracked by clever hands. Whether Letty Reinhardt was her great grandmother or not, her terrible fate ran straight into Van's mother's in ways she could no longer escape, and her father was implicated.*

*Why didn't you ever tell me what was wrong with her? I know enough by now to think she was frustrated in some critical way. I remember she used to write. I think she might have even talked about going back to school to study poetry. Weren't there a few of her poems published in The Wisconsin State Journal? This is all so vague. Nothing of hers was saved. After she died, you cleaned her room out so fast it was like she had never existed. Anyway, we had stopped talking by then. Was she really crazy? Or was she like so many women of her era, a housewife stuck at home in a suburb with nothing to do but watch television? Or was she always a bit depressed? You were never around. Did you abandon her? I think you might have. I am sure you did.*

Van felt young and sad. Had she ever grieved her mother's death? What did it mean to grieve anyway? There were books on the subject, stages of grief, support groups, but there had been no one to guide her, comfort her after her mother died. Not that she would have accepted it. Her father dug deeper into his work hole and took the bottle with him. Van had had pressing issues to deal with that had to do with Len, and then he had disappeared. She postponed her scholarship for a semester. What happened after Mother's death was mired in secrecy and shame, and Van did not want to dredge the murky bottom of that swamp. Van suddenly realized she was lonely. She had always been lonely. She had thought it was normal. She pulled out a used Kleenex from her pocket and blew her nose.

"Are you all right, dear? Do you have a summer cold?" Marion looked concerned.

"Probably allergies," Van replied. "Lots of pollen in the air this season."

"I found the article on Mrs. Reinhardt. I have to warn you, *The Chronicle* was a real tabloid and featured sensational stories. At least there were no photographs with this one." She handed Van a copy. "I have a box of Kleenex at my desk if you need it."

### DEMENTED WIDOW JUMPS FROM TRAIN

On July 31, Mrs. Adam Reinhardt of Maple Grove, being under a delusion, attempted suicide by jumping from the train coming from Ida Grove. Dr. Wiedersheim of Ida Grove has declared her insane. According to his report, the widow had been deranged since her husband's death last year. In a dramatic scene in the Ida Grove courtroom, she attacked Judge Mallett and was escorted to the train station by local deputies. The train was not at full speed when she jumped, and she was hospitalized with abrasions and lacerations but no broken bones. Mrs. Reinhardt has subsequently been committed to Saint Anthony's Insane Asylum in Dubuque. Our heartfelt thoughts go to the family.

Van shuddered. Her first thoughts were how awful it must have been for her children to have their mother be the subject of such a small-town newspaper story. Time collapsed. Past and present fused in an instant. If her father knew about Letty's insanity, was it part of the reason he ran? Of course, this had happened before he was born, and even with such public exposure a family could hide behind silence. He did. And her mother did, too.

Van recalled the woman in Charlotte Perkins Gilman's *The Yellow Wallpaper.*

She had included the short story in her course on female captivity narratives to demonstrate that there were many ways a woman could be held captive. Gilman's tale had a sinister twist because the woman protagonist was held hostage not by Indians, but by a treacherous alliance between husband and doctor. She was forbidden to put pen to paper, forbidden to write, as if writing were the cause of her madness. Van never fully understood why *The Yellow Wallpaper* had given her nightmares, but now she wondered if she had chosen that story because it was close to what happened to her mother.

Mother had never talked about her childhood. Her mother was an only child whose parents had died young. Was it a car accident? There were no photographs. Her obituary, written by her father, consisted of a few sentences using her married name. She never even knew the correct spelling of her mother's maiden name. Was it Kurtz or Curtis?

What Van inherited from her parents was a manual for running away and a trainload of unopened baggage. "Ask Vangie to do some research." Did he have any idea what she would find when he wrote that note? If her father knew his family's history, maybe he had been overwhelmed by it, out of his depth, over his head. Just as he was helpless to know what to do with his wife beyond what the doctors prescribed for her. Her mother's mental illness—could she call it that?—had no specific origin she ever knew of except Mother's unfulfilled urge for expression.

It was possible her father wanted her to discover this family history so she would understand him, have some compassion for the kind of man he became.

She couldn't face going into Dee Dee's. She still had trail mix and bottles of water. Emergency food she carried in the car when she traveled. Well, she was lost in the wilderness now, and this qualified as an emergency. She drove back to the motel and signed up for another night. Tomorrow would be Sunday. It was the end of the week she had allotted for this project. She could drive over to Black Hawk State Park, and maybe take a swim. She picked up the phone and dialed Em's number.

"Dr. Cooper here."

"Hi, Em, it's me."

"What's up? I thought you might be headed back to Madison by now."

"Is Mister okay?"

"The question is, are you okay? You sound a little shaky."

"I fell into a rabbit hole—or maybe quicksand. You know, the harder you try to get out, the deeper you sink."

"Okay, Van, just checking. Rabbit holes and quicksand sound bad though. Do you want to talk about it?"

"Not right now, Em. Maybe when I get back, when I know more. I was just checking on Mister."

"Mister's fine. He seemed a bit lonely so I brought him over here. You'll love this, he remembered all his favorite napping places."

Van felt her throat close. Tears stung. She swallowed. "That is really sweet, Em."

"Seriously, Van, your voice sounds a little strange. Catch a case of prairie fever?"

Em was teasing her. A familiar tactic. It worked for a moment.

"Well, the good news is I've had a lot of help from the women at the library, the courthouse, the town office—and

Dee Dee at the diner. Great coffee. It's good to hear your voice, Em. Not to worry. I think I just got trapped in a time warp—you know, it's an occupational hazard for an historian."

"Anything I can help you with?"

Van wasn't ready for a heart to heart. In fact, her heart was in pieces.

"It's too much to talk about now. I'll tell you more when I see you."

"Okay, Van. Give me a heads up when you're heading back. Mister and I will be waiting for you."

"Thanks, Em. Give Mister a pet for me."

Van hung up the phone. Hearing the concern in Em's voice brought stinging tears. She opened her map and located the route to Black Hawk State Park. Tomorrow was Sunday, everything closed on Main Street. A good day to camp out.

# MAPLE GROVE, IOWA

## August 1902

THE NIGHT AFTER KOHLER and Wiedersheim's visit, I went upstairs to see Letty. She examined the bruises and scratches on her hands and looked at me with a pitiful frown as if she recalled nothing of what happened. I tried to purge anger from my voice, but I was livid. Letty's gross breach of our secret agreement made me look incompetent and gave those men power over our lives. Surely, they wanted Letty put out of sight, but did she really need to be locked up?

"Letty, in a few days you will be going on the train to Dubuque. Dr. Wiedersheim has arranged for you to be taken to a comfortable place for a rest cure. You will be well cared for and will return to us soon enough." Letty squinched her face. "You need to cooperate with this plan. It is for your own good," I insisted. What a misery it was to be lying to her in this way, how our betrayals were compounding by the day.

In a fit of defiance, I protested in the only way I knew. I had not administered Wiedersheim's sedative potion as he instructed. Instead, I brewed a powerful infusion of prairie anemone to aid Letty in her recovery from shock. It was the least I could do for her. Within several hours Letty's color had brightened and her eyes had lost that dull stupefaction induced by Wiedersheim's medicine.

I looked at the list as to what Letty should bring with her to the hospital—three calico dresses, three chemises, three pairs of drawers, four pairs of hose, three nightdresses, three cotton flannel skirts, handkerchiefs, collars, one pair of shoes, one pair of slippers, one shawl or cloak, one hat or hood, and four aprons. Four aprons? Why on earth would she need four aprons? These instructions did not tally with what I thought she might need, but what did I know, having never been in an insane asylum myself? In a fury, I packed it all.

\* \* \*

Letty touched the right side of her face. It was still tender, and her right eye felt swollen and bruised. She inspected her scratched arms and hands. No bones seemed to be broken. Despite her injuries, on the afternoon Kohler and Wiedersheim came to the house, she had crept close to the staircase where she could hear every word.

Kohlers's wheedling voice was recognizable and she heard how he twisted Wiedersheim against her. She grew incensed. What a scandal, sending her off to some godforsaken place across the state of Iowa—punishing her for the accident on the train as if it were her fault. They said she jumped from the train. What a lie! She was pushed!

Under Wiedersheim's whiskey-laced tonic her tongue had grown so thick she sounded stupid. No one understood or believed her. She had tried to be truthful, but her only proof was her certainty, which was not worth a pinch of dirt these days. From the voices coming from downstairs, it seemed even her older girls had turned against her. And didn't Jacob's silence betray him? Why didn't he stand up for her? "Jacob was stolen," the woman on the train had hissed like a snake. Maybe she was right. Only Tante Kate's voice made the strongest objection with her most emphatic "*Nein!*"

"*Nein! Nein!*" Letty whispered along with her. But no one heard. The blood pounded in her head until she was about to explode.

A rest cure. There was no mistake in Letty's mind where they wanted to send her. An insane asylum. A place for lunatics. This was the very limit. There was no way to fight Kohler's cruel verdict. She was defeated and his minions had won. Was this not exactly what the woman predicted—first you get taken off your land, then they steal your children and remove you and lock you up far from home?

Worse yet. The blanket woman had abandoned her, too. Letty had not smelled wood smoke or heard a peep from her since she had shoved her off the train.

At least Tante Kate's concoctions did not make Letty drunk. With her last bit of energy, she devised a plan, and once she had it, she felt calmer than she had since Adam's death. Before dawn, she lit a candle and tiptoed down the stairs in her nightdress. On the kitchen counter she spied the big butcher knife, the one they always kept well sharpened. Her heart banged so loud she was sure it would awaken everyone. Hurry. Hurry. Hurry. There is not much time left to take matters into your own hands. Better to go to your maker or the devil himself than be hauled off to some insane asylum. Letty desperately needed release from the pressure and build-up that made her head hurt and her heart pound. How peaceful to open her skin, let the blood flow from her body, drain away all evil thoughts. How hopping mad those voices would be to get dispatched in such an easy manner. The chance of being cleansed of their vile influence made Letty's lips curl.

The knife weighed more than she remembered. The blade was cold as a sliver of ice when she pressed it across her wrist. She clenched her jaw and bore down as if slicing through chicken skin. A thin, hot stream of blood trickled onto her hand. Clammy perspiration chilled her body as hot blood blossoms appeared on her nightdress. Like pouring water in an anthill, the damning voices set up a hullabaloo. She could not bear them another minute! Let it be over! She took the knife to her neck, made a frantic cut, and screamed.

Tante Kate appeared with a lamp. "*Gott im Himmel, Was hast du dir angetan?* What have you done to yourself?"

\* \* \*

Jacob woke to the sound of pounding on his back door and Lizzie's high-pitched voice crying, "Jacob, Jacob, come quickly, Mother has done something terrible!"

He stumbled out of sleep and into his clothes pulling his suspenders up as he ran with Lizzie through the back alley to their house. Lizzie had just turned fourteen and her resemblance to Mama Letty was unnerving. At times Jacob felt she was Mama Letty and he was still a boy on the old farm, the similarity was so strong, not just in looks but in her darting blue eyes and how she moved so quickly, like a little sparrow. Jacob dreaded what new disaster had now befallen.

They ran through the side doorway and into the brightly lit kitchen where Mama Letty was slumped over in a wooden chair, her uncombed hair hanging down, her white nightdress stained with great blotches of fresh blood. Jacob immediately saw the instrument of her injuries; a blood-stained butcher knife lay on the table. Tante Kate had wrapped torn sheeting around Mama Letty's wrist and was holding a compress to the side of her neck. Blood was leaking through the bandages and Mama Letty's face was blenched so white Jacob thought she was dying right then and there. Tante Kate shot him a look that said what he was feeling. This was the end. At least it marked the beginning of the end, if such things could ever be marked and measured.

Jacob struggled to find his love for Mama Letty. Was she not his very own mother? What a tangled thing—fear for what she had just done, and hatred for the god-awful mess she was making for all of them. He could not see her in this wretched condition without feeling the hammer of judgment, an accusation that he was somehow responsible for this fresh horror. Papa Adam was dead, and it looked like Mama Letty was not far behind. Could he have prevented all this?

Mama Letty snapped at him, "What are you staring at? This blood is not your blood! You belong to the savages!"

She was demented. Nobody in their right mind would take a kitchen knife to their own body. But her words cut through him just the same, like the sharpened knife that had cut through her skin.

Dr. Wiedersheim appeared in the kitchen freshly shaven, his clothes pressed, and hair neatly combed. Jacob wondered if he always went to bed fully dressed, prepared to be pulled out for middle of the night disasters. Wiedersheim inspected Mama Letty's wounds and put on clean bandages and applied a thick gauze compress to her neck. He went right up to Tante Kate and in a fierce voice he snapped at her. "This never would have happened if she had been properly dosed like I prescribed."

Jacob was stunned to hear the doctor reprimand Tante Kate. He glanced at the kitchen door where the children stared wide-eyed with alarm. Lizzie stood frozen in place with fists pushed to her mouth. George held his younger sisters back. They had seen their mother bleeding and bandaged and then heard the doctor scold and humiliate Tante Kate. Nobody ever spoke to Tante Kate like that. Jacob had balked when Kohler and Wiedersheim proposed the asylum in Dubuque but at the meeting he found no words to follow his feelings. He had held to the possibility that she had somehow slipped and fallen from the train; never mind what crazy errand she had been running. But taking up a knife against her own person proved that she had passed far beyond their ability to care for her. They had the younger children to consider, too. The effect of seeing their mother in such a state of self-violation was agonizing.

Mama Letty had sealed her own fate. Surely not the one she had in mind.

Wiedersheim quickly reinstated his sedative prescription and recommended that the departure for Dubuque be postponed for a week to give Letty's wounds time to heal. The older girls agreed to help with their mother's care and Jacob arranged for the four younger children to stay with his family. His wife and children kept a normal, if slightly topsy-turvy routine during the summer, and would not mind having the children as company on their outings.

Each evening after he changed from his work overalls, Jacob checked in on Tante Kate. He never saw Mama Letty. "She is sleeping," Tante Kate groused in a tone that Jacob understood to mean, "She is drugged."

The night before Mama Letty was scheduled to leave for Dubuque, Wiedersheim paid Jacob a brief visit to make sure everything was set for the following day.

"The children should not be present for their mother's leave taking," he advised.

After witnessing Wiedersheim berating Tante Kate, Jacob was reluctant to go against the man's admonition. But it had become his duty as the oldest son to stand up for the family's wishes, a burden he felt ill equipped to bear.

"I am sorry. The older girls and I have decided otherwise. We have suffered so much loss already. Even though our mother is being sent away, the young ones need to understand she hasn't died like their father." It was a long speech for Jacob.

Wiedersheim was sympathetic. "As you wish. You can tell the children that Saint Anthony's is a hospital where their mother can get proper treatment for her kind of malady. Given the right amount of care and rest she will return to normal."

Jacob nodded. What the doctor did not know, and Jacob could not explain to him, was that Letty had probably never been normal.

The morning of her departure Mama Letty's wounds had not completely healed. The angry red gash across her left wrist was still wrapped in a bandage and covered by the sleeve of her shirtwaist but the wound at her neck, although shallow, looked puffy and inflamed.

Mrs. Good, the nurse companion hired to accompany Mama Letty, was unknown to the family. A stout woman of middle age with a gruff voice that brooked no foolishness, she was all business and efficiency. Her stern look discouraged any show of emotion; her firm manner felt too rough for such an occasion.

Under sedation, Mama Letty's eyes drooped and her mouth was slack. She followed Mrs. Good's directives like a dumb animal going to slaughter. The nurse grappled a bewildered Mama Letty, hustling her out the door and toward the waiting buggy. Jacob recalled the auction. The cows separated from the calves. Everyone bellering. But here, no one knew what to say. The little girls held each other's hands making breathy sobs, while the older girls wore grim masks of determination. Otto was not there. Jacob put his hand on the shoulder of George who stood stiff as a ramrod. Tante Kate was absent. She had refused to witness the departure. Nor were Wiedersheim or Kohler in attendance.

After the buggy pulled away, Jacob heaved a sigh composed of relief and sorrow. He had no idea what would become of Mama Letty. His thoughts turned to Papa Adam. Surely this would not be happening if he were still here. His large stalwart frame had given Mama Letty shelter and protection from whatever had tormented her over the years. With Papa Adam still alive Kohler and Wiedersheim would never have wielded so much power. Without Papa Adam's presence they were all left naked and exposed, and there was no possible way that Jacob could ever take his place.

\* \* \*

Wiedersheim's medicine had addled Letty's brain. On the train to Dubuque, her thoughts flew like crazed crows eating every word before she could utter it. Was the hideous woman assigned to accompany her going to push her off the train, or had that already happened? Letty pulled her shawl over her eyes and shuttered herself deep inside her mind's darkness where tiny pinholes of light only served to blind her. When the carriage arrived at Saint Anthony's, she awoke in high nervous alert. Surely this enormous red brick monster with its many barred glass eyes sparkling and flashing in the sunlight was about to devour her. Its four-story head had a dark hole for a mouth supported by white columns like giant teeth and on either side were vast brick wings outstretched to embrace her. Once she entered the mouth of this monster there was no chance of escape. Letty had no fight left and the nurse was rough as a man although she was wearing a dress. Letty could not resist as the nurse pushed and pulled her into the gaping orifice and the spring-bolted door snapped shut.

Inside this monster people had her in their clutches. They chewed her apart piece by piece, asking the nurse companion for all manner of details about her existence as if she was not present. What did that woman know about her? Nothing but what she was told by those whose wicked plan this was. Then they stored her up on the top floor in a tiny room with a little iron bed bolted to the floor and one high, barred window that kept its pale eye on her.

Letty retreated to the ceiling and peered down on her bound and bandaged body—her hands and feet had been tied with heavy canvas straps to the iron bars of the bed. All she had wanted was to be put out of her misery. Such a hopeless failure. Now she was condemned for creating this commotion. A leaden shroud of remorse crushed her. Poor Jacob. She had meant to tell him more, had meant to say he should ask Tante Kate where he came from because none of us were ever told. But her tongue was a thick creature that clogged her mouth. Voices floated in and out of her room, whispering. She searched their faces, but they faded into the shadows. *Adam, Adam, are you here?* How she longed for his voice. But wanting him was worse than sticking the knife into her heart. Shame twisted her mouth into a grimace. How could she have withheld affection from her husband, the one person who had really loved and kept her safe? Surely, she deserved punishment for all her dark sins.

# BLACK HAWK STATE PARK

## June 18, 2000

FATHER'S DAY. HOW IRONIC. A holiday her father had showed
no interest in and they never celebrated. Van took off her
watch and released herself from being a slave to clock-time.
She drove the paved road through mesmerizing acres of corn
and soybeans, soybeans and corn. In the late afternoon, she
pulled into Black Hawk State Park and campground, and
even though she had already paid for the room at the motel,
she forked over five dollars for a tent space near the east side
of the lake, far away from families in campers. She was eager
for a swim. Maybe she would camp; the tent and sleeping bag
were stuffed in the back of her trunk.

Martin wasn't the only man on her mind. Len was still
tailing her. She had dreamed of him again, or a shadowy
figure that might have been him. Black Hawk Park provoked thoughts of him. She could hear Len saying, "It's
pretty strange, isn't it? How those Indians got shoved off
their land and massacred when they put up resistance, and
then they become American icons, and everything gets
named after them."

He had used Chief Black Hawk as a case in point. Once hated and pursued back and forth across the Mississippi River, Black Hawk was an American symbol—a fierce warrior, a noble savage that Americans celebrated with statues and memorials because, brave as he was, they had defeated him. After he died in the mid-1830s, his grave had been vandalized and his bones displayed in a museum. Shortly thereafter, his bones disappeared when the museum mysteriously went up in flames.

Other Indian bones had been dug up by archaeologists and given to museums, where they sat for years in dusty boxes. What were people thinking when they wanted those bones to begin with? Talismans? Relics? Like pieces of the true cross or fingers of the martyred saints? Or did they just want to make sure Black Hawk was dead and accounted for and that he had been vanquished?

"The whole prairie is a boneyard," Len had declared. "Bones buried high on the cliffs above the great rivers are at peace, they have sung their death song and are on their spirit journeys. But other bones are scattered, left where they fell from starvation, disease, or massacre and those bones are not peaceful, their spirits are deeply disturbed, and destined to wander restlessly until given proper burial."

Van was reminded of recent legislation to repatriate stolen Indian bones back to the tribes. Repatriation. Was that what this trip was all about, retrieving her ancestors' stories and bringing them back, restoring them. For whom? What tribe? Or was she a grave robber herself, disturbing the Reinhardts by digging into their lives after they had died? Maybe she had offended their spirits. Maybe she should leave them buried with their secrets and silences.

From day one of this trip, her own history closed in on her like a pack of hungry ghosts. She recalled the night before she and Len had left for the Boundary Waters. They had a big fight—Len always grousing about injustice, Van always on the defensive. After jamming her thumb hard while pushing gear into the trunk of the car, she finally broke down.

"What if somewhere, sometime, your people and my people not only killed and stole from each other, what if they actually fell in love? We know that must have happened— Mary Jemison lived her whole life with the Seneca. They say she was captive, but she stayed with them because she wanted to, even when she could have left. Those Native women married to the French fur traders, some of them must have loved each other. Look at us—aren't we history, too, doesn't our tiny story live inside a larger one?" She held her thumb. She was crying. "These perpetual wars between white people and Indians, good and evil, men and women, humans and animals, are what break us."

Unused to letting anyone see her cry, she was mad. "Hard edges hurt, Len. I want the in-between, the borderland, where there is warmth and love, where blood is mixed and we are all a part of everything."

It was the last time she used the word love. What a romantic idealist she had been. She was young. She was pregnant and didn't know it. Now she felt sorry for that younger self, for how terribly alone she had been. Then her mother had probably overdosed. Her father became a drunk. And Len had disappeared. She always expected Len to reappear someday, but he never did, except in unwanted memories and dreams. He had left a small splinter of pain in her heart and she felt it festering. What was she supposed to do about that? It had been thirty years. And why in hell was all this past misery chasing her down the cornfields in Iowa of all places— somewhere she had never been in her life?

Water. She needed to get into the water to clear her mind. Brown with leaf tannin, the sweet lake water beckoned like a bowl of root beer. Back in the car, Van slipped out of her cutoffs and changed into a black tank suit. She pushed off from the rocky bottom and with cupped palms separated the water's coolness with the warmth of her body. She parted the lake's gleaming skin by fanning her arms open and pressing the water toward her body. She was a strong swimmer, unafraid but respectful of water's elemental nature. The water caressed like a cool swath of silk. She rolled onto her back and let her floating body rise and fall with the rhythm of her breath. The blue ceiling of sky was decorated with puffs of white clouds. She let her body open, her bones disarticulate, and then she rolled over and reached arm over arm in a vigorous crawl. She grabbed a sideways breath and blew it back through her nose, syncing her arm stroke and percussive kick with the melodious sound of bubbles. Back on shore, she felt clarified, light as air, transparent as water.

The campsite had a small fire grill. Van gathered twigs and birch bark and lit a match to them to ward off mosquitoes, then toweled off and changed back into her cut-offs. The scrape on her leg from the Dumpster fall a week ago was a faded swatch of pink. She pulled her get-away gear out of the trunk. That canoe trip with Len was the last time she had used the equipment, but she never got rid of it.

"Transitional objects," her psychologist friend, Pam, once told her when Van showed up at her office with a ratty stuffed tiger cat from her childhood. "We hold on to those things that give us comfort."

Well, the camping gear had not given much comfort at the time it was used, nor buried for years in the back of her closet. After Len, she had never slept in the tent. What was a transition, anyway?

At the last minute Vanhad thought to buy a can of black bean soup at a convenience store. She emptied it into the blue enamelware pot and set it on the fire grill. She ate the soup out of a chipped enameled mug while the fire burned down to embers.

On a flat spot she shook the tent open. It was musty and moldy from years of disuse, so she decided against sleeping in it. A pack of American Spirit cigarettes had fallen out, a leftover from the Boundary Waters trip. She lit one on the embers. The aromatic smoke was sweet, not offensive in the open air. She inhaled the smoke and blew it out. "Here's a blessing for you, Len, wherever you are. I hope you are alive and if not, I hope your bones are at peace." She tossed the tobacco into the fire where it flared and went out.

When the sun set, Van poured water on the twig fire, rinsed her pot and mug in the lake, put the moldy tent in the stuff sack and tossed it along with the old sleeping bag into the large trash barrel outside the campground. She drove back to the motel, took a long hot shower and slid between cool clean sheets and slept.

# PART THREE

# Return

# MAPLE GROVE, IOWA

## December 1909

EIGHT YEARS AFTER ADAM REINHARDT DIED in his office, Kohler's symptoms had not abated. If anything, they had become worse. Wiedersheim had come to the end of his expertise and suggested a consultation with a highly regarded specialist in Chicago. At his wife's urging, Kohler made the trip and returned to Maple Grove with a suitcase full of expensive remedies, tonics, and powders, but no diagnosis of his ailments. He had lost almost half his previous body weight. His wife had long since given up altering his good suits and passed them on to her portlier relatives. If he had cared to look, Kohler was certain his skeleton protruded under his skin, but he preferred not to investigate how far gone he was. The memory of widow Reinhardt's accusatory letters woke him in the middle of the night. Ghastly dreams of women with hands outstretched, begging for food, for corn and potatoes, haunted his sleep. He had hoped the well-paid doctor in Chicago would determine both cause and cure but the man shook his head, stroked his well-trimmed beard and finally conceded that he had never encountered anything quite like it. He would have to study on it. He would let him know his conclusions in due time.

Not only had Kohler's ability to take nourishment been deeply compromised, but he was also besieged by a fear of the very nature of eating itself. Seeing roast beef swimming in red juices immediately put him in mind of Adam Reinhardt. He could not eat anything that bled. The garden fruits and vegetables his wife so carefully prepared turned on him and he could only ingest the ones that were completely without bruise or blemish. The slightest discoloration instantly turned to rot in his mind. Wormholes especially were an abomination. Soon the very presence of food led to unwholesome thoughts of decay, and he absented himself from the family dinner table. The products from his dairy farm, the heavy cream and fresh cheese and sweet butter that he once prized and savored, turned rancid in his mouth. Easily overwhelmed by nausea that could barely be quelled, he made liberal use of purgatives. He felt cleaner and lighter without the heavy weight of decomposing food in his body. He avoided the dairy operation altogether, preferring the cleanliness of his hardware store with its inoffensive smells of sawdust and nails. But lately, he could hardly abide the presence of his customers, or even his own family. He could smell the odors of food emanating from their bodies and their breath. He had taken to frequent washings of his hands and person in order to avoid contamination. He sought the solitude of his home office where he did accounting, finding it to be the one place where he was free from such troubling anxieties. The evening of his return from Chicago, his wife prepared a delicate vegetable broth diluted with pure spring water, and he retired to his office to catch up with accounts that had accumulated during his absence.

The first order of business was to file the overdue annual report to the court on the Reinhardt business. For the past seven years he had not only been the executor of Adam Reinhardt's estate, but also the guardian of the widow whom he had declared insane and confined to the asylum. Really, he was handling the affairs for the whole family. He prided himself on the fact that he had leased their farmlands to Cyril Hoeffelder who agreed to pay $1000 for the use of the two hundred acres. Ironic that Hoeffelder, the poor widower farmer who had brought Adam Reinhardt's body to Kohler's house to die, had benefited to such a degree from the tragedy. One man's loss, another man's gain. Kohler supposed that was the way of the world, not that he himself had profited from these unwanted duties. Instead, he had paid dearly, with the loss of his health.

In his own estimation he had done quite well for the Reinhardts. But what a thankless task. The older girls continually petitioned him for more money to keep the family in groceries and necessities. Their extravagant penchants for fine woolen cloth and silk thread was not within their budget. They also insisted on sending the younger children to the Catholic school and, between the tuition and the annual pew allotment at St. Bernard's, things added up. Even old Katharina had the luxury of receiving two German newspapers sent from Chicago. Kohler duly listed the items in his annual reports. He wanted no penny to go unaccounted for. He felt justified taking a small annual stipend for his trouble. Especially since he was frequently required to visit the old farmstead to assess the need for repairs to the barn and fencing and such. The court allowed him the stipend without question. And he needed it, as his medical bills had been mounting up.

For the year 1909, Kohler resorted to the typewriter for the annual report. The tremor in his hands had caused his impeccable penmanship to deteriorate.

In the District Court of Iowa in and for Ida Grove
County
In the matter of the Guardianship of
Elizabeth Letty Reinhardt, insane.
J. Kohler, Guardian.

Balance on hand from the Estate: $341.00
Payment of the yearly rent for the year 1909
$1000.00
Total taken in by the estate: $1341.00

As qualified and acting guardian, the aforementioned
Josephus Kohler has expended the following sums for
and in behalf of said estate of Elizabeth Reinhardt, a
person of unsound mind:

For the care of Mrs. Elizabeth Reinhardt at
St. Anthony's Asylum: $172. 00
Groceries and merchandise for family in Maple
Grove: $125.03
To Millers Bros. for meats etc. $25.00
To Fox County Mutual Telephone Company for
telephone rental: $12.00
To St. Bernard's for school, pew rent and church
dues: $45.
To Kohler Hardware for materials and repair at farm
and town residence: $45.70
To Bowman Co. For coal and drayage $14.00
To H. Sorenson for cobs: $2.50
Two subscriptions for German newspapers $3.00
To German Savings Bank, interest for $200.00 on
loan: $14.00

After adding up other miscellaneous items, the balance for the year was $478.00. Kohler took a small satisfaction that despite his declining health he had met his obligations. He sorted the remaining stack of incoming mail by category and noticed a thick envelope from St. Anthony's Asylum in Dubuque. Assuming it to be their yearly bill and report to him as the guardian of Mrs. Reinhardt, he set it aside, although he questioned why it had arrived so much earlier in the year. He also noted that the return address was changed from St. Anthony's Asylum for the Insane to St. Anthony's Sanitarium.

When he got around to opening the envelope the next morning, he was thunderstruck.

*December 10, 1909*

*To Mr. Josephus Kohler, Guardian of Mrs. Elizabeth Letty Reinhardt.*

*Dear Josephus Kohler,*

*We are pleased to inform you as the appointed Guardian, that Mrs. Elizabeth Letty Reinhardt, who has been under our care for approximately seven years, is now in such an improved condition that we are ready to release her out of our custody....*

Kohler's hands shook uncontrollably. He skimmed the rest of the letter, barely comprehending its message. The last paragraph rendered him speechless.

*Since it is so near the joyful season of Christmas, we suggest her release take place immediately so she may be brought back into the family home for the holidays. Please make all necessary arrangements and wire us as to*

*when you plan to pick her up. If you cannot come your-
self, you may send a trusted family member in your place.
She does not require a trained nurse at this time.*

*The final bill for her stay and our services will reach you
after the first of the year.*

*Sincerely Yours,
Dr. Stanley Pierce, Sanitarium Administrator
Dr. Howard Handley, Staff Physician*

Kohler was thrown into a nervous panic, the very thing
the good doctor from Chicago had advised against. Trembling,
he jammed the letter back into its envelope. The yearly reports
from the asylum had always been routine. He did not recognize the doctors' names. Had they undergone a change in ad-
ministration along with the change in name? He had never imagined Mrs. Reinhardt's release, much less her return to Maple
Grove. The doctors declared her harmless. He did not believe it.

He hastened to summon Jacob Reinhardt to discuss the
situation. Jacob could relay the news to the rest of the family.
Speaking with old Katharina in his delicate condition was out
of the question, and the very thought of traveling to Dubuque
to collect the widow was beyond his worst nightmare. Despite his misgivings about Jacob, at least he was a man, and
Kohler was sure he could be counted on to do this duty for
the family with the least amount of unpleasantness. He put a
brief letter to Jacob Reinhardt in the post.

That night Kohler took a double dosage of the new sleeping draught, yet it did not prevent him from a frightful dream
of being pursued by a menacing dough-faced woman carrying
a glistening tray of noxious frosted cakes and glazed pastries.

* * *

With Letty sequestered in Dubuque, I was occupied with the greens and browns of everyday life, each day strictly apportioned—washing, sewing, mending, cleaning, baking, cooking and gardening— my past years on the farm relegated to distant memory. Occasionally I grew lonesome for the cow barn—the *Kuh* cathedral, quiet and solemn in its purpose, the twice a day communion with the warm beasts who offered their nourishment. The *milch* cows with their brown, heaving bodies gave a pleasure whose name I could not find, and I missed them. The dray delivered our milk in glass bottles. Wherever were they now, those compliant cows? I daren't think. The same for Letty.

Seldom did we speak of her. The older girls were taken up with their growing families. Lizzie had moved to South Dakota with her new husband. George worked odd jobs and still lived at home, Margaret started high school and Lena would join her in the coming fall. Hadn't I done my best with them? Since Letty had been forced from my keeping, I found it hard to recall her. Well, that was not exactly true. I fought to forget the events of her last days with us—like a bad stain, her actions left a permanent mark that could not be scrubbed out.

In the middle of December, Jacob came to the house by himself in mid-week, which was unusual. His face was ghostly pale and drawn. I braced myself for tragedy—an accident, an illness, an untimely death.

"*Was*? What has happened?"

"I have been out to see Kohler," Jacob said, his voice faltering. "He requested that I take the train to Dubuque to bring Mama Letty home for Christmas."

"*Was*?" I repeated several times, cupping my hand to my ear as if I were deaf.

"Kohler has gotten a letter from the asylum in Dubuque assuring him she has had a full recovery."

"*Was?* How? How is that possible? We have had no word of it. There must be some mistake."

Such an absurd request, as if Kohler was suggesting bringing her back from the dead. Not dead like Adam, or Jacob's baby daughter Florence, or even little Johnnie under gray stones in the cemetery, but dead to our lives as if she were a pickle jar stored on a shelf in the root cellar. Not exactly forgotten, but not at our daily table, either.

I narrowed my eyes. "Is Kohler behind all this? Did he arrange her release because he no longer wants to pay for her care?"

"I doubt that's the case. The man was quite beside himself. He looked deathly ill at the thought of Mama Letty's return. I truly don't believe he had this in mind."

Jacob stood in front of me, his mouth partially opened, as if I could save him from this woeful task. In his big workman's hands he held a fistful of dollars. "Kohler gave me this roll of cash, money for the train and a hotel in Dubuque. I'm to leave on the weekend," he mumbled.

I was tongue-tied. I couldn't find any words to reassure him. None of the family had ever made the long trip to Dubuque to visit Letty. We were all taken up with the tasks of everyday living, not to mention that even thinking about an asylum for the insane filled them with horror. The older girls wrote Letty an occasional dutiful note, announcing the birth of the latest babe or some other such notable event. Letty made brief replies thanking them, but she had given no sign as to how she was faring, or what her life or hopes for her future might be. And what could they possibly have been?

After Jacob left, I reconsidered Kohler's motivation in Letty's return. It was rumored that the man was suffering from some kind of wasting disease, no one knew what. It could not have been cancer or he would be dead by now. But surely something was chewing at him. The last time I saw him coming from his hardware store in town, he looked disheveled, pale and thin as last year's turnip. Not that I was inclined to spend any sympathy on him. The whole town of Maple Grove knew how our family had to petition and account to him for every penny spent. It was disgraceful, not so much for me as for the younger children, as if they were a case for charity, which they certainly were not. Adam may have died, but he did not leave us wanting. I never trusted Kohler's intentions, but at least I could tell from the looks of him that he was not eating up our profits.

As much as I had protested when Kohler sent Letty off to Dubuque, I dreaded her return. Over the years, I helped the family seal the wounds Letty had inflicted by never speaking about her last days. There were scars to be sure, but under my management as the titular head of the household, I felt no need to point out the damage. I had covered my shame at losing her with a determination that we lead a peaceable normal life. I was surprised to find there were benefits to her being gone.

For one thing, Jacob had found more time to visit. Every now and then he came over on a Sunday afternoon and occasionally he brought one of his children. They had seven children, not counting little Florence who had succumbed to influenza. My heart softened to see Jacob with his little boy, Johnnie, who had just turned three in October. Although he never said it, I believed Jacob named him after baby Johnnie who died so long ago. Jacob's Johnnie was my favorite, and he knew it for he climbed onto my lap, where he sat like a little prince. His features favored Jacob's, those dark almond-shaped eyes, and such a bright and handsome boy among all those girls.

The pleasure of Jacob's visits was not without its pinch of sorrow. Such sweet affection unfastens a rusty door where fleeting thoughts of how my life would have turned out if things had gone differently. If I had claimed Jacob as my son, he would know me as his true mother and his children would know me as their grandmother. But that life never happened, and I cannot sustain the thought of it, and my heart objects strongly to be reminded. I reproach myself but cannot weep tears that had long since gone dry.

On the Sunday afternoons when Jacob alone seeks my company, I occupy the upholstered chair with my mending and Jacob sits in the rocker with his pipe. I sense a melancholic streak and suspect he has taken to drink. One time I glanced his way and saw his face wet with tears. There were so many possible reasons, but I did not inquire as to their cause. I presumed the anguish of Letty's last days was topmost, although we had an unspoken agreement to never refer to what happened. Unspeakable. At least Jacob had never seen fit to question me any further and that was a mercy. Maybe he had forgotten.

I was always a whisker away from speaking with him, but I feared the aftermath and did not see how any good could come of it. How could I explain something to him that I did not understand myself? The past was past, and silence was the only weapon I found to defend myself. Jacob had lived more than forty years without this knowledge. Why start something now? I could not undo a decision that was made so many years ago—like unraveling a complex knitting project long after the work had been completed. I couldn't start over. I had written against that silence in my travel memory book. Not that anyone would ever read my words.

As if I had let the reins go slack on a wandering pony, I pulled my mind to the present. The older girls were in a fluster at the prospect of their mother's return and the younger children were confused and fearful. Seven years is enough time for a Biblical feast or famine but not enough time to erase the memory of the day she was sent away. Contrary to my desire to banish thoughts of her, they went to the night Letty attempted to take her own life with the butcher knife, and how she had disavowed herself as Jacob's mother, saying he belonged with the savages. *Gott im Himmel!* How had she ever come up with that? It was completely *unheimlich*, uncanny. I could have killed her, right there on the spot, helping her finish what she had so badly botched. Luckily, she went no further and her delirium was quickly discredited as the ravings of an insane mind, a woman under a demented spell.

I did not relish faintheartedness or rehearsing Letty's madness. On hearing the news of her return, I quickly took matters into my own arthritic hands. If Letty was coming home for Christmas we would make the most of the holiday.

Against Kohler's strenuous objections, I instructed the older girls to purchase a new dining table and chairs for ten dollars and we re-papered Letty's old bedroom walls with a cheerful print of blue flower sprigs. We mopped and scoured and scrubbed every inch of the house. Letty would return to a home that was spotless, filled with smells of freshly baked Stollen with raisins and lemon citron, and sugar dusted *Pfeffernüsse*. I would make *Maman's* little French jam tarts. We would have a real Christmas tree with candles and all the children would get a fresh orange. It would be what the older girls called an "old-fashioned" Christmas.

I supposed I was old-fashioned, but this was the only kind of Christmas celebration I had ever known as a child in Heidesheim. With Adam's death and the move off the farm, everyone forgot the old ways. Hardly anyone spoke good German anymore except maybe in the privacy of their homes. The Chicago *Wochenblatt* reported a growing problem with Germany and the Kaiser, and all German speakers in America were urged to learn English and to become good American citizens. I had no objection. I could grasp the language well enough. The French I had spoken so many years past was kept stored in my travel memory book. They say old people can forget what they had for breakfast that morning, but they can remember clearly what happened fifty years ago. They call it a second childhood or some such thing. I judged my mind to be sharp as a tack although my tongue had lost some of its edge. Surely at seventy-eight, I qualified as an old person, but it was not my childhood I was remembering. It was as if the stone wall I had erected to contain the past had crumbled and the wild weeds of memory had worked their way into every crevice.

The day Jacob was scheduled to return with Letty, I pulled the travel memory book from my apron pocket where I carried it during the day. I wanted to recall the past, and not think of what was coming toward me.

*In the shadows of the cabin, I saw old grand-mère Lucy in her worn calico dress and moccasins. She was chewing on cedar twigs with her few remaining teeth and hummed to herself in a low whining voice.*

*For days Pascal put off our leaving. "We must help them put in the summer garden." I did not mind or make objection for, in truth, I was happy with these two peculiar women in their rude little cabin with its chinked walls and rough plank floors, and I could see there was much work to be done. I had grown much stronger in my body and the digging of the garden was not a chore. We planted corn and squash and pumpkins, dropping the seeds into a pretty little patch of rich dark earth. Marie spoke to me only about what was at hand, and the old woman, Lucy, spoke to me not at all. But I believe she watched me for sometimes I would catch her and our eyes would meet for a tiny moment.*

*The two women kept up a constant banter with Pascal, their voices pelting him in French and Indian. I sensed the pleasure he brought them, and I must admit I began to get a little drunk on it myself, as if I were imbibing from the finest spirits to be had. My heart had known no feeling with which to compare. This joy betrayed no trace of obligation or duty, not insured by any binding ties. It was, I came to know, a love whose very freedom gave it life.*

*In the first days of June, after the garden was set, Marie and Lucy began the seasonal work of cleaning inside the cabin. With Pascal's help we hauled out all the bedding, the mattresses and ticking, the old blankets and quilted covers. We strung up lines and hung out their winter weary covers so they could freshen in the warm dry breezes of early summer. The straw mattresses were arranged on the new greening grasses outside the cabin to let the warmth and cleaning rays of the sun enter them. There was such an air of gaiety as all the somber gloom of winter was shaken out and sent away. It was as if we had turned the little cabin inside out like an old gray sock and in the little patch of yard, the many-colored quilts and coverlets bloomed like a fresh flower bed of blue, red and yellow calico. The air was warm and fragrant with the blossoms of crab apple and wild cherry.*

*All of us fell into such a giddy state that it was soon decided it was time to cook and eat our evening meal outside, something the two women did all summer long to forego the heat inside the cabin. It was like a summer picnic we might have had in the old country. But I could not compare as the food was of this land. Marie made a stew thickened with dried corn silk, a handful of the rice that grows wild, mixed with some strips of dried meat to which she added great handfuls of fresh spring greens Lucy and I had collected that day. We sat on the spread of blankets—Pascal in his natural* cross-legged way, Marie and I content to be on the ground with our legs folded under the skirts of our cotton dresses. Old Lucy sat with one leg tucked under like a girl, her other leg stretched straight, a moccasin and ancient legging peeping from beneath her dress of faded blue calico.

The twilight gathered around us as the last evening bird made its song and the night opened its dark cloak. Slowly, the two women took their bed quilts and headed back into the cabin to sleep. Pascal asked me in his joking way if I minded sleeping out under the stars in the sweet evening air as had been our habit on the trail. I agreed to his proposal, and we made our bed with the freshened mattress and remaining coverlets; the night sky overhead was darkest blue of indigo, and the stars were scattered in profusion above us.

Pascal and I had learned to find our way into sleep together for many nights on the trail, but this was the first night we found our way into each other's arms. He drew me close and when I laid my head upon his chest it was as if my ear were placed upon a drum, and the steady beat of his strong heart sought and found my own and the very earth did send its pulse to join us, and the sky made a wondrous starry blanket overhead. My body lost all sensation of solidity and hardness as if my bones had disappeared, leaving me with a softened pelt within which I could wrap my Pascal. My mind let loose like milkweed thistle in the wind, and it blew away like feather down on the soft, night breeze.

Pascal spoke, and his words reached up into the deep night sky and called the stars to come closer in their brightness. His words fell over me like soft evening dew and I was laid open like the freshly turned garden, and I felt the same eagerness of the earth for greening life in my own body. Pascal brought down the Milky Way and wrapped me in its silken gauze. The nearby trees whispered in the gentle night winds *and Pascal's voice joined them. My breath was all I knew of who I was, and it met and combined with his and we became one, breathing with the nighttime earth and sky. Marie's old dog lay at our feet. For three straight nights we slept in this way and Pascal showered me with stories and his love and I did gratefully receive all he had to give.*

A life lived in another language. How had I ever found those words? Nothing before or since had opened such a vein of poetry. Was it possible to keep a single year alive, a winking timeless sparkle amidst the dull aching of my drab days?

Church bells rang the noon Angelus, and I stashed my book and pencil stub into the apron's deepest pocket. I felt dizzy. Whatever was I thinking? There was still so much to be done before Jacob returned with Letty.

*       *       *

The pink blush of dawn announced a good day for travel, although it felt particularly cold for early December. Jacob dressed in his flannel long johns, woolen pants with suspenders and the jacket he wore to church on Sunday; he tucked the fob watch into his vest pocket and went downstairs. No one was awake in the household at such an early hour except for Elizabeth, putting cobs in the cookstove. She handed him his brown wool coat and a small package wrapped in brown paper tied with string.

"You will need nourishment for the train ride. I made a lunch with some slices of fresh bread and German beef sausage and hard yellow cheese." At the doorway she gave him a sympathetic pat on his arm. "Be strong, Jacob, dear."

At the train depot, Jacob bought himself a round-trip ticket to Dubuque and a return ticket for Mama Letty. The station was a new addition in Maple Grove. It was clean with solid wooden benches, and a big potbelly stove whose pleasant warmth warded off the December chill. There had not been any large snowfall yet and the day promised to be clear, so he had no worry about reaching his destination. He sat on the bench with the early morning travelers and waited for the train to arrive from Nebraska, the small suitcase resting on his knees. He felt alone, awkward and out of place. He had not travelled farther than a town twenty miles from the farm since he was a boy. It was the first time in his married life that he would spend a night away from home.

A piercing whistle announced the train's arrival as it pulled into the station with brakes screeching and plumes of steam blowing clouds into the winter air. As soon as it stopped the few local passengers began to board. Jacob was relieved that no one recognized him, as he did not want to explain the purpose of his travel.

He found a seat by the window and settled in. The aisle seat remained empty. Good, he thought, no need for unwanted conversation. Jacob suspected that Kohler had appointed him for this mission because he himself was not up to it. Jacob could not blame him. He deeply dreaded the undertaking. Who knew what he would find at the other end? The long hours of the trip home with Mama Letty were something he did not relish. What would they have to say to each other after all this time?

He still felt the sharp sting of her words when she said he was not of her blood. Oftentimes he had thought to question Tante Kate as to what Mama Letty had meant by that outburst. Questions formed and unformed in his mind like passing clouds, but he could never find the desire for answers strong enough to let them take shape. He never asked. He chalked it up to Mama Letty's deranged state of mind and it seemed best that he avoid any mention of that terrible night.

Jacob felt unfit to enter the place where Mama Letty had been locked up for all these years. It frightened him to imagine large numbers of insane people inhabiting the same building day after day. What fiendish howls of misery and hellish suffering must come out of such a place. The prospect was terrifying. He opened his suitcase and found the pebbled glass bottle of Old Guckenheimer he had secretly wrapped in his flannel nightshirt.

Jacob and Otto met regularly in town. They never found much to say to each other, but Otto always brought Jacob a welcomed jug of homemade hooch from his establishment in Early. When Otto learned he was going to get Mama Letty from Dubuque, he must have felt extra pity for he gave Jacob a bottle of real Scotch whiskey, quite a gift since you had to travel out of state if you wanted expensive liquor in a bottle instead of a jar. The whiskey warmed him, and he closed his eyes. It was going to be a long ride. At Maple River Junction, he changed trains and boarded the Cedar Rapids and Missouri line that would take him due east to Dubuque.

The day was clear, and the sky was a brilliant winter blue. The view from the window drew Jacob's attention. He scarcely recognized the land he remembered from his boyhood journey. Back then the high, rolling prairie grasses had stretched out toward the horizon with very few signs of human dwelling or enterprise. Now that vast range had been plowed and planted and made into farm fields that lay cheek by jowl, no open space between them. The yellow stubble fields had a fine dusting of snow. Clusters of farmhouses, barns and outbuildings sat like small ships anchored in the pale, rolling sea of cultivated ground. The train stopped at towns where church steeples, water towers, and grain elevators poked into the heavens.

It was a wonder to behold how the prairie had turned from nothing but prairie grasses into farmland in his lifetime, as if the land had fulfilled her promise to those pioneers who emigrated to the western prairie. Papa Adam had declared it a new Eden—a land of milk and honey, he had said. And for some, Jacob supposed, this was true. It took men like Papa Adam to endure the early hardships and not despair when disasters befell, though some misfortunes were harder than others to bear. Jacob was strong in his body, but he was not built like those men; his heart was not wed to the land like a farmer, and it never was or would be. Since his vision of the drought at the creek, he'd rehashed this again and again—always the same questions of why, but never any new answers. After Papa Adam died, Jacob watched the family farm break apart like a chicken coop in a high wind and knew he could do nothing to save it.

His own family was growing in number. He and Elizabeth had seven living children—only little Florence had succumbed to the epidemic of influenza. Such a heartache, and how the sorrow of her death reawakened the memory of little Johnnie who had died in such agony. Losing a child could easily break your spirit and make you question a merciful God. Deeply stricken, Elizabeth was not completely undone by their little girl's untimely death, as her attention was on the next babe she was carrying. Jacob took it harder. He desperately missed little Florence, even though he had the five other girls to keep him happy. And then there was his boy, Johnnie. The older girls doted on him—boys being a rare commodity. Having a large family to care for gave him a secure feeling although it took every ounce of effort to make ends meet, and most often they barely did.

All these thoughts passed through his mind as the train chugged and rattled east towards Dubuque. The rhythm of the rods and pistons lulled him, and he took another long draw on the whiskey bottle, hoping to forget the desperate errand he was running. His body slackened with the sway of the compartment as if he were being rocked in a large cradle. A great weight lifted from his shoulders and in its place came a heavy fatigue. He submitted to its direction and surrendered in resignation to his mission.

As he nodded off, a pulsing sensation like a heartbeat sounded as if someone was whispering, "Jacob, Jacob." Half asleep, he glanced about but could not locate the source of the voice and thought he had been dreaming. An elderly woman had boarded at Maple River Junction and occupied the seat next to him. Tightly wrapped in a knitted shawl, her head tilted toward his shoulder in sleep. He reached into his left pocket where he had stashed the bottle and took another long swallow. Soon the rocking motion overtook him.

Behind the curtain of his closed eyes, the land flew past, following the rise and fall of the gently rolling prairie. Suddenly the farmlands were gone, and all that was visible was the thick tough mantle of prairie grass as if all the little houses and barns and fields and livestock had been swept away by a great cleansing wind. The wide-open sky with gray and white shreds of racing clouds and the outstretched curves of the land were all that existed, and it was not desolate or wild, it was alive, fresh, and singing.

"Jacob, Jacob," the voice whispered, *"This is the land we once knew, the land that was pried from our hands piece by piece until we no longer lived on any of it: Beginning at the upper fork of the Des Moines River, and passing the sources of the Little Sioux and Floyd Rivers, to the fork of the first creek which falls into the Big Sioux or Calumet on the east side: thence along a line to the north west corner, thence to the high lands between the waters falling into the Missouri and Des Moines, passing to the high lands along the dividing ridge between the forks of the Grand River; thence along*

*the high lands or ridge separating the waters of the Missouri*
*from those of the Des Moines, to a point opposite the source*
*of Bayer River, and thence in a direct line to the upper fork of*
*the Des Moines, the place of beginning.*

"*Our ancestor's bones are buried everywhere on this land,*
*but they cannot rest; the plow constantly claws at them, the*
*cows live on top of them, the cornfields press down on them,*
*the people that live here know nothing, their spirits are covered*
*in grey shrouds of ignorance. We are heartsick and lonely for*
*this land like a child that has lost its true mother. Our children*
*will never know the rivers; the small streams that run like little*
*life-giving veins, we can no longer send them out on the hunt.*
*What will become of us? All is forgotten. All. All. All.*"

The train brakes pumped and shrieked to a stop at the
depot in Dubuque. Jacob looked around. He must have heard
the conductor call out the station stops along the way and put
them into the disturbing dream. The old lady next to him, her
shawl loosened, her head touching his shoulder, was loudly
snoring. Jacob patted her arm to wake her and then rubbed
his eyes and ears to clear away the dream. Frightened that
his mind had become unbalanced, he blamed it on too much
drink. His legs ached. He had been working too hard this
past fall, and this trip to collect Mama Letty had pushed him
past his limit. Suitcase in hand, he stumbled from the train.

The streets along the river were lit by lamps and filled
with horse-drawn carriages and even a few automobiles. The
great waters of the Mississippi were clogged with steamboats,
their lights sparkling and inviting in the cold night. He had
heard from Otto that people could gamble and drink in those
boats, as the laws of the land did not apply to the wide waterway. Feeling like a bumpkin, he stood with mouth agog as
folks bustled about this famous river town—a hodge-podge
of Irish, Swedes, Norwegians, Germans, of course, and so

many eastern Yankees. Across the street from the depot was Hoffmeister's, the German hotel that had been recommended by the train master. Jacob carefully signed his name on the register. His throat constricted, and he swallowed hard against the lump of sadness. He was a long way from the cozy warmth and the comfort of his wife and children.

Jacob asked for the cheapest room available, and once inside, he sat on the edge of the single bed, snapped open the suitcase, unwrapped the brown paper parcel, and ate Elizabeth's packed lunch. On the wooden washstand he found a glass tumbler and filled it with a long pour of whiskey. The burning heat spread quickly through his body. He was ever so grateful for Otto's generosity. Foregoing his nightshirt, he undressed down to his flannels, slipped in between thin sheets and a rough blanket, and was carried off to dreamless sleep.

The next morning he paid the bill and asked for a livery to take him to St. Anthony's. The hotel clerk glanced warily at Jacob as if the very mention of that place gave him the shakes. Under the clerk's scrutiny, a hot creep of shame made his cheeks burn. When the livery drew up to the gate of St. Anthony's Asylum, Jacob saw iron railings surrounding the great brick building and understood the clerk's reaction. He felt an overwhelming desire to turn away. Surely it was the largest building he had ever seen in his entire life. How had Mama Letty managed to stay alive in such a place for seven years?

Jacob approached the stairs to the great double doors and rang the buzzer. He announced himself and his mission, and a silent woman in a white veil accompanied him into a waiting room where he sat until someone called, "Mr. Jacob Reinhardt."

A cold draught entered with her. Surely, they had made a mistake. The woman they escorted into the admissions office was not Mama Letty, but someone else. He was about to call attention to the error, but his tongue stuck in his mouth. She came toward him as if from a very far distance and even when she was right in front of him, she was far away. Her approach felt like death itself coming to meet him. How pale she was. Her eyes had lost the sharp blue of cornflowers, replaced by the blue of a bleached-out sky. Her hair, no longer dark auburn, had gone to ashen gray, giving her the overall appearance of a specter. Only her body, fuller and rounder than ever it was before, lent the impression of solid substance. But the extra weight gave her an unnatural gravity, making her movements slow and deliberate. Her ill-fitting woolen coat was too small to button around her swollen body. How different she had become in this place: the old fluttering sparrow-like motions, the quick, intense darting eyes, the fingers flying away at her tasks were replaced by a heaviness that felt unwholesome, bloated, disastrous.

The nurse and doctor shook Jacob's hand, congratulated Mrs. Reinhardt, and showered them with good wishes for the holiday season. Jacob took up the pen that was offered and with a hand that felt like wooden stumps put his signature on the two release documents and received in exchange an envelope containing her discharge instructions. The nurse ushered them through the polished wooden double doors that snapped locked behind them.

Slowly, as if in a dream, he held Mama Letty's elbow and descended the wide set of marble steps to the large circular driveway where the livery awaited them. Jacob was taking Mama Letty home. He still did not believe it was really she.

# MAPLE GROVE

## JUNE 19, 2000

MONDAY MORNING. Van gave Dee Dee her order for an egg salad on whole wheat to go.

"You can't survive on egg salad and black coffee, hon. How about some onion rings or fries to go with it?"

"Fries sound good." Van checked her watch. "I'm off to Ida Grove. Shirley's combing through documents for me. I hope to finish this project soon. It's been a bit depressing."

"I guess that's what happens when you go digging too deep into the past. You never know who or what's going to turn up. That's why people are buried."

Van was relieved that Dee Dee didn't press her for more details. Dee Dee was in on the town's happenings but she was not a gossip. She had her job and stuck to it. She wrapped the sandwich in wax paper, put the dill pickle on top, and put the fries in a paper cup. She handed Van her lunch. "Here you go, hon. I'm not used to making food to go. Most folks want to sit around and talk while they eat. Which reminds me, Helen is back from South Dakota. She would like to see you, wants to talk. She's usually here in the late morning."

274 | PATRICIA REIS

"Did she say what about?"

"Nope. She just said tell Van Reinhardt I want to talk with her the next time she's in."

"Thanks, I'll stop by tomorrow morning." Maybe Helen had remembered some tidbit about the Reinhardts after all, and then Van could leave. She was itching to put this trip behind her.

Van drove back to Ida Grove to see what, if anything, Shirley had found. After swimming in the lake and eating soup from a twig fire she felt refreshed, back in her body in a fundamental way, ready to be done with this search that seemed to lead only deeper into darkness.

Shirley was waiting for her. Dressed in a grayish sweater and slacks, she was still a drab bird. Her eyes batted furiously behind her black frame glasses and the two creases in her forehead had deepened. She did not look like the bearer of good news.

"What do you have for me, Watson?"

Shirley handed her copies of documents. "I kept going through the early 1900s looking for stuff on Kohler and found these. Read them in order," she directed. "And read them here. I want to know what you make of this."

Van took the papers and sat in the chair that Shirley offered. A trill of anxiety pulsed.

St. Anthony's Asylum for the Insane
Dubuque, Iowa
1902 Record Book: page. 63

Admission: July 31, 1902
Patient #8837.
Age: 46 years. Birth Date: 12/31/1856
Height: 5' 6." Weight: 100 lbs. Eyes: Blue. Hair: Brown.
Marital Status: Widow

Dependents: 4 children under age 20.

Occupation: Housekeeper

Education: Common School

Religion: Roman Catholic

Nativity and Occupation of Father: German, Farmer, deceased.

Nativity and Occupation of Mother: German, Housewife, deceased.

Guardian: Josephus Kohler, Maple Grove, Iowa

Report: Mrs. Reinhardt was brought to Saint Anthony's Asylum in a poor mental and physical condition. She had tried on two different occasions to commit suicide by jumping off a moving train and by attacking her own person with a knife. She shows the effects of her rash act by scars on her neck and wrist. She was placed in isolation and kept absolutely quiet for a week. Her condition improved sufficiently for her to be allowed the freedom of the lower floor and she was also allowed to mingle with the other patients.

The patient remains deranged and is operating under an insane delusion much of which seems directed at her guardian and others whom she thinks are stealing food and land from herself and others. She also believes her husband was caused to suffer mortal injury by those who were plotting against her.

Prognosis: Poor. Patient will remain in asylum custody.

Admitting Physician: Dr. Hamilton R. Danvers

"Sounds like she was pretty far gone. Paranoia. Looks pretty hopeless," Van said. "I doubt this was all that unusual, women going off the rails with too much hardship and tragedy. Didn't they use to call it Prairie Fever? It's sad. She probably spent the rest of her life there."

"That's what I thought, too, until I read the next document. It was written seven years later. Get a load of this. No more Asylum for the Insane."

St. Anthony's Sanitarium
Dubuque, Iowa
*December 10, 1909*

*To: Mr. Josephus Kohler, Guardian of*
*Mrs. ElizabethLetty Reinhardt.*

*Dear Josephus Kohler,*

*We are pleased to inform you as the appointed Guardian that Mrs. Elizabeth Letty Reinhardt, who has been under our care for approximately seven years, is now in such an improved condition that we are ready to release her out of our custody. She has shown no signs of her initial unbalanced behavior, nor has she demonstrated any tendencies of violence toward herself or others. She is neither melancholic nor overly elated in her moods. She is free from all irritable restlessness and notions of conspiracy. She is, on the whole, meek and docile. She has acted kindly toward the other patients on her ward and has expressed only good will towards her caretakers. In sum, it is our considered opinion that she has responded well to our treatments, and, with the following restrictions and requirements, we feel confident that she may resume her place within the bosom of her family.*

*She must be kept to a strict routine regarding her habits of sleeping and eating. This has proved most beneficial during her stay here. She has gained a full fifty pounds under our regimen. She must take a daily walk in the fresh air no matter the weather. She must be kept away from spicy foods, hot baths, and any excitable people or situations. We recommend that you remain in the position as her guardian until such time that she no longer requires your services.*

*It is not often that we see such a recovery in these cases, and we are certain that when her family sees how greatly improved she is they will gladly welcome her home. Since it is so near the joyful season of Christmas, we suggest her release take place immediately so she may be brought back into the family home for the holidays. Please make all necessary arrangements and wire us as to when you plan to pick her up. If you cannot come yourself, you may send a trusted family member in your place. She does not require a trained nurse at this time.*

*The final bill for her stay and our services will reach you after the first of the year.*

*Sincerely Yours,*
*Dr. Stanley Pierce, Sanitarium Administrator*
*Dr. Howard Handley, Staff Physician*

"Whoa! Do you think they actually cured her? After all those years? After their dire prognosis?" Van wrinkled her nose. "Something doesn't add up. There must have been an effort to modernize their treatment practices. Probably some well-meaning reformers were trying to do that. I wonder how it worked out for Letty. Quite the bombshell for the family, I imagine, having her come back to live with them after all that time. Strange."

"I can't believe it was for the best," Shirley said. "I don't believe they were really looking out for the patient's interest. It might have been more a financial matter."

Van raised her eyebrow at Shirley's skepticism. But then she was privy to people's private documents and must know more than most about the darker side of their motivations. Could Kohler have finagled a release instead of having to pay for her care? Reading his careful accounting, Van had felt a twinge of sympathy for the executor and his ever-increasing responsibilities for this unfortunate family. Maybe the family wanted the extra money.

"Okay, Watson, what's next?" Now Van was flirting. She missed Em and was so grateful to have Shirley as a comrade to keep her steady in this increasingly bizarre turn of events. She trusted Shirley in the same way she trusted Em—both of them practical, unflappable, seen-it-all, no-nonsense women.

"I think you should go back to the library and search *The Chronicle* microfilm for December 1909, and January 1910, too. This was just the kind of story they would be eager to report. 'Mrs. Adam Reinhardt Returns from Insane Asylum.' I'll give Marion a call and tell her you'll be there in an hour."

Van checked her watch. She could make it back to Maple Grove in time. She put the papers in her pack and spontaneously gave Shirley a hug, surprising them both. Shirley's body felt bony and stiff, but when Van apologized, Shirley patted her arm. "I know, dear, this must be very stressful. Be sure to let me know what you find. You take care, now."

Back in her car, Van turned on the air conditioner. She felt buoyed by Shirley's camaraderie. It was like the old days with Em when they discovered some little-known fact that was the key to a larger mystery. Maybe writing detective novels would be a good choice for a second career, except there always had to be a dead body in the first five pages.

So, after seven years Letty had been sprung from the asylum. There were questions. How did she swing it? Was it possible she had recovered? How did the family adjust to her return? Van was drawn to the spaces between the known facts, and her imagination was all she had to go on. She was past the week she had promised her dad. She felt released from his directive and was working for herself now. She had Shirley and a team of women working with her. It made her happy.

The corn had grown at least a foot in the past week. Wasn't that the old saying? "Knee high by the Fourth of July?" The drive was mesmerizing, and she let her thoughts go to Letty. Was it possible that she had been cured enough to be sent home? Maybe she wasn't crazy after all. *Maybe Mother wasn't, either.*

# MAPLE GROVE

ON THE TRAIN RIDE BACK TO MAPLE GROVE, Letty tried to recall her family. They must be wondering how she ever managed to win a release from such a place as St. Anthony's in her mind she rehearsed what she would say to them. Truly it was not all that difficult, but it had taken years to accomplish.

Once Letty ciphered the code of which actions and behaviors the doctors and staff attendants desired, she made every attempt to conform herself into a model patient. After the initial stay in solitary on the top floor, she was brought to Hall 6 where she was allowed to mingle with other women who were proclaimed insane but not so completely that they could not function with manners proper to human beings.

It was obvious what was not desirable—excessive shows of emotion, constant wringing of hands or incessant weeping, loud or riotous laughter, humming, singing of hymns or popular songs, no yelling, or shouts of profanity. Of course, there was always plenty of that kind of commotion. Nor could they be completely silent. Speechlessness was viewed with great suspicion. Nor could they complain or vent any malice toward those who had seen to their incarceration, no matter the amounts of violation or injustices that had been applied to their person. They could not bemoan the loss of home and children. After all, hadn't they been sent to Saint Anthony's because they were incapable of keeping house or caring for their families?

Proper behavior was not the only standard. The good doctors required adherence to strict hygiene. Certain practices were deemed particularly wholesome—a forced eight hours of sleep, even for those incurable insomniacs whose illness would not let them rest, and three large meals a day, even for those who could not bear to swallow a morsel of food and often regurgitated into their bowls. Any form of food refusal was met with vigorous reprisals of forced feedings. They wanted the patients to eat. And so Letty ate, every single bit that was placed in front of her, and sometimes off her neighbor's plate at the table if she could do so. Eating required effort as the weekly round of meals was repetitive, and much of the food ill-prepared and of a starchy quality with very little meat and no sauces. But Letty ate and ate.

Along with a robust appetite, personal cleanliness ranked high on the list of wholesome virtues—if a person could manage to bring such a thing about. God forbid if a woman showed herself incompetent in that direction, she was automatically consigned to Hall 9. Letty had never been sent there, but she had heard of its dungeons from the few sorry refugees who had managed to make their escape. The staff's treatment for offenses against hospital regimens was swift and often harsh—heavy doses of chloral, along with cold baths that continued for hours, and lock-up in a dimly lit solitary room for days. These were assigned to the unfortunate ones who could not meet the standards. Letty quickly ascertained that a model patient was required to show a meek and compliant disposition along with complete adherence to all prescribed regimens. Especially approved by the staff were small polite phrases and occasional praise for the caregivers, no matter what ill treatment they dispensed; good wishes expressed toward families, whether or not they deserved such; and any offering of aid and assistance to those patients who were incapable of turning themselves into normal-looking and ordinary-acting human puppets.

What happened next, she would tell no one. She had been a resident in Hall 6 for one week when she smelled wood smoke. Certainly there were no fireplaces allowed in the asylum. And nobody else seemed to notice the distinctive odor. Letty clutched her arms against her chest. A new inmate had been brought in, and she could not believe her eyes. There she was, the Blanket Woman, her old informer and tormentor; her brown face was lined with age, her lank grey hair twisted into loose braids that hung down over a baggy, hospital-issue dress. Letty couldn't help but stare as the woman caught her eye and glared. She was mute, never a good sign. Probably waiting for a chance to pounce. The next day she was sheared, her long braids cut into a short hospital bob.

Whenever they were in the hall together, she never took her black glinting eyes off Letty, the two of them stuck together in some wicked way. Letty was pinned under the woman's gaze like a bug under glass, and could not escape her glowering looks or make a complaint without drawing unwanted attention. After a week of this silent persecution, Letty never saw her again. With the woman gone, the wicked voices that had pursued her with such vicious purpose also quieted, and Letty redoubled her efforts to win a release.

Soon she discovered a useful occupation, one that put her in good stead with the attendants, but also opened her heart that had been clamped tighter than the bolted door that locked them all away. A recently instituted law allowed in-habitants of the asylum to write and receive letters complete-ly uncensored. Well, Letty did not believe that to be true. She was certain the letters would be scrupulously inspected. But since she had once schooled herself in a letter's proper style, she made herself available to those poor illiterates who des-perately wished to send messages home.

What tales of woe and sorrow, what pitiful pleadings for a small visit from loved ones, what despondent and hopeless petitions for release. If half the things in their letters were true, anyone would have been driven mad. Of course, Letty did not partake of this privilege of letter-writing for her per-sonal use. Her futile attempts at reaching Josephus Kohler through letters and her shameful failure at convincing Judge Mallett of her cause burned brightly still in her mind. But now letter-writing served another purpose. Like every wom-an entering the asylum, Letty had lost everything of a wom-anly nature—she could no longer cook, serve meals or clean, she was not able to iron, mend or fold, she was no longer known as a wife, mother, or grandmother. Her sole accom-plishment was that she could read and write, and for this skill those who badly needed her help sought her and she learned to care for these hapless women. Feelings she thought were forever gone came alive again the minute she felt needed and useful. Of course, the doctors took notice, too.

Time had no meaning. How long had she been there? She could not recall. She counted seven years, but they all ran into each other in their tedium. Every day was regimented. Only the admittance of a new woman, or the removal of another, created the occasional stir. Behaviors once thought bizarre became commonplace and hardly worthy of notice. Season-al holidays passed, marked by the staff's meager attempts at celebrating. Family visits were often the cause of additional weeping and hollering. Letty was grateful she had no visitors to remind her of her former life, so she was befuddled when the staff pulled her aside one day in early winter.

The doctor was pleased to announce that she was scheduled for release by Christmas. Her mind went blank. She recalled working toward this outcome, then giving it up as a hopeless pursuit. It was common knowledge that the only people who left the ward went to the cemetery or another hall for the more deranged. Hardly ever did they hear of someone released home, especially after being incarcerated for as long as she had been. Rumors had been whispered about reformers who were changing the practices for treating the insane. But Letty was sure their plans never applied to her case.

In her efforts to conform, she had successfully molded herself into a person who could survive the torments of hell and even find usefulness there, but she did not feel capable of meeting the uncertain requirements of the world outside. How could she re-enter a world she no longer knew anything about? She had so accustomed her every thought and action to align with the dictates of the asylum, to the doctor's and the staff's routines and regimens that she was not capable of returning to her old self.

Well, wasn't that old self what got her sent here to begin with? Strange to tell, she had settled into this godforsaken place. The chiding voices in her head had receded and she never heard one peep from that old blanket woman with her ceaseless laments. Letty feigned cheer and gladness to hear of her good fortune, while sheets of terror like summer lightning coursed through her body and rivulets of cold sweat pooled beneath her breasts. Who would they send to fetch her home? She prayed it would not be that hideous nurse.

When the day for her release arrived, she was astonished to see Jacob. At first, he did not appear to recognize her. Well, he did not look like himself either, a little bleary-eyed, older, and quite stiff in his joints. Letty felt the familiar throb of love for him, feelings that she knew were not simply maternal, maybe even unnatural, although who was she to say? He was hers, had been given to her as a gift when she was not yet a woman, like the Virgin Mary at the Annunciation. Such a blasphemous thought. She was as possessive of him as if she owned him, desirous of his admiration, as if he were a suitor. She loved him differently than her other children, and in ways she probably shouldn't have, but it was too late now to change all that.

Of course, Letty wanted to go home with him, but she was terrified of the others, her children, and especially Tante Kate. How would she receive Letty after all this time? Letty pretended to be docile as a baby lamb while Jacob assured the doctors that he would care for her and that the family was glad she no longer needed to be in their custody.

"She would never harm anyone," he said. "After all, she has nine children, and although one died, she raised up all eight of them, including myself." Letty smiled with pride when he spoke to the staff and signed her release papers. Wasn't she right to teach him manners and how to sign his name? How eagerly the staff turned her over to her eldest son, no questions asked. Letty acted the part as if she had rehearsed the script. Observing herself from a far distance, she saw how easily the two of them left the locked premises arm in arm, making such a pretty picture, a middle-aged man gently holding the elbow of his elderly mother, escorting her from confinement.

Once outside the asylum gates, pandemonium broke loose—noise of buggies and vehicles growled on the road like vicious beasts, smells of gasoline mixed with horse droppings made her gag, the sunlight blinded, and at the train station people pushed past her as if she had no substance. The clamor of people moving freely without any watchful eye monitoring their every move made her weak in the knees. Jacob held her arm as she flinched and shuffled. There was no place to hide so she shrank into the smallest, darkest corner of her mind. They did not speak one word during the train ride back to Maple Grove. Letty pretended sleep.

Her situation worsened when she entered the house in Maple Grove. The smells of cooking and baking were hurtful reminders of what she had lost during the years away. She pinched her nose shut against the offending odors. And what had they done to her old bedroom? She didn't recognize the chintz wallpaper, aggressive blue twigs tossed in a snowstorm. The piercing ring of the new telephone installed in the kitchen hallway shot through her like dry lightning. Nothing was as she had left it. Everyone was misshapen and unreal as if seen through a warped glass. Their mouths moved and smiled but their words came from far away and did not match up with the bodies. Someone gleefully shoved a new babe into her arms who immediately set up a ferocious howl. There were other children she did not remember who hid behind their mothers' skirts and stared at her with fearful looks. Jacob was downcast and apologetic. Everyone walked on eggshells. Her youngest boy, George, had become a young man. He stuffed his hands deep in his pants pockets and could not look at her, while the girls made a pretty sham of light pleasantries. It was all wrong. Every last bit of it. Especially Tante Kate.

How very old she had gotten—shriveled, shrunken, an arthritic crow. But more shocking was how everything now revolved around her, how all the family, from Sister Kate to the younger grandchildren, looked up to her. She took her seat at the head of the table like some wizened queen on a throne. The very worst was how she and Jacob had grown so very cozy and familiar, how they had zipped up some gap between them in Letty's absence, how Jacob's attentions went to Tante Kate as if she had become his mother.

Letty's mind had no room for such an idea. Had not everyone called her Mama Letty and agreed he was Letty's from the beginning? She was enraged that Tante Kate had had the pleasure of Jacob's company all the while she had been locked away. But it was more than that. She had the distinct impression she had been purposely kept locked in another kind of dark. What if the arrangement they all had lived with since she was a young girl was an enormous deception? Wasn't she listed as Jacob's mother in the census, in Adam's obituary? No one had objected. How could Tante Kate have the temerity to sustain a falsehood like that for all these years? Maybe even Adam knew more than he ever said. Had she been purposely misled? Allowed to believe an untruth? Even encouraged? If she was not Jacob's Mama Letty, who was she? It was unbearable. She was determined to take the matter up with Tante Kate.

A few mornings later in the kitchen, Letty confronted her. "I want you to tell me the truth about Jacob."

Tante Kate's head snapped around and she gave me a look full of pity. "*Nein, Nein. Was nutzt uns solches Gerede?* What good is talk like that for us?"

Letty pressed on. "If you will not tell me, it is the least I can do to speak to Jacob myself."

Tante Kate stared at her as if she truly was deranged.

Letty countered her look by saying, "I am right-minded enough to know I am not his true mother. And I do believe you know more than you have ever said. In fact, I do believe I have been deceived. It may be too late for me to know the truth but it is not too late for Jacob. It is his right to know where he came from, and if you do not tell him, I will."

"*Schon gut, Letty, schon gut.* All right," Tante Kate replied in an unusually submissive tone. "After all the hubbub of the holiday celebrations and your birthday is over, we will sit down and have a little talk about it."

Tante Kate's agreement came a little too quickly. Letty immediately suspected it was a ploy to shut her up. She had used this trickery before when she tried to tell her about the starving children. This time Letty did not fall for it. She took satisfaction in holding something over Tante Kate, and it gave her a small thrill to think she could command such dominion after all these years. But her surge of power was a damp match and quickly fizzled leaving her without will to pursue the matter.

During the day, Letty wandered the house while the family went about their lives as if she weren't there. Since everyone thought she needed rest, they gave her no useful work, no way to be helpful in the running of the household, and this compounded a feeling of worthlessness. Parked in the upholstered chair in the living room with her mother's patched and mended quilt wrapped around her legs, she stared at the large, framed family portrait that hung over the sofa. She searched it carefully for some clues to her old life. She had a dim memory of her husband but could not recognize the children or recollect anything about the woman seated in the center of the photograph, staring off into space, a demure smile on her lips. A complete stranger. Letty addressed her: "Why should I continue to lend myself to this life when there is nothing left here that is mine? No one needs me. Do I still have any duty to live?" The woman stared into the blank silence with her enigmatic smile. An enormous chasm opened between Letty and the woman in the portrait. She wanted to smash the glass that separated them but was much too weak to make such an effort.

A few days after Christmas, people were talking in the kitchen, and Letty assumed they were making plans to

celebrate her birthday at the turn of the year. The voice of
Josephus Kohler squelched that thought. A freezing chill descended when Kohler came into the living room to pay his
respects. Letty purposely sat like a wrapped mummy dragged
from a tomb. She pulled her face into a grimace and stared at
Kohler without uttering a single word. Why should she speak
to him? What did she have to say to this man who had locked
her away and then even more cruelly brought her back to
suffer this new humiliation—a person responsible for the untold suffering of so many, a man who had refused to answer
her letters. Her grim-lipped stare was meant to convey that
she would meet him some day on her own terms, later when
she was ready, not now in this feeble condition. The thought
made her mouth twist into a smile as she could see right off
that he was not prospering; indeed, he looked quite peaked
and liverish. If she had not identified his voice, she would
never have recognized the man at all.

Kohler made his brief address and quickly retired into the
kitchen where the older girls and Tante Kate spoke to him as
if Letty had lost her hearing.

"She is not doing well. She is losing ground daily. She
doesn't speak. She is so strange. The aberration of her mind
continues. We do not believe she is making the necessary ad-
justments."

"*Nein, Es ist nicht gut*! It is not good. We cannot keep her
here," Tante Kate concluded. Then Josephus Kohler uttered
the words Letty feared were coming.

"It is just as I suspected. It appears her return was prema-
ture. We will have to send her back to St. Anthony's. I will
discuss it with Dr. Wiedersheim in the morning and set up
the arrangements. I am sorry this plan has not worked out as
expected."

Upon hearing these words, Letty knew if they sent her back

she would never return. Worse, she would be consigned to one of the wards for the most insane for the rest of her life. She thought the hateful voices had left her in Dubuque. With this turn of events they swarmed her mind like a plague of chinch bugs, eating up all green hope. *She wants you sent away. You should never have confronted her about Jacob. She never wanted you back. She is taking her revenge. She has won.*

That evening, Letty told Tante Kate she wished to sleep downstairs on the davenport. "I will rest much better by myself," she lied.

When the whole household was fast asleep, Letty pushed her mother's quilt aside, put her bare feet on the floor and crept past the kitchen onto the back porch. She had checked it all beforehand and knew exactly where everything was. It wasn't that she wanted to die. It was the only thing that would bring her peace of mind and the only means that was at hand. She unscrewed the top of the can. Fumes filled her nose; the smell was terrible. Quickly, she poured the kerosene down the front of her nightdress, surprised by how cold it felt. And then she lit the match.

\* \* \*

Kohler was bedridden for days with a high fever that burned his skin and brought terrible hallucinations. He could not purge the news of Mrs. Reinhardt's horrible death from his mind. His wife collected dishpans of fresh snow and bathed him with cool water as he raved.

His fever spared him from attending Mrs. Reinhardt's funeral, but he did feel a momentary pinch of sympathy for poor Father Storch who was due to retire in the summer. This funeral was probably one of his last duties. Kohler was sure Storch had to wrangle with the higher-ups for permission to give a Catholic burial. The clergy abhorred suicides and strictly speaking were not authorized to bury them in the Catholic cemetery. Storch probably called the death "accidental." The family's agony must have been taken into consideration, because the church officials had agreed to give the widow a final resting place next to her husband.

The morning his fever broke and the cold clarity of reason returned, a powerful resolution had taken hold. His first words were to his wife.

"Pack up everything. We are leaving this town."

With that plan in motion, Kohler felt himself purged and purified in a way that had eluded him for years. It was more than the fact that he was no longer in the throes of the fever; something deeply fundamental had shifted.

Kohler entered his home office that was not as yet disassembled. He needed the desk to complete his final paperwork. Before she left, his wife had set up the makeshift cot and the room was warmed by the woodstove. All in all it was actually quite cozy and adequate to his needs for temporary quarters until he finished out his business.

Kohler steered his mind away from thoughts of the last person to have occupied the cot in his office, and gave himself over to the accounting. He called Augustus Schmidtz for assistance in preparing the papers for the final probating of the widow's estate. Of course, Mrs. Reinhardt had been in no condition to leave a will. But he did not imagine this would pose any problem. Since he had all the pertinent information on the family already, he assumed this final executorship closure would merely be a matter of signing off on the paperwork.

Kohler came close to a relapse when a document arrived by special post. He read and reread the petition made to the court. Jacob Reinhardt had called for the court to make an inquiry into Kohler's doings along with a request to be appointed executor himself.

In a fury, he posted an urgent notice to Jacob Reinhardt demanding a meeting at his earliest convenience. He had to nip this idiotic plan in the bud. He was not going to let these people destroy him at this late date. He had no intention of leaving Maple Grove with a bad name trailing behind him like some foul odor. Not after all he had already done for this family. What a disgrace! He was overcome with indignation and worked to control himself. His stomach had already soured and was primed for another attack of dyspepsia.

Jacob Reinhardt appeared for the meeting the next day, and Kohler politely offered his condolences. He could see that Mrs. Reinhardt's death had beaten the man down. Kohler's persnickety nose told him that Jacob had already fortified himself with strong drink. He must have been under the influence when he petitioned the court. How did he think he could take things over by himself? He could not even read. Kohler was sure of it. Nor could Jacob afford the court's required bond or the expensive attorney that had probably helped him prepare the petition. No doubt in the immediate aftermath of Mrs. Reinhardt's horrible death, Jacob was looking for someone to take the blame. Kohler understood such feelings well for he had them, too. But try as he might, he could not find one person on whom to hang any accusation and make it stick, not even on himself. He had made a scrupulous examination of his actions. In the end, he concluded, no one was innocent, everyone was culpable, and so no one could be charged.

Everyone was overripe with recriminations. Letty's horrible death spared no one; it had blasted them all. He found himself glad to have called this meeting for he hoped that a rational discussion of his past actions and intentions would put Jacob's mind at ease and settle this unfortunate challenge to the executorship before it went any further. In an unexpected upsurge of paternal concern, Kohler reached out his hand.

It was as if Mrs. Reinhardt's death opened a door between them that had been previously locked. Kohler lost his prior irritation and took great pains to explain to Jacob what the transactions had been over the course of the last years since Adam Reinhardt's death and outlined his plans to settle Mrs. Reinhardt's affairs as she had died intestate.

"As far as I can tell, you are a duly appointed heir and stand to partake of the profits from the sale of the farmland. This whole thing could be a fairly simple matter for all concerned."

Shamefaced, Jacob confided, "Mr. Kohler, my family is in dire financial straits and we would greatly benefit if I could be paid off early."

So this was what he was after. The appeal was objectionable to Kohler's way of thinking, but wanting no further trouble, he explained, "It will mean you might not get as much money in the long run."

"I understand. But my needs are immediate. And I wish to settle the outstanding loan of eight hundred dollars against Adam Reinhardt's estate, minus the interest, if you are agreeable."

Despite his prior judgment, Kohler saw Jacob Reinhardt in a different light. Here was a man who had been caught in hideous events not of his own making. Not that he was blameless or above reproach—none of them were. But it appeared he had taken the brunt upon himself, and it had clearly taken its toll. Of course, no one had forced him to have so many children. He could have done something about that liability. But by all accounts, Jacob was truly devoted to his large family and did not appear to resent their claims on him. Kohler was aware that Jacob labored strenuously for their sake and he admired that in the man. Although he still questioned why he had moved off the farm, Kohler was certain it was not because he was lazy or wanted an easy life like his brother, Otto. He had no wish to pursue this line of questioning with Jacob. Nor did he see fit to pursue the circumstances of Jacob's birth and parentage. These interrogations were no longer a matter of consequence.

Mrs. Reinhardt's death made them strange comrades. It was as if they had been in a terrible war, fighting each other on opposing sides. Now that the war was over, they could meet as two men. There was nothing left to do but respect the other's courage, the battle having come so close to nearly killing them. Like all wars the originating cause was lost, forgotten. The only thing that mattered now was the ceasing of hostilities and a peaceful settlement.

By the time the sun had gone down and the electric lamp turned on, Kohler and Jacob Reinhardt emerged from their meeting with what each of them needed—-Jacob had the promise of money soon to come, and Kohler had the outstanding debt of eight hundred dollars settled and the hope of quickly finishing this business and joining his family in Colorado.

That night as Kohler was filing the final reports, he felt the presence of Adam Reinhardt. For once, he did not feel haunted by him. Instead, he felt the long-awaited release of the arrangement made while Reinhardt lay dying in the very room he was now working in. Everything Adam Reinhardt had labored to create was about to be sold off to others eager to pursue their own aspirations. His heirs would be flush with cash money but not with land—a sorry end to the immigrant farmer's hopes and dreams. What his children would make of their inheritance was anybody's guess. It was not Kohler's concern anymore. He was done. After finishing his paperwork, he reached into the back cubbyhole of his desk and retrieved the stack of pale blue envelopes that Mrs. Reinhardt had sent years ago. Although it had been within his rights, he never pressed charges against the widow for sending threats through the mail. He opened the woodstove. The dried paper flared and curled into black, flaking sheets. Kohler shut the stove door. He was surprised to find himself a bit peckish and imagined how delicious it would be to have a piece of toast spread with a thick layer of fried liverwurst.

# MAPLE GROVE

## June 19, 2000

Marion Grob was waiting for Van at the Library. Her lips were pursed, and from the way she held the copy of newsprint between her thumb and forefinger, Van surmised she held something nasty.

"Shirley called this morning and I was able to get to the obituary just now. You might want to come into our staff room. You'll have more privacy."

Van had the distinct feeling she was about to get clobbered. What now? "Misfortunes never come alone," was the saying. Was there no end to the Reinhardt calamities? She followed Marion into a cramped back room behind the stacks where a small refrigerator, cupboard, mugs and a coffee maker were installed. At least there was a window next to a little table that looked out onto maple trees. Marion handed her the copy.

"I'll be at the front desk if you need anything. You can help yourself to coffee; milk's in the fridge. There's a box of Kleenex on the counter over there."

Marion slipped out. The room was suffocating, and Van felt smothered by Marion's caretaking. She took a breath and forced herself to read the newspaper clipping.

## SUICIDES WHILE INSANE

Pouring kerosene oil over her clothing and touching a match to it, Mrs. Elizabeth Letty Reinhardt, a pioneer resident of Maple Grove, literally cooked herself at an hour shortly after three o'clock yesterday morning. She lived only a few minutes but suffered the most intense agony while the flames were eating her body away.

The room spun and Van swallowed against the nausea that was rising. She spread her hands on the table and willed herself not to faint or vomit. She gazed out the window where the afternoon sun dappled the trees.

"Here, I am here," she whispered. "I am here."

But whom was she addressing? Tremors rippled through her body as if everything had just occurred. It's the year 2000, she told herself. This happened almost one hundred years ago—in the past, not now. This is history. She read on.

"What prompted her action will never be known. She had been insane for a number of years, but was recently released from a sanitarium in what was believed to be an improved condition. She lived with an aged aunt, a son and two daughters. It had been customary for her and the aunt to sleep together but Tuesday night she announced her intention of sleeping alone. The son, George, occupied his room upstairs along with the aunt and the daughter. Mrs. Reinhardt slept on the davenport downstairs.

"Shortly after three Mrs. Reinhardt arose unheard by the balance of the household and procuring the oilcan, she saturated her clothing. She then applied the match and was instantly enveloped in flames. The pain became so intense that she ran screaming up the stairs. The son, George, heard her and seeing her flaming form snatched up an old quilt and wrapped it about her body. She was so severely burned about the face and body however, that by the time he had extinguished the flames she was dead. In his heroic efforts to save her George's hands were badly burned and he is in a serious condition. A physician was called in, and a horrible sight confronted him. The body and face of the unfortunate woman were literally cooked and the flesh was dropping off in places. All that could be done was to administer to the needs of the son and to place the dead woman in the hands of an undertaker.

"Mrs. Reinhardt was the widow of Adam Reinhardt, who died some years ago from injuries received in a runaway wagon accident. They were a pioneer couple and lived for many years on the farm in Sioux Creek, which the widow still owned at the time of her death. Her death under such circumstances is most unfortunate and distressing and the family has our deepest sympathy. The funeral was held this morning at ten o'clock and burial made in the Catholic cemetery."

Van was blindsided by the amount of detail in the news report. Letty's death was intentional, calculated. She had planned it out. What possessed her? What had she signified by putting such a violent end to her life? Van's mind raced with possibilities. Rage, fear, despair, fury, burning hot or smoldering, all the unacceptable passions of a woman who lacked a voice—the final act being the one thing that says it all. Was her father ever aware of this? He was born five years later. Maybe the family clamped their mouths shut and never spoke about it. *If you don't speak it, it never happened.* But how shameful for them to read this in the newspaper with such agonizing details. Judged insane, women like her were locked away from civil society so what they saw or knew or felt was never acknowledged. *Don't we still do that—lock away our wretched secrets in the madhouse of our minds?*

From her backpack, Van brought out the family portrait and studied Letty, a forty-four-year-old woman seated in the midst of her family. Try as she might, Van could find nothing to indicate such a catastrophe in the making. Letty's Mona Lisa smile was a little creepy knowing now what had happened after the portrait was taken—jumping from the train, going after herself with a knife, the asylum, the self-immolation. Something had broken Letty—something more than her husband's death or losing the farm or commitment to an asylum. Van was certain there were secrets buried within secrets, like one of those Russian dolls that opens to reveal another doll and yet another hidden within that one. Letty left no evidence, no letters. Something unspoken had driven her to a horrendous last act.

Was that what happened with Van's mother? She had never believed Mother's death was accidental. Deep in her gut she knew that was a cover-up, a lie. For years Van had hated her mother for ending her life—such a *waste*, such a betrayal, so arrogant and absurdly self-centered. Her mother's unexpressed anguish was a sucking blackness that shut down any need Van had for maternal attention and care. The early years of darkened rooms and TV dinners, her mother's hospitalizations and her ambiguous death had impaired her, afflicting her with a long-standing distrust of women and a sense of unworthiness lodged deep in her bones. *I was her only child. Hadn't I been worth staying alive for?* Apparently not. Mother's suicide—she could call it that now—left Van profoundly bereft of a mother. But it was also a broken treaty—the basic human agreement that life must be lived, that we are bound to help each other to live. She would never know what her mother had signaled by her final act. She hadn't left a note, unless her father destroyed it, which was possible.

What had transpired between her parents was silent and

deadly. Van had blamed her father and never forgave him for whatever part he played. Had he driven her crazy with his coldness, his lack of feeling? They never openly argued or even raised their voices with each other. Their resentments, disappointments, unbridgeable chasms of misunderstanding were never spoken. Was he tormented after her death? Guilt-ridden? Afterwards, all she knew was his bitterness. Whatever occurred between them, she had absorbed its toxic influence and like a slow seep of radiation, it had caused invisible damage. She had never felt it so clearly, could no longer deny it.

She was so young when her father muttered things in answer to her childish questions about the people in the family portrait. Who were they? What did they do? Were they rich? Her memory was more feeling than actual words spoken. When she begged him for stories about his parents, he pointed out the Longfellow book and his mother's love of poetry. Why she was named Evangeline. His father was a working man who couldn't read or write. Then as an afterthought, he said, "He was a drinker and when he drank, he cried."

Another time he mumbled to himself, "Kohler was a swindler."

"Who was *Kohler*?" she had asked. Or did she make that up? Hard to know.

Her father had changed the subject, annoyed at being pestered by his nosy daughter. Then he refused to talk about them at all. He certainly never mentioned suicide.

Again, she questioned whether Letty was Jacob's true mother. Was that the ruinous secret? If so, who had extracted the vow of silence on that matter? Who told the foundational lie repeated in the census and obituaries, the deception that probably turned her grandfather, Jacob, into the man he became?

She had never heard Kohler's name again until she came upon it in the probate documents and it rang a bell. Had

Kohler really been stealing from the family, or was this just a fantasy arising out of the family tragedy and Letty's madness? Was it based in truth? It didn't look like it from all the probate records and court accountings over the years. He was a careful man, finicky and precise. That was apparent from his reports to the court. She had gone over them a number of times, scrutinizing them for any possibility of fraud, but there was none to be found. Clean as a whistle. Van even felt moments of pity for Kohler who had accrued mounting responsibilities for such a hell-bent family. Where did the whole notion of stealing come from?

Without a doubt, there were so many thefts, thefts of bones, of land, like Len always reminded her, but there was more than that, she was certain. There were stolen truths. Like what did Letty knew? How does maiden aunt, Katharina, figure in this family? Absent from the family portrait, she is only present in the census records and the obituaries. How did she survive the grievous deaths of her brother and then Letty's suicide? She was not buried in the cemetery.

Where did Jacob come from, who were his parents, and who were the ancestors, and what happened between them, really? Ghosts inhabit empty places, black holes composed of secrets and silences, sufferings and injustices, and Van thought, *this is what I inherited, what got passed on to me, the unwitting descendant.* She wasn't quite ready to believe that the actual dead returned, but she was certain their unnamed and undisclosed suffering, their unfinished business, does. Witnessing is required, but also, as Len frequently told her, there is a need for justice. Whether or not it ever comes in time, and it probably never does, justice is what we owe these ghosts of the past. But how was she supposed to do this family justice?

She pulled her journal out and finished the entry she had started.

*Okay, Dad, I don't know how much of this you ever knew. But here it is in a nutshell. Letty was committed to an asylum in Dubuque for almost eight years. Your dad went to get her when she was released in 1909, who knows in what condition. Shortly afterwards, Letty died by suicide in a horrible way. She was buried in the cemetery, so they probably said it was accidental, although* The Chronicle *wrote a ghastly version. All this before you were born. If you didn't know the details, you must have grown up inside a cloud of shame and secrecy. Didn't you ever see your Uncle George's burned hands and wonder about their disfigurement?*

*No surprise your dad took to drink, or that he cried, as I recall you once saying. I wonder now if this Reinhardt misery is what drove you to run, to reinvent yourself. I don't blame you. You know I have run from my own past, too, and now it comes back to haunt me. I always thought Mom's death was your fault. But really, that was just an easy out. Honestly, I think Mother was like Letty, that what she needed in order to live out her days was beyond anyone's comprehension. I don't think I will ever find out who or what drove Letty off the edge. Like Mother, it was probably not having a voice or being believed. I guess in some ways we are both to blame for Mom's death—along with whatever so-called treatment she received. I think you probably did your best. I'm not sure I did. I am still thinking about that. Also, let's get one thing straight. I don't believe Kohler was the cause of anyone's suffering. I imagine he was crushed by all the tragedy. He probated Letty's estate and then left town for Colorado.*

*Okay, the week I promised you for this project is up. You might not like what I found, much less where I'm think-*

*ing of taking it, but as the song goes, "It's my life and I
ain't gonna live forever."*

*Your daughter, Van*

Van found it hard to imagine Martin ever being able to
reconstruct this family story. He was a hard man of hard science. Facts and figures. He never could have done it. Maybe
he knew that. "Ask Vangie to do some research." Well, she
had done it—up to a point. There were still unanswered questions that needed answers.

Along with the promised week, Van felt larger things ending. For one thing, the narrative she had made of her personal
history was in need of revision—orphan, independent, single
woman with a cat, career as an historian, even a feminist historian. Her tumultuous struggle between her creative mind
and the tyranny of archives and documents had been wrestled
to the ground. Neither side won. Just as there are silences in
families, she knew there were silences in history, too. Archives,
like personal biographies, often had a self-serving agenda, and
both official and personal narratives depended on who was doing the telling. What appears as agreed upon consensus often
covers up deep conflicts and injustices. For years she had challenged traditional history, contending that rationally packaged
facts put a safe distance between the present and the truth of
the past. What is the nature of history, if not human stories
set into tight boxes with all the blood removed, like a corpse
in a casket? Unreliable. History was bloodless compensation
for the dead. It wasn't justice. Behind the looming shadow of
history, something more elusive beckoned her. Not memory as
such, but amnesia, the lack of memory.

In her professional work, Van was quick to demonstrate
how women's stories were hidden in the shadows behind the

manmade edifice of official history. A few sparse letters and diaries shone a dim light onto women's intimate lives. They were tiny histories, coveted treasures, few and far between. Even with such scant evidence she was able to generate new narratives. Even silences can sometimes be made to speak for themselves.

But there was nothing of that sort to illuminate what had happened to the Reinhardts. All the known facts of the family were found in public documents, and they ended with obituaries, and the obituaries carried deceptions and passed them on. The trip to Iowa began with a request from her dead father she had felt compelled to honor. She had not expected to be confronted with lingering ghosts, the restless dead, unsolved mysteries, much less her own buried secrets. Truth and lies are buried together.

The word that came to mind was *palimpsest*, the ancient practice of recording a text on parchment and then scrubbing out the words in order to inscribe another text over the original. Often, traces of the previous words bled through. Stories layered upon each other through time, her own story over-written on the surface of an effaced past.

She had never considered before how she had lived without knowledge of her own forbears—no one on her mother's side, no information on these Reinhardts until now—and how that personal vacancy had probably fueled her drive for historical research. She thought again about Jacob Reinhardt, who might have lived his whole life without knowing where he came from. Who was Jacob's mother, and how could Vanever prove it? And further, who was his father? Though her nose was pressed to the ground, Van had lost the scent. She reached for the Kleenex box.

Was she the last person in this lineage to shed tears?

# MAPLE GROVE, IOWA

## JANUARY 1910

LETTY'S DEATH RUINED EVERYTHING. I could not believe I
was still alive. Sometimes your own dying comes too late. The
sight of Letty's burning body would forever scald the rest of
my days. No one could possibly have foreseen this horror. It
surpassed all imagining. Not taking one's own life, no, we all
had more than passing knowledge of such an event. But by
such outrageous means! When Letty returned from the asylum, I had taken extra precautions with the knives, but I had
never considered the kerosene. If I couldn't have imagined it,
how could I have prevented such a *Katastrophe*?

I took to my bed but could not sleep. In my mind I went
over and over each day, looking for ways I could have foreseen and prevented her terrible end. Letty had been hard to
fathom and everyone in the family harbored fears of her despite their determination to fold her back into the family. Her
lack of speech seemed understandable at first. Everything had
changed in her absence. It would take time. I understood silence, its purposes and necessities, but Letty's silence was a
malignancy that grew from a darker and more foreboding

place than I had ever known. Letty was not only withdrawn; it was as if some malevolent spirit had taken over. I forced my mind away from such superstitious nonsense and strove toward keeping a level head.

When Letty had accosted me in the kitchen with questions about Jacob's parentage, I was flabbergasted. Of all possibilities, why had she chosen this topic to loosen her tongue? We had never spoken of it in the years we had lived together. Why was it of such importance at this late date? What was done was done. Had I not made the most advantageous choice years ago? Had I not agreed with Adam to let Letty claim Jacob as her own child, seeing that it was the most practical thing to do? Was the arrangement not done for the good of all? Was not my very silence on the matter a sign of consent?

After Letty left the kitchen that morning, I had an unbidden impression of Jacob's life—how he had been stolen over and over again, first by my own actions, then by Letty who practically thieved him when she was still a girl in braids and pinafore, years before she and Adam ever married, and then by his wife, Elizabeth, who snatched him away from the family and the farm. True enough, I had doubts about the prudence of keeping the secret over the years, but they were never strong enough to go against the thing I had set into motion by relinquishing my claim to Jacob. Where was the sense in going back? Surely this request was another one of Letty's derangements and I felt both fear and great pity for a mind so tortured.

I was also furious that Letty threatened me with breaking the pact. Hadn't she already shown herself capable of such a thing during that ill-fated meeting with Kohler? So I relented and against all better judgment agreed to talk later. Did my reluctance to speak of these matters at that moment push Letty to her end? Or were my words to Kohler what finished her? Did I have some part in Letty's gruesome ending? None of these questions came with ready answers.

In the week after Letty's death so many things clamored for immediate attention—making funeral and burial arrangements, nursing George's burned hands, throwing out the charred patchwork quilt that he had used to wrap around his mother's body, repairing the fire-damaged kitchen, arranging insurance claims, signing court papers and documents. Thankfully, the older girls had taken over everything and tried to keep up a good front and a normal routine for the children's sake. I made some effort but stayed in bed for days and slipped out of time for longer and longer periods.

One morning the older girls were speaking about me as if I could not hear them. They said the shock of Letty's death had made me senile overnight. They said I had stopped speaking to them in English and would only talk in some strange mix of French they could not decipher. They said I stared into space for long periods of time and it looked like I was hearing voices or seeing things that were not there. They were not prepared to cope with another demented person, they said, and I heard their plans to send me to Armour, South Dakota, where Lizzie lived with her husband. The money designated for me in Adam's estate would cover all the expenses and give Lizzie some extra funds for her care. They did not expect me to live much longer.

It was convenient for me to let the older girls believe these things, and make their plans. I did not mind moving from this doomed house in Maple Grove where Letty had died. It made no difference to me at this point where I put my head down at night. But I was frantic about my travel memory book. My darning basket was on the shelf and when everyone was away from the house, I sewed a secret pocket in both my daytime dress and my nightdress. Wherever I went, my book would travel with me. After supper I asked Sister Kate to fetch Jacob. I wanted to see him before leaving for Dakota, before I was pulled into another life, one not marked by clock or calendar.

Sister Kate lit the bedside oil lamp. She pulled the blanket over me and placed a kitchen chair next to her bed. "Jacob will be here within the hour. I'm sorry the house still smells of smoke. I don't know how we will ever get rid of it." She opened the window a crack. "Do you need anything?"

"Rest. I need to rest."

"Of course. I will be in the kitchen if you want me."

As soon as Sister Kate left the room, I reached under the mattress to retrieve the travel memory book and pencil. Although the older girls think me senile, my memory for the past was still acute. In German, I scribbled a note in the margins of the memory book. My fingers were stiff and arthritic, my once beautiful penmanship crooked and almost illegible. The pencil had hardly any lead left. This will be the last entry.

> *Dear Book. Maybe there will be a reader someday. But I am not ready, not ready at all to have my words exposed to the eyes of another soul. It cannot be Jacob, although by rights it should be. Maybe I will take it with me wherever I go after I die. They say hell has plenty of incinerating fires.*

Through cloudy eyes I made out what I had written so many years ago with that fine Staedtler pen whose whereabouts, like so much else, was lost to the ages.

*I did not leave with Pascal on his journey up the river valley. I could not even remember my reasons for wanting to continue north. If I went with Pascal, I would only slow him down and perhaps become a burden. If I stayed, I reckoned he would return more quickly—before the snow flies, he promised. I did not want this parting, but he was restless to go. Before he left, he took the money I had once given him from his leather pouch and handed it back to me. "You will need it. Use it to take good care of my old women until I return." It was as if money no longer tied us together. We had found something so much stronger than that roll of cash dollars. It became a little joke between us. When the two women were not looking, we embraced.*

*One day in early fall, Lucy put her wrinkled brown hand on my stomach and with her fingertips she traced little circles and made a toothless grin. A jolting shock ran through me. Was it fear or was I stunned to find that my body had begun its own journey and I could no longer change its direction? The door of my life flew open and slammed shut as if a wild wind had suddenly blown through me. It took weeks to let the full meaning of this knowledge settle. I felt the joy and sweetness of this new beginning life like liquid honey running through my veins, and along the very same pathway ran an icy stream of dread. My thoughts went to Adam. How would I ever explain this turn of events? My body was stronger than it had ever been, and Lucy constantly plied me with special teas and mashed up plants to strengthen my constitution. Marie seemed happy, too, but anxiety twitched her mouth. Her rosary beads were never far away.*

*The garden gave us an abundance of good nourishment and when the leaves turned red, we put up food for the winter, dried apples, cut-up strips of pumpkin and squash were laid on wooden drying frames in the last warmth of sun. The cabin ceiling was decked with wild plants and herbs, red raspberry twigs, wintergreen, chokecherry leaves, and cornhusks hung from the rafters. We set a feverish pace to ready ourselves for Pascal's return, the winter and the birth coming after the turn of the year.*

*When the snow began to fly, we settled in. Our stores were set, the woodpile stacked, and the cabin snug for the com-*

*ing winter, but Pascal's absence troubled us, although we did not speak of it. Lucy busied herself with making tiny slippers from the rabbits she had snared, and Marie knitted a blanket from woolen yarn she had salvaged. The old dog groaned from his bed close to the wood cookstove. We grew quiet and inward turning, each giving herself over to her own thoughts. Lucy kept up her unceasing singsong humming.* Weh, Weh, Weh. *Then it snowed—for days and nights. When Marie went for wood, we tied a rope to her waist so she could find her way back to the cabin door. The whole world grew white and silent, and we were afraid.*

*Pascal did not return, but his pony did. The good beast was in a terrible condition with deep cuts and scrapes in his hide and eyes white and wild, as if the creature had lost a part of himself and did not know where the missing phantom went. Although in disarray, the saddlebags were still in place. Old Lucy wrapped herself in blankets and put on snowshoes and went to talk the horse down from its frenzy, gentling him in her language, walking him in the deep snow, soothing him in a questioning tone as if the pony could answer our most pressing inquiry. Where is Pascal? Lucy brought the saddlebags inside. The old dog sniffed at them and whimpered. Inside those ancient leather bags were all that Pascal owned which was so very little. There were no official documents so we knew he had discharged his duties at the agency. One bag disclosed several makuks of maple sugar and Indian rice so Marie knew he had made his way to the far reserve up north and was probably headed home. How close he was, we did not know.*

*Deep inside one bag Lucy fished out a grayish, woven length of string. A closer look revealed a faded plaited band made up of different colors. Marie said Lucy had braided it when Pascal was born. It was his token, all those streams of colors woven together. He always carried it with him. Beyond that there was nothing. We took up our private vigils. Marie turned an ashen color, but she said Lucy was certain that he was not dead. How she fathomed it, I did not know. The two of them were alert for the sound of his returning and I placed my hope in their watchfulness. If the horse had spooked and Pascal had fallen from him, it was possible he had found his way to an old trapper's shack. Pascal knew his countryside, as I knew from our travels together.*

I could read no more. My breath was shallow, my heart flittery. Maybe I was dying. Can a person die from memory? It seemed possible. And where will I go when I die? Who will come to meet me? Or was that just a fanciful notion made up by priests as a stay against terror? I put out the bedside lamp and stared out the window. The night was coming on with tiny winks of stars. Pascal's voice arrived with a wind that rattled the windows.

*Eh,* ma cherie, *it was a fine January thaw when I set out and thought I could make good time if I crossed the river at its widest point rather than making the longer journey down to the usual portage. Pascal, what a fool you were! When I fell through the ice and the water lynx grabbed onto my leg I cried like a boy for Toussaint. My good pony could not get to me, and I sent him on to find his own way back. I was not far from our cabin. I hauled myself onto the bank, but I didn't know where to find shelter where I was. And the great north bear descended, and the river ice cracked like a huge drum. It was the only sound I heard except for the short white puffs of my breath and my pounding heart. The full moon was streaming her silver light and the trees made purple shadows against the glowing snow. Mon Dieu! I was so cold, my teeth were breaking against each other and my blood was going to ice, and my bones clacked. Kate, you were my sun, my warmth, the one bright place in my heart and I was going on a journey without you and it was so very, very cold.*

*Eh! Where was Toussaint? He warned me not to try and make it back to you. He told me that the river ice would not hold me at this point in crossing. He said I had lost my head and my good senses as a voyageur over the love of a woman and that was the most dangerous thing for a man like me. He said I was a* très fou, *love-crazy, softhearted, French-Indian for sure and that you would truly be my downfall. And then his spirit disappeared.*

*But wait! A long grey shadow approached! Ah, at last, here was Toussaint shining and decked in his finest array, his fringed jacket and a scarlet sash tied round his waist. Merci, merci, he had not forgotten me, his foolish great-grandson. He came to take me on the journey to Grandfather Tate, the one who sits at the entrance of the trail to the great Milky Way. Eh, Toussaint, a grand voyageur that always knew his way, guided me to the ghost lodge. This time I obeyed his instruction. He put the crooked log down and made a bridge for me to cross the stream to the other shore. He said the proper spells, so the bear and owl spirits let us pass on the pathway to the stars. I sang my death song. Look for me always in the nighttime sky. Adieu, ma cherie, my best love.*

> *To the Spirit Land I am going.*
> *Tate, Old Grandfather, to your lodge I am going.*
> *In the great dark night my heart goes out to you.*
> *I am going.*
> *On the Spirit Trail I am going.*

The stairs creaked with the heavy sound of a man's ascending footsteps. With a jerk, I pulled myself back from the edge of that other world. I was one step away from leaving with Pascal. Reluctantly I relit the lamp, clearing the place of phantom visitors and shoved the travel memory book deep under the covers. Jacob entered and sat quietly next to my bed.

# MAPLE GROVE

## JUNE 19, 2000

"Hi, Em, it's me. How's Mister?"

"He's missing you. You said you would only be gone for a week."

"I know. Would you mind keeping him for a few more days?"

"Actually, Mister has made himself quite at home. I'm the one who is missing you."

"Oh." Van caught her breath. "Well, I miss you, too."

"Van, what's up?"

"Honestly, I can't begin to tell you because I don't know myself."

"That doesn't sound like you. You are coming back, aren't you?"

"No worries about that. It's just that there are still some unanswered questions."

"Have you been crying?"

"Well, to tell you the truth, I have been." Van felt the sob move up her throat. "There is so much loss and sorrow in this story."

"Can you tell me?"

"I want to, Em. I really do. But not on the phone. It's too much. When I come back."

"And that will be soon?"

"In a few days. I'll call before I head out, so you'll know when to expect me."

"I'll be waiting for you. Day or night doesn't matter. Then you'll tell me everything, okay?"

"I promise. Let me talk to Mister."

A loud purr came through the receiver. "Hi, Mister, it's me. I'll be home soon."

Van hung up the phone and pushed her head into the motel pillow. Waves of longing rose and fell as if she were drowning. Pressure in her chest made it hard for her to catch her breath. She yawned, then put her fists to her mouth like a child. Great sobbing heaves started in her belly and moved up and through her throat. She gave over, knowing only the necessity and not the meaning nor the bottom of her sorrow.

In the morning, she swam up through dark layers of dreams. Like a kaleidoscope, images coalesced and disappeared, leaving only frustration. As a solitary child, puzzles were a favorite activity. She would beg for the most difficult ones, the ones with hundreds of small pieces, with scenes that could not be distinguished until the very last piece was fit into place, mountain scenes with twenty different colors of snow and shadow, the Grand Canyon with complex shadings of red, orange and ocher. When some pieces went missing, hidden under the sofa or taken up by the vacuum cleaner, she would make the missing pieces out of cardboard and crayons. But the puzzle remained accusatory in its incompletion. She felt that way now, a sense of work unfinished. Aren't we all complicated, unfinished puzzles made up of thousands of pieces, many of them lost to us forever? The thought offered cold comfort. The Reinhardt puzzle was missing some critical pieces, and her own identity was in disarray.

Before heading to Dee Dee's, Van stopped at the town office. Lillian was helping another customer, a sweating man with a stylish haircut, sporting a linen suit and flowery tie. In their interchange, she saw another side to Lillian—brusque, sour, cranky. The man was irritated. He left in a hurry and Van raised her eyebrows.

"What kind of dope does he think I am? I'm not about to give this guy from Chicago any inside information on who's thinking of selling out their family farm. Besides," Lillian huffed. "It's unethical."

Moral fiber, Van thought. Along with her great kindness, Lillian possessed moral fiber. A rare quality ingrained in the women she had encountered in Maple Grove. Solid to the core. Martin had had it, too, a sure sense of right and wrong, but somewhere along the line his moral fiber had hardened, became a weapon.

"Sorry, dear, but these people drive me nuts." Lillian wiped her forehead with a damp white hanky. "Now, what can I help you with today?"

"I'm wondering if you can look up an old address for Jacob Reinhardt, my grandfather. He lived in the same house in Maple Grove since the late 1890s. He died quite a while ago, in the early 1940s." Van's voice cracked a bit. "I think my dad grew up in that house."

"I have to warn you, if it's still standing, it probably won't look anything like it did. People always think they have to remodel, even when a house is perfectly good. They add extra rooms and porches and garages, make improvements." Lillian was still a bit cranky.

"I know, Lillian, but the land is still the land, right? I would just like to put my feet on it."

"Of course, dear. I got so riled up by that city fella, I forget myself. Certain people just knock me off my perch. Give me about fifteen minutes."

Lillian disappeared into the back room. Van pictured it crammed with ancient file cabinets, some probably unopened since the turn of the century. Jacob's house, her father's childhood home, was not listed in his file folders. She was doing her own research now. By standing on the ground where her grandfather lived and her father grew up, she hoped to catch a glimpse of something beyond the official documents.

Van pushed her braid to her back, repositioned Lillian's fan so it blew in her direction, and took a seat on a wooden bench. She recalled how Len used to tease her about her prairie ancestors. He said she was picking up the bones of the dead. *Is that what I'm doing?* But I am a stranger here and whose bones am I searching for? And where was home?

Lillian emerged from the back room, her face flushed from the heat. "I found it," she said. "I know that house. It's on Fourth Street across from the public school. No need to drive; you can walk from here."

"You're the best, Lillian."

"Bosh. Anybody can do what I do. I just happen to be the one here."

"You're still the best."

"Well, thank you. I guess you'll be heading home soon?"

"Probably tomorrow."

"Well, it's been a real pleasure, Ms. Reinhardt. I hope you found what you've come here for."

"Couldn't have done it without you, Lillian."

Lillian brushed the compliment away, but Van could tell she was pleased.

The house was a small non-descript two-story with dormer windows—beige vinyl siding, bikes in the yard, cracks in the cement driveway. Unlike the remodeled farmhouse, this house was well-worn and weary. Van wondered again if a house held memories. And she wondered, too, how this house could have held Jacob's large family. Where did they all sleep? She pictured her dad coming home from the school across the street. She imagined him plotting his escape. She checked her watch. Almost noon. She still had time to go to the library and ask Marion for Jacob's obituary from *The Chronicle*. She didn't expect any surprises, just the standard obituary that repeated the same stories, the same deceptions.

Marion was behind her desk wearing a freshly ironed blue and white gingham dress that reminded Van of something her mother might have worn when she was younger. Her brown hair had recently gotten a gold rinse and perm. Van suddenly felt self-conscious in her jeans and tee shirt, her sun visor and thick damp braid.

"Glad to see you, dear. Now, dear, what's on your agenda today?"

"I've got one more obituary to go—my grandfather, Jacob Reinhardt. Died 1947, I'm not sure of the month."

"That should be easy to find. I'll be back in a sec."

"By the way, your hair looks really great. Where did you have it done?"

"Hazel's Beauty Parlor. Just down the street. A little past the library. It's the place everyone goes. Actually, it's the only place in town to get your hair fixed. You don't need an appointment."

Van considered what she had learned about the Reinhardts. She had done her research. Their story, and how she thought about it now, did what official history could not—create interior lives, desires and longings, hopes and losses, for people who were once living. Wasn't history just another form of fiction? An unbidden thought rose fully formed. What if she used her sabbatical time to write about the Reinhardts? Not as history, but as story. She had enough of the puzzle. She could fill in the missing pieces like she did when she was young, crafting pieces from her imagination to complete the picture.

# MAPLE GROVE, IOWA

## June 1924

Elizabeth walked toward the back garden with a news-paper in hand. "Jacob, dearheart, Tante Kate's obituary was in today's *Chronicle*," she said. She took a seat next to him on the bench. Jacob stared at the freshly turned-over garden soil. The bleeding hearts had just flowered; their stems arced under a burden of delicate pink blossoms.

Elizabeth read the obituary aloud. There was not much else to say. More than fifteen years since the older girls had shipped Tante Kate off to live with Lizzie in South Dakota, and now she was gone. Jacob recalled the last time he had seen her. Sister Kate had rushed over to his house saying Tante Kate was calling for him. Even more surprising and peculiar was what happened next.

Jacob sat on the chair placed next to her bed. The window next to him was open a crack and he could feel a sharp sliver of winter air. Still, he flushed. The intimacy of her bedside felt immodest. He had never seen her in a flannel nightdress, her brown unsilvered hair in a loose braid. He had only ever seen her fully dressed. Black dresses, wool in the winter, and cotton in the summer, her hair pulled tight against her skull in a bun. He flinched when Tante Kate reached for his hand, but he could not escape her grip. She was not in her right mind. He could not cipher her words, a jumble of German mixed with bits of what he thought was garbled French, names and language he did not recognize. Maybe she was talking with her long-ago people from Germany. People said that sometimes happened when a person was close to dying. He heard his own name mentioned, and she seemed to be addressing him. Her eyes were closed. There was nothing to ask or say.

In the past, Tante Kate had hardly spoken more than a few sentences in a row. Now he let the flood of strange words wash over him and did not strain for their meaning. He sensed she had saved up these words for a lifetime and was making a long-held-back confession. Her wrinkled cheeks were wet, like faded rose petals drenched with dew. Ill at ease, he felt duty-bound to remain by her side for however long it took to unburden herself. The next day they sent her to South Dakota on the train. It was the last time he had seen her. Lizzie rarely mentioned her in the infrequent letters she sent to her sisters, and memories of Tante Kate merged with the bleak recollection of Mama Letty's last days.

With the two women gone, there were few places of comfort and refuge to be found in those difficult years, but Jacob had stumbled upon several. Some were more harmless than others. He withdrew from most company, while his need for Elizabeth had increased. She often read poetry aloud. He enjoyed the music he heard in the words she spoke. He took shelter in her common sense and clung to the warmth of her body. The result was they made more children but that was not a bad consequence—their last child was a boy they named Martin. With Elizabeth's tutoring, he was destined for higher learning.

Jacob could still read the weather, although it was much harder to do in town—the signs were more difficult to decipher through the maze of trees, telephone, and electrical wires, and the skies were not so easily scanned as they were in an open field. The moisture in the air was compromised by the amount of heat, coal and wood smoke coming from village chimneys that made an artificial climate and interfered with his ability to register what the true measure of vapor might be. Even though it was not a necessity, he still made note of what kind of rains were coming in the spring, how much snow they would be likely to get in the winter, and how hot the summer was going to be. His predictions were not always accurate.

Alcohol had turned him into a man of tears. He found it was the only thing that gave the certain kind of solace he sought. Later, Otto told him where to get his supplies, and Jacob made it a regular practice to head out in late fall with his old suitcase, taking the local train to the border of Iowa and crossing into East Dubuque, the very same train he had taken so long ago to fetch Mama Letty from the asylum. But this errand was of a different sort. Elizabeth, who had supported Prohibition, a teetotaler averse to any kind of strong spirits, did not approve of this activity; she pursed her lips and frowned, but never took any steps to stop him.

He built a garden bench, and placed it next to the backyard flower gardens, and sought his refuge there from early spring until the end of October. When he was not on his knees gardening, he sat on the bench and took a pull or two from the bottle and smoked his pipe. All his current cares washed away, and he would hear the great singing symphony of the flowers, the chirping birds, the robins and the meadowlarks, and sometimes at dusk, the three-noted bob-o-link. Underneath the bird song, like a string section of an orchestra, came the melody of busy insects, humming bees, and flies, and in late summer, the steady sawing of cicadas, and a murmuring *Wey, Wey, Wey.*

One early spring afternoon in 1947, along with the sighing wind coming off the western prairie, another voice rode on the beat of his blood.

*Eh, Jacob, my boy! She was a wild one! Mon dieu! Who would guess an old girl come all the way here from that country could be so wild. You wouldn't know it to see her. She was straight and stiff as an old barn board, but she rode on the back of the pony, her hair flying in the wind as if she were one of my grandmother's people. No woman I ever had, and truly there were many, gave me such a time! And she was not young then, but she was clearly famished.*

*I never trafficked with women for long, as they could easily become a burden on a man like me. Don't get me wrong. As I said, I had my little amours. But my living as I was making it determined that I could not be tied down in any way. I had no scrap of settler in me, not in my blood nor in my inclination. She was an* aisaca, *what my grandmother's people called "a bad speaker," the sound of that German tongue as offensive to their ears as the smell of their cows and pigs and their greed for Indian land. She could see I was no farmer, had no silent woman at my side, no big eyed solemn-faced children swarming around me.*

*I was clean-shaven and had sat myself in the big copper tub full of hot water at the hotel. I do not believe I looked dangerous and indeed, I was not, although, Mon Dieu! I could have been! For one thing, I did not take spirits. Non! Never! I had seen too much hell and destruction come from the whiskey bottle. It had ruined many of my grandmother's people and destroyed my father, too, although there were oth-*

*er circumstances beyond the bottle that led to his untimely demise. Drink was the less vicious, in his case. The evils that whiskey had wrought kept me busy working, carrying words, arbitrating, and negotiating between parties, but I myself refused to partake of it. You should know this.*

*I was used to strange requests and orders, discharging them without giving much judgment as to what was asked of me. I did not question who was doing the asking, I was not inquisitive about their intentions or their motives, I was only interested in carrying their petitions to the desired recipient and getting paid for my trouble. Eh! It mattered not to me whether I carried orders in English and delivered them in Dakota or even Ojibwe, or translated French trader lists into understandable American speech for the merchants or took a Dakota chief's complaints to the agency men, or explained to the young, full-blood warriors where they could now hunt and where their presence was no longer acceptable by terms of the latest treaty.*

*Oui, oui, all those tongues were mixed in me and sometimes it proved a great travail to keep them from making a large tangle in my mind. I even knew some Dutchmen talk and I could take the foreigner's words and translate them for my grandmother's people so they could be forewarned about those farmer's notions and purpose. Eh! Maybe I even believed I could do the sacred parley with the animals, but their voices were so very far away I had lost my touch. In a dream the deer-people told me where they would be heading for the summer, and I had to tell my grandmother's people living along the Mississippi and that was where I was headed.*

*"Take me with you!" she said in a whispery voice. "I can pay!" she insisted, holding out her fist full of American dollar bills, and because I was so trained by the habits of my trade and because I needed that paper cash, I simply replied, "Oui! Bon."*

*What a surprise I brought my mère and grand-mère. I wanted to draw them away from the sour taste of grief and loss that was their daily bread and help them to forget the hungry spirit that slipped into their little bed at night under the old quilt like a will-o'-the-wisp, filling the small space between their curled-up woman bodies.*

*Mon Dieu! I never thought I would lie with an* aisaca. *In those days, Old Toussaint, my grandfather, prowled close, a restless revenant, hounding me like an Indian dog, filling my mind with worries of how this would all end. That old trapper was busy sniffing out a woman's snare, not wanting me to get caught like a little foolish rabbit. Aiii, Toussaint! Give a man some rest! I cried. For three nights, Kate and I slept out in the open and for three nights I poured my stories into her ear. Come, my son, and I will tell them to you.*

# MAPLE GROVE

MARION GROB EMERGED from the back room and handed Van a copy of *The Chronicle's* obituary of her grandfather Jacob.

JACOB REINHARDT was born January 18, 1869, to Adam and Letty Reinhardt and died in his home in Maple Grove April 8, 1947, at the age of 78 years.

At the age of eight he came from Illinois with his parents to pioneer a farm in Ida Grove County. In 1894 he was united in marriage to Elizabeth Konrad and shortly thereafter they moved to the town of Maple Grove where he spent the remainder of his life. Eleven children were born to them. A daughter, Florence, preceded him in death. Mr. and Mrs. Reinhardt celebrated their golden wedding anniversary in 1944.

A great lover of music and flowers, Mr. Reinhardt enjoyed a variety of music on his Victrola and he was an ardent gardener, cultivating many pretty flowers that he shared with his friends and neighbors. He contributed much to Maple Grove in the many nice gardens he maintained. No task was too difficult, and he often worked beyond his endurance these last years. He will not only be missed by his family but by his friends for his cheerful, friendly greetings and his help in time of trouble.

The first thing that struck Van was that Jacob died in early April, almost to the day as her dad. Probably just a coincidence. The next was a sucking sensation of loss. How she wished she had known this gentle man. His love of flowers was a surprise as her father had an aversion to flowers. Cultivated or cut, there were never any flowers in her childhood home. Nor was there music. WHA radio and later the television were strictly for news programs, *Huntley Brinkley, CBS Evening News, Face the Nation*, and for her mother's late-night company, more often than not, a flickering blue screen. She had to go to a friend's house if she wanted to watch *Marshal Dillon* and *The Twilight Zone* for entertainment.

She vaguely recalled her father saying that his father was a drinker, probably depressed or in grief given the family tragedies, maybe illiterate, but there were other softer qualities that Martin shunned. She pulled the family portrait from her backpack and studied Jacob. Sensitive features, a rather lost look, a fish out of water, dreamy. The obituary carried on the old deception of his parentage. This was the gaping hole in the Reinhardt puzzle and without the missing pieces, the picture remained incomplete, off kilter. Van had her hunches, but no confirmation. All the documents carried the same story, but the truth was buried. For more than a week, she had happily trotted down the trail, digging for clues, even found the church records for Jacob's marriage license. Now she had lost the trail. No birth or baptismal records. She hated leaving town without this crucial piece.

Since arriving in Maple Grove, she had become used to having more than coffee for breakfast. She walked down to

Dee Dee's to say good-bye, maybe find Helen, and get some food to go.

The diner was packed, the air conditioner going full-blast, folks at their usual spots fanning themselves with laminated menus. Van was third in line to place her order. Helen pulled up next to her.

"Hi, Helen, I was hoping to see you. Dee Dee said you wanted to talk."

"I was so afraid I'd miss you." Helen's face was flushed pink, and she was a bit breathless. "Whew! It's a scorcher today. Do you have some time? I told Fred if I saw you I would be late coming home so he won't be expecting me."

"Sure, Helen. Let's go to the back table. Nobody ever seems to sit there except me. Can I order something for you? Coffee?"

"I'm too jumpy for coffee this morning. Maybe some Raisin Bran."

Dee Dee dished up a plate of hash browns, ham and eggs to take to a customer. She looked up expectantly. "I see you two found each other. What can I get for you today, Helen?"

"No offense, but it's too warm for a hot breakfast today. Can I have some Raisin Bran and black tea?"

"Make that two Raisin Bran and coffee for me," Van said.

"Easy enough. I'll get that to you pronto."

A few familiars waved hello as Van and Helen staked out the back table.

"I'm not even hungry," Helen whispered. "But I don't want to come in and not order something. It's just not polite." Helen took the menu and started to fan herself. "I never get used to the heat."

Dee Dee brought two bowls of Raisin Bran, a pitcher of milk, a cup with a Lipton Tea bag and a mug of coffee. "I hope you girls have a nice visit."

Van was on edge. She could not remember ever eating Raisin Bran. Helen poured sugar and milk in her bowl and put a napkin over a tan faux leather pocketbook that took up most of her lap. Van sipped her coffee.

"You won't believe what I found out when I visited my sister Eunice last weekend. Dee Dee probably told you she is ninety-five—seventeen years older than me. She's the oldest and I'm the youngest in our family. She's in a nursing home in Armour. I try to go up once a month. Fred doesn't mind the drive, says it gives us something to do."

Van nodded at Helen, encouraging her. Her Raisin Bran was getting soggy; she stirred it with her spoon.

"So there I am sitting in Eunice's room, trying to come up with something to talk about. Her room is actually quite nice. The nurses are very considerate. Mostly farm wives looking to make some extra money. Eunice lived in her own home up until several years ago. Never married. She worked as a nurse in Armour for most of her life. We grew up there, I moved to Iowa when I got married to Fred. Now, where was I? Oh, yes. Eunice asked about the news from Maple Grove. Well, you can imagine, most of what happens in our town is in the obituary column, and nobody had died recently, so I happened to mention that you had come from Madison and were looking for your father's family, the Reinhardts. I said I couldn't recall anyone with that name."

"'Well, I do,' she says. I almost fell off my chair!"

A current of electricity shot down Van's arms. Nose twitching. Ears up! "I didn't know any relatives lived in South Dakota."

"You have to understand, our family was pretty poor, my dad was laid up with a back injury for most of his life and my mother took in sewing and such to make ends meet. You can imagine their surprise when I was born. Talk about a caboose!"

Helen took a spoon full of cereal and poured more sugar in her bowl. "You have to have a lot of sugar to make this stuff palatable. They say bran keeps you regular, so I eat it."

Van steered Helen back to her subject. "What did Eunice have to say about the Reinhardts?"

"Because we were so poor, Eunice started taking care of sick folks right out of eighth grade. It's how she got started on her nursing career. She made a pretty darn good living. A neighbor asked Mother if Eunice could take care of her elderly aunt, a woman they called Tante Kate who lived with the family. Apparently, they had some funds to pay Eunice for daily visits to the old woman. Eunice said that Mrs. Hebenstreit—I think the woman's name was Lizzie—was mean to the old aunt, kept her in her room, fed her oatmeal, never called the doctor for her aches and pains. To this day my sister is still a very mothering type of person, and she was so even at that young age."

Van's foot was jiggling, impatient for Helen to get to the point. But there was no rushing her.

"Eunice just loved that old lady. Doted on her, bathed her, got her dressed, took her out on the porch if the day was fair, just like she was an old baby. The family said she was senile, but Eunice didn't believe it. The old woman didn't speak good English, some smattering of German, from the old country. She showed Eunice how to do fancy sewing even though her hands were crippled from arthritis. Right before she died, she gave Eunice a little leather-bound book that she had written in. What a shock. It was all in French, written in faded ink and pencil. We were Norwegian, so Eunice couldn't read it, but she kept it in a drawer. Her patients often gave her little tokens to remember them by. She had always meant to find someone to translate. Anyway, Eunice forgot about the book until she moved into the nursing home. She was hoping one of the old-timers there could read it. Not that Eunice is any spring chicken herself."

Helen was out of breath. She poured milk and sugar into her tea and took a sip.

Van felt like she was in a movie. It all felt unreal, disorienting.

Helen pulled a faded brown leather book from her purse. *Reisealbum* was engraved on the title page—a travel memory book. The yellowing pages were filled with barely legible French script, a few German phrases, and notes on the margins. Faded ink and pencil. Stuck inside was a pale blue envelope with the name Katharina Reinhardt written in a spidery script. The envelope had been sealed but over the years the adhesive had deteriorated. Van lifted a very old sepia tone photograph from the enclosure.

Van gasped. "Oh, my God! It's her! Katherina! The lost matriarch of the Reinhardt family."

"Do you recognize her?" Helen asked in surprise.

"I've never seen a picture of her—only recently read about her existence in the census records." Van felt as if she were looking at herself from another lifetime. "Look at the set of her jaw—an exact replica of mine. And her nose! I'm certain she's my great grandmother."

"Oh, my," Helen said. "I had a hunch this was something important."

Van touched the photograph with her fingers, lightly moving them over the image. Katharina Reinhardt must be Jacob's mother. "I'm sure she is my dad's grandmother, not his great aunt, as the census said. And that makes her my great grandmother."

"How exciting," Helen said. "I never imagined such a thing. My sister led such an ordinary life. Will you be able to read the French?"

"Yes, of course, it's old-fashioned script, but yes, I think I can. I've studied the language for years. I can't thank you enough, Helen." She didn't realize she was crying until she wiped tears with the back of her hand.

Helen patted her hand. "I can't wait to tell Eunice. This will just make her day. Maybe you can visit her. She still has all her facilities—well, you know what I mean. It's only a three-hour drive north from here."

"Yes, I would like to do that. I was planning to leave to-morrow but I can go there first. Can you give me her address and a way to reach her?"

Dee Dee came over with the coffee pot, poured a refill for Van and looked askance at the soggy bowls of Raisin Bran. "You girls still working on those?"

"Oh, my gosh," Helen said. "We got so caught up in talking. You won't believe what my sister Eunice gave me."

Van held up the book. "It's a journal written by my great

grandmother. I had almost given up on figuring this family out. Such an unexpected find." Van dabbed at her eyes with a napkin. "It's all very emotional. A kind of miracle, really. I'm used to working with official documents, census records, and stuff like that. I never imagined finding anything like this."

Van couldn't remember the last time she cried in public. Probably never. She didn't know if it was seeing the picture of Katharina or the genuine warmth and interest from Dee Dee and Helen. Probably that, and a lot more.

Dee Dee touched Van on the shoulder. "It's not every day that life hands us a miracle, hon. The Raisin Bran's on the house today." Dee Dee cleared the table. Helen wrote Eunice Harkens's name and address and the phone number of the nursing home on the back of a telephone bill envelope and handed it to Van.

"Do you have any idea what year Katharina Reinhardt died?"

"Eunice said she started taking care of her when she was thirteen." Helen touched her forehead. "The old lady was in her nineties then. I have to think she died sometime in the mid-1920s."

"I'm going right over to the library and see if there happens to be an obituary in *The Chronicle*. I can't tell you how much this means, Helen."

"I'm just the messenger. My sister is the one who should be thanked."

"I plan to do that in person, Helen."

Van's car was still parked in front of the town office. She walked over to the library. Marion was surprised to see her.

"Back so soon?"

"Just one remaining request. It's a long shot. I'm not sure if *The Chronicle* will have it, but can you see if they ran an obituary for Katharina Reinhardt? She lived in Maple Grove for years, but died in Armour, South Dakota, probably in the early 1920s."

"I'll get right on it. Do you want to wait?"

"I think I will. It must be 100 degrees outside."

Van took a seat at the long table. She took the memory book from her backpack and studied the photograph of Katharina Reinhardt. Formidable. Even in those corseted fashions, the shape of her body felt familiar. Again the sharp sensation of electricity ran down her arms. Stuck between the middle pages was another photograph that showed an older Katharina seated on a chair with a young man at her side, most likely her brother, Adam. There was no indication of when the picture was taken; probably after they had arrived in America. In the second photograph, Katharina looked very dour, her mouth turned down at the corners. A very stubborn woman, Van thought. She must have dominated everyone. From the family portrait, Letty looked like a puppy in comparison. What a struggle those two must have had living together for forty years.

Katharina's French script was scratchy and old-timey. Translation would be slow going with the faded ink and pencil. It was like small lights were being turned on in the library of her mind, recalling all the research she had done on early Prairie du Chien, where the documents were often in French. But why did Katharina write in that language when the prevailing language of her background was German? The penciled notes in the margins were in German and looked like they had been made at a later time.

Hungrily, Van opened the brittle pages towards the end of the diary. This was so unlike her usual style, which was straightforward and methodical, beginning to end. Never mind. She wanted to see where and how Katharina's account would end. Then she could go back to the beginning.

*I was not prepared for the pain. When it first began, I bore it silently until the great rush of waters broke open. Old*

*Lucy saw everything and she began to make preparations for the birth and she helped me into an old cotton shift. We had just had a bit of thaw in the weather but now the winter clamped down hard with icy fingers. The little cabin was snug and warm. Marie brought in plenty of wood and she boiled snowmelt in the big iron pot on the black cookstove. Lucy made infusions from the bloodroot twigs we had gathered months ago. The old dog became restless and whimpered at the unusual activity until Lucy spoke sharply to him in Dakota and he retreated to his place near the stove.*

*When the pain took me over, Lucy kneaded my great swollen belly with her expert hands, so soft and yet so knowing and strong. All the time she sang low in her singsong fashion—Wey, Wey, Wey— as if she was telling the babe how to make its way into the world. She handed me a piece of clean cloth rolled up to bite down on when the pain overtook me and spooned tea into me when I could rest. She had probably done this many times and there was comfort to be had in her knowledgeable hands. Marie's fingers flew around her rosary beads and her twitching mouth was busy making prayers although she made no sound and her face was pale and full of fear. I could hardly look her way. I do not know the number of hours that passed; I only registered the movement from light to shadow.*

*Suddenly everything stopped. A great chill descended as if the door had been flung open and a bitter draught of icy air came blowing through. I thought maybe Pascal had finally returned. In my delirium, I heard his voice.*

Van paused at the names. Pascal was probably a common French name. Her eyes narrowed. Where had Katharina been living during this time? Was it possible she was somewhere near Prairie du Chien, or near the "half-breed" tract that Marion had mentioned? She felt the galaxies swirling, sweeping her into another world. All of a sudden there was more than a Reinhardt puzzle at stake. Is there a point where we are all deeply interconnected to each other? Where no one is really an orphan. Isn't the human gene pool vast and inclusive? In her journal, Van drew a line from Tante Kate, Pascal, to Marie Pascal, to Jacob, to her father, to herself. Van caught a scent and was back on the hunt. Her eyes went back to the script; she would fill in details later when she had more time.

With one swift gesture Lucy undid her braids, letting her iron-grey hair flow down her shoulders in ragged streamers. She began a low chant. Seeing her thus, Marie let out a piercing howl, joined by the old dog, and then mine own voice let loose coming from a place I never knew existed and, in that moment, your high-pitched cries were added to this ungodly chorus. All our voices met and curled together like smoke and flew up the chimney, reaching for the stars in the nighttime heaven. Pascal was gone from us.

Using her sharpest skinning knife, Lucy cut the cord that joined the babe to me and hung it near the stove to dry. She spooned a mixture of cohosh and shepherd's purse into my mouth and soon the afterbirth arrived and was put into a bowl to be buried later. Lucy said some Indian words over the babe. She changed my birthing bed and laid the infant on my breast.

We withdrew into our private worlds since the mysteries of life and death and love and loss differed so greatly for each of us. We had been marked and bonded forever by this moment, yet I foresaw how our trails were destined to part.

The work of mothering a newborn does not allow for being overcome by life's tragedies. With Pascal gone, it was life that called us forward as reluctant as we were to keep going. Lucy helped me, as I had so little knowledge of these matters *and when the babe cried she placed him in a hand-made sling she used as a cradle and as she rocked, she sang her one-word song—Wey, Wey, Wey— and he always fell asleep. She never braided her hair and she wore the same tattered dress day after day. I do believe her mind had become unhinged and she thought it was her own child that she tended. Marie was going through the motions of life like a ghost with her rosary in hand or around her neck. She was in a constant state of grief as she muttered her Hail Mary's. When she took the infant in her arms, her eyes betrayed a fierce mother hunger.*

Van took a deep breath. The travel memory book was akin to winning the cosmic lottery. For the first time in her life, she felt chosen. Anointed. By whom or what she couldn't say, but that didn't seem to matter. Katharina's story was a blessing. A direct transmission from great grandmother to great granddaughter. An assignment from the ancestors. She couldn't wait to tell Em. There was no one else who could understand how much this meant for Van.

Marion came in with the microfilm and handed it to Van. "Here you go, my dear. *The Chronicle* never missed a beat. Hope this is helpful."

The obituary was dated May 28, 1924.

Word was received yesterday of the death of Miss Katharina Reinhardt at the home of her niece, Mrs. Lizzie Hebenstreit, at Armour, South Dakota. Miss Reinhardt was about ninety-four years old at the time of her death. She was born in Germany. When about forty years old she came to Ida Grove County with her brother, Adam Reinhardt. In 1901, after the death of Mr. Reinhardt, she continued to make her home with his widow, Mrs. Reinhardt, in Maple Grove until the latter's death sixteen years ago. Funeral services will be held at Armour, Friday morning.

"Thanks so much, Marion. This fills in a big missing piece in the Reinhardt saga. Very helpful."

"Does that mean you've found what you were looking for here in Maple Grove?"

"More than I ever imagined." Van held up the *Reisealbum*. "Can you believe this? Helen Stumpf's sister knew my great-grandmother Katharina. She gave Helen's sister this diary before she died."

"Oh, my. Now that qualifies as a found treasure."

"It's written in French, so it will take some time to translate. But it is completely astonishing that this old woman kept a diary. I'm hoping to visit Helen's sister in the nursing home. She might have stories of Katharina."

"How exciting. I am just thrilled for you."

"Honestly, I could not have done it without your help—and Lillian's at the town office, and Shirley in Ida Grove, and of course, Dee Dee and now Helen Stumpf. I wish I could bring you all back to Madison with me. I have never had a better research team."

Marion smiled. "Bet we would have a blast in Madison. Maybe you'll make it back our way again?"

Van felt a small tug in her heart. For the first time, she felt she was of these people; they had welcomed her, helped her, showed interest in her project. Did she owe them something in return?

"After I go to Armour, I have to head home." Van hesitated, "I may come back later this summer, just to say, hi, to see how everyone is doing. I feel at home here."

"You know you are always welcome, dear."

"Thanks, Marion. I'm going to sit for a while and translate more of this French."

Katharina was now using the familiar *tu*. Was she addressing her baby?

Marie took me aside in the late spring and said she was closing up the cabin and taking Lucy back to the big reserve up north. She wanted to take you with them, to where you could be cared for by everyone. It was your place of belonging, she said. It was like you were their payment for losing Pascal. The plan was firm in her mind and I found no argument to go against her. What was I going to do at my age; a single woman with only a younger brother who I hoped was still waiting for me. I pondered on it for a day and then conjured a plan of my own. I would let Marie and Lucy take you north and return to that miserable migrant town from whence I had come. I would find Adam and insist that we leave that town and find someplace else to settle. I would never tell a living soul what had transpired. I would close the door on this brief life and never allow myself to remember either its pleasures or the pain of loss. It was over.

I counted out the remainder of the dollars that Pascal had left with me and I gave Marie more than half for their travels. The rest of the money I kept for myself. The morning we departed, Lucy lifted an ancient deerskin pouch off the nail in the far corner of the cabin. She was barely a shadow now with her old patched up dress and apron, her moccasins nothing but worn through pieces of hide, her long, gray hair still unbraided hung down her back like some ancient animal skin. I followed her to the back of the cabin, not to the outhouse, but on the other side of the horse shed. There, she picked up her gardening shovel and proceeded to a place where the white birch trees grew like pairs of thick white legs and she dug a hole.

Kneeling on the ground, she carefully placed the pouch in the little grave, tamping it down with handfuls of dirt and singing a song in her usual fashion. "Weh, Weh, Weh." I knew she was saying good-by to everything, and I even said a little prayer myself. She did not see me. Her eyes were turned so *deeply inward she was like a blind person feeling her way through her last days. She was surely dying, but slowly, bit by bit, like the big trees that fall apart in the forest, and I prayed for your safe journey to the reserve in the North Country.*

*I packed up the few belongings I had brought when I first ventured forth with Pascal. I was still in possession of the small pouch that Lucy had handed to me shortly after the birth. It contained your dried umbilicus. Stubbornly, I refused to give it to them, saying it was part mine and I wanted to keep it, all the time I determined to give it a quick burial as soon as I was able. Maybe that was my biggest mistake. Marie told me that the Indians had a superstition that a person who didn't own his original connection to life was in danger of losing his way on this earth. That person, they believed, would spend their whole life searching for something. She said that's why Indians thought the white people were so lost. I ended up sticking it into the branch of a thick pine like a strange Christmas tree decoration, hoping some bird would find it and make good use of it as nest material. I could not bring anything from this life back with me.*

*Marie made arrangements for the widow Josie Flambeaux to close and shutter the cabin and keep watch over it while she was away, and gave her the old dog and two good ponies in exchange. Josie hitched up her team and wagon and we all clambered in back, sitting on clean hay. I wrapped you in my woolen shawl, like Lucy showed me, and in this way I could bring you to nurse without inconvenience. Lucy had made clean rag pouches of maple sugar water for you to suckle on during their trip north, so this would be the last nourishment I would give you and my milk carried my hopes for your life along with my sorrow. It took us the good part of the day on those rutted roads to reach the village where proper transportation was to be had. Once we arrived at the place of our parting we climbed from the wagon and assembled our few belongings as if we were merely out marketing for the day.*

When Marie held her arms out for you, a voice not of my own making uttered, "Nein." Marie cowered in surprise like a faithful dog that had gotten an undeserved beating. Lucy's eyes were glinting knives that cut my heart. I clutched you close to my breast and quickly turned away, as I had no words to explain myself. They would not openly contest me in public. Two elderly Indian women wrangling with a white woman over a babe was unthinkable. I quickly flagged a waiting buggy to transport us to the train depot. When I turned, Marie and Lucy were shuffling north; two gray-haired figures, their arms joined like a hook and eye.

I mingled with the other travelers preparing to board the train going south. Seated on a worn wooden bench in the depot, I brought you out from beneath my shawl and smoothed your dark hair. I heard myself speaking to you in German, "Mein Kind," and in that moment the German words came tumbling forth like an unblocked stream, washing away all traces of country French and the few fragments of Indian I had learned. With the German words, my practical mind took over, and I shifted the weight of my body until I composed myself into a respectable, German-speaking woman of middle age, a matron carrying her child, a woman beyond suspicion.

The approaching train whistle pierced my ears and brought me quickly to my senses. I carried you on my shoulder and walked onto the platform. In doing so I had to step over an ancient, toothless Indian woman wrapped in a shabby blanket. She had conveniently placed herself on the ground with her back up against the outer station wall, her moccasin-clad feet stuck straight into the thoroughfare of ticket holders. She pushed her wrinkled brown hand shaped into a shallow cup forward, begging for any bits of generosity that could *be loosed from the travelers who crossed her path. Most of what she acquired were looks of contempt and revulsion and sometimes words to match, along with a few stray pennies. I had to look down so as not to step on her and our eyes met briefly as I pulled my skirts aside.*

*Then I heard her ragged voice as she rasped in broken English, "Where did you steal that papoose from?" A wave of fear shot through my body and I turned from her impudent inquiry and quickly hid you back into the folds of my shawl. I knew in that moment that I would have to counteract any possibility of this knowledge revealing itself again and so purged my own mind of memory as best I could. This book tells what I do not wish to forget.*

Marion had flicked the lights on and off, signaling the library would close in fifteen minutes. Van had sat there for hours. She turned to the last page in the book to see where Tante Kate had ended her diary. A separate paragraph looked like it had been written later. No date was written on it. The first sentence was stark in its simple declaration. *I named you after Jacob in the Bible.* There it was, written clearly so many years ago. Katharina addressed Jacob, but she had never given the book to him or any others in the family. She doubted he could read English much less French or German. Illiterate, her father had intimated long ago.

Van skimmed the last page.

*The old woman who helped deliver you gave you another name at birth. I am the only one who carries the memory of your hidden name, Little Blue Clouds. I was told it was meant as a charm for the protection of small children. You were never baptized in a church. There were many reasons I never told this story. If the old woman gave you a secret name to keep you safe, I reckoned my silence on these matters was the best pro-*

*tection I could offer you and I admit it was easier for me that*
*way, too. Maybe it is too late now, but I must acquit myself of*
*blame before I die. I will not carry this story to my grave.*

Van closed the book. The leather cover was stained and creased, the pages brittle, the spine loose, the words faded in places. She held it in her hands like a holy text, kissed it and pulled it to her chest.

"Bless you, Katharina Reinhardt. The chances of finding your words are beyond imagining. They are revelations, direct dispatches of truth, as if you had written them for me to find so many years after your death, after everyone's death." Katharina's story rippled in her blood like a spring river infusing her with a new vision of herself.

"I'm making a vow to write your story, Katharina—yours and Letty's and Jacob's. "

She pulled her journal from her backpack. A great heave of sadness left her chest. She missed her father terribly. How she wished they could sit together and knit this story into a narrative that would provide comfort and relief. That was her assignment now.

# MAPLE GROVE

JUNE 20, 2000

*You sent me on this assignment, Dad. The beautiful women in your hometown of Maple Grove have helped me beyond measure. The heavy burden of the Reinhardt legacy that you carried to your grave has been lightened. I feel oddly emboldened by what I have found. You had no way to know any of this. Here are the facts.*

*Katharina, Adam's older sister, was really Jacob's mother, your grandmother, my great grandmother. She left a diary telling her story. Your grandfather was called Pascal. He was métis a French and Native man. Katharina kept this a secret her entire life, yet she still felt compelled to write her story. I don't believe any of this was ever known to the family. It explains a lot. Maybe not everything.*

*Truth-telling unties the dark knots in a lineage, no matter how much time has intervened. With Katharina's diary as my inspiration, I will finally unburden myself of something I never told you.*

348 | PATRICIA REIS

*When I came back from the Boundary Waters all those years
ago, I was pregnant. Then Mom died and Len disappeared.
You were unavailable. I was really alone. I postponed graduate school. You held that against me. I could never have been
as strong as Katharina, bringing a child home. Even she gave
Jacob over to Adam and Letty to raise as their son. The times
were different. A complicated miscarriage spared me a very
hard choice, but I was a wreck afterwards, spent days in the
hospital, and had a hysterectomy. I have never told a living
soul about this. With great grandmother Katharina as my inspiration, I want to declare the time of shame, secrecy and
silence is over. I only wish you were alive. I want that so much.*

*Most of all, I hope you will forgive me for not being a bet-
ter daughter. I hold nothing in my heart except love for you.*

*I am going to write the Reinhardt story using documents
and my imagination. I am going to dream them into life
on the page. This is the only way I can honor all those
who have suffered from secrets, including Mother, who
was not able to fully realize her gift for words.*

*Your daughter, Evangeline Reinhardt*

Van waved good-bye to Marion and walked down Main
Street to Hazel's Beauty Parlor. A few women in curlers dozed
under silver helmet dryers, limp magazines rested on their laps.
   "I would like a haircut," she said to the woman at the desk.
   The woman eyed Van's braid. "You want me to trim the ends?"
   "No," Van said, "I want it cut—short."
   "Are you sure, dear? Looks like you haven't had a haircut in years."
   "Time for a change," Van replied.

Back at the motel room, she propped the family portrait on
the dresser. "No more secrets now," she told them. "I'm going

to tell your story from what documents I have gleaned, from what I imagine, and from what Katharina wrote in her journal. As the last living Reinhardt, I promise to do our family justice. I am no longer a stranger raising your bones from the earth."

She touched her head. The feathery lightness made her grin. She needed to get on the road. She had plans. But first, call Em.

"Dr. Cooper here."

"Hi, Em, it's me."

"I know it's you, Van. Where are you?"

"I'm checking out of the motel. I'm going to drive to Armour, South Dakota, to find my great grandmother's grave. I can't wait to tell you all about what I have found."

"When's that going to be?"

"I should be back tomorrow night. How's Mister?"

"Mister and I are doing just fine."

"Well, tell him I'm on my way. And Em?"

"What is it? You sound pretty jumpy."

"Just a warning. You might not recognize me."

"Now you are being a tease."

"Well, you'll know when you see me. There's something else. I have a big writing project in mind for my sabbatical. I'll know more when I see you. But there is more."

"Okay, Van. Let me have it."

"I just talked with the real estate agent. Dad's house sold. It's closing in two weeks. I've lived in my rented studio apartment for all these years. I want a real home, a house on the lake, a place to write. Will you go house-shopping with me?"

"Sounds like fun. I'll start checking the papers."

"And one last thing." Van took a deep breath. She was a different person now. She could say what she felt. "I love you, Em."

"I love you, too."

"Maybe we could try again, Em. I never really gave us a chance."

# AUTHOR'S NOTE

*Unsettled* is a novel based on the lives of my pioneering German ancestors, a rural gothic tale set in the prairies of western Iowa, that covers a span of fifty years, from 1875 to 1925.

Many events in this story actually happened, yet it remains a work of fiction. Some places in this story exist, some do not. Most people in this story existed, but some did not. I have kept the first names of my ancestors but given them the patronymic surname of Reinhardt. With the exception of some letters and the fictional journal, all census records, probates, and obituaries are historical documents.

Although drawn from available facts, the intimate lives and thoughts of the characters have emerged from my imagination. This is not a disclaimer about the story's truthfulness; it is merely to say that memory and history are like fraternal twins emerging from the same womb, yet carrying different genetic material. For this work I went swimming down the spiraling DNA of my ancestors, going past historical hindrances and misleading markers, to find the place where memory, history and imagination embrace and open into something lucid that feels like truth.

In the beginning, an old family photograph, and a trove of public documents wove themselves into a tragic yet discernible shape. Delving further, I encountered discordant webs of deception; confusing contradictions in the census records; a family portrait that belies the given ages of the people pictured; obituaries that name family members wrongly by leaving certain people out; whiffs of mystery that carried a depth charge of something unspeakable, noticeable only out of the corner of an eye as a disturbing ghostly aura.

These gaps in the ancestral record drove my desire to write this book. What I discovered is that the patterns from the past have already been woven—the empty spaces, gaps in the record, the question marks, and silences are simply apertures through which secrets can still slip. Reweaving the web of memory takes imagination and heart. These are the threads that mend the tears left by history.

—PR, Portland, Maine

**Enjoy more about *Unsettled***
Meet the Author
Check out author appearances
Explore special features

# ABOUT THE AUTHOR

Author Patricia Reis is a Midwesterner at heart. In the mid-1800s, her German immigrant ancestors pioneered a farm in southwestern Iowa and their portrait gave her this story. She has lived on both coasts and currently resides in Portland, Maine where she is active in Maine Writers and Publishers. She spends six months of each year in Nova Scotia. Reis holds a BA in English Literature from the University of Wisconsin, an MFA from UCLA and a degree in Depth Psychology from Pacifica Graduate Institute in Santa Barbara. She also maintains a private practice of psychotherapy for women.

Reis's memoir, *Motherlines: Love, Longing, and Liberation* (SheWrites Press, October 2016) won a gold medal for memoir from Independent Press Publishers. Along with numerous essays and reviews, she has published several nonfiction books. *Women's Voices,* includes her in-depth interview with naturalist and writer, Terry Tempest Williams; *The Dreaming Way: Dreamwork and Art for Remembering and Recovery* (recently translated into Korean, 2019); *Daughters of Saturn: From Father's Daughter to Creative Woman* (1995, 2005) with a forthcoming Russian translation.

# ACKNOWLEDGEMENTS

Before sending *Unsettled* to my agent, I had a dream: It is night. In the back of my house, beyond the stonewall, a dark shadow is rummaging in brush. I yell, "Are you a grave robber." This dream gave me pause. In writing this book, I had been digging up my ancestral dead for almost twenty years.

Margaret Atwood says, "Everyone can dig a hole in a cemetery, but not everyone is a grave-digger. The latter takes a good deal more stamina and persistence. ... As a grave-digger, you are not just a person who excavates. You carry upon your shoulders the weight of other people's projections, of their fears and fantasies and anxieties and superstitions." Yes, I am a dedicated grave-digger. But a grave-robber? That is a different occupation.

Canadian author Michael Crummey offers an extended meditation on a fiction writer's responsibility to historical people when "making visible the dark matter at the heart of human history." *Unsettled,* with its noble intentions of truth and justice, is not without its moral ethical dilemmas, in particular appropriation and exploitation, two forms of robbery a writer can perpetrate on what Crummey calls, "the defenseless dead." I assume my dream was bringing that potential into my awareness.

As a child, I used to study the Reis family portrait that hung in my family home and is featured in the book. The formal photograph has accompanied me in the years of writing the family story. Stamina and persistence, as Margaret Atwood says, are necessary for the grave-digger's occupation. Research, innumerable conversations, various attempts to shape and reshape narrative structures, many readers and editor's comments followed as the work was buried and exhumed numerous times before reaching its final destination.

*Unsettled* is necessarily a work of fiction. Even with the help of artifacts and official documents, I was tasked with imagining the lives of my pioneering ancestors, not just the obvious hardships and victories, but the inner workings of their psyches, their private loves and fears, their quirks and desires, their weaknesses and courage. Above all, I had to put them into relationship with each other, to sense the family dynamics that informed their lives. I have changed the family surname to Reinhardt in case there are living relatives who might object to the story I tell.

A book with a gestation of almost twenty years has accrued many debts. Anne Furan Spartz gets my first bow of gratitude. A second cousin in my paternal lineage, she is a dogged genealogist, a trusty Sherlock to my Watson. In the mid-eighties, she visited my parents and interviewed my father about his Iowa childhood. She came bearing documents, obituaries, census records and newspaper clippings. The obituary of Elizabeth Reis who took her own life by way of self-immolation haunted me. My father, a great storyteller, never knew the truth of his grandmother's death until then. As a child he had been told that she got to near the wood stove and caught on fire.

Anne Furan Spartz provided me with a treasure trove of old photographs, copies of newspaper articles, family trees. Indefatigable, she chased down the lineage for clues of my grandfather Jacob's parentage. Census records proved surprisingly deceptive. Only intuition and imagination would solve that mystery.

In 2001, I had a visitation, something many writers talk about but I had never experienced. It was a woman's voice saying, "It wasn't that I wanted to die, but I was so damned mad and it was the only means at hand and the only thing that gave me peace of mind." I knew immediately that it was Elizabeth speaking and I wrote her words down on a yellow legal pad.

Several years later, my brother Willy Reis and his wife Pat, drove me from Madison, Wisconsin to Iowa. Intrepid travelers, they happily scouted the Iowa countryside so I could get a feel for the area. Anne Furan Spartz met us there. We found the cemetery and located the plat map of the old farmstead where the ancestors pioneered a farm in the late 1800s, and the house where my grandparents lived and my dad grew up. With my forensic nose for hidden stories and buried truths, I got my shovel out.

Carolyn Megan came to this project at a crucial moment. Her ability to enter into the narrative with a grasp of its intention and an understanding of its shape often surpassed my own, and was what delivered this work into its final form. Earlier, Genevieve Morgan added insight and helped me condense the number of my characters. In the early days, Suzanne Strempek Shea cheered me on and gave me valuable directions on writing fiction.

Literary agent April Eberhardt, my tried and true benefactor and friend, has stayed the course. Without her steadying hand at the plow, *Unsettled* would not have found its home, nor its cover. She is the one who sent me a picture of the John Rogers Cox painting, *Grey and Gold*.

Asking people to listen or read a long work of fiction is daunting. For their cheerful willingness, I thank Alexandra Merrill, Leah Chyten, and my creative process group, Jackie Reifer, Julie Searles, Joan Lee Hunter, and Arline Saturday-born. Gratitude goes as well to all the friends and acquaintances who patiently listened to me read and describe this project. The list includes many and I hope you know who you are and that you know that your interest built muscle for the long haul.

Three residencies at Ragdale Foundation, my writer's deep home, has facilitated my work. With its acres of uncultivated prairie land, I cannot imagine a more inspiring and welcoming retreat space for a woman with Midwestern roots. Gratitude abounds for the privilege of its bounty, including all the dedicated writers and artists who formed the ad hoc community in residence.

A big shout out to the publishers of Sibylline Press, Vicki DeArmon and Julia Park Tracey and their team. Their combined experience, warmth, humor and vision have created not only a perfect home for *Unsettled*, but a welcoming spirit of community and collaboration for authors.

Closer to home, *Unsettled* is dedicated to my father, John, who instilled in me a love for storytelling, beginning with his made-up bed-time stories and introducing me to Thomas Hardy whose novels we read together when I was an adolescent. The opening scene of *The Mayor of Casterbridge* at the country fair is a scene that remains memorable.

I am deeply grateful to my sisters, Elizabeth Johnson and Ginny Reis, who have been steadily on the sidelines cheering as I ran this marathon. My partner, Jim Harrod, has been with me in more ways than one through all the iterations that this project has undergone. Hand at my back, wind in my sails, my heart's true home.

Gratitude goes as well to Michael Lesy for his generosity and friendship. For all the friends and acquaintances who patiently listened to me read and describe this project, I hope you know who you are and that you know that your interest built muscle for the long haul.

Many traditions have a practice of propitiating the dead by feeding them. In that spirit, *Unsettled* is an offering to my ancestors. May you feast on my words, savor the sweet, the bitter, the sour, and spit out any uncooked, strange or indigestible bits.

# BOOK GROUP QUESTIONS

## *Unsettled: A Novel*

### BY PATRICIA REIS

1. Why is Van motivated to fulfil her father's last request, especially when they were so painfully distant? How does Van stand to benefit from seeking out her family history?

2. Whose voice do you find the most compelling in this novel: Van's contemporary voice? Tante Kate's secret history or silent observations? Letty's internal confusion? Jacob as a child or a man?

3. How do the many women assistants and keepers of records aid Van along her way? Could they be compared to angels or muses or sibyls along Van's journey?

4. What are your thoughts on keeping a secret diary, especially one so full of explosive truths? As Tante Kate's was nearly lost to time, what are the dangers of keeping your diaries a secret?

5. How was mental health and illness portrayed or faced in earlier times? Home care, asylums, hospitals, treatments like eating or art, the use of straitjackets or manacles, etc.? Could the Reinhardt family see that Letty was ill and did they ignore it or avoid it?

6. Family secrets always seem to come out at inconvenient times—but others are lost to history? Which do you feel is better in the long run—let sleeping dogs lie or bring it out of the shadows?

7. How does the genealogical road trip appeal to you? Have you gone to a different state or country to explore your roots, and have you uncovered any secrets or mysteries along the way?

Sibylline Press is proud to publish the brilliant work of women authors over 50. We are a woman-owned publishing company and, like our authors, represent women of a certain age. In our first season we have three outstanding fiction (historical fiction and mystery) and three incredible memoirs to share with readers of all ages.

## HISTORICAL FICTION

### *The Bereaved: A Novel*
### By Julia Park Tracey

Paperback ISBN: 978-1-7367954-2-2
5 3/8 x 8 3/4 | 274 pages | $18
ePub ISBN: 978-1-9605730-0-1 | $12.60

Based on the author's research into her grandfather's past as an adopted child, and the surprising discovery of his family of origin and how he came to be adopted, Julia Park Tracey has created a mesmerizing work of historical fiction illuminating the darkest side of the Orphan Train.

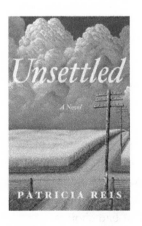

### *Unsettled: A Novel*
### By Patricia Reis

Paperback ISBN: 978-1-7367954-8-4
5 3/8 x 8 3/4 | 378 pages | $19
ePUB ISBN: 978-1-960573-05-6 | $13.30

In this lyrical historical fiction with alternating points of view, a repressed woman begins an ancestral quest through the prairies of Iowa, awakening family secrets and herself, while in the late 1800s, a repressed ancestor, Tante Kate, creates those secrets.

## MYSTERY

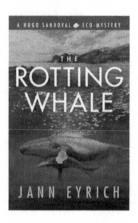

### The Rotting Whale: A Hugo Sandoval Eco-Mystery
#### By Jann Eyrich

Paperback ISBN: 978-1-7367954-3-9
5 3/8 x 8 3/8 | 212 pages | $17
ePub ISBN: 978-1-960573-03-2 | $11.90

In this first case in the new Hugo Sandoval Eco-Mystery series, an old-school San Francisco building inspector with his trademark Borsalino fedora, must reluctantly venture outside his beloved city and find his sea legs before he can solve the mystery of how a 90-ton blue whale became stranded, twice, in a remote inlet off the North Coast.

MORE TITLES IN THIS ECO-MYSTERY SERIES TO COME:
Spring '24: *The Blind Key* | ISBN: 978-1-7367954-5-3
Spring '25: *The Singing Lighthouse* | ISBN: 978-1-7367954-6-0

## MEMOIR

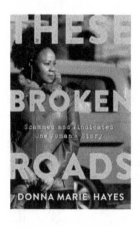

### These Broken Roads: Scammed and Vindicated, One Woman's Story
#### By Donna Marie Hayes

Tradepaper ISBN: 978-1-7367954-4-6
5 3/8 x 8 3/8 | 226 pages | $17
ePUB ISBN: 978-1-960573-04-9 | $11.90

In this gripping and honest memoir, Jamaican immigrant Donna Marie Hayes recounts how at the peak of her American success in New York City, she is scammed and robbed of her life's savings by the "love of her life" met on an online dating site and how she vindicates herself to overcome a lifetime of bad choices.

### Maeve Rising: Coming Out Trans in Corporate America
BY MAEVE DUVALLY

Paperback ISBN: 978-1-7367954-1-5
5 3/8 x 8 3/8 | 284 pages | $18
ePub ISBN: 978-1-960573-01-8 | $12.60

In this searingly honest LBGQT+ memoir, Maeve DuVally tells the story of coming out transgender in one of the most high-profile financial institutions in America, Goldman Sachs.

### Reading Jane: A Daughter's Memoir
BY SUSANNAH KENNEDY

Paperback ISBN: 978-1-7367954-7-7
5 3/8 x 8 3/8 | 306 pages | $19
ePub ISBN: 978-1-960573-02-5 | $13.30

After the calculated suicide of her domineering and narcissistic mother, Susannah Kennedy grapples with the ties between mothers and daughters and the choices parents make in this gripping memoir that shows what freedom looks like when we choose to examine the uncomfortable past.

## Sibylline
PRESS

For more information about Sibylline Press and our authors, please visit us at **www.sibyllinepress.com**